R. Thomas Sheardy, a retired professor of art history, has taught classes in Native American, Asian and Islamic arts. His professional publications include *Searching for America: Essays on American Art and Architecture* (Cambridge Scholars, 2006), for which he served as editor. His fiction has appeared most recently in the Write Michigan 2016 Anthology (Schuler Books and Chapbook Press, Grand Rapids, MI), a juried competition. He has done archaeological work in the jungles of Yucatan and is an avid traveler. He is also an artist, maintains a large English garden, and raises orchids. He resides in Crockery Township, Michigan.

For VikiSu—Always in my heart

R. Thomas Sheardy

SLOW DANCE IN A
WINTER GARDEN

AUSTIN MACAULEY PUBLISHERS™
LONDON * CAMBRIDGE * NEW YORK * SHARJAH

Copyright © R. Thomas Sheardy 2023

All rights reserved. No part of this publication may be reproduced, distributed, or transmitted in any form or by any means, including photocopying, recording, or other electronic or mechanical methods, without the prior written permission of the publisher, except in the case of brief quotations embodied in critical reviews and certain other non-commercial uses permitted by copyright law. For permission requests, write to the publisher.

Any person who commits any unauthorized act in relation to this publication may be liable to criminal prosecution and civil claims for damages.

This is a work of fiction. Names, characters, businesses, places, events, locales, and incidents are either the products of the author's imagination or used in a fictitious manner. Any resemblance to actual persons, living or dead, or actual events is purely coincidental.

Ordering Information
Quantity sales: Special discounts are available on quantity purchases by corporations, associations, and others. For details, contact the publisher at the address below.

Publisher's Cataloging-in-Publication data
Sheardy, R. Thomas
Slow Dance in a Winter Garden

ISBN 9798886931846 (Paperback)
ISBN 9798886931853 (ePub e-book)

Library of Congress Control Number: 2023906368

www.austinmacauley.com/us

First Published 2023
Austin Macauley Publishers LLC
40 Wall Street, 33rd Floor, Suite 3302
New York, NY 10005
USA

mail-usa@austinmacauley.com
+1 (646) 5125767

Much appreciated is the help and encouragement of my long-time friend and former writing instructor Jean Pataky. Quotations are from Joni Mitchell's lyrics to the song, *The Last Time I saw Richard*, (1970) from the *Blue Album*, and from Neil Diamond's *Play Me* (1972) from the *Moods* album. Nathaniel Hawthorne's late novel, *The Marble Faun* (1860) is also cited. Comments on art and history, and on Hawthorne's philosophy, represent the author's views and do not necessarily represent conventional interpretations.

Part I
Winter Gardens

Unquestionably, this gentle, kind, benevolent, indulgent and most beloved and honorable reader, did once exist for me...

Nathaniel Hawthorne, *The Marble Faun*, Preface[1]

---

[1] My citations from *The Marble Faun* come from the Gutenberg Project's Centenary Edition of the Works of Nathaniel Hawthorne, copyright by the Ohio State University Press, 1968, and as reprinted in a Penguin Classics edition of 1990.

One

He could even remember, time was, he actually liked women. He used to enjoy their company, both in public and in private, both in the barroom and the bedroom. He often talked of it when he was younger and would often think of it in his later life, spending long winter hours watching memories come and go, emblazoned upon sunny windows—like pictures recalled from a book he'd once read—how much he had liked women. He'd thought of it most of his life. Even as a child, lingering by icy window scenes hanging on the walls of his memory, watching the women walk by on the snowy sidewalks. Even as a twenty-something sitting at his old manual typewriter clack-clackiting away at some inane piece of fiction in faded type—since he'd forgotten to buy a new ribbon and had rewound an old one retrieved from the wastebasket in the kitchen, still textured with coffee grounds. The woman who lived with him puttering about the stove, raising dust clouds of flour: Alison; his lover—

No. Those were not the words he was looking for. Caleb put down his pen and paused to stare out the window into the sunny landscape. The deep green hills and tawny valleys of Tuscany were trundling by as the second-class train plied its way from tunnel to tunnel on its course toward Rome. He was using his laptop as a writing desk. "I know I'm old fashioned," he thought to himself. "I still prefer to write it out in long hand. It seems less likely to require lengthy revision that way."

That was it: that's what he'd tell the committee.

"I know they have emailed me already, wondering if I've finished the first chapter yet." He glanced down at the yellow legal pad on which he had been writing—ever since having left Venice. In fact, Chapter One was nearly finished. He read the first lines again, smiling. He liked those opening lines.

"He could even remember, time was, he actually liked women…Especially that one woman, crazy as she was…After all, she was just a woman, almost a child. Not her fault. He could even remember, time was, he might even have *actually* loved her."

No. Those were not the words he was looking for. Afterall, the first couple lines of a novel should be compelling in some way. Hook the reader, as they say. He screwed up his face as he tried to decide what to do about it. He scratched out some of the words and wrote between the scratched-out lines. John and Alison. Characters he didn't like very much. They were in the kitchen of their small house on a Friday evening in Winter, some forty years prior. They had been arguing for the last ten pages or so. Why didn't he like them? Of his own making. What could he do to make them more likeable? He had better come up with something soon. He was hoping to finish that first chapter before arriving in Rome.

"That gives me about two hours."

1

He could even remember, time was, he might even have actually loved her. Alison. His lover.

"Why," he wondered. It wasn't just sex, as some might have thought. He was good looking in those days and could have found a bed partner easily, a different one every night had he been so inclined. He repeated the question to himself as he had many times over the years, and especially then, as he paused in the sunny kitchen, bent over his manual typewriter: why was she here? Was it merely to have something to constantly compare himself to? Like Adam? Having to invent a name for the other person in order to comprehend his own existence? Is that all it amounted to?

But still—wanting her was better than being her, he thought to himself as he watched her puttering at the sink in those ancient of days. It hadn't occurred to him that he might not have known who he was then, much less who she was. As far as he was concerned at that point in his life, she was just a woman; second in creation's value. And her puttering at the sink was distracting him from his work.

"What are you doing?" he asked, annoyed. The billowing flour cloud was etched with her sun-struck profile as she turned toward him. She carried her great breasts like loaves of bread in the crooks of her arms. "Huh?"

He leaned on his elbows, his chin on his fists, blinking his eyes as he bent forward into the square of light that reflected off the lake and through the window into the cloud of flour. She had hesitated at the sound of his voice, as she normally did when brought back to reality from one of her private little fantasies. She even seemed to have forgotten what she had been doing as she paused to stare into the sunny reflection from the lake. Then she sighed and sat down opposite him at the small kitchen table where he sat behind his typewriter sipping his cold coffee. Her red hair was glowing with sunlight. Her soft, pink face made its own light when she smiled. "What?" she wondered.

"What the fuck are you doing?"

She stopped smiling. "Nothing."

She stood and returned to her work. Her hands were covered with flour. She wiped them on her dress. She must have been baking something.

"You have your dress on inside-out," he observed, flat voiced, no longer amused at her antics.

She pulled it out from her bosom and stared down at it. "I know. I didn't want to get it all covered with flour." He merely rolled his eyes and turned back to the typewriter, silently wishing he had a room of his own in which to work. "Anyway," she went on, and he remembered that she had been talking about something for the past several minutes while he had been trying to write. A story he was never to finish.

"I can still taste that chili. I swear, John; that was the best chili. I wish I had their recipe. Most college cafeterias aren't that good, you know? I mean, have you ever thought about how lucky you are?"

John stopped typing and stared at the painted yellow wall before him. She went on. "I was surprised. I mean, how good it was. I guess that must be the first time I ever ate there at the college with you. It was nice, you know. We should do that more often. I enjoyed meeting your students." She had paused to look out the kitchen window into the yellow sunlight. John could see her reflection in the decorative copper pans that hung on the painted yellow wall. Alison never used them to cook in even though John had bought them for her as a Christmas gift. That was two years ago. They had remained there ever since, where he had hung them, collecting dust. She must have considered them some kind of interior decoration, he guessed.

"There's another storm coming in over the lake," she was saying. "Just what we need. More snow. It is pretty, you know, but I was hoping the tulips would be blooming by now. I mean, it's already March and—Did you know you can see Lewis's cottage from here? Sort of behind the trees, I mean." She had stretched over the sink almost to the steamy glass. "I never noticed it before. Just the roof. I think it's his place. Looks kind of precarious from here, right on the edge of the dunes. Is that the right word, 'precarious?' You're the writer, not me. I wonder if he can see our place too."

"For Christ's sake, Alison, I'm trying to write!"

Then he felt bad. Then she was quiet. For a while.

"What's it about," she asked, not looking back from her place in the sunshine. "You've never even told me what it's about."

"It takes place during the war," was all he said in return.

"Which war?" she wondered, innocently enough, he had to assume.

"I don't know," he admitted. "Perhaps the last one."

"You don't know anything about being at war," she scoffed.

"I know what it's like being in a bad relationship," he said, his voice having taken on a mean timbre.

She was undeterred. "Is that what it's about? A bad relationship?"

"Yeah." He paused and looked up to her. She had turned toward him quarter-wise so that the sunlight filled her fluff of red hair. "While the main character is fucking some native girl on some remote island his wife is back home dying in childbirth."

"Oh, God," she sighed, turning back to the window. "How awful for her."

"Yeah," he said, going back to his typing. "Awful, isn't it?"

Alison was, thankfully, quiet—for a while. She stood at the window for a long time, her floury hands raised before her like one in penitence. Her silence and her presence touched him, and he turned his eyes up to look at her at last. She was absolutely angelic; the way the sunlight gathered itself about her like a mandala. The way the itinerate glow etched her profile in silver. The way her hair—

Aware of his scrutiny, she lowered her head and went back to work, raising a cloud of flour that darkened the aura like a shroud thrown over her. He closed his eyes for a moment, sealing in the image. It was quiet in the kitchen, then: for a while. John sat, his fingers poised above the keys. Alison stood, her hands in the sink. Each stared at whatever it was had come to confront them. It was chillingly quiet. For a while. Then, the sun moved, and the room darkened abruptly. John went back to typing and Alison to washing out the dishes.

"Mother called today."

John turned once again toward the light at the window. "What, Alison?"

"Do you eat there often?" She asked not looking back at him. "The cafeteria?"

"No. I don't like the food."

"Oh. Did I tell you that Mother called today? I must have exceedingly perturbed her. Is that the right way to say it?"

"Perturbed exceedingly; if you must use superlatives."

"She hung up on me."

"I'm sorry. Anything else?"

She shook her head "no." He turned back to the typewriter.

"I'd like to read it someday, John, what you're writing. I wouldn't understand it and I probably wouldn't even like it, but I'd like to read it anyway."

"Alison," he said, "sometimes you baffle me."

She grinned back at him. "Do I?" Then, she asked him to read out loud what he had just been writing. He told her it wouldn't make sense out of context.

"Seems to me it should," she said.

John went back to typing and in the same moment, as if on some other afternoon and in some other context, Alison asked, "Have you seen Cutler lately?" John stopped typing. He sat back in his chair and raised his hands as if pleading for mercy. "Why?" he posed, wearily.

"Just wondered."

"Why?"

"Curious," she said. "Think he'll be there tonight?"

John was not about to bite. She had been dropping hints all day about something going on that evening as if she were just waiting for him to ask about it while he was bound and determined not to. She had opened the oven door and its pungent warmth wrapped momentarily about his shoulders. "Okay," he said at last, turning to face her again, "what are you baking?"

"It's for tonight," was all she said. She looked back at him from her place at the sink. It was the only place free for her to work so she was mixing up the ingredients there. "But listen," she added all at once, "I really don't care if you don't want to go, John. I'm going whether you do or not, you know, and I'd like to use the car. Seems I haven't been out of this house in weeks."

"Fine with me," he said. "You know I hate to drive at night."

It would be nice to have the place to himself, he thought, watching her puttering at the sink. He'd probably go for a long walk on the beach. He did his best thinking while walking on the beach in the middle of the night. Alison hated that he knew. She always complained about him crawling cold into bed and wanting her to warm him up. He smiled. It wasn't very considerate, he guessed. Still curious, he asked as casually as he might what she was planning to wear.

She seemed surprised by the question, as simple as it sounded. "Why, John?"

"I thought you might want to wear my serape."

She started to laugh. "I don't think that would look very good with my red pumps, but thanks, anyway."

Pumps, he thought. Now he was curious.

"Will you be late?"

She shrugged into the floury cloud she was once again raising. He was wishing he hadn't asked the question, so he decided to distract her in some way. He went to the sink to rinse out his coffee cup, but she had it filled with mixing bowls and measuring cups. She asked him how his typing was going as he set the stoneware cup down on the porcelain draining board. He told her he couldn't concentrate and that he was going for a walk.

"I may not be back before you leave."

She kissed him on the cheek. She told him she'd see him in the morning, and he left, slipping into his old cloth coat as the plastic-wrapped screen door slammed shut behind him. He suddenly wanted to be as far away from her as possible. A chilly wind blowing up from the water then whipped wet snow into his face. He shuddered within his clothes and started down the long line of stairs that pointed to the frozen shore below. John was shaking his head, wishing to himself he still loved her. Alison. His lover.

2

The sun was still brilliant in the west, a flat yellow disc, foretelling of spring. The earth was dark with moisture though the air had chilled in anticipation of nighttime storms, the embryos of which were forming at the edges of the sunset. The lake spread out from the littered shores like an empty platter, hollowed by the weight of the very atmosphere and buffed by winds to a polished aluminum sheen, a delicate filigree of waves along the beach; a film of water sliding over a film of sand. Clumps of stiff grass were festooned with tufts of snow and dead things left from winter's rages. Closer to the water, the sand was smooth and hard, laced with frost at the water's edge. Delicate splinters of light glanced off the turning waves as the sun flattened out along the dark cobalt blue horizon in preparation for its daily death by drowning.

John walked alone on the very hem of the lake. The great water on one side, slipping away, the image of a woman on the other—pursuing. His small house poised above him on the bluff of sand and displayed in a jewelry box window the smiling ruby of Alison. He turned away from the crystalline image toward the liquid sea. Her smile remained in his sight; distant, still enticing. It was what he hated most about her; he couldn't stand to be away from her. She was like the beckoning of the softly curling waves. He wanted to be more then with her. Like the big water, he wanted to be more than just beside her. But lately, that was all it was: beside her, not really with her. The lake comforted him in his self-imposed state of loneliness. Not like Alison, it was constant and beguiling, its silence, and its immortality notwithstanding. From everlasting to everlasting. A continent of water that divided masses of land like a bundling board. He stopped in his ambling, unaware that he'd walked into the water, his feet sinking into the wet sand.

Alison was baking something up there. She was going somewhere that evening. Wearing her best shoes. He could picture her in the tiny bathroom putting on her make-up, probably humming some song she'd heard on the radio the night before while he was trying to sleep. She must've known he had to get up early that morning for a Saturday class, but she claimed nighttime was the only time she had enough room in the small cottage to do the laundry. That didn't make sense to John, but then, little of what Alison said or did made sense to him. He had to shave that morning in a tangled forest of hanging lingerie. He couldn't understand why she washed it so often, she never wore it that he knew of, not even panties. Alison hated underwear. He laughed to himself. It was one of the things he found most charming about her.

"Gawd!"

He looked down at his wet and bitter cold feet. "Silly bitch," he grumbled, "wearing her dress inside-out so as not to get flour on it."

As he lifted each leg to shake the water out of his shoes, he noticed he was wearing two different colored socks, one red one and one blue one. And he'd worn them all day that way!

"Shit."

"No wonder the chancellor was laughing when I left his office." It had been dark in the bedroom that morning. Allison had been up late. John hadn't wanted to disturb her. At least she had laid his clothes out for him. He sat down on a log and took off his soaked tennis shoes. He wrung out his socks and put them back on. He wasn't sure if he was mad at her or not. He smiled. It was kind of funny.

"I wonder if she did that intentionally." He put his socks and shoes back on and returned to the red stairway that pointed like a vulgar finger toward the house at top of the hill. Why hadn't she told him about the socks? He could just imagine her answer.

"I thought you wanted it that way," or, "I kind of like it that way."

He kicked at the hard sand only to remind himself how cold his feet were. He should go up and change his shoes but then, he'd have to tell Allison what had happened. He could picture her standing in the bathroom door in her slip and laughing at him. He'd wait until she left.

He paused in his dialogue with himself to glance up at the warm house where there were dry socks and comfortable slippers. The little cottage set atop the bluff in precarious splendor against the mauve sky. The windows still reflected a golden memory of the sun though the cedars that hugged them were black as night and the red stairway draped like a tired animal's tongue over the lip of the hill. That was one of Alison's crazy ideas, painting the stairs red. Thirty feet of scarlet enamel stretching from sea to sky. She had sat there day after day complaining of the sand in her underpants (that was when John had finally suggested she not wear any if it bothered her so much) painting that damned stairway. He was wishing he could have painted it in invisible paint, so Alison wouldn't be able to follow him on his nightly walks. He was certain she did that sometimes.

An urgent thought came to his mind. Where was she going? What was she baking? Was she leaving him? She had said something about her mother calling that afternoon and she was baking something.

"Alison hates baking!"

He decided to return earlier than usual from his evening walk. He started up the stairs. Maybe he'd catch her before she left with his car, surprising her in the kitchen, her suitcase in hand, her hands covered with flour. Maybe she'd just be pulling out of the drive or maybe he'd meet her face to face in the open doorway. Then she'd have to tell him where she was going. He mounted the steps three at a time; then paused. He pictured Alison standing at the kitchen sink and crying.

No. That was then. The day last summer her mother had come by. They had quarreled. She and Alison. John had arrived home from his walk just as Mrs. Wundelund was driving off. He knew it must have been her. He could see the silly little pillbox hat she always wore like some geriatric Jackie Kennedy. Alison was standing at the sink, her arms elbow deep in gray dishwater, and she was crying.

Alison never cried, not even at those silly soap operas she watched. But she cried that day, all afternoon. John had finally thrown his hands in the air, knocked over his chair as he'd jumped up from the typewriter, and stormed from the house. She was still crying when he returned later that evening, having walked for most of three hours on the beach. She was in bed, crying when he came into the bedroom. He sat in the front room and watched television. But all he could hear was Alison, crying herself to sleep. Things were different between them after that.

The front door to the little house was wide open. "It's winter out here," he shouted toward it. The door swung shut with a loud thud. He went to it and found it locked. He pounded on it. It opened with a glimpse of Alison's red hair disappearing into the bowels of the small house, pungent with baking smells and the subtle fragrance of make-up and clean laundry. He followed her into the tiny bathroom, pausing in the doorway, sharing space with her in the steamy mirror.

Alison jammed her fists into her hips. She was wearing a slip. John tried to see if she was wearing panties underneath. "Now, John, are you going tonight or not?"

He was afraid to ask. He became uncomfortable when Alison got assertive. "Where?"

"Shit," she said, brushing past him into the bedroom and its array of gilded mirrors. Another one of Alison's interior decoration ideas. John found himself automatically speaking in whispers in the bedroom. Alison held a red silk tie-dyed dress with red fringe up in front of her.

"You were the one who wanted to go," she was saying as she pirouetted, glancing from mirror to mirror at herself. "The invitation was sent to you: and guest."

"Invitation?"

She squeezed by him into the bathroom. "I laid out some clean socks for you."

"I have to wear socks?"

"Unless you want to wear those wet ones," she said.

"Oh, Christ," he moaned. "It's Lewis's birthday party, isn't it? You were baking him a cake." He was thoroughly embarrassed, and Alison was loving every minute of it, he was certain. She turned to face him in the bathroom doorway. She was smiling, not unkindly. She kissed him.

"Get dressed, Sweetheart. I have to finish brushing my hair."

"Sorry," he said in a pathetic little voice.

"I know," she said. Then she started singing along with Joan Baez.

John was wondering half aloud if any of the college administrators might be there.

"I thought you got along fine with the deans," she said from behind the half-closed bathroom door.

He was dropping his pants. "I do. But some of the others don't. Especially after that war protest march last fall. I always seem to get myself in the middle of something."

"I can't imagine Lewis asking the deans if he doesn't get along with them."

"He's black, you know—"

She paused in the doorway, bending into the room. Her hair was ratted into a great billow and backlighted by the ruddy sunset on one side and the bathroom light on the other. John stared at her a moment, enthralled. "I mean; he has a tendency to kiss up to the dean. Do I have to wear socks?"

She turned her back on him, the glow in her hair having coppered and then bronzed as she passed by the front window. "Think of it as a costume party, John," she said.

He sprang to the bedroom doorway as she threw him his overcoat. He caught it over his head, banging his knuckles on the doorsill. "Ow! You know I hate to drive at night, Alison. We'll probably have an accident."

"It's only a mile, John." She was waiting in the opened front doorway, a gray and brown view of the dusky sky behind her, silhouetting her tarnished mop of ratted hair.

"A lot can happen in a mile. Aren't you going to finish your hair?"

"In the car."

"I was kind of thinking of making love to you in the car."

"It's only a mile, John."

"What about the cake?"

"Didn't turn out."

He had paused, facing her in the opened doorway. He mumbled something about heating the outside as he pushed his face into her hair. "Too bad about the cake."

It had started to snow. Great puffs of it settled in ragged clumps on the hard fenders of the sports car. Alison was sticking out her tongue as far as she could. John reminded her that the snow was probably polluted with carbon monoxide, or something, and she shut her mouth and slid into the cold vehicle. She jumped at the icy touch of the leather seats, which squawked as she sat. She tightened her coat about her, thinking to herself how little fun John was lately. How he used to compete with her in catching snow on the tongue, and now he seemed bent on spoiling the game. Now he seemed to annoy her, whereas before, he'd made her laugh. He'd been into his writing so completely lately that he didn't even hear her anymore when she talked to him. She'd been discussing the party at Lewis's for over a week. He apparently hadn't heard a single word of it. She let slip a pathetic sigh that manifested itself in a steamy breath, then she turned to gaze at her own reflection in the frosty window.

She sighed again as the motor turned over within its cold, steel jacket. John was talking to the motor, encouraging it to keep going. She glanced at him sideways. God, he was handsome! She looked away quickly lest she begin to fall in love with him again. She was just beginning to get good at not being in love with him and she didn't want to spoil it. But she could still see his face in her head, imprinted on the reflection of her own face in the glass. The headlights exploded silently onto the black fir trees across the drive and both images faded.

It's his mind that's homely, she thought. His stories are about twisted people in hard times trying to cope with doomed worlds. She'd never told him how much she disliked his stories. She'd always nod and say, "Hmmm. Neat,

John. Really neat!" It was enough, it seemed, to satisfy him, but it made her wonder how it was he saw her. As one of his bizarre creations or as the real, flesh and blood woman she was trying to be.

The headlamps moved over the lack-luster view and glanced off the sooty snowbanks as she glanced over at John, sort of sideways. She covered a giggle. He was hunched over the wheel of the little steel monster like some misplaced time traveler, grimacing with each flash of the headlights off the falling snow. She grabbed the door handle as the car spun to the side on an icy curve, a glimpse of the iron-black lake striking her eyes as the car righted itself into the abiding whiteness of the snowstorm once again. The amber lamps of Lewis's cottage glowed assuredly beyond the sloshing of the windshield wipers. The snow had turned to rain. The headlights jumped about among the parked cars in Lewis's yard. Alison smiled at the little display and then everything went dark.

"It's raining."

"I know, John."

"We're going to get our party clothes all wet."

"What do you suggest we do about it?"

He just grinned.

3

Lewis opened the door. "Oh, I thought it was John and Alison."

At first, Calvin and Beatrice Umlohr didn't seem to know what to say. They were standing on the little front step to the glassed-in porch, in the rain, huddling together under a misshapen umbrella and holding a small, wrapped gift out before them like an offering. Lewis laughed good-naturedly. "Oh," he cried, his eyes searching the dark parking area behind them for some sign of intelligent life, "You weren't supposed to bring gifts. Didn't I tell you?"

"Wouldn't be a birthday party without gifts," Beatrice said. She kissed him on the cheek and his first inclination was to wipe off the cold chill she'd left there but he directed his hand instead to take her coat, shake it a bit and toss it on the wicker settee near the French doors that led to the front room. The Umlohrs were both professors of music. He was short, and she was tall, and they resembled each other in other ways as well. Everyone called him "Cal" and her "Bea" excepting John, who called them "Calvin-and-Beatrice," all together like that, as if they were some kind of two-headed hybrid monster out of Greek mythology or the like.

Lewis was dark, especially in the company of all the northern European colleagues who now clustered around him. He had invited lots of people and nearly everyone he'd invited had come. He probably hadn't taken the time yet to wonder why, though John would be certain to raise the point upon his arrival.

"How much of this is curiosity and how much is tokenism?" he would ask in a palmed whisper.

Lewis would have to honestly admit he hadn't thought much about it until John had brought it up. Then John would accuse him of being naive and he'd feel bad for a while. It happened every time they got together, and Lewis now found himself wondering as he escorted the Umlohrs into his small living room why he had invited John at all. But, of course, John was still his closest and most honest friend at the college. That was why.

He introduced Cal and Bea to Mr. and Mrs. Deadman. They were docents at the museum where Lewis had done some co-op work while still a student at the very college where he was now in his first year as an instructor of art. The Deadmans (he could never remember their first names) were rather dull as party guests but they had been nice to him and had helped him get into graduate school. And they knew interesting people and often brought interesting guests with them which may be why they were not very interesting in themselves. Alison had observed once that they suffered from an advanced state of name-dropism: rather than simply dropping a name, they'd produce the person in the flesh.

Lizzie Tifgat. Their guest's name was Lizzie Tifgat, her married name, though she was now separated from her husband. Lizzie Tifgat was an authoress of some notoriety, more social than academic, and was recently featured in the news for having published her third novel, The Golden Tool.

"Interesting," Cal said. Then, "Where's the bar, Lewis. I brought my own bottle as you requested."

"Well, with so many here, I thought—"

"I brought one, too," Bea said. "Cal and I don't agree on what is proper to drink at parties. I drink Amoretto. I like it with orange juice."

"I'm not sure if I have any—"

"What's yours, Mrs. Tifgat?" Bea asked escorting her toward the kitchen. "What do you drink at parties?"

"Whatever is open," she answered.

Cal and Bea laughed. Lewis had been left behind as the others gathered at the kitchen table-turned-bar. He joined them. "I drink scotch, but—"

"So do I," Cal said. "Cutty Sark. Make sure you don't touch my bottle, now," he said, attempting a joke. Bea laughed. "Oh, you invited the new chancellor. How nice. Is his wife here?"

"Looks like everyone's here," Cal added as if answering for Lewis.

"Just John and Alison is all—" Lewis started to say.

"Oh, they're here," Bea cried suddenly, spinning about and knocking Lizzie Tifgat into the bar. The bottles and glasses clattered together. "Didn't you know?"

"It doesn't matter," Cal said but she went on, "I saw their Rolls in the driveway."

"Fiat," Cal corrected.

"Whatever," she said eagerly. "We walked right by it. I wouldn't have noticed except—"

Cal had succeeded in leading his wife away to talk with the new chancellor. Lewis was smiling. He rarely smiled but if anyone could induce him to smile it was John. Lizzie Tifgat had strolled to the front window, but Lewis assured her it was too dark to see anything in the yard. "My porch light must have burned out."

"I noticed," she said. She smelled very highly of perfume. "The Deadman's almost missed your place but for the cars parked there." She was wiping steam off the glass. It reflected her stiff, platinum hair and orange-red mouth in a soft, almost flattering manner. "One of the reasons I accepted the Deadman's invitation was to meet John Wilson."

"Yeah. You're both writers—" he observed blankly, but she was already walking away.

A small commotion across the room caught his attention. The front door was opening to the sounds of an argument on the porch. The partiers had quieted. Lewis and Lizzie Tifgat moved toward the door. John stepped into the room and a regimen of hugs and loud greetings. He seemed momentarily stunned by the gush of attention and when he caught Lewis's eye, he shrugged as if to ask, "What's this all about?" Alison stumbled into him from the porch, trying to pull her arm from her coat, which had somehow become all twisted about her. Bea Umlohr went to help.

"I must be caught in the lining," Alison was saying. Someone was twittering. John frowned, glanced at Alison who returned a raised eyebrow. John greeted his host.

"How was it?" Lewis asked, waiting for a response.

"How was what, for Christ's sake?"

Someone else laughed then and John shuddered. The partygoers had clearly discovered what he and Alison had been doing in the little Fiat Spider. No easy feat in so small a car, Lewis had observed casually. Laughter. John was clearly annoyed. A dozen people were standing in a semi-circle around he and Alison, smiling and waiting for something to happen. Alison was finally getting out of her coat. She looked up and smiled triumphantly as laughter finally overwhelmed the little horde. John asked what the fuck was so damned funny when his eyes met with those of his host. He turned cautiously toward his lover, and blurted out in front of everybody, "Good god, Alison! You put your dress back on inside-out."

Two

...we may see a flight of broad steps, descending alongside the antique and massive foundations of the Capital, toward the battered triumphal arch of Septimus Severus, right below. Farther on, the eye skirts along the edge of the desolate Forum (where Roman washer women hang their linen to the sun,) passing over a shapeless confusion of modern edifices, piled rudely up with ancient brick and stone, and over the domes of Christian churches, built on the old pavements of heathen temples, and supported by the very pillars that once upheld them. At a distance beyond—yet but a little way, considering how much history is heaped into the intervening space—rises the great sweep of the Coliseum, with the blue sky brightening through the upper tier of arches.

Nathaniel Hawthorne, *The Marble Faun*

The second-class train pulled into the main terminal in Rome: *Roma Termini*. The two hours had slipped by as seamlessly as did the landscape, from lush countryside radiant with sunshine, to a tumblescape of concrete apartment buildings. Caleb stood by the window, his notebook in hand. Try as he might, he could not finish the chapter. There was noise and activity all about him. Trickity-clickity, screech and trundle. Throbbing, wobbling, turning and ducking under a lackluster trophy of Imperial rubbish; shoulder to shoulder in the squawking jam-packed *carrozza*; a second-class car filled to overflowing with holiday visitors descending on Rome.

Caleb tried to see between the bobbing heads a glimpse of this city-of-graves so powerfully pungent in its presence. The train was passing the brick and lichen ruins of what was once the uterine temple to the virgin goddess Minerva, who the Greeks called Athena, a sooty dusting of snow notwithstanding. Shoulder to shoulder with a crowd of nervous Italians yack-

yackiting in antiphon with the trick-trackiting of the trundling steel wheels, he sighed a blessing in reverse, "What the fuck am I doing here?"

The car jerked forward in halting hops under the sparks of its electrical umbilicus. Ceeee-ack-a-lack-lack-lack. Screeching. Grinding. Roma Termini, the speakers buzzed. Roma. Termini! "Ack!" Someone had just kneed him in the nuts!

He is John Caleb Wilson. He is the hero of his other stories as well as this one. He is the victim of the pen as much as she is; of the very pen he holds as he writes on his little pad in the cramped quarters of the compartment, awaiting the train's final destination, the final exodus from these crowded confines to the open air of the platform. The last descent from transience to immovability, Dante's Third Level of Hell, as far as Caleb was concerned. He is a writer, one of those odd people who seek to uncover a kind of divine wisdom in the everyday doings of ordinary people. In this regard, his profession was not unlike that of the taxidermist.

He was not happy with what he did though he couldn't help but do it. And he had been doing it most of his life—writing. Unable to sleep as a child, he used to tell himself stories, the sounds of the television in the other room where his parents languished, serving as *cantus firmus*, like the drone of an organ behind the words of the preacher. For Caleb then, there was always music behind him when he was writing, even if only in his head. In grade school, he'd write novellas in the margins of his notebook during arithmetic class. In high school, rather than being active in sports or with girls, it was stories about football players and cheer leaders being carried off by aliens and in college he took creative writing classes with a protégé of Faulkner who both talked and wrote with a southern accent. His favorite word, both in his writing and his lecturing was fuck. Caleb used to call him Professor Fuckner. He barely passed the class with a "D."

"You're not a very good writer," the professor had told him. "Maybe it's time to consider another outlet for your creativity. Sculpture, maybe."

"I don't like getting my hands dirty." Professor Fuckner was not amused.

That was then. This is now. Over forty years and several un-published novels later. And for some reason he could not even remember what had happened to most of them. Those yet to be published great books. One was buried in the ground somewhere. Another had lain in his dresser drawer under his underwear for so long he had come to look upon it as just another pair of boxers. The other half-dozen or so—lost causes.

He tried to move as he pushed his way into the corridor but slammed his shoulder into the rugged rucksack flung over the burly back of a German tourist. He and his Nordic paramour had pushed their way in front of him as if the American did not exist in their worldview. People with other things on their minds do that sort of thing, he mused, still writing in his head. Caleb was almost always in his head and had been there for so long a time he no longer cared to try to tell the difference between real life and the life he wrote about.

Holiday visitors had pressed into the narrow space of the train's corridor to toss valises out the opened windows to shouting relatives on the platform. Caleb tried again to move but a large group of small children all dressed in their holiday finery had pushed in front of him to wave out the window at tearful parents and grandparents. He tried once more to move and found himself face to face with an oversized nun who was ushering a troupe of teenage girls down the narrow passageway at the expense of everyone else's comfort. One of the girls smiled back at him, a kind of apology, he assumed. Her sweet warm face showed fleetingly among the flock of nun's caps. They were flaring and white like paper geese alighting on black shoulders. In the gangway, the nuns clustered and talked and laughed together like *real* women. They too toted shopping bags glittering with wrapped gifts as they leapt joyfully from the crowded train onto the equally crowded platform. The schoolgirls had formed themselves into a neat line on the quay awaiting the orders to march, their red caps and gloves, their blue skirts and blazers flash-flashing like semaphores as they moved through the pulsing crowds.

The same girl glanced back at him as he stepped at last onto *terra firma*. She was perhaps amused at his apparent confusion, and she smiled the wine-dark smile of a Mediterranean. Her skin was almost the color of his dark hair. His skin was the color of her starched blouse. He studied the back of his hand against the blur of activity on the platform as if it were a clue to his own misery. He felt suddenly sickly pale compared to those about him; like seeing the snowy Alps from the vineyards of red clay or the black Adriatic set against the walled shores of Albania.

No matter. The girl was gone. The crowds had moved on. He was suddenly nearly alone on the platform. He heaved a breath of relief, took up his leather bags, one over each shoulder, leather against leather, and numbly followed the line of pilgrims that pointed toward Rome.

Roma Termini: more crowds; December crowds descending on Rome. Advent. Bad attitude. Sad, pressed and late, having no reason to celebrate; he paused. Having no time for ancient mysteries, he kept his eyes in his pockets. Elbowed and shouldered, a beating of wings as pigeons took flight in the vast atrium of the station, a flutter of foreign tongues, a feathery taste of impending tragedy; he sighed again. "What am I doing here?"

A surge of that shorter, darker race pulsed just beneath the surface of his vision. It moved in rippled waves through the great concourse of the Fascist era monument to modernist efficiency, in imitation of Imperial crowd-pleasing splendor. Named for the Roman thermal baths nearby, the Stazione Termini was originally built in a pseudo-Renaissance style employing columns arranged according to Vitruvius's architectural standards. Like the Coliseum, the lower floor was in the Greek Doric order and the upper floors in the Ionic and Corinthian orders. But that venerable edifice was replaced under Benito Mussolini with marble modern. Caleb let out another sigh as he paused to gaze about.

"Now, what; I wonder?"

That was it. The train-ride! He was weary. He'd come down from Munich on an all-nighter. Packed. It was a Sunday. The weekend before Christmas. He'd stood up most of the way. Having purchased a reserved seat in Venice he then had to evict an old woman who pretended not to have understood the "prenotato" sign over the seat. None of the Italians in the compartment spoke to him the remainder of the trip. The old woman continued to stand in the doorway of the compartment and glare at him. He tried to sleep for a while and did achieve a facsimile thereof, but a bad smell attended him the entire way and he assumed it was some trace left by the old woman as a curse upon his reserved seat. He could see her glaring face even with eyes closed.

That was when he decided to ignore her and to write instead of sleep. Monsters can produce a sleep of reason, from time to time! He was still writing in his head when he stumbled from the terminal into the soft, late-afternoon sunshine of wintry Rome. He could sense the sun's presence though he could not see it. It was reflecting off the plastic signs that lined the terminal concourse. He moved instinctively toward the light. The smell followed him, and he wondered if he'd not caught it from having sat in the same seat as the evicted old hag. Italy is filled with witches, he had been told, ever since they were driven out of Spain. Or was that the Jews?

He pushed his way through the crowds until a cool sun struck him at last in the eyes. He stopped, surveying the vast tumbled streetscape; hawkers and busses and the pitiful remains of Imperial rubbish carefully protected in their chain-link sanctuaries, plastered with Communist posters, nonetheless. There were hawkers and busses everywhere. There was also a ridiculous looking man parading about with a magic-marker sign on a stick over his head. He was a short, bald man, as wide as tall, and the sign was in English: "Academy San Marco This Way." The man spoke no English. He simply nodded at Caleb's question, obvious as it must have been, and pointed him toward a blue and white van in the parking area, its nose poking out from behind a crumbling wall-relic. The nuns and schoolgirls were boarding it. The man with the sign had moved on, seeking others to lead astray.

Caleb tried to scratch his head in confusion but for the weight of shoulder bags that cramped his arms all the way down to his wrists. The best he could do was to move his fingers in a scratching manner at his side. Then the blue and white van pulled away and revealed the Word, "Academy San Marco," in gold, bold italics on a tan van. Bland fascist architecture in Mussolini modern stood beyond, and beyond that, crumbling Baroque facades crusted with pigeon shit: split pediments, mixtilinear arches and massive wooden doors. A waste of wood, he thought. A waste of everything!

The light turned red, but the van did not stop. It turned green and it halted to let an old woman cross the street. Red, go. There were two other sleepy less than cordial fellows in the van, well-spaced apart. There was a man, seen from the rear, with ruddy hair and thick body. And there was a woman, already seated near the back when Caleb had boarded, her head inclined against the dirty glass. She hadn't noticed him when nodding a greeting in her direction. He dropped one of his shoulder bags to the seat and she noticed him.

"Need some help?"

He shook his head, unimpressed with the sound of her voice and her unexpressive eyes. "Writer?" he asked casually.

"Poet."

Figures, he thought. "It's going to be a cold, dry winter."

He sat a few seats in front of her, enjoying the silence, hoping it would last a while longer. Silence was the reason for his being there, in Rome, at the

Academy, in winter! It was a respected retreat for the gifted, a safe haven for the creative mind, that repository of hope, memory, and remorse. It was also there, he was certain, where *she* dwelt, no longer of the flesh, but in perfect splendor among those other relics of former times.

He fought back a sob. He'd been doing that too much lately. Regretting.

The little bald man was driving the van, his sign cleverly propped against the seat, tucked under the lip of a little fan, unnecessary in December.

"December!" Caleb thought. "Rome in winter! Fuck."

The ancient metropolis lay silenced under a transparent veil of snow and low riding clouds. The tan van moved through the grey eminence like a gondola along some old waterway. A heavy mist had settled about the taller palaces on the Via Cavour. They seemed frayed at the upper edges, as if their upper stories had been torn off by time and circumstances. The tattered remnants of Roman glory slipped past on either side as the van plied its way between the Then and the Here-and-Now, the ruins on one side, the busy street on the other. Rain washed across the windows, smearing their grimy lenses with an even darker gray. The silent riders seemed to almost tip toe past the Theatre of Marcellus and on toward the eternal River Tiber. The dark river was lost within its own mantle of fog and the Domes of Christendom seemed to float on a sea of sooty clouds beyond the leafless plane trees. Rain patterned the view, streaking the already streaked window glass. Caleb heaved a pathetic sigh and closed his eyes. They crossed the Tiber into Trastevere.

The Academy accepted only a few winter fellows. He was among them. The directors had promised him a quiet and restful haven. It was to be a protected and productive place; just what he needed, a lack luster trophy at best. It seemed at that moment in time an appropriate place: a gift for the gifted; quiet, cold, distant and unforgiving. He'd won the scholarship along with a prize for the best possible first novel of the new millennium—Or something like that.

He opened his eyes as the tan van made its way through narrow streets flanking the Tiber in all its dull splendor. Old Rome shimmered like a home movie beyond the dirty glass. Not even Christmas with all its paper trimmings could dress it up as far as John Caleb Wilson was concerned. He was instead reminded of his mother, a bored and colorless woman who blamed him for herself having grown old and alone. She was a homely bride, his Roma.

They had crossed the bridge. They had traversed the Tiber Island and left the old city. They began their ascent into the trans-Tiber hills. Even in winter, Trastevere was a fantasy place of deep green cypresses punctuated with the paler greens of palms, the greenless branches of plane trees and figs, and in amongst the greenery, architecture; Italianate architraves, cyclone fencing and asphalt driveways. He rubbed his eyes. Was he still in Rome? Here were slumbering neighborhoods, tree-lined alleyways, private gardens behind walls of stone rubble studded with broken coke bottles. He found himself smiling at the sight. It was nothing short of a real imitation of tasteless California in the Tiber-shed hills. Far below, and, thankfully, out of sight, obscured by the fumes from its own decaying body, lay Rome.

The Academy was lost on its own expansive grounds like so many pasteboard Hollywood mansions, here duplicated in marble, pure white and exquisitely ornamented. Like plaster-of-Paris geese grouping on the lawn, it was an arcade of wings surmounted by long neck towers and orange bill-tiled roofs. He found himself smiling again, this time in delight. He looked about to see if the others had taken notice, but each was lost in his own imitation of sleep.

"Yes," he thought, "this is perfect; the perfect place for fakes like me to escape the real world of flesh and blood. I can live here."

He took up his leather bags, one on each shoulder, leather on leather, and stepped from the tan van onto the dark dirt of the Academy cloister, an imitation of the very cloister, the cloister of the mind. Ah, yes, that was it! This is the place, the very place, the place in which she dwells in perfect synchronicity with all that is tragic and beautiful. He stepped forward, his hand in his heart, his eyes upon those of the sycophants who had come out to meet him, the young men in blue frocks who took up the luggage like crosses to bear on behalf of the sinners of the world. He watched them go, seeking meaning in their every deed. Then, he took his vows from the trustees assembled on the steps and, entering the foyer, took leave of the world of the flesh, there to reside in the perfect world of his imperfect imagination.

The three supplicants paused to admire the grand staircase as pointed out to them by a black-bearded man in a white sports coat. They were admonished to let their eyes soar to the ceiling and lose themselves among the vaults where stucco cherubim cavorted, and voluptuous Olympians leered down at them from the gilded cornices. The woman poet laughed, and her twittering resounded off the archivolts to the dismay of the hosts. Everyone looked at her in silence and she grew quiet.

The fellows were then conducted to their simple quarters on the third floor. Their stiff city shoes pounded on the gentle marble stairs. It suddenly seemed the only noises that existed in this sacred precinct were those the Americans had brought with them from their homeland.

The young men in the blue smocks carried their luggage, each into his own room. Caleb wondered if he should tip the porter, but he'd left before he was able to arrive at a decision. He had closed the door behind him, and Caleb found himself alone in the small room. He breathed carefully, afraid to move. There was a narrow bed, too short for a six-footer, a wardrobe and a sink. Electric wires ran around the room at about shoulder high like a molding, attached to the plaster surface with staples. A single naked light bulb dangled from the high ceiling. There was also a table with a desk lamp, and a Renaissance style scissors chair awaited him near one of two shuttered windows that seemed to overlook a garden. He opened the shutters. The glass was dusty on the inside and rain-streaked on the outside. He opened the casements. A damp breeze invaded the small cell.

It was indeed a winter garden over which the window looked, blighted by winter, its orderly heaps of snowbound herbs overlapping the walkways. Rain striped the view of shadowy cedars beyond with diagonal hatching. A damp chill gripped him by the hands and drew him to the bed. Having left the window open, he sat, pressing his hands into his groin to warm them. Someone, somewhere, was playing a cello.

"And besides," he said to himself, "she had put her dress back on inside-out—"

Three

1

And besides, she had left the door wide open. A damp chill had gripped him by the hands and drew him to the front window. He turned to close the door and went back to his typing.

Alison was always doing foolish things, like leaving doors open in winter, and John was always trying not to let it bother him. He would go secretly about the house and yard correcting her little mistakes lest she find them out and blame them on him. That was one of his morning tasks: the corrections. Alison nearly always slept in close to ten or eleven no matter what time she had gone to bed the night before. She nearly always slept in and John appreciated that. It gave him just enough time each morning to go about the place and correct Alison's little mistakes from the day before. Little things. Things that drove John crazy. Not the big things like using the vacuum cleaner on the hearth when there was a fire blazing there and sucking fire into the bag and practically burning the house down before throwing the thing out into a snowbank where John would find it, still smoldering, on his way in from work. No, he could almost understand the big things as they might happen to anyone under certain conditions.

It was the faucets left dripping. The stereo left running with no record on the turntable. The closet lights left burning with the doors closed; places where there shouldn't have been lights in the first place. It was doors left open in winter.

They were little things, but they seemed almost too regular to be mistakes and that bothered him most. It had never occurred to John during his daily rounds that Alison might have been making all those little mistakes on purpose. For his sake. To give him something to occupy his time while she slept a few hours longer. To keep him out of trouble. That would have been her answer. Or, to contribute to the personal mystique she had been cleverly crafting over the past months as a means of assuring his continued interest in her. To remind him, if nothing else, that she was still there. In his house.

He had shouted at her because the door had been left open to the winter. The house had smelled of baking things and she had refused to tell him what she was making. But she was smiling about something and that had bothered him. What had she done now that she was waiting for him to discover? He tried to correct the error by pretending to be indifferent to her, disinterested in her evening plans. She said her mother had called, but he knew she was fibbing. He watched her pick out a party dress. Silk tie-dye! That was a mistake he had no control over. Alison's taste. Now he stood in the damp draft from the opened door to Lewis's house watching the guests making fun of Alison in her inside-out dress. There was no way he could correct this latest mistake either.

"It's all the rage," Alison was laughing. "Everyone in Paris is showing their seams this year."

John turned away. Something had caught his eye. A blonde woman near the punch bowl, leaning on the table so that the lip of varnished wood cut into her thigh just at the hem of her short velvet dress, and she was watching him. Her entire body, from mid-thigh to shoulder was corseted in deep purple velvet and her hot-pink go-go boots just as tightly bound her calves. She wore a pink headband and curls of her ash blonde wig gathered like epaulettes on her shoulders. She had turned toward him all in one movement as if it were not possible for individual parts of her body to move independently.

My God! It was Lizzie Tifgat.

She was looking directly at him, into him, but he had lost himself in his obsession with Alison once again. He was thinking about the morning, the beginning of the day now ending, and he was wondering if the day was going to end differently than usual. Even before he had finished correcting the past day's mistakes, even before he'd finished his second cup of coffee, Alison had come stumbling into the kitchen still clutching the remains of her recently interrupted dreams. He'd smiled a silent good morning as he was not accustomed to speaking to her so early and his voice hadn't responded to his will. She dropped into a hard kitchen chair. He pushed an empty cup her way and she pushed it back. Her hair fell over her face and she made a weak gesture at pushing it aside. One delicately blue eye peered at him through the tangle of tawny locks.

"Jesus," she sighed.

"You're up early."

"It's Saturday."

Her response hadn't made sense, but he'd let it go.

"Don't you have a morning class or something?" she wondered in a cracked voice.

"Ten o-clock."

"Will you be home for lunch?"

"Sure."

"There's some cold cuts in the fridge. I should be back in time to get everything done."

"Good." (What the fuck is she talking about?) "Maybe we should do something tonight."

She had looked up suddenly with a quizzical look on her face.

"I mean; we haven't gone out in months."

She interrupted him with a harshness in her voice he didn't understand. "And what do you suggest we do, John?"

"Uh—Whatever you like?"

She sighed and took the cup to the counter where the percolator hissed and gurgled indifferently.

"I'm sure whatever it is I'll only end up doing it by myself." She turned to face him, leaning her butt on the counter so that the varnished lip cut into the soft folds of her cotton gown. She held the steamy cup before her and, strangely, smiled sweetly at him. He involuntarily smiled back, wishing he hadn't. He agreed sullenly that she probably would end up doing something by herself. He got up from the table and went into the bathroom. Alison watched him go. He watched her through the crack in the half-opened door as she dumped her hot coffee into a nearby planter and returned to the bedroom. He shook his head as he ran the buzzing razor over his chin.

No wonder that plant wasn't doing so well.

Lizzie Tifgat was still staring at him. He snapped his mind back to the present. Here was another mistake he could not correct. He grabbed Lewis by the sleeve. He was still laughing.

"Why did you invite her?"

"I thought she came with you." More laughter. "Or did you come first?"

John lowered his voice to a hard whisper. "I mean Lizzie Tifgat, you imbecile! Why did you invite her?"

"I didn't." He pulled away from him angrily.

"I thought this was to be a faculty only affair."

"So did I," he returned, abruptly, "but I don't have much control over my own destiny, it seems. Someone told the chancellor about the party, and—"

"Jesus, boy! Is he here?"

Lewis scowled and started away. "Don't piss me off, John."

"Sorry." He took him by the arm once more. "It's been a trying afternoon, Lewis, but—How did that Tifgat woman get here?"

Lewis was still angry and was clearly losing interest in John's little palace intrigues. "How should I know? She came with the Deadmans. Christ sake, John! What was I supposed to do, bar the door? Besides," he hesitated, suddenly interested. "Why should you care who I invite?" John was searching for something in his pockets. "I sort of know her—"

Lewis was starting to smile. "Yeah? Tell me about it?" They moved a little way off. John was especially fidgety. Lewis was losing his patience again. The whole scene was one of tense discomfort. John's body stiffened. Lewis glanced over his shoulder, in the direction of John's harsh gaze. Lizzie Tifgat was moving in their direction with three drinks clenched in her hands.

"Later," John coughed. "The Queen Bee is about to arrive with stingers."

"No," Lewis said, looking around. "The queen isn't here yet." John scowled at him. "I don't mean him! Jesus, Lewis! No bias in you, is there?"

"Bias?" Lizzie Tifgat wondered, extending the drinks. "Me? I'm no feminist, John, if that's what you two men are afraid of. You, of all people, should know that."

"You two do know each other—"

"I was referring to my friend Lewis, here, Mrs. Tifgat."

Lizzie looked Lewis up and down. He asked nervously, half-jokingly, "Does it show?"

"Well," she said, "not yet."

Lewis showed the whites of his eyes as he rolled them heavenward, accepted the glass of liquors, and asked anxiously, "So. How do you two know each other?"

They each answered at once: "Casually," John said.

"Intimately," Lizzie said.

Lewis nodded, his eyes on John the entire time. Lizzie was asking John how he had been. His answer: "Fair."

Her response: "Not from what I've been hearing."

His reply: "That depends on who you've been hanging around with lately, I suppose."

"And what do you hear about me?"

"I don't get out much."

Lewis interrupted. "Sounds like I happened upon a conversation left unfinished from some earlier time. Think I better—"

"Yes, you should," Lizzie added. "Alison is taking cuttings from your African Violets."

Lewis was walking away, confused and muttering. "I don't have any African Violets—"

"Bad joke," John said.

"It served its purpose," she said; then, "Well. Imagine this."

"Imagine," he returned, looking away.

"Nice to see you, too."

"Funny," he added, looking back, "I was just thinking how nice it's been not seeing you."

"It has been a pleasant if uneventful interlude," she agreed. "Nice party, huh? Having fun?"

"Bored to tears."

"Yes," she agreed, her lips at the rim of her glass, "it is getting that way, isn't it?"

"I'm certain things will get livelier," he said, looking directly at her. "The Deadmans don't know you very well, do they?"

"Not very. But I have changed—a little."

"Which parts this time?"

She smiled. "Just the hair. That's a god-awful shirt, John. Birthday present from Alison?"

"Uh-huh. I don't remember your boobs being that round."

"It's the dress, John. Not as attention getting as Alison's, but I like it."

"We all try, don't we?" He yawned.

"Bored again?"

"Silly games bore me almost as much as faculty parties, Mrs. Tifgat."

"John," she said, seriously. He turned to her. "Bored people are usually the cause of their own boredom."

John bowed. "Touché," he said, smiling, but a little.

"Don't bend any lower, dear heart," Alison said from behind him. "You might split something."

"You must be Alison—"

John was trying to usher his paramour away.

"We've met before, Mrs. Tifgat," Alison said over her shoulder, surprising them both. "I used to do your hair. I'm a cosmetologist, by profession, you know."

John was baffled. "You are?" She rolled her eyes. Lizzie Tifgat was nodding. "Yes," she said, "I remember you. Why, Alison! You used to do a beautiful job! I've not been able to find a girl I like half so much as you. Why did you stop?"

John had stopped listening. Another mistake he could not correct. Lizzie Tifgat and Alison actually liked each other. They were destined to become allies against him based on their own individually warped perceptions of him as a man. He was doomed.

"—and I love your dress," Lizzie Tifgat was saying with a laugh. "It isn't many people who arrive at a party with their insides already showing." She eyed John then added. "I commend you."

"I like yours better, Lizzie," Alison said, "but I'm too shy to show that much of my body in public."

"Do you really like it? It isn't very comfortable."

"It would be better without the long-line."

Lizzie was smoothing her fingers over the fabric. "You may be right. You want to trade?"

"Love to."

And they were off to the bathroom. John finished his drink and moaned very audibly. What was it about him that attracted the weirdos of the women's world?

2

Bea Umlohr had come in from the porch and, seeing John, had waved a friendly, "Hi."

"Hello, Beatrice," he said, seeking an out. "Where's Calvin?"

She merely shrugged. "Nice to see you. Is the chancellor still here?"

John admitted he did not know. "Was he here earlier?"

"Kitchen. Dorothy Deadman has been monopolizing his attention all night. I just had to step out for a joint," she concluded in a whisper.

"Bored, Beatrice?"

"I hate faculty parties," she said with a guilty giggle. "Isn't that a hoot?"

John responded that Bca and Calvin always seemed to have such a good time at faculty parties. Still whispering, she admitted it was because they were usually half in the bag by the time they got there. Then she laughed.

"But then, we're nearly always half in the bag, as they say. It's the secret of our happy marriage, John."

"Everybody has a story, Beatrice."

"You should try it."

"I should try something."

She had slipped her arm through his. "Not having a good time, John?"

He tried to wiggle out of her embrace. She was ushering him toward the kitchen. As they strolled, she asked, "What's your story with Lizzie Tifgat? I understand she practically begged the Deadman's to bring her."

"We were lovers."

"Before Alison, I presume—I mean—"

"I was a teenager."

"You were never a teenager," She grinned. "Why haven't you ever had an affair with me?" she asked suddenly, stopping them in the doorway. "I'm married. And older. You apparently like that in a partner."

"Lizzie was a mistake," he said, immediately wishing he hadn't said it. (Did he say, mistake?) "I mean. I was young. It was a bad relationship. It has haunted me ever since." Why was he telling her all this. She seemed genuinely intrigued. Nodding. Biting on her thumb. "And, besides, Beatrice, I've never felt particularly attracted to you."

"Oh." She seemed suddenly distracted. "Where's the god-damned bathroom," she asked, breathlessly. He laughed. "That shit always does this to me," she explained, as she started toward the closed door of the bathroom.

John was still laughing. "I think it's occupied," he said. "But there's a half bath off the front porch." He pointed the way.

"Oh," she gasped. "These cottages are so quaint, aren't they?" She started toward the French doors, still talking as she went. John had stopped listening.

She stepped out onto the porch, calling over her shoulder, "And what was it you and Alison were doing out in that little car or yours, John?"

"You know Alison," he said, as his paramour, in a purple, velvet mini and go-go boots, came out of the other bathroom, "she's always losing something."

Beatrice mentioned breathlessly as she slipped into the half-bath that Alison had probably lost that long ago.

"Lost what?"

"Your virginity."

"How dare you discuss my virginity with Beatrice Umlohr."

"New dress?"

"Like it?"

"Looks better on you than Lizzie Tifgat."

"I look better out of it, too," she said.

John merely sighed. Someone had turned up the volume on the record player and other couples were dancing to a ballad of some kind. John wasn't really paying it much attention. Alison's mouth was moving but he heard nothing. "What?"

"I said, Lizzie told me you two used to sleep together," she said.

"It's a lie," he said. "We didn't just sleep together."

The bit of silence that followed was dark and red with tension. Instinctively, John and Alison put their arms around each other, and they began to dance despite the hard silence that accompanied them. Then, as the smell of her shampoo began to awaken his senses, as the swell of her body began to warm his own flesh, as that seductive something hidden deep down inside her began to work its spell upon him, John pulled her yet closer to him, allowing, at the same time, the sound of the music to fill the space vacated by the silence.

Something had occurred to him, but he had decided to think about it later. It had something to do with loss and he knew it was his relationship with Alison of which he had been thinking all that time. He'd been thinking about it for weeks but had not actually identified the real meaning of his preoccupation until having seen Lizzie Tifgat that few minutes earlier. She always reminded him of loss, for some reason. Even when he was first sleeping with her as a college student in her writing class, she had somehow symbolized loss to his awakening consciousness. It was an emblem he had embraced in those days as necessary to his spiritual growth, as pilgrims embrace empty reliquaries. It was when he had grown tired of, or perhaps afraid of that icon of loss that he'd left the older teacher and struck off with another, younger woman; one less marked by the stigmata of age. That would have been—Nancy? Or was Wendy first? It didn't matter much. They both looked more or less alike. In memory. Except that Nancy had magnificent boobs. Or was that—

It was all too confusing to think about right then, especially with Neil Diamond as accompanist. He felt suddenly sad, so he moved reality to the back of his mind and stepped in behind it. Or, that is, he thought he did.

"Don't you feel like dancing, John?"

Her question had rung with the plaintive timbre of an oboe. John was struck by the woody sound of her voice and was moved to sympathy. "I guess not. Sorry."

"You're writing, aren't you?"

"What do you mean?"

She smiled thinly. "I can always tell when you're writing."

He pretended not to understand her, but she went on, gently prodding him with her sincere words and her wonderful depth of feeling. "You get a distance to you," she said, her eyes lifting into her head as she searched for the right words. "Even your expression changes. The kind of words you choose to talk with changes, as if it is another person's voice speaking through your mouth. It used to frighten me until" I learned that the other person is yourself, or some part of yourself, trapped deep inside and tapping a kind of S. O. S. on the back of your teeth so that your speech becomes rhythmical. Like in poetry."

"Even your body changes," she said. "It's like you get bigger, taller, harder. And you say things that are cruel and thoughtless, though, kind of beautiful, too. It is one of the things I love most about you, even though I will never have enough brains to understand it."

She had smiled very sweetly, and he wished he had something to say to her but all he could do was shrug slightly and force a small but hopelessly inadequate smile in return. (You are the words.) He still held her hand. (I am the tune.) The other dancers were moving about them, bumping them. (Play me.)

She began to back away from him, until at arm's length, finger to finger, her touch eluded him, and she was enclosed by the dancers and disappeared from his sight. The immediate sense of loss was exhilarating, and he reveled in the silence for but a split second, until his peaceful repose was interrupted by the glare cast off distant eyes.

Through the mob he could see her, even in the darkness that momentarily engulfed him. Though she stood behind him, he could feel the bite of her ravenous eyes. He turned to face her. She was smiling but not with delight. Hers was a lethal smile. She was wearing Beatrice Umlohr's flower print caftan. It was Lizzie Tifgat.

John had nodded toward her from where he stood near the French doors talking to Alison, and she had returned the gesture. Then, lest Alison was watching, he squeezed into the crowd of dancers and out the other side, up against the wallpapered wall. He was hoping he might blend in with the patterns and become invisible for a time but Beatrice, in Alison's inside-out dress was waltzing his way in search of a dance partner. A flash of white light slapped him in the face as Calvin stepped out of the wallpaper and into his sight. It was the bathroom door that had opened. Not only had Cal left the seat up, he had left the light on.

"Next," John said, slipping into the brilliant though watery atmosphere of the small john. He turned out the light. Someone was toying with the door handle. John pulled out his penis and urinated. He wasn't sure where. He had been blinded by the light and the darkness had left him confused. He did not hear the sound of water he'd expected. Maybe Calvin had put the seat down after all. Finished, he found the toilet tank handle and flushed the toilet for no apparent reason. He opened the door to the anxious face of chancellor Groen.

"It's all yours," John said.

"Christ!" came a voice from the closed door as John walked away. He moved cautiously down the darkened hallway toward the kitchen where the noise and activity of the partiers was made more raucous by the yellow walls and fluorescent lights. He paused. Watched from a short distance. Listening.

The heads of the revelers seemed to float on a thin sea of smoke while, below, their legs mingled with the legs of tables and chairs sprouting from the flowered linoleum like sea grasses moving to and fro with the currents of conversation. He retreated from the awful vision, slipping past the bathroom door and the cursing voice of the chancellor and back into the front room where dancers occupied the void of silence that still lay draped like a sleeping python in the hollow of the house. A crystal doorknob poked him in the ribs, and he let himself out onto the porch with its pots of dead geraniums and ferneries of sprengerii so often found in the obsolete summer kitchens of farmhouses in old country towns. The sun was just rising behind a fine, green maple tree beyond a garden vision of hollyhocks and larkspur. Colors everywhere were faded with age as in old photographs, but the forms were distinct and heavy with symbols. Everything was pointing up as if drawn by the ascending sun and settling mists of dawn. All but the young woman who was pleading with him to stop. Her hair was the color of the young sun. Her skin the blush of misty air. The red of poppies. And someone, somewhere in the soft distance, was playing a piano.

He took a breath and tasted the moist warmth of a summer morning, though the porch was dark, and a late winter chill filled the void of his departing memory. A fading keyboard arpeggio remained with him, but he paid it no mind. His writer's brain often left him with feelings akin to loss, to memories of events that could never have occurred in real life. His real life.

"What are you doing out here?"

It was Alison.

"Some air—"

"I hear a piano," she said, peering into the darkness where the cars were parked, glistening softly in the occasional bits of light that played across their metal shoulders.

"Don't be silly."

"Beethoven, I think."

How dare she enter into his private world of imagination! "Let's go back in. The others will think were screwing again."

She stared at him a moment in dark disgust. "My you've gotten romantic lately," she said.

"I didn't mean it the way it came out. Let's go in."

"Kiss me first."

Pause. "Why?"

She raised her fingers to her mouth. The whites of her eyes showed flirtatiously. "My lips are cold?" John laughed at last. He enfolded her in his arms and kissed her very gently and warmly. Then more passionately as his mind toyed with the phenomenon that but minutes before he'd been wishing she weren't there. He sensed through the depth of the kiss she'd been wishing the same thing. Wondering why it was she stayed with a man when her inner desire was for marriage and children. He knew she suffered guilt for that, but she knew his mind. He hated kids. And he had no intention of ever marrying Alison for any reason whatsoever.

"Do you love me, John?"

A whisper at her ear; "Always will, Alison."

She sighed audibly in the comfortable arms of relief as they returned to the warm heart of the house. Her head on his shoulder. His mind still at the threshold of memory. She sensed his distance once the light of the hi-fi touched his face with red. "What, John? What is it?"

His voice came with deep within him. "That porch."

"I don't follow you."

"It reminded me of something." He turned to face her head on. "But I don't remember, exactly."

"A photograph?" she wondered.

"Maybe. My grandmother, I think."

"What about your grandmother, John?"

"I don't know. But there must be a photograph somewhere. Do we have a box of old pictures, Alison? In the closet, or in the attic, maybe, or the cellar?"

He had asked in profound earnest and her response might have seemed foolish to anyone who did not know her as John did. "We might," she said, thinking, "if we had an attic or a cellar."

John went on. "The front closet. Overhead is a trap door. I have a box of keepsakes up there. If the squirrels haven't got to it."

"I didn't know you had keepsakes, John," was her odd reply. He merely stared at her, the party lights moving in ghostly patterns on the nearby wall. She was distracted by them. John had turned away from her. He was walking down the hall toward the bright kitchen and the bar. She watched him go, then followed, probably wondering why she was following him. She asked if he'd like to go home. He shook his head "no" but said he'd like to look for the keepsakes when they got home. Or tomorrow, perhaps. She said to herself, "If there is a tomorrow."

He had stopped, and she ran into the back of him.

"What?"

"Nothing."

"You're crying."

"Am not!"

She merely stood there in silence a moment or two, then said, "I think I'll find somebody to dance with me."

But Alison did not feel like dancing any more. She simply stopped and turned away. "Did you hear the singer?" she asked as they walked from the circle of other dancers. "He was saying something about freedom and children."

Lewis admitted he hadn't been listening to the lyrics. "You think a lot about children, don't you, Alison? I mean, that's what John's always—"

"No," she snapped. "It's just the music, is all. He's a terrific writer."

"Who?"

"Neil Diamond. His songs, I don't know. They touch me."

"Yeah. Well. Here's John. Just the guy you've been—"

"Crazy," Alison said.

Four

They had now emerged from the gateway of the palace; and partly concealed by one of the pillars of the portico stood a figure such as may often be encountered in the streets and piazzas of Rome, and nowhere else. He looked as if he might just have stept out of a picture, and in truth, was likely enough to find his way into a dozen pictures; being no other than one of those living models, dark, bushy bearded, wild in aspect and attire, whom artists convert into Saints or assassins, according as their pictorial purposes demand.

"Miriam," whispered Hilda, a little startled, "it is your Model!"

Hawthorne, *The Marble Faun*

John and Alison, characters he didn't like very much, had just arrived at a party. Why didn't he like them? She was a whiner. He a complainer. They had a pretty good life together, otherwise. Why couldn't they get along? Maybe something will happen at the party to shed some light on that question. Caleb chewed on the end of his pen.

"What happens next?" He asked aloud. How could he make them more likeable?

There was a tapping at the door, then, a whisper in the woodwork. Annoyed and relieved at the same time, Caleb put down his pen and looked up.

"Avanti?"

The door opened a crack, and a young woman stuck her head barely in. "Oh. You speak Italian." It was the bland blonde from the tan van. (He was still writing in his head.)

"A little," he said from where he sat on the corner of his bed, his closed laptop as a writing desk.

"Are you busy?" Before he could answer that he was, she stepped fully into the room. She kept her hand on the door should she have to make a hasty exit. Caleb shrugged as she asked if she might come in for a few moments.

"Don't mind the room. I wanted to finish this chapter—"

"You're working," she said, turning to go.

He assured her it was all right. "I just haven't the energy to unpack," he added.

"Nor I." Her voice was annoyingly week and hesitant, as if she were trying to advertise her virginity in advance of any possible propositions. Caleb was nearing sixty. She was what—forty? He was forcing himself not to look at her breasts. He gestured toward the chair. She paused to peer out the window before sitting.

"You have a view of the garden."

She sat on the very edge of the chair. "My window overlooks a school yard." She was fidgeting. "I wish there were children in it. It seems awfully lonely." Then she smiled genuinely. "Must all be home for the holiday."

Caleb nodded cordially. She went on. "As I should be, I guess. This is my first time away from home during the holidays. I'm used to being with my family. I'm not feeling very good about that, I guess."

Caleb interrupted her. The last thing he wanted to hear at that moment was a confession. "I don't have much of a family. It doesn't matter much to me." She was still wearing her cotton coat and scarf. They were as colorless as she was. "But why did they insist on our being here before Christmas?" she asked plaintively. "The tutors won't be here until after New Year's."

"The ambassador wants to show us off at some shindig," he said. "That's the way I understand it, anyway. You have a family?" Was she married? The question was one way to find out.

"My parents, is all, and a sister or two." She was standing as if making ready again to leave. "Doesn't seem fair," she said to her reflection on the rainy window glass, "being here.

You?"

"Mother and Sister. Not close," he said, trying not to reveal too much as he was also trying not to remember too much. How long had it been since he'd last seen them? Since that time he had made fun of them for believing in God.

The woman was fidgeting, hesitating, as if waiting for him to tell her to sit down again. "You have a nice view," she said.

"It'll be nicer in the spring, I suspect."

She was nodding. "Spring—" He felt sympathy for her, and he stood and joined her near the window. He asked her name.

"Jo Ashley, Joanna, actually—Ashley. I'm a poet. I won some prize—"

He interrupted her again. "John Caleb Wilson."

She registered surprise. "The Latter Day Venus," she said, in reference to his prize-winning manuscript. "I read about it, Mr. Wilson. It sounds like a good old-fashioned story! Like Hawthorne, you know. Potential to be one of the better first novels of the new century—"

"Millennium," he suggested; then added, "Call me Caleb."

She grinned with a little embarrassment. "But it sounds beautiful!" she cried. "Like a grand romance of the past."

Caleb was annoyed at her bringing it up. "Beautiful or not," he said, mocking her, "it's not going well." He turned away. "Too literary, one of the judges said. Anyway, they liked it enough to send me here—"

"That's a good thing, I think—"

He nodded, hoping to hide his own embarrassment better than she had hers. He admitted he didn't recognize her name. She laughed a little and explained that it was because she used a penname.

"Natasha Van Pelt. My family wasn't too keen on my becoming a writer."

"I know your book," he said, hoping to hide his disfavor. (What a bunch of feminist whining crap!) "Yes. I read it."

"Really?" She sat again and she started moving about in her chair as if trying to find a comfortable spot. "Awful, wasn't it?" she added, not looking up at him.

"No!" he returned rather too quickly. "I mean; it won a prize, didn't it?"

"Well," she said, looking about nervously, "that was nice, anyway."

"Yes," he mused, following her line of sight to the rainy garden beyond the dirty glass. Already, an early dusk had fallen, and the view had darkened to shades as colorless as were those of his visitor.

"It seems the only way a woman can get published these days is to write like Betty Freidan!" she was saying as if in apology. She giggled girlishly, moving toward the still opened door. She said it wasn't really her style and then she made her goodbyes and left the room, closing the door very slowly, as if hoping to be called back.

"What a fake," he said to himself as the door closed. "Doesn't even use her real name."

No. It was mutual. Like the world of fakes he had convinced himself he was escaping, Caleb was also a quack, a plaster of Paris duckling on the lawn of the middle-class home he'd left long ago. But something of that old house still clung to him, like the smell left by the old woman on the train from Venice. Some trace had stuck to his shoes only to leave a print on whatever ground he trampled. He had come to Rome in search of a reality he seemed to have lost sight of, one that may not even have existed. He had come in good faith, seeking truth, and like every other adventure of his life, he had begun his quest with a complaint. He punched his fist into the marble sill of the viewless window, then left the room, door ajar, and crossed the hall. He knocked, and Jo answered.

"Yes?"

"It's Caleb Wilson."

She opened the door with a wide smile on her face. "I can't invite you in. My clothes are all over the room."

"Let's go into the city, Jo. Let's take a cold walk through the streets of Rome. If that isn't enough to inspire a romantic writer and a Sapphist poet, then we're doomed."

She laughed lightly, eying him strangely. "What did you call me? A Sapphist?"

He shrugged. "You know: like—Sappho?"

She nodded. "Yes," she said. "But I'm not a Lesbian, if that's what you mean." Then, "and, yes. I'd love to walk through the rainy streets of Rome with you. I've never been—"

He stumbled pitifully. "For purely literary purposes, you understand." She merely smiled. She had a nice smile. At least, she had that going for her. He tripped over his feet as he crossed the hall and stumbled into his room.

"No," he was saying to himself. "Not with her!"

By the time they got off the bus at Colosseo Station, it was dark. The winter sun had set unceremoniously behind a bank of ocean hugging clouds and Rome had taken on a different life under the bronze tinted lamplight of the modern age. The Coliseum rose above the swirl of traffic on wings of halogen and cast its infamous silhouette against a dark brown sky. The rain had stopped, and the sky was clearing. Occasional stars showed in feeble imitation of the crackling floodlights. After pausing to gaze like tourists at the sight, they started out, only to be confounded by a homeless woman, sprawled across the sidewalk, her arms flung before her, like a penitent before a reliquary, begging for coins. They stepped over her body and walked on. A lull in the traffic provided an opportunity to absolve their sin by crossing the street, holding hands, and at a run, as if the begging woman was after them.

"My first time in Rome," Jo was saying as they stepped onto the curb at the foot of the ex-Temple of Venus and Rome. She hadn't stopped talking since they'd left Trastevere. But now, as Caleb had hoped, the brooding presence of the sprawling ruins brought her at last to silence. "My god—"

"Yes," he agreed, in a voice barely above a whisper.

They walked quietly up the old *Via Sacra* to peer into the Forum through the nearly perfect arc of the Arch of Titus.

"What better place to die," Caleb mused aloud, catching her attention.

"What?" Her voice carried the tone of suppressed anxiety.

"Now I remember why I am here," he said.

She backed away from him a few steps. "To die?"

"Or to commit a murder." She laughed and said something about him being a little too melodramatic for her taste. He hadn't heard her and was saying over top of her words that he meant the place was a perfect spot to reminisce, to be alone, in silence eternal.

She again asked what he meant, and he went on, gesturing like a preacher. "Look at this place. Look around you, above you, beneath your feet." She was doing so as he rambled along into verbal fantasy. "Above, there is a marble sky and below, an ocean of stone and there, scattered among winter's brittle bones, here and there, look you; a face, carved in stone, and yet," he paused for sake of drama then added, "those blank eyes are so full of longing."

"Oh," she said, suddenly, hugging herself and bringing his words to a stop. "I'm getting chilled."

"I'm writing," he said impatiently, as if that should have justified his continuing to ramble. She said something about wishing she hadn't come along with him. He turned to her, no longer writing, but apparently requiring of her some sympathy. But she had left him there, in the shadow of the triumphal arch. She was walking back toward the wide avenue and its endless streams of traffic. Caleb followed at a short distance. He was annoyed. And he felt suddenly abandoned, for some reason.

"I seem to be the innocent cause of other people's miseries, Jo. And I don't know what to do about it."

Jo stopped and turned to face him, the hulk of Constantine's Basilica sprawling behind her. "Then, stop thinking that way." She adjusted her fists to her hips. "You seem all mixed up to me, Caleb Wilson," she said. The confident tone of her voice caught him by surprise. "You're talking in circles. Am I mistaking the writer for the real man, or is it you who is doing that?"

He was quiet for a few moments. He felt hurt. She fidgeted. He looked away, toward the beckoning lights of the ruins; sighed pathetically. "I seem to have lost touch, I guess, with one or the other." He looked up with an embarrassed grin. "And I'm not sure which one."

She took his arm and began leading him up the street toward the great white monument to Italy's first king. "That's all right," she said. "It happens to all us writers from time to time."

She had taken control and Caleb tagged along like an obedient hound. The traffic had lessened, and a kind of quietude had settled upon them. After a while he said, "Recite me something, will you? While we're walking; recite me something of yours. Will you?"

As she took a short while to think he added, "Something comforting?"

"Give me a moment," she said, her eyes on the amber sky, her mouth tending toward a smile. "I'm writing."

They walked a while more in silence. The winter sidewalk was empty of tourists and even the street had cleared. The stillness that attended them was heavy and cold. They paused and looked across the vast tumble of ruins, illuminated as they are now by the modern age.

> "These big stones," she said,
> "How grand and old they are.
> Older still, is the small stone I carry in my hand.
> It is the heart of my friend,
> Given me for safe keeping
> While he flies in fantasy—"

She bowed her head. They walked on a while without talking, then paused again to stare into the old forum, the three remaining pillars of the Temple of Castor and Pollux standing like a semaphore against the curses of the past. Caleb let slip another sigh.

"Very nice," he said softly. "You are, indeed, a poet!"

"Thank you, sir. You are, indeed, my inspiration."

He turned to her with a smile. "Really?"

She nodded.

"I don't think I've ever been anyone's inspiration before."

"I can't believe you haven't"

They were standing very close to each other, almost breast to breast.

"Must be the ruins, don't you think?"

"Could be the man."

"Really?"

She looked toward the Forum. "Or the ruins—"

"Don't fall in love with me, now!" He was grinning playfully, and she returned the grin. She shook her head no, her eyes still on the illuminated relics of the Roman past.

"Not a chance," she said, very softly.

"Man hater?"

She shook her head again. "Smart."

"Oh." He smiled. "Same difference."

They laughed, a little. He suggested they walk to the top of the Capitoline Hill to look at the Forum from the cradle of Michelangelo's piazza. A chill attended them as they mounted the steps and paused to glance over their shoulders through the grand Arch of Septimus Severus. It was a deep, penetrating chill that attended them, as if the heaps of marble crystal strewn about were ice rather than stone and the draft emanating from the crypts had thus been cooled in passing. Jo and Caleb were in Rome but, like all American mid-westerners, they were destined to drag some relic of that frozen north-country with them wherever they went. And, as writers, they wore chunks of their past like epaulets on the shoulders for all the world to see.

From the paved heights, back dropped with medieval traffic and Baroque neon that flash-flashed in red and green on the archivolts, to the hollowed acres below, where the Forum lay like some misplaced graveyard, their eyes moved like living beings; touching, searching, penetrating the lights and shadows of the *son-et-lumiere* pageant. So struck were they by the imposing trash heap of exquisite marble garbage that they lingered there for some time, glancing over their shoulders as if only for a moment, frozen, like statues, having forgotten their chill.

What small dignity compared to this? What insignificant chill, what sadness? They sighed in unison with a passion that filled the vaults of their own crania with a kind of light, illuminating their own bones as if they too were relics of the past. Like the romance novels of Nathaniel Hawthorne, indeed, they were. Then they stiffened as if confronted by an icy wind.

They had each become aware at once of an intruder, not one walking between them, but, more subtly, dividing them, not physically, but with the precision of a glance. A man stood a short distance off, in the shadow of the brick-and-mortar palace that guarded the entrance to the piazza. He was a small man in a dark coat, hunched over against the coolness of the evening. He was watching them! One of his eyes showed even in the darkness of his demeanor. He merely stood there, neither moved nor blinked. He was breathing heavily. Jo grabbed hold of Caleb's hand. But he had started to hum a Joni Mitchell song of some years earlier. She was confused for a moment, then, she remembered the words and sang along with him as they walked on by:

They continued into the bright piazza atop the Capitoline Hill. As they went, they left the present behind them and entered into an unholy alliance with the very past from which they were each trying to escape; a contract so laden with fine print as to have become invisible to the rational mind. Rome can do that to a person, even one not so lost in mystery as was Hawthorne.

They held hands as if they were lovers, for something had driven them to each other's side, to seek comfort in each other, to offer up the other, should it prove necessary, to the flames of sacrificial desire. They paused at the feet of the equestrian statue of Marcus Aurelius and looked back.

Another man had followed them into the piazza. He was taller, older than the shadowy figure they had encountered on the steps. He had followed them boldly, in plain sight. He had stopped when they stopped, looking at them as they looked back at him. He was standing but a few feet away and was sketching something in a book. Jo looked at Caleb and Caleb looked at Jo. She started to walk away but Caleb lingered. He nodded toward the sketcher. She acquiesced. They went to see what he was drawing.

"Look," the man said in a deep and resonant voice, having sensed their approach. "Look how Michelangelo has created for us a place of impossibly perfect geometry rendered imperfectly and made to appear possible. It is a void on top of a hill, heavy with the impulse of that omnipotent heart." He turned to them and smiled. He moved his hand in a sweeping gesture toward the expanse of the ovoid piazza. His eyes remained in shadow. "He was a crude man," he added, "who bestowed upon us these gifts of pristine beauty."

He held up his sketchbook then and they both bent to look at it. It bore a likeness of Caleb, in profile, in heavily penciled lines, the Capitoline Palace, lightly rendered, behind him.

"It's beautiful," Jo said involuntarily.

"I hope you don't mind," he said, stepping back and out of the light. "I've been looking for a model like you?"

"Model?" Jo wondered.

"Why me?" Caleb was asking, suddenly and obviously uncomfortable.

"You remind me of *him*."

"Him?" Jo asked, seeking Caleb's arm to cling to.

The man answered as if it should have been obvious, "Yours seems an appropriate face for my mural."

"Your mural?" She was turning this way and that in an effort to see his face.

"The *Collegio di Arti Sacre*," he said, bending further into the shadow that attended him. "I'm doing a wall there. That's all. Thank you and—Merry Christmas."

"Merry Christmas," Jo said after him, her voice small and weak. Then, releasing Caleb's sleeve and moving a few steps away, she repeated, "Christmas, Caleb. I'd almost forgotten."

"A few days hence," he reminded her, his eyes on the place where the man had once stood.

But the man was gone, having sunk back into the night from which he'd emerged. They both stared for a time into the darkness beyond the piazza, the steps from which they had recently come, the thicket of old trees that arched over it.

"Who was that man?"

He shrugged.

"Was he one of your characters, Caleb, come to life, here in Rome?"

"Don't be silly—?"

"He had that tragic quality you seem so capably to have mastered."

"He gave me the creeps," Caleb returned rather quickly.

"It's this place," Jo said with a shudder, and looking about carefully. "This perfect geometry of Michelangelo's imperfect mind." She heaved a breath. "Let's get back to the twenty-first century, shall we?" She jiggled his arm to get his attention. "I'm hungry!"

He had hesitated though she had started away. He was still peering into the shadows cast by the Capitoline Palace. She waited, then returned and pulled at his sleeve once more. "Caleb?"

"Okay," he said. "I guess I could eat something."

He took her hand and led her back toward the darkness.

"Any ideas?" she queried.

"There's a restaurant near the Forum of Trajan. A favorite of mine."

"Lead on," she said cheerily, albeit not convincingly.

They passed beneath the brooding edifice as they descended the dark steps and retraced their earlier path, entering again into the light, the artificial light of halogen streetlamps. They had escaped the Evil One, and now they paused for one last moment in the lamplight of modern times to glance for a few last seconds into the mighty relic of Imperial Rome. Then, twice blessed, warmly dressed, they passed the Marmertine Prison, where Peter and Paul had once languished, and they strode boldly into the swirl of traffic on the broad thoroughfare. Beyond, sharing a portion of the silence that attends all ruins, was a small, glassed place overlooking the cellars of once proud basilicas. They asked for a table near the window. A host of waiters accompanied them. They sat in precarious splendor on the very edge of the ancient world, the modern one having been muted by the august presence of marble colonnades, their bases festooned with yawning cats.

"How are you coming with your novel?" It was an innocent question but, as Caleb did not have a ready answer he responded impatiently. "What novel?"

"The novel that's going to make you famous," she returned, half-seriously.

He admitted it was a more difficult task than he had expected. It's easy, he speculated, to write a detective story or even a romantic adventure tale, where lots of things happen. "Problem is, with realism, not much happens and it's hard to keep the reader's attention. She was wondering how he was expecting to address that issue." He shrugged. Maybe he should invent a mysterious stranger just to give the story a little punch.

"That man," Jo mused.

"What man?" Caleb was savoring his small cup of espresso.

"With the sketch pad. He seemed unreal, in some way."

"Like one of my characters, you said"

"I didn't say that," she insisted, looking up at him. "But didn't you sense it?"

He turned to gaze into the forum though the lights had gone out and all he could see was a mirror image of he and Jo looking back at him. "I've been trying not to think about it," he said. "It was all too familiar, for some reason, running into him there."

"You talk as if you've met him before."

He merely shrugged. She drew her fingers close to her mouth and stared at him by way of his reflection in the dark glass. Caleb had grown quiet. His eyes were on hers, but he was not looking at her, she must have known. He was seeing someone else beyond her, near her, in her. She knew that look; she'd certainly seen it in other men.

"Why doesn't anyone ever see me for who I really am?" she asked aloud.

He blinked his eyes and asked; his face screwed up into a strange expression, "What did you say?"

"I said, I think you're writing. I'd rather you were paying attention to me, but I think you are writing. Am I right?"

Caleb grinned. Then he shrugged. A second time.

"Yes," she insisted. "I think you are."

He leaned forward and smiled at her. "Why do you say that, Jo?"

"Because," she said blankly "there he is!"

He followed the direction of her gaze with his eyes. The man with the sketchbook had just come in the door to the little restaurant. His face was in shadow but one blue eye seemed to show, even from across the room. Caleb automatically sank down a bit in his chair but no matter, the man had stood in the doorway for no more than a few moments, glanced about, then tucked his sketchbook under his arm and left, the closing door making a dark shape where once he had stood.

Caleb continued to stare at the door for a long while. Jo fidgeted. Then they went back to their coffees and drank in silence. It was a dull silence that accompanied them the remainder of the evening. The lights in the forum had faded as the *son-et-lumiere* pageant came to an end and the tourists went home. The restaurant was nearly empty when they left, shrugging off a chill as the doors were closed and locked behind them.

"It's late," Caleb said as they walked away from the cafe, its lights going out one by one. "The Metro stopped at eleven. I hope we can find a taxi."

They walked quietly along the once bustling thoroughfare. Ahead lay the Piazza Venezia, still awhirl with Fiats and busses. They heaved a communal sigh of relief and quickened their pace. There were ruins on all sides. The brutally delicate Column of Trajan showed red in the traffic light. The domes of jewel box chapels lay silhouetted against the darker buildings beyond. To the left was the raucous, wedding cake monument to king Victor Emanuel, which stood in Baroque silence amidst the ancient clamor of the nearby forums. Busses came and went in the broad piazza. Caleb and Jo joined a small bus-waiting crowd at the corner. They turned and stretched to read the names on the fronts of the passing busses. Only a few actually stopped. They talked a little, meaningless things, mostly, gesturing meagerly, hugging themselves against the nocturnal chill.

Busses came and went. The crowd changed, swelled, moved, disappeared altogether, then reformed as more busses came and went, rending the crowds in twain, in two directions: to *Palatino* and to *Pincio*; Roman hills so laden with architecture they no longer rise above the piazzas like shoulders, but sag like old flesh. The Rome of the Vitruvian Man had been transformed by the Age of Reason, as Caleb might have put it, and now it lies ripped in half by busses.

Boarding at last, it was the last bus to Trastevere. It turned from the light and moved off. As the doors shut, a shout had caused it to pause, but then it trundled onward, leaving the would-be rider behind, sketchbook in hand.

"Tomorrow," Jo had said as she sat.

"What about it?" He had paused in sitting to peer out the rear window.

She was merely wondering what they might do tomorrow.

Caleb heaved a sigh and sat down. "I gotta write."

"It's Christmas Eve."

"Next day is."

He was stretching and turning to see out the rear window as the bus moved down the broad Corso Vittorio Emanuele. He was thinking of the man they had encountered on the Capitoline Hill. It was different, that thought. Caleb had never felt himself attracted to a man before. He wasn't sure what the attraction meant. "There's nobody else in my life. Hasn't been for a long time. Maybe I'm just lonely. What harm could it do? In six months, I'll be back in Michigan and Rome will be a memory, nothing more." The thought of it had given him an erection.

"Jesus—"

"What?"

"The church."

They were moving past the Church of Gesú, Caleb explained. The Jesuit church was designed by Giacomo dele Porta in 1575, intended to rival St. Peter's in interior opulence. She nodded at his words, turning her face toward the glass. He could see both her face and the lighted façade of the basilica at the same time, projected on the window. A smile had spread across his face against his will.

Five

1

It was in a garden that he first had wondered about it. His garden. Cutler Insbroek's garden. A strange haven for exotics under glass; foreign plants brought together in a small crystal palace behind the Chem Building on the old campus. Cutler cared for the garden in a loving manner, spending days of hours in its warm interior, checking on it between classes to make sure the temperatures were appropriate, and the misting system was in good working order. He'd pay close attention to each plant. The potted acanthus, its curling leaves longing for the Mediterranean sunshine, seemed soothed somewhat by the touch of the grower. The *spleenwart* bowed under the weight of its own sweat and drip-dripped on the variegated leaves of the dumbcane. The *monstera deliciosa* leaned itself back against the feathery *podocarpus* as if relaxing in the presence of the grower.

The moist touch of the silent plants comforted him as well. The *syngonium* and its African cousin named for Nephthys, the Egyptian goddess of mourning, draped lazily over the sills of the benches and the *laelia* orchid lounged in their embrace. Cutler held his hand above the sparkling blooms as if touching their fragrance with magician's fingers. It was a loftier paradise he tended with such care, a place of his own making, not one imposed upon him by external powers; not the one into which he had been thrust as an adolescent, that lanky boy trying not to outgrow his sexual self-image as regularly as he did his clothes.

The Winter Garden was a place out of time and space. It existed as much in an ideal state as it did in reality. None of these inmates belonged here. Not even the gardener. None would have survived outside the glass. It was a safe haven here, north of the forty-fifth parallel. Nor were the exotics themselves compatible, being, as they were, from disparate parts of the tropical world. The *spleenwart*, for example, the *asplenium flaccidum*, comes from the South

Pacific. The *syngonium* grows wild in the torrid jungles of Central America, while The similar looking *nephthytis* hales from tropical Africa. The dumbcane, or *dieffenbachia*, lives in Brazil. The *monstera* in Mexico. The *laelia* orchid, also from Mexico, is named for one of the Vestal Virgins of ancient Rome. Cutler knew all these things. He knew all the plants by name, and he spoke to them and comforted them as he passed among them. He felt at home in his winter garden.

But the glass behind the glistening foliage had gone black since he'd stepped into the sultry atmosphere of the hot house. He was late. He'd been invited to a birthday party at Lewis's. The chancellor might be there. He'd better make an appearance. He didn't want to go. Cutler was not a sociable person.

He pulled on his coat though he was sweating. Snow lingered in the lights beyond the glass. He paused at the door, anticipating a cold slap in the face when he opened it. But he didn't open it yet. Something had occurred to him and he knew, before long, he'd have to sit down someplace and think about it. Like the reflections in the dark glass, it wasn't clear enough to recognize and yet, it seemed familiar. That obscure thought.

He didn't want to go, but he did. He reached for the light switch, but the lights went off by themselves. He tried to switch them back on, but it didn't work. He checked the heating system. It was okay. "Must be the bulbs," he decided.

At the curb, visible between the Chem Lab and the old dormitory, rested his red '69 Triumph. It was still warm inside from his recent drive into town. Nonetheless, he pulled his scarf tightly about his neck, having been chilled by the snowy wind against his wet skin. He drove out toward the lake and into a snowstorm. He didn't pay much attention to the watery view through the windshield as he drove past nineteenth century Victorian homes looming over their snow-scaped lawns. The river was little more than a meandering, black rift in the gray and white sameness of the vista. He turned from the river road into the dunes, sliding to the right on a patch of ice, slipping off the pavement into the sandy shoulder and splashing slush up against the rear windows, startling him. He brought himself back to the here-and-now, his eyes back to the soft road, which was little more than a darker shade of gray between the sandy shoulders. He didn't want to go but he did.

He saw the lake then, a great empty void stretching to the invisible horizon, more in memory than sight. A row of lighted cottages festooned the dune-ridge like a string of baroque pearls. The last one, on the highest hill, was Lewis's. The first one was John's. He passed it by, noting it was still bright. "They must not be there, yet." John and Alison, his lover.

He could see the parked cars ahead in the low light of his headlamps. He could already picture John laughing at some racist joke or flirting with whichever woman was present, single or married or older, or—And he could see Alison becoming sillier as John became increasingly disinterested in her. He decided to have a drink at Evelyn's Bar first and he swerved his sports car hard to the right to just barely catch the road that fell as if by accident off the dune and then slumped to the beach below. He left his warm car in a dark parking lot since the streetlamp had gone out. Huddled against the lake wind and the cold rain it now brought, he rushed into the small bar. It was decorated with leftover Christmas lights. Beyond the windows, a thin gray line marked the horizon where clouds were pulling away from the recent sunset, a vestige of which remained in the collective memories of the older patrons who lolled about the scattering of tables like pieces of rustic décor. Cutler sat at the bar, his back to the others, his face in his hands.

"Cutler Insbroek!" Evelyn cried from her smoky station near the stacks of plastic glasses.

So much for anonymity. She leaned over the bar to give him a hug. She smelled of cigarettes and hair spray. "How's every little thing?"

Normal, he thought. As it should be. He exchanged a few small talk words with her and then, thankfully, she went to serve another patron. Cutler didn't feel like socializing. He settled back once more into the comfortable interior of his own body, behind his aging skin, into his warm organs. The quiet, almost tragic aspect of the bar and the drink and even the round-voiced Evelyn seemed to be just as it should have been. Everything was right, until he held up his glass to drink. He saw himself reflected on the windows behind the bar; windows whose daytime purpose was to admit a stunning view of the vast and shining lake. The glass also showed the rest of the bar as it was laid out like a display of relics behind him. His eyes shifted from one reflection to the other until they merged in a flickering afterimage like a ghost. His was a stiff and angular, unbeautiful face, an expressionless one, as usual, but not a bland one. It was not unlike the face of a corpse of one who had died a violent death having been calmed by the tender hand of the embalmer, a fragile essence of that violence still visible beneath the transparent skin. The still, plain face of Cutler Insbroek, the implacable visage of an outwardly quiet and contented man, was suddenly lined with tears. He hid himself behind the glass of liquor and lime. Evelyn had returned, continuing a conversation begun the last time Cutler had been there.

"…Well, she was too dumb, if you ask me, but she was determined. You remember Alice, don't you? She used to come in here with you a lot and now she's too high class, I guess." She paused to drawl out the word over a long drag on her profusely smoldering cigarette, then, went on, "Well. Out of the blue, guess who dropped in yesterday?"

"Alice Stricht?"

"Alice Stricht." Cutler nodded as Evelyn added with lowered voice, "Big as a barn."

"Fat?"

"Pregnant," she cried, collecting smoke like a hat around her head.

Cutler nodded and sipped his drink while she bit upon an already broken, lacquered fingernail to think. "Let's see, what else? It's been so long I've seen you I don't know what news you haven't heard yet. Big Dave died. You knew that. Florence quit, and Alice Stricht is p.g. I guess that's it."

"By whom?"

"What? Oh, Alice?" She shrugged. "Don't know." She bent over the bar and spoke softly. "Don't nobody know."

Cutler finished his drink. "I have a party to go to."

"Lewis?" She laughed. "God, was he nervous. Had three martinis here this afternoon. I finally had to practically push him out the door around four."

Cutler was already in the doorway. He waved back to Evelyn and left. Alice Stricht, he thought. The only woman he'd ever really felt attracted to for some reason. Her wit. She made him laugh, usually over sexy things she had the habit of saying under her breath in less than appropriate situations. In chapel. At the chancellor's reception. She hadn't looked pregnant then. Besides, they were good friends. If she were in some sort of trouble, she would have confided in him about it. Why didn't he know who the man was?

Her students used to call her Miss Trick, with emphasis on 'trick.'

"Pregnant? God, she must be forty if she's a day!" He was talking like Evelyn. Cutler had the habit of picking up the special idiosyncrasies of people talking to him. Alison had said it was because he had no idiosyncrasies of his own.

He started the engine and drove back up the dune. The water he turned his back on was one of those ice-blue lakes that sprawl in spilled-ink pattern across the continent. Clear, wide and expressive, they flow from shallow, pebbled westward shorelines in ever building waves to high-rise dunes that face the setting sun, having turned their humped backs to the sunset out of spite for the darkness. The liquid Cutler drank was gin. With that, he too could turn his back on what he chose not to understand. Nonetheless, the botanist in him was fascinated by the ever-changing line that marked the margin between the water and the dune, the liquor and the glass. It was the delicate, intangible threshold of that glistening membrane that intrigued him most. Beneath that film, among the ice cubes and lime or in the silky depths of a larger ocean, dwelt something beguiling. Either real or imagined. Or both.

2

A bit of commotion near the porch door caught their attention, John, Alison and Lewis. All three looked up *en suite* as Cutler Insbroek came into the room. Lewis rolled his eyes and went to greet the latecomer. Alison stepped in front of John. "I told you he'd be here," she said with a triumphant lilt in her voice.

"He won't stay long. He hates parties," John said.

"I thought he was your best friend," Alison said. "Why do you speak of him as if he's a pest?"

"Because he is one. Lately, anyway. I don't know. He's changed since he came back from France last summer."

"I thought he was in someplace called Provence," she added, pronouncing it in English. "That was the summer I moved in with you. Are you so sure it's him who has changed?"

"No," he said, impatience in his tone, "you moved in two summers ago."

"Really?" She started counting months on her fingers. "How long has it been—" She didn't finish her question.

Cutler had caught sight of the two of them and was trying to get away from the Deadmans and the Umlohrs, who had corralled him near the door to the kitchen. He nodded toward them with a smile. Alison, having stopped talking at last, waved enthusiastically at him. John flopped noisily into an armchair as Cutler walked over.

"Gosh, Alison, you look beautiful tonight," Cutler said, shaking her hand.

"Gosh," John mocked from behind her. When Cutler saw him, he flashed a smile of real sincerity and affection. John remained cool. He did not get up. They did not shake hands. Cutler stood a moment fumbling with his hands as if trying to think of something to do with them. Cutler was athletic, poised, tall and potentially handsome. He was also shy, hesitant and uncomfortable in social situations. The combination was an odd one in that people were attracted to him by his physical presence but soon bored by his manner. Only gregarious John seemed to find him interesting enough to engage in long conversations. When Alison asked him what he and Cutler talked about for such long hours, he would have to admit he honestly could not remember.

"John," Cutler began, "you got your hair cut." Alison had sat on the arm of the overstuffed old chair. "Isn't this nice," she said. "Look, Cutler, this chair is big enough for you to sit on the other arm. Sit!" She demanded. "That's what I like about this old-fashioned cottage furniture. It's made for farm families."

"That makes no sense," John said, standing. Cutler sat on the arm. "Yes, John, but you know what she meant," he said.

"Right," Alison said, also standing. "John never likes to give me any credit." John sat again in silence as if pouting. Alison had folded her arms with impatience and then sat on the arm opposite Cutler. Thus, they all sat, in silence, for several moments. The three of them might have seemed comical to onlookers, of which there were none. Perhaps for that reason, John and Cutler both stood at once, then laughed a little, and lifted their shoulders in jest. They decided to have a drink and walked away as if Alison had not been there at all. She remained sitting on the arm of the overstuffed chair pouting loudly.

John and Cutler walked in silence to the kitchen table bar. They each opened a bottle of beer and toasted each other without words. Cutler stared at the bottle for a moment and said without looking up, "It is good to see you, John."

"I've missed you, too, Cut. Seems we don't see much of each other anymore."

"Things change."

"You mean me and Alison."

"And me. I don't know. I've been moody lately. Not like me, actually."

"What's troubling you?"

He shrugged, turning his eyes up to the other at last. "Growing older? Something like that, I guess?"

"You still seeing Alice?"

"John," he pronounced, looking away. "That's been on hold for years. You know that."

"No sparks?"

Cutler smiled slightly. "Not even a glimmer."

"Maybe you should try another match," John suggested.

"Something happened in Paris last summer—" He had paused.

"I figured as much. Wanna talk about it?" Cutler's eyes had wandered back toward the overstuffed chair where Alison still sat, nodding her head to the music. John watched the little episode carefully. Certainly, Cutler had no feeling for Alison, other than friendship! John chewed on his thumbnail. Was he playing a waiting game? It was probably immediately clear to other people how painfully and obviously difficult a time Alison and John were having together. Everyone knew she wanted to be a legal wife and have children. She talked about it all the time, even to strangers she'd encounter in the Laundromat. But Cutler, if anyone, should have known how much John loved her—had loved her; could have loved her.

Long suffering Alison, John thought. How Cutler must be moved by that fantasy. To him she must seem like one of those special women who, through heritage or special favor from god, could accept all the sins of the world in one man and love him anyway. She was certainly no saint as far as John was concerned but he could easily imagine how one as naive and sensitive as Cutler might be fooled by her disguise.

Now Cutler was looking at him and a shudder passed through him. Was he letting his obsession with Alison transfer itself to the lover instead? Everyone knew Cutler didn't date much. Was John being naive himself in not recognizing the obvious in his friend? Maybe Lewis was right. Maybe Cutler was a fag.

John stopped himself in mid thought as Cutler was talking to him. John pretended to have been listening and nodded approvingly as Cutler rambled on. He was the only one he talked to very much and John felt it a courtesy to at least pretend to listen. He loved Cutler in an odd sort of way, but his affection had something of pathos in it that bothered him a bit, as if it was not a true affection but one put on like a gift sweater he didn't really like and wore only when in the presence of the one who had given it.

Cutler was talking about how bored he was with the party already. John reminded him he hadn't really done much socializing since he'd come in. "You're the only one I like here," Cutler said, setting the empty bottle on the kitchen-table-turned-bar. "You and Alison."

"So, why did you come?"

"Lewis invited me. It would have been rude not to." John was about to say that Lewis had told him he hadn't invited Cutler but stuck the bottle in his mouth instead. Cutler went on.

"Besides. I heard the chancellor was here and I thought I should at least make an appearance."

"He's on the back porch having a smoke."

"Who?"

"The chancellor."

"He smokes?" Then he said, "Let's get out of here, John."

"What?"

"I've got a fresh joint in the car. One of my students gave it to me."

"Sounds good to me, but—" After a moment's consideration, they started to leave. Alison was watching from her place on the arm of the otherwise empty overstuffed chair. As they ambled by, she called out loudly, "Where are you going? What about me?"

John had stopped. "I'm not really in the mood, I guess, Cutler."

"Nor am I," Cutler said softly. "It seemed the thing to do at the moment." Alison had come over and slipped her arm through John's, catching him off guard. "Didn't you bring a date, Cutler?" she asked.

John asked her if she happened to have seen one wandering around. Cutler sort of laughed. Alison went on. "Why didn't you? You knew we'd all be couples here."

"I knew you and John would be here, too," he returned with a little grin.

"We're a couple, aren't we John?"

"Let's put it this way," Cutler said. "You look like a couple. Besides," he went on, "Lewis is our host, and he didn't bring a date."

"Lewis said you weren't even invited," Alison said.

Cutler shook his head, seeking a way out of the conversation. "Who cares? I came because I knew John would be here and I haven't seen him in months. What's your excuse?"

"I'm with John so why should you care?" Alison said strongly. "What is it between you too, anyway?"

"We've known each other a long time," Cutler said.

Alison had placed herself between the two men. "How long?"

"We grew up together," Cutler said. "Didn't you know?"

"Then why don't you get along?"

"Because I grew up and John didn't." Lizzie Tifgat said from the shadow nearby, "Sounds like the perfect friendship to me."

"You still here?" John asked.

"It's all right, Alison," Lizzie said. "Close your mouth, Cutler. It is I. Anyway; as I was saying to Alison, I don't expect him to treat me any better than he does anybody else. I'm used to it"

"He's creative lately," Alison said. "At least, that's his excuse for his rudeness."

"You're writing again?" Cutler wondered.

"He's always writing," Lizzie said, "like any true writer."

"What's it about?" Cutler asked.

"He never talks about—" Alison started to say, but John had started talking, in a chant like manner, and she raised her hand to her mouth in surprise.

"And it all seems so familiar," John was saying, as if to himself. "But then it gets jumbled in my head and it isn't until I take the paper out of the typewriter and read it that it makes sense. It's almost like someone else is doing the writing, or some other aspect of myself, and I just happen to come along and find it already written."

"What are you talking about?" Alison wondered.

"Who is the narrator?" Lizzie asked.

"I don't know him very well. Though I should, I suppose."

"I don't understand," Alison whined.

"What happens to him?" Lizzie wondered in a deep and sensitive voice. He returned that he didn't really want to talk about it. Cutler had started to walk away. Lizzie Tifgat slipped her arm in his and ambled with him. "So, Cutler, what have you been up to these last few years?"

John turned to Alison. He was not smiling. Alison merely lowered her eyes. Cutler and Lizzie had started dancing. John was watching them. He took Alison by the hand and led her to the dance floor. He maneuvered them into the other couple then apologized gushingly. Lizzie asked Alison why she had consented to dance with one so rude as that.

"Haven't you ever screwed somebody just to get back at them?" she asked as the music ended. Then she looked directly at John and said, "Dancing is a lot like screwing."

"Well, screw you," John said. He walked to the door and out onto the front porch, closing the door behind him. Lizzie suggested to Alison they get something to eat. Cutler was alone in the middle of the dance floor. He heaved a sigh and started for the door though he had talked with neither his host nor the chancellor. John was watching as he grabbed his coat from the overstuffed chair where he'd left it, threw it over his shoulders and walked out. He went out to the front porch. Cutler was crossing the small yard. Frozen grass crunched beneath his shoes. A distant streetlamp reflected off the glaze of ice that shimmered on his car. Damn, he was heard to say. He didn't have a scraper with him!

John stood on the porch watching with a smile as Cutler scratched at the ice on his windshield with his fingernails. John chuckled. He liked Cutler. He didn't know why he treated him so badly. Behind him was the party and Alison and Lizzie Tifgat. Inside him was an urgent need he could not understand. Before him was Cutler Insbroek. He decided to leave the party. The screen door slammed behind him, startling the man chiseling at the ice on his windshield.

"What?"

"Let's go have a drink at Evelyn's?"

"I can't get the ice off my window."

"We'll walk."

"It's icy."

"It's winter."

"What about the party?"

"You mean, Alison? She knows how to get home if she misses me."

Cutler lifted his shoulders. "Okay," he said, smiling a little. His teeth showed in the bit of light that was bouncing around off the icy things in the little dooryard.

They started walking, the two of them, carefully at first as the earlier rain had left puddles on the roadway, which were now freezing in delicate crisscross patterns that glistened in the brilliantly dark air and crackled underfoot. Streetlights in the hills above, shining through bare trees, cast cubist shadows down the dunes and off the glazed grasses. The road made a black path through the reflections, sliding off to the left and down to the lake, which spread in even blacker hues to the starry horizon. Even here, halfway up the sand hills, the sound of water lapping gently on the hard shores sounded its plaintiff patter. Everything was stiff and poised just so. The world seemed to have come to a dead stop and John and Cutler ambled through it in quiet respect. John was about to tell Cutler he was sorry for treating him badly. He turned to him and said his name. Cutler turned his way.

"You guys in trouble?" They had paused on the edge of the glow of the lights from the house, such as it was. "When are we not in trouble."

"What is it? Don't you love her anymore?"

"Love?" He glanced back at the small house, its warm windows seen over top of parked cars. "Yeah. I do. But she drives me crazy."

Cutler laughed uncomfortably. "I thought that's what you liked about her."

"I'm serious," he said, taking him by the shoulder. "It's nothing I can put my finger on. That's what makes it so frustrating. It's little things that build up throughout the day and into the night. Constantly picking, constantly poking me until I lose my patience with her and I can't even tell her why. 'What did I say specifically to anger you?' she'll ask, or, 'What words did I use to upset you, so I'll know not to say them again.' Then I stand there stupidly, and she says in her mother-may-I voice, 'I'm worried about you, John.'"

"Cutler; she thinks I need therapy, or something." They had paused again, just in darkness. The sound of a screen door slamming caused them to look back. Cutler asked him if he thought he needed counseling and John shook his head. "I don't know. For living with Alison, maybe."

"Maybe you need to be away from her a while."

"Maybe."

The delicate moment was shattered by a call from behind. "Hey, you guys. Wait for me!"

She burst upon them, crashing between them, slipping her arms through each of theirs. She was talking even before she arrived and continued to talk all the way down the hill.

"And then Dorothy and Bea changed dresses and you should have seen that trick. Busty Dorothy and boy-chested Bea in each other's clothes." She took a moment to laugh and thus draw breath. "Well, I told Lewis he should have a cross-dressing party like this every year. I've been having so much fun."

The road became rutted as it neared the lakeside street, turning abruptly by a sign that pointed the direction with an arrow of glass beads. They walked carefully, the ruts were filled with icy puddles and the ridges were glazed and glossy. Cutler reminded Alison of the real meaning of the word 'cross-dressing.'

"Whatever."

Between the clumps of tall grasses that lined the lane they could see the flashing neon of Evelyn's Bar. It shouted in red and yellow silence against the black ear of the night. As they stepped into the nearly empty parking lot, the light suddenly buzzed and flickered off. The three of them paused and Alison stopped talking.

"Are they closed?" she wondered after a moment's silence.

Cutler was smiling. "Wait," he said. "Let's see if it happens again." John was annoyed with the circumstances. "What?" he asked impatiently. Cutler was walking back up the road. Alison asked where he was going. John suggested he might be seeking a quieter place to have a drink. She didn't understand. She gasped suddenly when the neon sign came back on. Cutler walked slowly back toward them and the sign flickered off a second time.

"I don't get it," John said."

"Neither do I," he admitted. "It happened last time I was here."

"What?" Alison asked, looking from face to face. "What happened?"

"The light," they said.

"Let me try it," John said. He walked away until he could no longer be seen. Cutler called to him that it wouldn't work with him.

"I've checked it out with other friends," he said, as John came back into view. "It only seems to work with me."

Alison suggested she could make it work. "I'm a bit of a mystic, after all." The two men rolled their eyes as she started away. Then they rolled their eyes to the sign. "It has nothing to do with mysticism," Cutler was trying to explain to them. "I'm certainly not psychic, John. You know that."

"No. I'd say your practical to the point of boring."

Cutler laughed. "It's true. But for this."

"I don't get it," John said again.

Alison was standing on the rim of their vision jumping up and down and waving her arms.

Cutler shrugged. "Certain lights; I don't know. When I walk past them, they go out. When I get a little way off, they go back on. I don't know why, John, but it is true! It's been happening off and on for the last few months."

"Since you got back from Paris."

"Started there."

"Ridiculous!"

"You saw for yourself."

John was thinking. Alison had rejoined them and assumed John's thinking pose for a moment. "Try another light," she suggested. A streetlamp burned a couple hundred feet down Lakeside Road. Cutler nodded and started walking toward it. John and Alison huddled themselves together as they watched after him. A chilly breeze was coming up on them from the lake. "This is silly," she whispered.

"It's entertaining," John said.

"For you, maybe."

"You're just upset you couldn't make the light go out."

"You're just upset I didn't let you and Cutler get away with abandoning me at the awful party."

"I thought you were having fun at the party, cross-dressing and such."

"I lied, John."

"Fuck you, Alison."

Cutler had disappeared as he had left the light of the little bar. He reappeared in silhouette against the streetlamp's glow.

"See?" Alison said.

Then Cutler disappeared again as the streetlamp blinked out. John laughed. Alison pulled away from him and hugged herself against the chill. Cutler could be seen coming back toward them. The streetlamp burst back into full brilliance silently, casting his shadow before him. Cutler was smiling broadly.

"I love it!" John cried.

"I'm cold," Alison sighed.

"I thought it might be vibration," Cutler was saying, "the particular rhythm of my walking? But, damn it, John, it even happens when I'm driving. It happened in the library the other day, too."

Alison had gone inside. Cutler told of how the stacks kept going dark as he walked through them. "It was scary. Those dungeons are dark when the lights are out. The faster I walked toward the exit, the faster the lights went out. I thought someone was playing a trick on me but when the librarian went back to search, she found no one there. So long as she was there the lamps stayed lit. Believe me, I was so shaken by it I went to the Campus Pub for a beer and wouldn't you know; the instant I sat down, the light over my table went dark! I tell you, it's creepy."

"You know, old man," John said, with a great smile, "you just got a hell of a lot more interesting."

Cutler scowled. "Thanks."

John threw his arm around him. "Let me buy you a drink, Cutler Insbroek."

"Now that I'm more interesting, you mean?" They laughed as they walked arm in arm toward the bar. Then John stopped. Cutler waited. "So?" he wondered, just as he was opening the door, "what are you going to do?"

"I don't know. I can't talk to her about it and believe me I've tried. She gets this condescending smile on her face and talks softly and sweetly, as if in her mind, she has to calm some savage beast." He spread his arms. "I may get emotional, Cutler, but I am not dangerous. She must know that after all these years."

He took a breath as he was about to enter through the door Cutler was holding open, then paused; he was very close to the other man. "She said I remind her of her father."

"The guy who beats her mother up."

"Yeah."

They were standing in the darkness of the burned-out light. No sooner had Cutler let the door close behind them, the neon sign flickered on again in all its garish splendor.

The sun had barely risen behind the distant mountains and the garden lay in darkness. Caleb rubbed his eyes. He had not been able to sleep. A different bed. A different place. The man with the notebook, encountered on the dark piazza, kept visiting him. In memory. And the face of Cutler Insbroek.

He stood before the window, looking out. A dark view of nothing in particular. What was he doing there, in that place, at that time? Rome. A new millennium. No prospects!

Part II
A Mysterious Travelogue

Six

When we have once known Rome, and left her where she lies, like a long decaying corpse, retaining a trace of the noble shape it was, but with accumulated dust and a fungous growth over spreading all its more admirable features—we are astonished by the discovery...as if it were more familiar, more intimately our home, than ever the spot where we were born!

Nathaniel Hawthorne: *The Marble Faun*

A cool grey sun rested atop the tawny tile roofs of the villa's east wing. Dark pigeons cut ragged chunks out of it as they flew from roof to roof for no apparent reason. A morning ritual, Caleb thought: a paltry pilgrimage.

He sat alone in the dining room. Though the winter sun was late in rising, the other academy fellows were later still. Caleb was an early riser. He found himself waiting alone outside the locked doors until the *cameriere* had deemed it right to open them, not even concerning himself to switch on the lights. Romans are, in general, late risers. Caleb drank his first coffee in the near darkness of shadowy dawn; shadows from his own past, mostly. The young waiter who opened the doors for the early rising American returned to his place by the kitchen door, no doubt wondering drowsily what this silly American was doing up so early and for no apparent reason. He had no job to hurry off to, no kids crying for their breakfast. There were no dogs barking in the piazza. No *motos* revving their motors in the *atrio*. Besides, it was Christmas week. He should be enjoying a little vacation, like the rest of the Christian world.

Ever aware of his silent presence, the *cameriere* would watch him sipping at his coffee and scanning hen-scratched pages in a bound notebook for no apparent reason. Sometimes Caleb would tear a page from the book and toss it aside as if it were garbage. He pictured the waiter collecting the scraps and tucking them in his pocket after all the Americans had left the room. They might be important someday, he probably thought. Why else would this man be putting precious words on paper if they were not important? He saw him trying to read the scraps he'd retrieved but his little bit of dining room English would prove inadequate at best. He had been told that the young man was from Sicily. He was probably proud enough that he could even read Italian.

"I'm glad I'm not him—" And, strangely, Caleb felt a little ill at ease under the watchful eye of the *cameriere*. He bent over his notebook as if to guard it, as if the precious words he'd scrawled there the night before, before drifting off into his own variety of sleep, had some value beyond the trifling cost of ink and cellulose fiber.

His cup was empty, and he wasn't sure how to order another. He eyed the waiter from the corner of his eye and noted that his eyes were closed. He took a moment to study him, for future reference. He was a small man, a clue to his southern heritage. He was thin, narrow shouldered and dark toned with tawny black hair and a trimmed Van Dyke in the style of movie stars and *futbol* players. He was a handsome kid in his late teens. He opened his eyes and Caleb turned away. It had never occurred to him the young man might have been watching him for the same reason—simple curiosity. This tall, angular American in ill-fitting clothes and wire rimmed glasses, this white skinned Mercury with pale blue eyes and but a shadow of virility on his upper lip: Caleb smiled at his thoughts as the waiter poured more coffee into his cup.

"Grazie," Caleb said clearly.

"Niente," the boy said, without smiling. (Nothing.) It never occurred to the writer as the kid ambled back to the buffet counter that the help also had stories to tell.

Piero had come to Rome to visit his aunt, who was dying in a hospital there. She lingered, so he took a job. There was need of a temporary waiter at the Academia San Marco for the Advent holiday, at least until Epiphany. Piero had never waited tables. His father owned an upholstery shop in *Siracusa*, on the ancient island of Sicily. But he was assured the job would not be difficult. There were only a few Americans attending the winter session at the academy, and, as they were Americans, they would not be demanding. He returned the coffee pot to the warmer and assumed his place by the kitchen door. How these foreigners could stomach coffee made in batches and left to warm on electric coils, the young man could never have understood. He was shaking his head when something caught his attention. An unattractive young woman had come into the dining room. No matter. She was not a coffee drinker.

The woman sat down, and Caleb seemed to forget about the young man with the coffee pot. It was the first of many mornings in which she would time her entry to the filling of the second cup of coffee. It was the cue for Caleb to stop writing and start listening to her. It apparently did not occur to him the waiter might be wondering why he was no longer important. The woman didn't drink coffee. Once she would enter the room the waiter seemed to disappear, as far as the American writer was apparently concerned. He'd continue to stand and wait, as it was his occupation. Others might enter and call him to their table, but he'd never be called back to the one he liked most.

"Why does he ignore me when the woman comes in?" he wondered. "Is she his wife? It's no reason. After all, I open the dining room for him, sometimes an hour early. I make him fresh coffee. He thanks me, but he never smiles at me. Perhaps he doesn't like me."

Then the room would soon be noisy with loud talking Americans—even a few Americans can raise the decibel level in a small room—and Piero would forget about the one he liked most. But when he'd leave, the woman with him still talking, he'd watch him go as if seeing a friend off at the station.

"I wish I were him—"

Then he'd go back to work, and the day would progress as usual.

"So, how far have you got with your story?"

Caleb was pretending he had not heard her question. Jo tapped him on the shoulder and asked again how far along he was. He replied as if talking to someone else about some other topic. John runs into a former lover at the party. His former writing teacher. He is not happy to see her. He takes her home and screws her anyway.

Jo let out a frustrated breath. "Why?" she asked. "What about Alison?"

"She had gone to the bar down on the beach with some of the other guests, I guess. That left him kind of vulnerable."

"Sounds like you kind of sympathize with him," she said, looking away.

"With John."

He merely shrugged and decided to change the subject. Said he'd been thinking about the man they had encountered the night before. She was making ready to leave. Had some writing to do. Again, she asked, "Why?"

"He seemed so lonely," he started to say, as he came up behind her. He nodded toward the young waiter as he passed him.

Jo was saying as they left the dining room that she had forgotten all about the man with the notebook.

Caleb explained that he just thought it had been an interesting encounter. For a writer, maybe. Then she added, "I thought you said he gave you the creeps."

"He's an artist," Caleb said, pausing on the first stair to look up at the painted ceiling of the foyer. She looked up too. Winged *putti* stared back at them; the Punishment of Prometheus, to which they served as witnesses, notwithstanding. A vulture tearing his liver from his battered body. He, writhing in exquisite pain.

"Artists are bound to be a little odd."

"And writers aren't?"

He tossed his hands in the air. "Writers, too—"

She had started up the stairs reminding him casually, "Don't forget the reception this evening."

"Course not." The words had been spoken as if he hadn't really been listening.

"I'll bet the guy is gay," she was saying, with a flip of her hand in the air.

"Why do you say that?"

"That sketch he made of you—"

"I'd like to meet him again sometime."

Jo spun about on her heels, nearly falling off the step. "What?" she snapped. "That makes you gay, too."

He grabbed her by the shoulders and lifted her off her feet. "You think?" he asked, grinning.

"Put me down." He stopped her mouth with a wet, tongue-filled kiss. She spit it back at him and started up the stairs, but Caleb had noticed that they had an audience. The young waiter was standing in the double doors to the dining room watching them dubiously. He grabbed Jo's ass in the Italian manner, and she shrieked.

"You pervert," she laughed, dashing up the stairs. Caleb pursued her but paused long enough to catch the waiter's eyes. He was smiling broadly, and Caleb returned the smile. He shrugged—in the Italian manner—and continued his chase. He caught her by the arm just as she had opened her door and the two of them fell into the room in a loud and lusty embrace.

"Jesus," she cried, kicking the door shut, "not in front of God and everybody!"

They rolled about on the hard, marble floor for a while, digging their hands into each other's clothes, kissing and moaning, and then, they stopped. Caleb pushed himself up and looked down at her. Her expression had gone blank. She lay, small, weak and vulnerable beneath him, her colorless hair spread across her face like a veil. She had even stopped breathing. He blew out a breath and rose to his knees.

"Sorry."

"S'all right."

He helped her to her feet. "I don't know what got into me."

"Me too."

He sort of smiled. "Was kind of fun, though."

"Uh huh." She turned her eyes away from his at last. He had raised his eyes to the window behind her. "I think I'll take a walk in the garden. Want to come?"

"Stuff to do."

He nodded.

"Right."

"Bye."

He pulled the door closed behind him as he left. The garden was still in darkness, the sun on the other side of the villa. The cypresses were darker still, glistening with rain from the night before, but their tops were golden, touched by the sun, and they moved ever so slowly on the light breeze that slithered about them. There was a row of about a dozen of them flanking two sides of a pea-gravel walkway. To either side were partiers edged in trimmed boxwood and laden to overflowing with last year's grasses and herbs. The path was scattered with laurel leaves and pinecones from the nearby stone pines and there were occasional marble benches along the way.

In one of the side gardens, there rested a lichen-clothed statue of a faun. Its eyes were blackened by age but water droplets on the stone gave them the appearance of life and they seemed to stare lasciviously back at the wanderer. Caleb paused. The faun's erect penis had long since been broken off by vandals or perverts. Nonetheless, he was grinning as if mocking the world of mortal flesh and blood.

Caleb sat on one of the cold stone benches. He turned his eyes to the statue nearby and asked pathetically, "Who am I, I wonder? What brings me here, and what is expected of me? Did I come here to die? Is that it, I wonder?"

The statue merely grinned as drops of dew slithered down its marble cheek in imitation of sympathetic tears.

Out of the choppy sea of tile roofs, a golden bubble appears, floating like a glass sphere in a tangle of nets, half above, half below the larger sphere of brick-and-mortar ocean. Like an uncommon relic, hidden from the metal laden streets, tucked into some gray corner of Italy's memory, its oldness affects even the atmosphere around it, aging the very air taken in by those passing by, for whom it is little more than a cement reflection of the universe entire that perches upon its spindle, like a clue to some unknown mystery. It is the Pantheon. The *Rotunda Maxima* of Imperial Rome.

Caleb studied its facade as if searching for hidden meanings. He scratched the dome of his skull in search of words. Finding nothing, he opened his dog-eared Michelin Green Guide on Italy, the tenth edition, page 172, and read: "…a masterpiece of harmony and majesty, is dominated by a dome, the diameter of which is equal to its height. The side chapels, adorned with alternate curved and triangular pediments, contain tombs of the kings of Italy and that of Raphael (on the left)."

He paused to look around. He was wondering where the stranger might be right then, the man with the sketchbook. Then he reprimanded himself for even considering such a question much less putting it into words.

He dropped wearily into a chair in one of the outdoor bars that line the piazza. They were all but empty in winter, filled to overflowing in summer. He waited. A shadow fell across him. A man in a white apron had come out of the warm interior and stood by waiting. Caleb looked around him. Most of the tables and chairs were stacked on the walk awaiting the milder weather of spring. There were no other patrons occupying the other few chairs that were scattered about for the Advent tourists. Nonetheless, the waiter waited.

"Café."

"Café," the waiter repeated, as if bored with his small task. He hurried off and returned with a small round table. He threw a cloth over it and hurried off again. He returned with a bowl of sugar cubes, a napkin and a spoon. Then, from his back pocket, he retrieved a small vase with a single carnation in it. Caleb thanked him with a smile, and he returned a bow, then hurried off again. Even the help has stories, he knew, but he'd not even taken the time to look this one in the face. He was preoccupied with something, but he wasn't certain what it was that was troubling him. While awaiting the coffee, he once again searched the sunny spaces and the long, cold shadows for something. He was sitting on the warm side of the piazza along with a few other intrepid tourists who stood nearby with their cameras at the ready, but most of the wide square was empty of life. There were a few pigeons and an occasional dog, and a shadowy figure lurked among the pillars of the Pantheon, but that was all. Caleb turned his face to the sun.

He once again opened his notebook and poised his pen. He needed to write something, but nothing came. The waiter returned with the coffee and hurried off once more. Caleb closed his notebook.

Something had occurred to him. He surveyed the nearly empty piazza, the few chairs scattered randomly about the central fountain, the one draped table, the imposing portico. Its monolithic granite columns caught bits of sunlight reflected off second story windows that shone like irregular blotches on their cold granite skins. The anachronistic chairs, the ancient, timeless pillars; the presence of these two realities in the same place and time had struck him with a kind of melancholy. One winter table. One writer. One empty piazza filled to capacity with the ghosts of millions.

It was in this piazza a few years before he was born that the local Jews were gathered for deportation to death camps. Caleb did not know that fact. He suffered a chill, nonetheless. He sipped his coffee to ward off the chill.

Without thinking, he had gotten to his feet. He rambled about the scattering of chairs, his eyes always on the portico and its host of shadows. He'd left his empty cup and his notebook on the one draped table and wandered off. From the warm comfort of the cafe doorway, the waiter had watched him go but had made no attempt to call him back. Waiters wait. It is what they are expected to do.

Caleb stopped to stand alone in a patch of sunshine. It felt good on his face, and he paused to close his eyes and bask a moment in the gentle warmth. Then the sun moved. A deep shadow fell over him and he opened his eyes. The sun had not moved but Caleb had, involuntarily, and the shade of the mighty portico now loomed over him. The icy grandeur touched him to his bones, collecting in the cold spots in his shoulders and his groin. He had crossed the square as a sleepwalker, had transcended the light and shadow of history, and entered, as if indeed somnambulating, into a sunny place near the portico of the Pantheon. He collided then with a warm and bulky body, chest to chest and cheek to cheek.

"It's you!" Caleb said. "My god! Here you are."

The man was already walking away. He paused and looked back. He was nodding and smiling. "So it seems," he responded simply.

Caleb too had paused. "But where'd you come from?" It was an odd question to ask. He was trying not to look at the other man. How differently he appeared in daylight. He hadn't remembered him being so muscular. In the light of day, he looked more like a rugby player than a painter.

The man answered with a slight spreading of his hands, "Here we are. Again."

Caleb glanced nervously about him. There were no other people in the portico, nor anywhere to be seen. "What are you doing here?"

"Raphael," was the reply. He had gestured toward the portal and Caleb started after him. He asked his name. From over his shoulder as he walked, he said, "Michael." He had passed into the shadow of the portico. "You?"

"Caleb."

"Faithful as the dog," Michael was saying.

"What?"

He paused and waited for the other to catch up. "Your name. It means faithful servant. From Exodus; one of the twelve spies sent into the Promised Land."

Not knowing exactly how to respond, Caleb simply returned, "really?" He nodded. Then, he walked on and disappeared into the shadow of the great portal until a shaft of light suddenly fell upon him. He had stopped and was spreading his arms as if to embrace the vast interior. Caleb passed through the portal and walked carefully up to where the other man stood.

"Look," Michael was saying, taking him by the arm then and leading him in. The silent globe of the old rotunda hovered on the very edge of their vision. A shaft of winter sunlight, having pierced the oculus above, split the cool interior with precise measure. Michael had led Caleb into its brilliant sphere. The building seemed to spring away from that point as if they, like the sun's ray, had inscribed it upon the face of the earth through the simple act of touch. Caleb turned his eyes to the hand that gripped his arm. There was something different in this man's touch. It was not of the physical realm; there was something different.

"Look," Michael said again, with a sweep of his other hand. But he was looking at Caleb directly, steadily, as if trying to figure something out about him.

"What?"

Michael let go of his arm and walked away. He glanced back over his shoulder, smiling. "Impressive, isn't it?"

Caleb shook his head. "It's okay." Michael seemed to have become distracted by the view.

"Another perfect creation by an imperfect mind?" Caleb posed. The other was undeterred. "It was conceived by Hadrian in the second century of our Lord, completed by—"

"Hadrian? Wasn't he the Roman emperor who had an obsession with a beautiful young man?"

"Antinous. He drowned in the Nile." Caleb stopped listening. Michael was rambling as if not really listening to his own words. Now he was talking about something else as glibly as a professor or worse, a preacher. Caleb was watching him as he talked, gesturing, smiling; pronouncing our bland language as if it were as lyrical as Italian. He scratched his chin in wonderment and Michael stopped talking. He was handsome, energetic, athletic, well educated, softly spoken. It was a combination as odd and sinister as that of the Pantheon itself in its modern setting. Pagan temple to the planetary gods, Christian church, national shrine, tourist trap all at once.

"Well, Caleb, you're not really interested in all this history, are you?"

"Yeah," was his quick reply. "'Course I am." Michael smiled at him thinly. It was an odd, looking-right-through-you kind of smile. Then he apologized for the quizzical smile and said, "Let's get out of here."

"But—I want to see the tomb of Raphael."

Michael seemed momentarily confused. Then he nodded, very slightly. "It is an appropriate request," he said. He pointed the way. They paused before a niche surmounting a low arch. There was a stone sarcophagus and a bronze wreath. Two brass doves hovered above the casket, and someone had tossed a white rose into the niche. There was an inscription on the face of the sarcophagus. Michael translated it in soft words.

Here lie the bones and ashes of Raphael of Urbino; Painter.

Raphael must have lived a life of opulent loneliness. He never married, and he died young. Handsome, in a childlike way, he had stumbled into the world of international fame almost as if by accident. He hailed from the small fortress city of Urbino and was trained by the little remembered Pietro Vannucci of Perugia. A gracious man, according to the biographer, Raphael was loved by everyone. Even animals loved him. Compared to the rugged Michelangelo and the strange Leonardo, Raphael was ordinary, which may be one reason why he was so praised in his time for his humility and his charm, as if, basking in the shadows of greater men, there was nothing else interesting to say about him. Poor man: great painter that he was, and the best we can say about him today is that he was a nice guy.

Of the other great bachelor artists with whom he is often associated by the biographer, his story is the least compelling. His womanless life was never the subject of controversy as were the lives of the other two. Leonardo had his favorite boys, one assumes, and Michelangelo, if he didn't actually fondle his models, he at least looked at them longingly. Why else do those beautiful nudes on the Sistine Chapel ceiling gaze so longingly into the nothingness of an empty hereafter if not with the pain of celibacy? As if awakening from the innocent sleep of childhood, only to discover the aloneness of adolescence, they stretch and yawn, yearning for the return of the painter whose touch alone can fulfill their unrequited desires.

But Raphael never painted men in pain, nor women in confusion. His figures, at very most, are oblivious to the real world of flesh and sex, having chosen to remain half asleep, thinking of nothing: mute, and beautifully indifferent to the cries and whispers of agony and ecstasy. Like the painter himself, they are gracious, charming, beautiful, and boring.

After a moment's silence at the tomb of unknown Raphael, they turned to go, but as they moved through the ancient void of solid geometry toward the great doors, the sun, having reached a place in the winter heavens predetermined by astrologer architects, and barely skimming the lip of the dome's open, turned-up mouth, glanced momentarily off the indented edge of a ceiling coffer and with one luminous finger traced an arc on the pavement before them. The fine line of reflected light etched the rim of a marble disc set in the floor.

"Solstice," Michael said softly. "I'd almost forgotten."

"It isn't Solstice," Caleb returned, but Michael had left the Pantheon. Caleb stood for a while on the porphyry disc, as if afraid to put his feet on the solid geometrical ground of the darker pavement. He moved toward the portal. Michael was standing in the sunshine of the piazza beyond the portico, the one draped table on which rested Caleb's notebook beyond. Caleb waited until the other motioned for him. He joined him in the sunshine.

"I don't understand," Caleb said.

"What don't you understand?" Michael asked, as if annoyed.

"How we happened to run into each other here."

"Tourists often find themselves in the same places," was all he said. He was looking about as if for someone else, more interesting. "Walk with me?"

"Why?"

"Why not?"

"My notebook," he said over his shoulder as he turned back toward the light in the piazza. Michael waited for him to return. They started walking the street that lay hard by the curving walls of the rotunda, following the slow-moving sun toward Trastevere.

"So," Caleb asked as they walked, "what now?"

"Lunch?" Michael ventured.

"Maybe."

"I know a nice place near Piazza Navona." Caleb had paused in a square of sunlight reflected off an unseen window and glanced at his watchless wrist. "Lunch?" It seemed a logical answer to his former question. Still studying his wrist, he asked, "You want us to be friends, Michael? Why? I don't have many friends and don't quite understand the value of having them."

Michael replied that he found that statement hard to believe. Caleb merely shrugged glancing sort of sideways and with skepticism at the other man. Thus, they stood for a while in silence, in that oblong square of reflected sunlight. At length, Michael asked where he had gotten such an idea about himself. Caleb looked away. "Former friends," he said.

They started walking again. Michael asked carefully if the friends in question had left on their own, "or did you throw them away?"

"A little of both, I suppose." His voice was especially soft, and Michael asked him to repeat what he'd just said but he didn't. They were walking very slowly, each watching the paved earth on which they walked.

"Is that why you're skeptical of my offer of friendship? You're afraid it will end in hurt?"

"We only hurt the one's we love," Caleb returned, smiling at the triviality of the words.

"More," Michael added. "We often ruin them as well." But those sounded like Caleb's words. He stopped walking a second time and turned to look the other man in the face. "Is that what is destined of our friendship, I wonder?" he asked, "Ruin?"

Michael had continued walking slowly through the shadows cast by old palaces, across the narrow streets, the sunny piazza as his goal. And he answered softly as he was walking slowly away, all the while looking downward, at the way his feet moved from paver to paver. Caleb did not hear his response. The other man had paused. He was looking away, as if Caleb were not even there, gazing at the walls of a church as if he could see through them to the paintings that hung inside. "Perfect," he said. Caleb yet lagged behind. "What is?"

"Caravaggio," he said in return.

"What about him?"

"He used to walk these streets." He turned to Caleb with a bright smile. "Just imagine! Caravaggio! You know his work?"

"I've seen the Matthew paintings in this church," he said.

"But, don't you see?" he asked. "That's it!"

"What's it?"

"It's what I noticed last night but it didn't register 'till just now. It's you!" He looked him steadily in the face. "You're right out of Caravaggio. Yes! That unruly dark hair—Those liquid eyes—That melancholy mouth." He stood back and nodded as if admiring one of his own paintings. "Caleb; you must have been a model for Caravaggio!"

"Don't be absurd," Caleb said, starting off once more toward the piazza. Michael caught up to him as he added, "I am nothing like a Caravaggio."

"Ever seen his painting of a young boy with a basket of grapes?"

"No. And, I'm not exactly a young boy." Michael agreed. "But look at yourself!" He had taken hold of his shoulders and turned him toward the windows of a restaurant. "I'm serious. Look!"

"I don't have time for your games, Michael," Caleb said, wresting himself from the strong grasp and walking on.

"My games?" He caught up to him, confronted him, the brilliant sun stretching across his upper body like a banner. His expression was intense. Caleb paused, still in shadow. Michael asked why he was there. In Rome. In winter.

"Writing."

He said he wasn't surprised. When asked why, he said, "This meeting seems too much like something one might read in a novel."

"Nothing I would ever write," he returned, impatiently. Michael grinned. "No," he said. "I suppose not." They walked in silence across the Piazza Navona, through the liquid sunshine, but Caleb was thinking to himself that this brief, possibly intense association could prove to be, if nothing else, interesting.

They had paused in the very center of the piazza, crowds of tourists and venders swelling about them, and Michael had him once more by the shoulder. He turned to face him and said, as Caleb rolled his eyes heavenward, "Let me tell you about this church. It was designed by Gianlorenzo Bernini in—"

Caleb listened patiently for a while and then started away. "Such talk," he said. "Such words—"

"I love this stuff," Michael was saying from just behind him.

"You get so passionate about it."

"I speak from my heart," Michael said. "Have you a better word for it?"

He glanced at the lights and shadows playing across the truncated marble facade. "Folly."

Michael had caught up to him. They walked side by side through the throngs of people. "That is an organ of the body with which I am unfamiliar," he laughed.

"It's situated just behind the heart, I am told," Caleb said, "and is often mistaken for the *real* heart by those of us who are unfamiliar with the anatomy of emotions."

"The fool's heart," Michael mused. They paused to look at each other and then back at the bustling piazza. Cars, people, pigeons and dogs came and went with purposes known only to themselves. The arena was awash with color-filled light and motion. Sounds of the city—motors grumbling, mouths talking, wings flapping, dogs barking—were appropriate here. Everything seemed in place and of its proper time. It is the heart of Rome, a folly of reason and history, the Piazza Navona. It is a place where the incongruities of the Eternal City seem truly symbiotic, suspended in raucous harmony with the rest of the known world. It is the center of centers, from which Western Civilization sprang and to which it will someday return, collapsing into itself and taking with it the rest of the universe as well.

Michael paused and looked over at the other man. He was massaging his slightly bearded chin with the fingers of his left hand. "Maybe you don't know," he said.

"Know what?"

"I don't know. I—just thought you might, is all."

"Know what?" he asked again, but Michael was walking away.

"I hope I can find the way," he was saying.

"Me, too," Caleb said, mostly to himself.

They left the piazza together and ambled the streets of old Rome in silence, pursued by shadows.

Seven

1

John sat in silence, leaning on his elbow, watching Alison and Cutler laughing over some inane story she was reciting. She had placed herself between the two men at the bar and proceeded to turn her back on John as if he weren't even there. He had been placing the order and Evelyn was filling him in on gossip she'd heard earlier in the day and when he turned to insert himself into the conversation, he discovered that Alison was taking Cutler on one of her magical mystery tours, all of which he was more than familiar with, so he had decided to simply remain behind and watch. He let his mind wander back a few hours. Seeing Lizzie Tifgat. Talking with Beatrice Umlohr. Insulting Lewis.

What had he been thinking? How could he have said such a thing? "Jesus, boy!"

Lewis had scowled and started away. "Don't piss me off, John."

He hadn't meant to say it. It had just slipped out. He tried to explain the comment away by saying he had endured a trying afternoon. John had never actually had a black friend before. He didn't know the protocol. They didn't teach those kinds of things in those days, he'd tell himself, later in life. How could he even begin to imagine how trying every afternoon must have been for Lewis E. Jonas. The only black professor in a nearly all-white college.

"I like it here, all right," Lewis had replied to John's question, posed one afternoon when the two of them sat together at the boat-shaped bar in Evelyn's. He was staring at the glass of beer he held tightly in his left hand. "Not very many people like me, is the problem."

Having clearly misunderstood, John had laughed. "I know what that's like." Lewis could have suggested the reason some people may not have liked John was due to his personality, not the color of his skin, but he said nothing.

How could he have made John understand how he felt? Instead, he laughed. Told about the day he had sat in the barber chair for two hours waiting for the barber to come over and cut his hair.

"What happened?"

"He just sat there," Lewis said, "in the other chair, reading a magazine. Some kind of gun owner's manual. Any time someone came to the door, at sight of me, they'd turn around and walk away."

John was suddenly interested. "My god," he said. "What did you do?"

He shrugged. Said he finally got up and left the barber shop. "There were men gathered outside. Frustrated patrons, I guess. I had to walk right through them. They wouldn't move out of the way. Not one inch."

His voice had softened. Took on the tone of distance, like one reciting a bad dream. John asked him very carefully if he had been scared. Lewis shrugged again, very slightly. Yes. He had been.

"Sorry."

"Shit happens."

They drank a while in silence. John wondered if he was planning to stay on at the college. Lewis admitted he didn't know. John suggested he host a party. Give the faculty an opportunity to get to know him better.

Lewis laughed, showing his gums. "I don't know how to host a party, John."

"It's easy. Just name a date and invite people. Tell them to bring their own drinks. If they ask if they can bring anything else, tell them to bring snacks."

Staring at his glass of beer again, he asked, "What if nobody comes?"

John assured him they would be there, all those curious white folks.

Lewis shuddered noticeably.

"That cottage I'm renting for the winter is pretty small," he said, after a time. "How many should I invite?"

John had suggested a couple dozen. Assuming half would show up. As it was, the little cottage was packed. Not only did everyone Lewis invite show up, several uninvited guests did as well. Oddly, John was thinking as he sat more or less alone at the bar, Alison rambling on nearby, nobody seemed to take the time to talk with Lewis. He seemed to be spending most of his time standing on the edge of small pods of conversation, listening. Always on the outside.

Maybe he should leave Alison and Cutler and return to the party, John was thinking, if for no other reason than to give Lewis someone to talk to. Except that he was no longer in a party mood. He had started rubbing his eyes with his knuckles. His eyes were sore and when they were sore, he didn't feel like being sociable. He could always tell when it was a Saturday, as his eyes would hurt him. They didn't bother him other days of the week, but Saturdays! It was from a week of reading, he'd always assumed, of studying, of looking and of seeing. He was always tired on Saturdays, as Alison so often reminded him, but not just tired: tired of looking, wishing not to have to look anymore. Next day was Sabbath. A day of rest for his eyes. John never read on Sundays, not even the paper. And he was sad on Saturdays. He didn't know why but it always seemed to be so. Sundays held happy memories of childhood games and walks on the beach, but Saturdays bothered him for reasons he did not fully understand. His sore eyes, the sadness; Saturdays did that to him.

A flash of Titian Red hair startled him, and he realized Evelyn had materialized before him. She stood just beyond the narrow boundary of polished wood, wiping her hands on a linen towel and smiling an orange-lipped smile. Light reflected off her glasses and the rhinestones that dangled from her pink ears. She raised a smoldering cigarette to her mouth and took in a great gulp of smoke. Her mouth was moving beyond the smear of smoke that she exhaled. "Another drink, folks?"

John checked his watch but the other two had already answered and she had gone to make the drinks. John was ready to go home. To bed. To sleep. Perchance to dream. He glanced at his wrist. He wasn't wearing a watch and hadn't since he'd lost it years before. He raised his wrist to his ear instinctively but heard no ticking. Evelyn had set another bottle of beer before him. Alison was drinking some blue thing and Cutler was sipping coffee.

"Besides," she was saying, "he didn't even know me, but he must have thought he did."

John smiled at her words and stopped listening and excused himself. The other two looked to him as if annoyed at his interrupting them. "Toilet," he said, and they went back to Alison's little fantasy. He could still hear her voice as he walked away from the bar.

"But how did he know your name?"

"That's just it, Cutler. He must have thought I was someone else he knew named Alison."

"It's not a real common name."

"I know! Isn't that a gas?"

John shut the door to the men's room behind him and reveled in the silence that followed. At the urinal, there was a lingering hint of Cutler's cologne and he shook his head.

"Are you still here?" he asked the porcelain presence. Then, at the mirror, he looked carefully into his own eyes, trying to understand the sadness that had overtaken him earlier that evening. His eyes hurt so badly he decided to take out his contact lenses. With a flip of his forefinger, he spun the lethal disk of crystal out and into his other palm. He rolled his other eye toward the light and poised nervous fingers on the rim of his vision. This one always gave him trouble. He spread his lids with careful fingers and popped the lens out and it fell into the sink. He blinked his eyes several times and squinted to see better as he searched the white expanse of enamel glaze for a glint of light off minute glass edges. He found it and tucked it carefully into its case then sighed in relief at the new freedom his eyes were experiencing. When he returned to the bar, he discovered that someone else was occupying his stool.

"Alison?"

"Oh, John. I thought you'd left, or something."

"Or something?"

The stranger excused himself and moved to the next stool. "I thought it felt a little warm," the stranger had said with an embarrassed laugh.

John sat with a sigh of impatience and took a sip of his beer. He could hear Cutler's voice over the sound of the jukebox. Normally quiet, when he got excited, which often happened when talking to Alison, his voice would grow louder and higher in pitch. Even after it faded behind Alison's as she continued with the protracted tale, it remained lodged in John's mind, an unwelcome guest just the same.

It was Cutler's adolescent voice, a song that had dwelt in John's memory for many years. It was the voice of the little boy, having grown early into a tall man's body but still wearing that child's face. It was the voice of John's childhood, his only real friend in junior high, and his burden. Cutler was shy except with John. None of the other boys liked him because of his strangeness. His obsession with death and his high-pitched voice, a voice much too small for a boy his size. He'd conduct funerals for roadkill animals and invite the neighborhood kids over with handwritten notes, but John was the only one who ever attended. Otherwise, Cutler would have had to conduct the services all by himself. His little graveyard grew larger by the year but after John got into high school, he stopped attending the services for fear his upper-class friends would find out and think he was as weird as Cutler. But their friendship never ended, and John never really understood why it hadn't. They had nothing in common—except a shared history, an ancient history at that.

He chuckled to himself. There were so many funny things about Cutler to recall. He often wondered if all those strange events hadn't been done just for his own amusement. He wouldn't have put it past Cutler. He was, after all, a very clever man, despite his strangeness.

Alison had spilled her drink and Evelyn was there, suddenly mopping it up and accepting her apologies. The sound of water splashing across the bar had brought to John's mind another unwelcome guest, a memory that bothered him though it was one he cherished, one he hoped to someday forget as he could never look at Cutler and not remember it and the recollection of it had shaded the color of his love for Cutler for many years.

It was summer. All bittersweet memories are of summer, he thought. It was high summer, one of those hot, yellow days when nothing can cool you off but water. They were swimming at Cole's Dock, an old wooden structure at the butt end of Lake Street, where the only paved road in town in those days came to an abrupt end at the beach. The dock was left from World War II days when it was used to board a car ferry that stopped at some of the road-less settlements along the lakeshore. It was private, but John and Cutler used to swim there often, jumping from the pier in hopes of avoiding sunken abutments and rocks. They'd let themselves sink to the bottom and see who could stay down the longest. John always won. Then he'd burst through the surface with a gasp of delight at the brilliance of the air and the excitement of victory. He'd shake his head to free trailing drops of water from their hairy bonds and then he'd hold Cutler under until he'd struggle to be free. Then he'd laugh.

"Damn it, John, someday you're going to be responsible for somebody's death!"

"Jesus, Cutler, it's only a game!"

Cutler was sore. John didn't like what he'd said to him. He turned his back on his friend and started up the ladder. He paused about halfway, his feet still in the cool water, sensing something sad. He turned to see if Cutler were following him, but the other had turned and was swimming into deep water.

"It's only a game," John said again.

He stood on the end of the dock watching Cutler swim away toward the hidden horizon, hidden in the haze of a warm summer afternoon and an ancient memory. He called his name but there was no response. He adjusted his hands at his hips, waiting for Cutler to turn around and head back toward shore so he could go on home and get away from him for a while. But Cutler continued to swim out into the lake.

"Damn it," he said as he dove from the dock. He dove too deep and scraped his belly on the rocks below water. He was a strong swimmer, better than Cutler. He sprinted after him in an overhand crawl, popping his eyes open occasionally to make sure Cutler was still in sight. He took a hard slug to the shoulder as Cutler passed him on his return to shore. He stopped for a few seconds, treading in deep water, looking about. Cut was racing back to the dock.

"You son-of-a-bitch!"

He started back, already winded. Cutler had never beat him before. He couldn't let it happen this time, especially after what he'd said to him a few moments before. He glanced up. Cutler's tanned body was already emerging from the water at the ladder. He could see him through the froth, his long legs and arms bending rhythmically, his white ass moving up the ladder. He ducked his head into the cool and sloshing water. The view there was gray and silver, shimmering with fishlike darts of sunlight. When he lifted his head again, shaking it to clear his vision of water, he saw Cutler's legs hanging over the edge of the dock above him. He climbed the ladder and lay down beside him. They were both exhausted. They breathed heavily and in unison. They were quiet for some time.

"So, why are you pissed, Cut? You know I'd never let you die."

Cutler sat up, his glistening back to his friend. "I'm not pissed," he said softly.

"Well, something's bothering you. What is it?"

Cutler talked into his lap, his head bowed away from John. "It's just—Sometimes I think you don't like me, is all."

John sat up next to him. "What makes you think that? We've been friends since kindergarten."

"I know." He was moving his fingers over his abdomen as if searching for an itch to scratch. "Sometimes I think you're making fun of me."

"Oh, that," John said, uncomfortable with criticism as he was. "I make fun of everybody, Cutler, you know that. I even make fun of myself."

Cutler sighed. "I know. I'm sorry I said anything." He stood and walked back to where their clothes had been left, two little piles of shorts and tennis shoes and baseball caps. When John came up to him, he saw that Cutler had a hard-on. He stared at it until Cutler suddenly sensed his scrutiny. He hadn't realized himself what had happened, and he was suddenly embarrassed. He pulled on his shorts and grabbed his shoes and ran to his bike before John could think to say anything. They were probably fourteen. What happened wasn't so uncommon for boys at that age, John knew now. But it was after that day that their friendship changed. They hardly saw each other after that. During high school, they'd wave or nod to each other but never spoke. John was always afraid someone would find out what had happened that day in summer and think he and Cutler were weird or something. They lost touch completely during their college years and John almost forgot about Cutler Insbroek and the day at Cole's Dock.

Then they found themselves both teaching in their hometown college. John had thought to himself upon first seeing Cutler again that Fate had played a dirty trick on him for his having ignored the one person She had deemed to be his faithful, lifelong friend.

2

Alison was laughing. John blinked his eyes and involuntarily plunged his hands into his groin. For some reason, he had an erection. He sensed the scrutiny of the man sitting next to him. They locked eyes and the man picked up his drink and moved down another stool. John started to laugh. He hadn't realized at first that Alison and Cutler were standing and getting into their coats.

"You going back to the party?" he wondered.

"Cutler has some good grass," Alison said, too loudly. "Wanna' come with us?"

"You know I don't do that shit," John said in a frustrated whisper.

"Yeah, I know." She had started for the door, Cutler just behind her.

John asked after them, "How long will you be?"

"Not long," was Cutler's terse response.

"Well, I'm tired."

"See," Alison was saying to Cutler. "I told you he'd say that."

Cutler went to the men's room. John and Alison sat in silence for a time. She was first to speak, in soft words, that seemed to come from some other person.

"I had a cousin committed suicide. Did I ever tell you that?"

He shook his head no. "How?"

She didn't know. She was young at the time. Maybe only five or six.

"I didn't know her very well but—"

"What?"

"I remember how it shook up the family, the whole family. Even my parents. You know, how everybody seemed to think they could have done something to prevent it."

He wondered why it was she was telling him that story. She said it had been on her mind lately for some reason. How it shook up the family. "Still does, I guess."

They sat a while longer in silence. Cutler came back to retrieve his coat from the hook under the counter. Alison leaned over to kiss John lightly on the cheek and then, she and Cutler left. His voice could be heard as the door slammed on the wind. "I'll bring her back to your cottage, John."

"How you gonna get the ice off your windshield?" John called after them. He glanced over at the man who had been sitting next to him.

"Looks like you've been bird-dogged," the man said.

"My best friend," John said.

"The man or the woman?"

John simply scowled. "Both of them," he said softly.

He stood to get into his coat. Evelyn asked if he was leaving though it should have been obvious he was.

"Three dollars," she said.

"What? Oh."

He handed her a five and told her to keep the change.

"Nonsense," she said with a broad grin. "You're one of my best customers. I don't take tips from my best customers."

He smiled. "Thanks," he said, feeling better. John stepped into the cold wind, the door slammed behind him and the streetlight at the top of the bluff went dark. Cutler and Alison must have been passing by, he thought.

He pulled his jacket about him and decided to walk home. It was about the same distance back to Lewis's where his car awaited but he might have to talk to someone if he went back there. He started down the beach toward the little speck of light that marked his bedroom window. The bedroom he shared with Alison. He swore he could hear her laughing and when he looked up the hill toward Lewis's he saw that the streetlamp was burning once more. He saw two beams of light play across the cedars that hugged the dune-top road. "Must be Cutler and Alison," he thought, "going for a hayride."

The wind was at his back. The sand was packed and solid due to the cold and the walking was easy. As he went, he let himself slip back into his story, the one he'd been writing most of his life, the one without an ending.

John's legs were bitter cold. He was sitting on the ice hard beach where the ripples of the nocturnal lake lapped gently among the crystal shells that rattled softly together like bones. He got to his feet. He could see the lights of his small house flickering among the wind-blown cedars. He walked slowly toward the feeble beacons. Waves of dark clouds dipped and swirled behind the dunes. He paused at the base of the red stairway, black in the non-light of mid-night. He started up, noticing how the fragile moon, recently released from the grip of the clouds, tinted the edge of each stair tread with a delicate line of luminescence. The steps were icy, and John slipped, crashing down hard on one cold knee. Rubbing it, standing, he started up again. The lights left burning in the house urged him on though there was something less comforting about them than usual. He paused, wondering. He almost wished he had gone back to the party. The house was empty. He sensed it. Alison would not be home tonight.

He started up again, stamping his feet on the landing to shake off the sand from his shoes. His feet were soaked, his pants wet to the knees. He looked at his feet incredulously as if he could not understand why they were so cold. He stamped them again and crossed the small sloping yard to the house. There were no mysteries this time, no late model automobiles speeding away, no radio music sounding in the kitchen, no baking smells. There was, in fact, no mystery at all in John's life. So intent was he on inventing lives for his mythical characters he had neglected to construct a life of his own.

He stared at the house for a while as if he expected it to do something, but it simply rested there, on its precarious perch above the shining lake, awaiting a painless and gradual death by rot and neglect. John did not go into the house. He sat down in the yard as if waiting for something and he would have remained there the night long had not the cold and the loneliness driven him in. He didn't go into bed. He sat on the sofa where he could watch out the window. He would have remained in that position until dawn except that sleep and sadness soon overtook him. He laid his head on the back of the sofa. Then he slipped off to sleep.

Eight

The spectre himself here settled the point of his tangibility, at all events, and physical substance, by approaching a step nearer, and laying his hand on Kenyon's arm.

"Inquire not what I am, nor wherefore I abide in darkness," said he, in a hoarse, harsh voice, as if a great deep of damp were clustering in his throat. "Henceforth, I am nothing but a shadow behind her footsteps. She came to me when I sought her not. She has called me forth and must abide the consequences of my reappearance in the world."

Hawthorne, *The Marble Faun*

"I've lived all my life in small towns," Caleb said. "This city is a new experience for me."

"Do you like it?"

"I'm not sure. I only just arrived. Give me a day or two."

"I grew up in a city," Michael said. "But I've lived in small towns since college."

"What do you do?"

"I'm a priest." He was pointing toward a sunny street beyond the piazza, an alleyway, at best, situated in such a way as to catch the sun's full attention at midday. "The restaurant is that direction. Hungry?"

"I thought you were an artist?"

"That, too."

"Famous?"

"Hardly."

"Then, why do you do it?"

"Why not? Hungry?"

"I guess."

They walked on. "I've never known a writer, before," Michael was saying. "I'm curious: How does one become a writer, anyway?"

"One does not *become* a writer," he answered. "Why did you become a painter?"

"Same."

"I don't follow," he admitted, though he was following him up the dark lane.

"I was born that way. My family was never happy about that. They just wanted me to be a priest." Michael said, as if it should have been common knowledge. He was the youngest boy. It was logical in his parent's minds, he go into the priesthood.

"Did you want to?"

He paused only briefly, as if looking for the right alleyway off the main street. "Not especially. This way," he pointed, then, he added, "They'd been grooming me all my life. I don't suppose they really thought I had any choice in the matter."

"What happened?"

"What?"

Caleb shrugged. "You know. When you chose not to be a priest." Michael smiled. "I didn't do that," he said lightly. Caleb paused, a shadow falling across his face. "Then, you *are* a priest?"

"It made them happy. They're all gone now, anyway." Caleb asked if he had never slept with a woman. The sun poured generously upon them as they had paused in a piazza; more a swelling of the street where an alleyway joined it. Michael pointed toward a small bistro at the end of the alley. He had nodded.

"What happed to her?" Caleb asked from behind him. Michael had paused. He looked back briefly, smiled strangely. "She died, Caleb." Then he said, "Let's eat, okay? I'm starved."

"Me too."

But Michael had not heard him. Caleb watched after him a moment, then followed obediently, like a pilgrim. They went into the antique *taverna* and found a table in a square of sunshine by a window. It was warm and pungent inside. It was quiet and sad. Caleb set his pointed elbows to the table and laid his head in his opened hands. "I'm sorry," he said. "I didn't mean to pry."

"It's all right," Michael said in return. "It was a long time ago. It is part of my history, now. Nothing more. Everyone has a story, Caleb." He was having difficulty with the words. "You, most of all, must know that. Some stories are interesting, some ordinary, I suppose. Some are simply—"

He had stopped talking and Caleb stole a glance at him. He had turned toward the sun light, his profile limned in gold. His eyes had filled with water and his mouth had come at last to rest. Caleb reached across the table and clasped his forearm. Michael smiled slightly and let a tear fall. It crashed to the linen tabletop with the maximum speed of memories in free fall, a silent explosion of the heart. Caleb was writing.

After a moment's silence, Michael turned back to him. "My life has been prescribed on my behalf by the powers of the past," he said, "family and church. Your life seems to be free from those things, Caleb. It rests within your own hands as does your chin at this very moment."

Caleb had not been listening. He sat up suddenly. "What?" he asked.

The expression on Michael's face had taken on a beauty associated with expectation. "I want to live your life," he said, leaning forward a bit, "at least for a few weeks. Is it so much to ask?" Caleb stood up. "What?" Michael repeated his words. "Is it too much to ask?"

"Yes," he returned abruptly, sitting again, and shuffling about in his chair.

Michael seemed momentarily stunned. "Don't you understand?"

"Yes, but," Caleb tried to appear nonplussed. "No one can live a life through someone else," he proclaimed.

"Why not?" Michael wondered. "You're a writer. You do it all the time."

"That's different," he heard himself saying. "I don't live other people's lives. I invent those people. The lives they lead are multiples of my own, of my own imagination, my own creation, I suppose, but they're not real people—with real lives."

He went on. Real life wasn't important to him, he said. "It's what I *make* of it that matters. Don't you get that?"

Michael was nodding, smiling, as if knowing something Caleb did not know. He leaned ever closer, spreading his hands across the table. "And, who gave you the power to recreate the world as you would have it?" He did not wait for Caleb's response. "If that power is truly Divine, as I believe it is, does that not obligate you to share its possibilities with others?"

"It's why I write."

"Bullshit!" Michael said, without expression, and sitting back. "You haven't a clue as to why you write, Caleb Wilson."

He was looking especially smug and that made Caleb angry. He turned away, and then, just as the waiter was pouring the wine, the dark red blood of

Italy's mountains, he stood and turned his back. He stood there for a while, as if planning an escape. In his mind, he could still see Michael sitting there across from him, in a sunny square of light. He was watching him. Curiously. His head in his hands. Caleb punched himself in the lats and turned to sit again. When he sat down, Michael turned his face away. He said nothing.

"I'm sorry," Caleb said. "Truly. I don't know why I did that."

Michael nodded. Caleb tried to explain; something about not being used to people hitting him where he lived, in the region of the heart. He laughed. "Of course, there are those who claim I have no heart." He could say no more.

"I don't expect you to understand me any better than I do you," Michael was saying, "though, as a writer, I somehow thought you would."

"I've disappointed you."

"Not in the least." He kept his eyes away from him. "It was childish of me to believe in the possibilities of what some call fate."

"Don't say those words," Caleb pleaded. "Some things are possible. I'm just not the one who can make them happen for you, is all."

He looked up at last. "Have you any idea what it is like to be lonely to the point of non-existence?"

Caleb bit his lip. "You're talking to the man who invented the concept." He turned his eyes toward the sunny alleyway. "But I believe we create our own loneliness, even though we may not mean to do it. Some of us, it seems, have no other skill than that!"

Michael was nodding. He raised his glass and toasted in silence. Caleb did the same. They drank.

"Such words, Michael." He paused at sound of his own words. *Such* words! After taking a breath he smiled. The other had turned again into the sunlight that illuminated their small space. He nodded, his profile outlined in gold. Caleb handed him his glass for refilling. Michael refilled both glasses.

"To you, my friend. May you ever thrive."

Caleb returned the toast. "May we both."

He tasted the wine for the first time. It was sweetly pungent but bitter in the back of the mouth. He set the glass down and took up the menu. He wondered casually what was good. Michael suggested the veal *alla Romagna*.

"The proprietors are gay," he said behind his hand. "They are very good cooks."

As they walked the quiet alleyways of Old Rome, Caleb felt a sensation of tension in the air; a reflective instance, the cause of which lay beyond comprehension. Something in the vast realm of Being had moved and all subordinate creatures twitched with a brief and diluted anxiety. Michael's face too had lost all feature, like a marble statue left to the eroding power of the winds. Had he taken leave of his body? Not even Caleb's staring eyes had registered on the other's projected consciousness. Had his mind left the physical shell altogether, or simply withdrawn from the surface to its inner depths? He continued to walk and react to the environment as he passed through it but not as one aware of his own presence.

"Michael?"

"Yes, Caleb."

"Are you all right?"

"Yes. But did you not notice it?"

"What?"

He only smiled. Could he have been speaking of the same sensation, that vague and fleeting feeling of futility that had brought Caleb himself to pause?

"I was thinking of that neighborhood I grew up in," Michael was saying, but Caleb had stopped listening. He too had drifted into a state of memory. He didn't hear the story of the other man's family, the great sadness they'd shared and how they'd communicated that sorrow through time and space to one another and any other who happened to be near. He didn't hear how the family members one by one had died off, excluding Michael from that final communication; to live on alone, sharing nothing, slowly to be drained by time and space of every joy he'd ever known; of every good feeling he had ever possessed.

Thus, Michael remained as an empty case, waiting to be filled. Nor, as Michael talked in unusually protracted metaphor, could he have known Caleb's thoughts and the story of his own family, one that yet thrived in that small dying town of his fading memories. It was a family he had chosen to ignore for the sake of blessed loneliness, a loneliness that Caleb wore like a stitched badge on his garments because, in his generation, to his mind, it was the thing for a writer to do. It was a loneliness that none other would be expected, in his mind, to comprehend or appreciate, like cancer. The only person it really has any meaning to at all is the host in which it elevates itself; a self-consuming Eucharist; an invention of Modern Times, to his mind, unknown to anyone not born of the Great Depression and the World War and all those other dreaded bedpartners of our indifferent parents. Certainly, Vincent Van Gogh had not been lonely. Certainly, Strindberg had not been shunned, nor Wilde nor any other blindered poet of that pre-civilized age.

And yet, there it was: the small town, great and beautiful to the stunned and stunning child of beauty Caleb had been. Small, decrepit, and old to him now, like his mother, once tall and stately, like those doomed elms that once lined the street named after them; now broken and bent, offering no shade in summer, nor even from her outstretched fingers, nor to catch the golden edge of sunshine in her hair anymore: nor to be young. Caleb could not think of his little town, without thinking of his mother, shrunken with age as she now languishes, for he knew her from better times, and he knew she was now dying a slow and painful death. Oddly, he blamed that demise on himself. The town thrived when he was young and then he left and never went back and that marked the beginning of the end, his mother along with it.

"Had I never been born," he thought, "she would never have to grow old and die, at least not as far as I would have known."

The sun had lost itself behind ancient buildings. The narrow, twisting alley lay in deep shade. An old, musty chill attended them as they walked, not talking. They rounded a corner, the bright piazza in sight, the sun in their eyes, and a dark figure crashed into them, pressing between them, having come around the corner from the other direction. Michael jumped suddenly to the side, saying something in Latin under his breath and marking the cross on his chest. The shawl-draped old woman paused and looked up at the two taller men.

"*Scusi*," she said simply, and hurried on.

Caleb did not watch after her as the other man was doing. He was staring instead at the look of horror on Michael's face. He asked him, "What?"

He sort of shook his head, smiled with embarrassment, and started walking again toward the piazza. He had mentioned casually in passing he had thought it was someone else.

"Who, for Christ's sake?"

Michael merely walked on in silence. Caleb followed a few steps behind. When they entered the piazza, the low sun having cut it in half, dark on one side and bright on the other, they paused. The warmth on their shoulders revived the conversation.

"It's almost Christmas," Michael said, in reference to the lights strung across the open spaces.

"The academy is throwing some kind of party this evening."

Michael was already walking away. Caleb said that he had enjoyed their time together, but that he had better be on his way. Michael offered casually that he would be occupied for the next several days himself. Church duties. He had paused and turned to face him. "Lunch, sometime, do you suppose?"

"Next week? Monday, maybe?"

"The Church of Jesus."

"Noonish?"

He had stood for nearly an hour in front of his closet, trying to decide what to wear. He hadn't brought a sport coat with him, and his only pants were blue jeans. Finally, the sound of music coming up from below, he went across to Jo's room. He knocked. Asked through the door what she was wearing. The door opened. She wore in a brightly colored dress and had her hair up on top of her head. She wore make up and jewelry.

"You look pretty," he said.

She observed that he wasn't dressed, and he explained his predicament. She offered to help and followed him back to his room. She asked if he had a nice sweater and he pointed to the shelves on the side of the wardrobe. She poked her fingers into the stacks of sweatshirts and sweaters. The one she chose was a deep red in color, with a cable pattern down the front. She suggested a white shirt and black jeans and then she stood back to watch him dress. Dropping his pants, he glanced up at her and grinned.

"Like my skinny legs?"

She turned to go but he called her back. "I don't want to go down alone," he admitted.

She nodded. "I'll wait. But, hurry, will you?" Dressed, hair combed, and cologne splashed on his face, he turned to her with a bow. She took his arm, and they descended the broad marble stairs to the hall below. It was filled with people; patrons, students, sponsors, professors, wait staff. The regents wore evening clothes, their decorated women hanging on their arms like ornaments. The profs wore frock coats, the staff, white linen jackets. In a bay near the front portals, there was Christmas tree and a quintet, fumbling its way through American show tunes. At the foot of the stair was a draped table festooned with greens and roses and over laden with cheeses, fruits and candies. The cafeteria waiters stood close by, ready to pour glasses of sparkling prosecco.

Taking a glass in hand, Caleb admitted that the reception might not be so bad after all. Jo laughed, and they toasted. They stood on the edge of the small well-dressed crowd. A man in an Armani tuxedo was speaking to the group in Italian. He was welcoming the winter scholars and thanking their patrons, naming each of the monetary contributors as a way of reminding everyone how much it cost the city of Rome to run the academy. Caleb translated as best as he could for Jo, and the two of them were soon surrounded by the other American fellows, each leaning in closely to better hear. The speech ended, the crowd applauding, Caleb and Jo returned to have their glasses refilled. Piero smiled warmly, and Caleb gave him a thumbs-up. The small gesture seemed to have elated the young man greatly.

"I like your first two chapters," Jo was saying as they ambled again to the edge of the small crowd.

He nodded a thank you. She commented that the use of a story within the story was a good move. "John and Alison," she mused. "Good names."

"I saw Michael today," Caleb stated flatly over a sip of sparkling wine.

"Who?" she asked absently. She was wondering at the same time what happened to the story that the character named John had been writing. "It sounds like it could have been a good one in and of itself."

"Dead and buried," was his reply.

Jo did not register that she had even heard him. She was smiling strangely and then she waved at a white bearded man standing on the other side of the room. "That's Ben Hallick. Our current poet Laureate. I'll be working with him."

She turned to look at him. He avoided her eyes. "Why?" she asked then, on another topic.

"Don't know."

He said again that he and the man named Michael had run into each other quite by accident, but she was shaking her head. She said she had been asking about the story; why hadn't he done something with it? Then, she rolled her eyes and walked away from him, joining a small cadre of equally ordinary looking American women writers, poets and musicians gathered about a manly matron of huge proportions. Caleb watched after her in silence. Sensing eyes, he glanced over his shoulder. The Sicilian waiter was watching him with a slight, knowing smile on his face.

"*Le donne*," Caleb mouthed in his direction. Piero nodded, though he probably did not yet know the ways of women personally. He came over, ready to pour more wine. He was saying, in his own dialect, that Caleb should look for a prettier girl. They laughed.

A prettier girl. There *she* was again! His mind went blank as her face flashed across his vision. He turned from the crowds and wandered away. There was a mirror on a nearby wall. He paused before it, standing in front of himself, divided by the mirror. Behind him lay the room, in reverse. Dark paneling segmented by moldings framed the standing women in their slender dresses, their pastel reflections shimmering across the polished marble floors as they moved in imitation of dance. Men in dark, paneled suits shadowed them in ties and vests that rivaled the slender dresses in their gaudiness: beiges and mauves and deep-breathing maroons. Dark coiffeurs and dark eyes, and in front, Caleb's white face captured in the glass. He didn't want to be there, neither in the decorated room nor in the reflection of it.

Even when Caleb did not have a mirror handy it was how he saw the world around him, always in reverse and doubly distant from his eyes. This was how he saw those assembled; the regents, the decorated women, the professors, the fellows; each a reflection of the other, each colder, glassier and farther from sight than the other. He finished his glass of sparkling wine and went for a refill. Thus, the evening flowed, each glass a memory, each memory an afterthought, a delayed reaction resulting from another action of equal or lesser value.

Grouping themselves about the spindles of conversation that moved across the room, gyroscopic words spun sentences into images; dull but somehow alluring images that mingled on the orbits' edges into blurs of meaning through which Caleb passed. Always avoiding the black holes at the centers, into which the images collapsed, preferring the spectral strands of space that lay between galaxies, on the periphery of consciousness.

"And you have come all the way from Iowa?"

"All the way—"

"Nevertheless, it's Europe's market that is causing America's problems—"

"If the academy is to survive this financial crisis—"

"Yes, I love Italian cuisine."

"How do you feel about French *cucina*?" Caleb asked as he passed by. He paused again before the mirror, tipped his make-believe hat to the reflected crowd of decorated people, and returned for a refill. He dropped a few Euro into Piero's hand, and glass in hand, he walked away and started up the stairs. Piero was watching him. He must have recognized in the other man's expression a pain he could understand; that empty feeling that attends a loss. His own feelings changed from empathy to sympathy. He no longer wanted to be like him.

"He is too sad," Piero thought to himself. Then he turned away from the stairs to pour more wine for the young woman whose name he did not know. She stood in silence, watching after the writer. Then, she followed him. Piero was smiling at the thought of it. She was ascending the stairs, a few steps behind the unhappy American.

The bed was bounding about like a carnival ride. Caleb rolled over and reached for Jo. She wasn't there. He sat up. Someone must have been going at it in the room next.

No. That room was empty. He was feeling sick to his stomach, so he got up and went to the window lest he have to hurl. He grasped the marble sill with both hands. The lamppost in the garden was swaying this way and that, as the tall cypresses do on the gentle breezes that often move up on them from the Tiber valley below. Caleb smiled.

"Earthquake," he said.

It had been almost silent, but for the bounding of the bed, an arrhythmic, rolling feeling. It was soon over. The lamppost was still swaying, but less so, and the bare branches silhouetted against it had stopped moving altogether. Gradually, the post came to rest once more, and all was silence and simplicity.

After a few moments Caleb returned to bed, lying awake for some time, staring at the ceiling, and the way the tree branches were reflected there in delicate equilibrium with the painted angels who hovered at the corners. Two hundred kilometers away, in the medieval mountain hamlets of L'Aquila and San Gregoriano, hundreds of people died that night.

The greyest of mornings lingered beyond the stone-framed window, like a drape drawn, as if the marble casing itself had grown shut during the night. An impenetrable mood filled the hallway where a maid mopped in slow motion the already immaculately clean floor. Caleb left footprints on the dry stairs. The grand vestibule was always bright, even at night, with reflecting surfaces; travertine, glass and chandeliers, and—but for the security guard—was nearly always empty. A colorless woman came in as Caleb came down the broad marble stairs. She carried a great cornucopia of dazzlingly brilliant flowers: carnations, gladiolus, roses, and heather. She dropped them casually into an awaiting vase on one of the mosaic-topped tables and left. Their colors made the day seem greyer still.

Caleb waited until the women had left the vestibule and then he went to the table and began to arrange the stems so as to better show off each bloom, each separately placed to balance out its form, shape and hue.

"*Non tocare!*" the security guard bellowed, overly loudly, so that the words echoed around the room and rang in the portals.

Caleb stood back abruptly. To his surprise, the guard was immediately reprimanded by the housekeeper, who had come in at the sound of his shouting. She was telling him cordially that the young man seemed to know what he was doing. Then she smiled his way, but he did not return the smile. He left the flowers as they were and walked on past the guard and into the small dining room. Resting there in a loose circle were linen clothed tables and beyond, a segmented view of the gardens where young men in dark clothes were shoveling manure from a barrow into the empty beds around the dry fountain. Caleb was late this morning and his favorite table, next to the double doors that led to the patio, was already occupied. Jo was already up and waiting for him at another table. Everything was wrong that particular morning.

He sat down, and they nodded to each other. She knew by now that he was not very communicative when first out of bed. He glanced about furtively. A few other fellows sat at other tables, drowsily sipping their coffees and teas.

There was Paul at his favorite table, in the dark corner, well away from the windows and the other fellows. No one spoke to him in the mornings and even in the afternoons, he was less than cordial. Too bad, Caleb thought. He was young, attractive, well-built and had a reticent kind of charm. Caleb used to speak to him regularly upon encountering him in the hallways or the gardens. He'd been greeted in each case with a silent, "What do you want," expression on his face and Caleb eventually stopped speaking to him. To pass someone daily on the stairs or in doorways without speaking seemed to him as almost immoral. Too bad.

Then there was Nathan, a cellist. He sat by himself at a table near the windows, perusing his sheet music. He would have been expected, by virtue of his high-browed instrument, to be smug and distant but was in fact, genuine. He was tall, unattractive and beautiful all at once, with a surprisingly graceful manner, despite his basketball-player arms and legs, his cello-playing hands and mentality, his confining Jewishness, his lengthy balk, his astonishing music.

Jo liked him; it was clear. She often commented upon him, what he was wearing or what he was eating. He was one of the few cordial men in the winter academy. Jo was one of three women. She did not like the other two. They always sat together, talked and giggled like schoolgirls, and complained loudly about everything from the food to the indifference of the waiters. They were dual images of the rich, spoiled, daddy's girl and professional student for whom academic study was a pastime. Though the academy was competitive, it did admit practically anyone who had the funds. Come spring and the two women would surely be gone.

Jo made it a point to speak to them when she went for another helping of yogurt. "Betty and Veronica," she said. "Good morning." Caleb actually laughed out loud. One of the women complained that Jo did not even know their names yet.

"Sorry," she said. "My memory is shit." She returned to the table grumbling under her breath. "I hate having to be nice to people who don't like me," she said at his ear. He was still chuckling. "But, you're so good at it."

"Years of Catholic schools," she said.

The two women were making ready to leave. As they passed by, they each made it a point of speak to Caleb. One of them winked over her shoulder as she left the room. He went back to his coffee.

"Just your type," Jo was saying, "according to your novel, anyway; blonde, pretty and air-headed."

"You're wrong," he said, getting up to leave. "I don't particularly like blondes."

She laughed. She took hold of his hand. He paused, asking over his shoulder, "What?"

"Help me make my bed?"

"We did make kind of a mess of it, last night, didn't we?"

She simply nodded, grinning.

Nine

1

John had left the bar without her. Alison asked Cutler if he'd take her home. He helped her on with her coat and pulled the stool out from the bar for her, but she did not wait to be led to the door. By the time Cutler left the building, she was on her way back up the hill to Lewis's house. The streetlight went out and she paused, reaching back for his hand.

"You and your tricks," she complained. "I can't see a god-damned thing!"

"Sorry."

"Oh, Cutler, you're such a wimp."

He merely started up the hill, the streetlights blinking out one by one as he went. Alison followed at a distance. She was trying to figure out why it was she was going with Cutler. He wasn't much of a conversationalist, but then, neither was John, lately. Cut was a good listener, though. That's something John was not, and never had been.

"Wait up." She called. "I mean it. I can't see where I'm going."

She came up alongside him. "Take my hand?"

He did. They walked in silence. He took very long steps, and she was having difficulty keeping pace on the icy pavement. He was a bigger man than John. She noticed that as if for the first time. His body loomed like a great shadow against the dark gray sky and his shoulders were broad and strong looking. He worked out at the gym John had told her. The only thing John ever picked up was a pencil. Nonetheless, she rather liked his bony body.

By the time they reached the top of the hill, she was struggling for every breath and Cutler had let go of her hand.

"You're not very romantic, are you," she said softly.

"Romantic? Why should I be? You're John's girl."

"Girl!" she cried suddenly. "For one thing, Cutler, I'm nobody's anything, much less a girl."

He signed heavily. "Don't play wifey games with me, Alison. I'm not John, after all. Besides, you know what I mean."

"Oh," she said, with a little shrug. "Yes. I know what you mean. Thing is—I'm not so certain I still am John's girl."

He moved a little closer. A touch of sympathy colored his voice. "You guys having problems? I mean, more than the usual?"

She lowered her head. "I guess."

"Want to go someplace?" he asked.

"Someplace?" She wondered.

"For a drive, or—something?"

"I guess so."

Their words had grown secretively soft. They were standing very close to each other in the dark chill of the frosty dooryard in front of Lewis's house. There were still some cars parked on the icy lawn and party sounds still emanated from the house from time to time, in syncopation with the distant whisper of waves on the beaches below.

"Maybe I," she began, barely above a whisper. "Maybe I should wait here in case John comes looking for me."

He nodded in dark silhouette. "Yes. I suppose you should."

Neither of them had moved.

"But thanks anyway for the offer, Cutler."

"Sure." She started back toward the house. She could hear his feet crunching in the crust of snow as he walked to his car. She heard the car door open as she reached the steps. She heard the wipers slapping back and forth on the frosty windshield. Then it was quiet again as both of them had paused in their labors. She glanced back at him. He was standing in the light of the opened passenger side door. She turned from the steps and followed the path of light etched softly on the snow. Ducking under his arm, she slid into the cool leather seat. He closed the door, and the light went out. It smelled sweet and smoky inside the car; the scent of aftershave lotion and burned marijuana. She stiffened at sound of the other door opening. She pressed her hands into her lap as if anticipating something. A breath of cool air slipped in next to her as Cutler slid into his seat. He was holding the lighter before him, a red spot that seemed to dance about in the air. A smear of aromatic smoke filled the small space between them as he passed the joint to her. She breathed in as he slipped the shiny key into its metallic orifice, clacking gently. She passed the smoke back to him, but he waved it off as he was just starting the car. The cold engine grumbled a bit, rolled over and got up and tip-toed away and down the hill toward the lake. He took the smoke from her and blew it back toward her. The lake was shining as if from its own lamps.

Alison took the reefer back and touched her full lips to its wet tongue. She could taste Cutler's spit as she swallowed. Smoke trailed from her mouth and nose like a small shining ghost. As she passed the thing back to Cutler, she saw that he was smiling. It was a wide and beautiful smile that dispelled the darkness and illuminated her trembling fingers as she pressed the joint between his lips. She was smiling too, freely and openly, the first time in days.

Her hand had paused in air, then came to rest on his where it held the wheel, then it fluttered to his leg and alighted on his thigh. Heat radiated from between his legs, and she dipped her fingers into the space to warm them. She noted again what a big man Cutler was and smiled again at the thought of how big he must be in the groin. The joint was coming back to her, from Cutler's large fingers to her eager mouth. Reaching for it with her teeth, she leaned yet closer, her hand moving of its own accord into the hot spot under the flap of his coat. It came up against a solid mound of denim, pulsating within her grasp.

Cutler was driving very fast. The wave-streaked lake was rushing by at light speed. He was not the shy driver John was. He took the curves along the shore with a precise energy uncharacteristic of his normal reticence. She had started to laugh, and he was smiling all the more. She breathed in his smoke and blew it back at him by way of the moist mouth of the joint. She was no longer able to discern the landscape that sped by her window as Cutler had shifted into hyper drive and the cottage lined beach front was little more than a blur of sparkling lights intermingled with washes of frothy waves.

The tighter she held him the faster he drove.

Cutler wasn't smiling anymore. He was bent over the wheel in serious discussion with the road. His hands clutched the wheel and his fingers flexed and drummed as if he were playing an instrument. The passing streetlamps flashed on and off as the auto topped the crest of a hill and then plummeted down the other side. Alison bent over in her place and pressed her face into Cutler's lap. She blew the last gulp of smoke out between his legs, then began moving her lips over the stiff seams and folds of denim. The passing lights reflected into her eyes off his belt buckle. She rested her head on its side and turned her eyes upward. She could see his chin, rippling with each breath he exhaled. His throat convulsed with each dry swallow, and a light from somewhere had gathered about his temples.

She sat up and leaned back in her seat.

"Good shit, Cutler."

"What?"

The car was slowing.

"I said—"

He had started to laugh.

She smiled. "What?"

"You."

She laughed with him. "Oh, that." More lights moved upon them as they drove along the lakeshore, a random line of old cottages scattered among the forested dunes. Alison noticed how the lights played over Cutler's beautiful face, how they splashed one by one across his cheeks and spiraled down his shoulder. She turned back from him and leaned against the cold window, her hair, spreading out on the glass. She withdrew her hand from where it had been resting on his thigh. He glanced over at her. "You all right?"

"I feel fine," she sighed. She could clearly see houses now, each illuminated on its own little patch of snowy lawn. She could feel the motor shifting into lower gears as the car paused at a flashing yellow light. The jumping colors seemed to hurt her eyes and she closed them. The light continued to blink though, in her memory. When she opened her eyes again, she discovered that the car had come to a stop. The scenery beyond the windows was no longer moving of its own accord. Cutler had parked the car in the nonexistent shade of a maple tree by the side of the road. She sat up to look around. The engines hushed, and it was quiet again.

"Where are we?"

"My place."

"I thought you lived with your mother."

"I do. She's having a party. Want to go in for a while?"

"Why did you bring me here?"

"This is where I was going, Alison. I live here, remember?"

"But I don't—"

"We don't have to stay long. I just wanted to say hi to some family friends, is all. Would you prefer to wait for me here?"

"I thought we were going to make out, or something," she pouted.

"Alison," he said.

"I know!" she snapped. "You don't have to remind me. I'm John's girl, aren't I?"

"At least for the time being, you are," he said, carefully.

She let out a breath and glanced his way. "I guess so."

She waited for him to open her door because she knew he would. She stood up into the cold air and looked about cautiously. All she could see was the humped shadow of the car and the way a nearby porch light made crooked blue patterns on the snow. Cutler took her arm and guided her to a gate in a low brick wall beyond which was a shoveled walk leading to a brightly lighted portal. They passed through a black and blue garden of trimmed hedges and burlap-wrapped shrubs. Near the house, the air was filled with crystalline light and there was music sounding, like a scratched record playing in an old movie house. Cutler opened the arched wooden door and the music defined itself. Someone was playing a piano in an inner room. There were people milling about in a small foyer, and voices came and went with introductions only half heard and quarter registered. Someone took Alison's coat.

"Who was that?"

"The maid."

"The what?"

She reached out for his arm as he started away. They passed through several doors with no rooms between them. Crowds of smiling faces filled the doorways.

"This your place?"

"I told you. I live here."

"Big, isn't it?"

"It's my mother's. She's always managed to marry well."

They had paused in a large room. Voices out of the vastness were calling his name and he was nodding and laughing. It was a Cutler Insbroek Alison had never seen before and she was fascinated.

"Who are all these people?"

"Friends of my mother's, I guess."

"They seem to know you, too."

"Some of them."

"Will I meet your mother?"

"That's who I'm looking for."

"You live with her?"

"Yes."

He had opened a door and switched on a lamp. It blinded her a moment. She blinked her eyes and tried to concentrate on what he was pointing at. They were in the doorway of a small, ornamental bathroom.

"I thought you might want to—"

"Yes," she said suddenly. "Thank you."

As she stepped into the small room, she watched his smiling face in the mirror until it was cut off by the shutting of the door. Piano music drifted in as she turned her attention to her own reflection. She was trying desperately to understand what was happening. She flushed the toilet, splashed some water on her face, and opened the door with a smile. Another smile greeted her.

"Cutler," she said. "This is a lovely house."

He looked about disapprovingly. "Mother's decorating," he said.

She pushed her wet hands against her hair to dry them. "Do I look presentable?"

"You look fine," he said.

"Really?"

"Honest." He marked a cross on his heart.

He offered his arm. They strolled down the hall and into a bright room. Her other hand rose of its own accord toward her own heart. They had entered a large, gothic ceilinged room warmly lit with masses of candles and smoldering logs in a stone fireplace. The walls were paneled in light oak and there were floral carpets on the floors. All the furnishings were of pickled oak and white leather upholstery. There was a white piano in a bay of leaded windows on the lakeside of the room: a concert grand, it stretched lavishly into the room and the entire hall was hushed to near silence by its presence as it sweetly contemplated the beauty of its own meticulous voice. A white-haired man in a tawny hued sport jacket was playing a Chopin nocturne. It was very slow and deep, in contrast to the gaiety of the room. The man was very old, with nearly transparent skin and huge hands, and he bent over the keys, nearly embracing them, and with his eyes closed. Alison left Cutler's side and moved as if by instinct toward the light of the piano music. The delicate atmosphere of the nocturne opened like a gate and the old man looked up at her with a transparent gaze. The music continued at the tip of his fingers as he smiled her way. His face was as white as his hair and was softly creased and folded about his alert ice blue eyes. He wore a thick mustache and his smile hollowed out his cheeks. He slid over on the stool and nodded for her to sit beside him.

She glanced back at Cutler like a happy child and sat next to the old man.

"Cutler was right," he said to her as she sat. "You are beautiful."

Alison's heart nearly leapt from her body.

The man continued playing then as if nothing had happened. Alison sat quietly watching him, aware of Cutler's presence a few feet away. Something about the act of sitting. Something about watching the old man play. Something brought back memories of another time. It was to become a cherished but sad memory. It was the day she first began to notice the change in her life with John.

2

She sat down quietly and waited for him to finish. His fingers were flying feverishly over the keys, clacking out thoughts as precious as Chopin's. The carriage stampeded to one side, flung itself back and stampeded again and she marveled at his fingers' antics. And his face: How John attacked that typewriter! With each return of the carriage, a grimace, each period a blink, a swallow for each change of mood and a change of mood for each character. How they must have been fighting on those pages. Or, perhaps, they were making love.

He let out a breath and pulled up the page to stash it aside, looked back at her and relaxed a bit, smiling. "Hi," he said.

Her body began to warm within her clothing. Beyond the window, behind him, it was snowing, and the ink-sketched branches were clacking against the windows.

She breathed with him, knowing him as she did, and displayed her palm to him. He touched sensitive fingers to it and she clasped them.

"Miss me?"

"I always miss you when you're traveling."

"Traveling?"

She shrugged with a little girlish embarrassment. "That's what I call it when you're writing."

"I do drift away sometimes, I guess. I get so lost in the story it almost becomes real life to me."

Alison frowned, then threw it away in place of a smile. "I hope I'm in there someplace," she said in a small voice.

"Every page," he said.

"That makes up for the traveling," she said. "If you ever stop writing about me, it probably means we're finished. Huh?"

"Don't be silly," he said, from behind the typewriter. "You're sounding too much like a woman."

She admitted she was doing it on purpose. "Just to remind you," she concluded with a grin. She stood up. She knew she had already intruded upon him for too long a time. His eyes were beginning to wander back to the page between words. She walked into the front room, assuming her usual place on the sofa. She could still see him through the kitchen door. She could feel the coolness from the window on her shoulders. It was her usual place, halfway between John and the lake. She took up her book and turned down her eyes. They were playing Chopin on the radio, and something occurred to her.

She put down her book and turned up her mind. A vision crossed her consciousness; something familiar, distant but recently recalled, came and went in but an instant. A second or two of spring, bright with flowers, had glowed on her winter brow like a crown and she paused in her reading to recall it again, but it was gone. It must have been important to have impressed itself upon her like that and she tried again to recall it. She closed her eyes, shutting out the view of the room and of John within it. It was a distant memory, older than the sum of all her years times the sum of all her recollections and she marveled at its antics as it rolled about the meadows of her mind.

Something about crossing the room and picking up her book just then had loosened the fragment from her unconscious. She felt the warmth of a tropical sun and smelled the exotic spices of southern lands. She caught a glimpse of a bright seaport. She saw sails and tasted salt in the air. There was music and possibly the fleeting image of a beautiful dark-skinned woman flipping cards, the laughter of children in a courtyard filled with pots of blooming plants. And there was the lingering lilt of foreign words spoken with a smile.

But the memory was fleetingly brief and left but an aftertaste of itself in the back of her mouth. It troubled her. She got to her feet and turned to face the white vista beyond the icy window. Deliberately keeping John out of sight, she slipped past the kitchen door and into the bedroom, but even that act brought feelings back to her from some other time.

The array of mirrors stopped her in the doorway. The music had changed. A delicate snail trail of trumpets glistened in a field of trombones. There was a fragrance not so easily forgotten as words: A woman, thin and mature, pale yellow from head to foot, lay before her, stretched prone in midair. The fragrance was flowers: Lilacs; like the cheap colognes that languished in pretty bottles on her commode under the small window.

She sat on the bed and looked at herself in multiple mirrors. She sighed. Her bare feet had tangled themselves in something soft and familiar. It was a pair of John's under shorts. He always left the last day's pair on the floor by the bed to mark the spot where they had dropped the night before. She picked them up and looked at them. When she was first living with John, she used to wear them all day under her housedress after he had gone to work.

He was standing in the doorway watching her. He asked her if something was wrong.

"I was just contemplating the laundry," she said.

He laughed at her. "Well, if you come to any conclusions, please let me know." She frowned at him, and he went back to his typing. She tossed the shorts into a basket behind the door. It was only half full, but she needed something to do so she took it up, like a baby in her arms, and went out.

"I've come to a conclusion," she told John.

"Laundromat?"

"Seems appropriate."

He seemed confused. "Want me to go with you?"

She was halfway out the back door. "I've only a little to do." She had forgotten it was snowing and she didn't have her coat on. John was watching her from the window as she rushed to the car, sort of hunched over to keep the snow from going down her neck. The keys were in the car. It was still warm inside from morning shopping trips. She eased the car onto the road, and it slid sideways down the hill toward the lake.

Once on the main road, driving wasn't bad. The snow was light near the water and in town the streets were clear and glistening, reflecting the bare trees that arched over them. The Laundromat was empty. It was a Saturday afternoon. She dropped in the coins and the washer began to grumble and slosh about, fondling John's underwear with warm water and suds. Alison leaned on the trembling machine and stared out the steamy window. The view beyond was glossy and slick with ice and water. Dark coated people, huddled against the speckled wind, moved furtively between cars and buildings along Main Street.

Someone was crying. Alison looked about carefully. A young woman with dark hair stood at another machine, her back to her. She was taking things out of a washer and placing them on a nearby counter, crying all the while. Alison frowned, annoyed that her quiet time had been interrupted. The woman seemed especially disturbed about a wad of sheets she kept holding up to the light. Finally, she stuffed them into the washer again. In so doing, she had caught sight of Alison. She wiped her eyes and smiled a little.

"I can't seem to get these things clean," she explained. Alison remained where she was. "Maybe you're not using enough soap," she offered, thinking to herself it wasn't a thing worth crying over.

"No. It's the bloodstains. I can't get them out and they're my favorite sheets." Alison merely nodded, wishing to be left out of the little melodrama but the woman was holding the cloth up like Veronica's veil, so she went to look for herself.

"Looks clean to me," she started to say.

"No!" she insisted, crying again. "I've got to get it clean or my husband will be angry."

"I can't imagine that."

"He will, I tell you! I don't know what to do."

Alison had shrugged and started to walk away but the woman went on. "He's a nut when it comes to cleanliness."

Alison had paused a few machines away. The woman had pulled the sheets from the washer again and was laying them in wet piles on the counter.

"Well, I don't see any stains there, so I don't think you have to worry."

"You don't?" the other asked, turning her tear-streaked face to the light. Alison shook her head and returned to her machine. Light beyond the windows had dimmed and the street had become a flickering backdrop for mirroring the laundry room itself. The woman could be seen in reverse now, stuffing the sheets back into the washer and the sounds of her sobs rose above the rumble and slosh of the machines.

Why do things occur in one's life, she wondered, as if planned by strangers? She had started thinking about her mother. It was a topic that usually meant she was about to sink into an abyss of guilt. The two things had become connected since she had moved in with John: Mother and guilt. And another thing: it happened that so long as she stayed with John she could stave off the guilt. If she should ever leave him, if he should tire of her, well: she didn't want to think about that possibility. She'd have no place to go but home to Mother and—Guilt!

She hugged herself as if cold and leaned her butt against the warm, throbbing washing machine. Outside, ink sketched branches were clack-clacking against the reflecting windows. Mother sat in her usual place, on the sofa, watching Alison as she waited at the kitchen table. The teakettle whistled and they both jumped. Alison reached for a hot pad, took the pot to the table and filled the little hand painted teapot her mother had given her on her sixteenth birthday. She swirled the tea about and then poured two cups. She sighed and carried the cups into the front room, glancing nervously at the window for sight of John's car.

"Thank you, dear. Isn't this nice." She sat on the floor near the coffee table and pushed a plate of cookies toward her mother. Mrs. Wundelund was wearing a tweed suit left over from the past and a hat with a stuffed bird perched atop her white-blonde hair.

"A nice surprise," Alison said, trying to sound sincere.

"I hope you don't think I was trying to interfere."

"Of course not."

Silence.

"You're—going out?"

"John and I are going to a reception at the college tonight."

"John's still teaching, then."

"We're not on welfare, Mother."

Mrs. Wundelund nodded. "John's not here, then."

"No. How's everything?"

"The same, I guess." She seemed very uncomfortable. "I've not seen you in so long, I—"

"I'm glad you stopped by."

"I was in town for a funeral and—"

That was the end of the pleasantries. Alison had turned her eyes to the window, hoping not to see John's car. Her mother was staring into her lap.

"You remember Carolyn Bannyn."

"Of course, Mother."

"Wasn't she in your class? I thought so. She married young, you know, right out of high school. But, oh, she was happy. You could tell just by looking at her. How radiant she looked. They have a beautiful son, you know. Well, the divorce wasn't really a surprise to anybody—"

Mrs. Wundelund had a habit of not finishing her sentences.

"Carolyn?" Alison asked at length. "Divorced?"

"Yes, dear. He was miserable to her! He actually tried to wean her away from her family; imagine that! He was too intellectual for people like us, that's what your father says. But family ties are stronger than books. Even the Bible —"

"The Bible is a book, Mother."

"Of course, the divorce was hard on both of them. Anytime you break God's rules like that, you have to expect to suffer guilt, seems to me. That's what your father always says. Our punishment of ourselves is usually worse than any society can put on us. Anyway, they're both running around now, different partners every night! Isn't it a shame that—"

"What would you have them do, Mother, continue living together in misery?"

"Oh," she gasped ceremoniously. "Who am I to say how other people should live? I have my own family to worry about."

"Since I'm your only child, I guess that means it's me you're worried about?"

Mrs. Wundelund looked up in silence. "I am a little—" Since she was given to not finishing her sentences, most people who knew her had learned to finish them for her. "Worried about me?" Alison asked. "Don't. I'm happy with John. I know what I'm doing. And I love you for caring."

Mrs. Wundelund nodded and set down her cup. That was the sign that she was about to leave. She stood up and Alison went to fetch her coat from the front closet. They stood in silence a while at the front door, Alison keeping her eyes from her mother's gaze.

"I didn't want to come, you know."

"It was Dad's idea?"

"He wanted me to bring you home."

"And now you have to tell him you have failed."

"Yes."

Alison embraced her mother, surprising her. "I'm sorry," she said. "I know how difficult he can be if he doesn't get his way."

"I'll be all right," the other said, shrugging out of the embrace.

"I hope he doesn't hurt you."

"He can't hurt me any more than you have—"

"Mother. I'm your ally, remember?"

She suddenly threw her arms in the air. "Ally! Then why did you leave me? Why do you make me face him alone? What kind of a daughter are you?"

Alison covered her open mouth with her hand. She had forgotten the way her mother often used her as a receptacle for her anger. She merely backed away, not knowing what to say. Mrs. Wundelund had calmed a bit, nodding a silent apology. "I have to go."

"I know. I wish our visit could have been different."

"It will never be different," her mother had breathed as she left the house. Alison stood in the opened door and watched the old Chevy move down the road toward the lake. John's Fiat passed it on the way. Alison returned to the sofa. John raged into the house complaining about her leaving the door open to the weather. She had started to cry. She cried for three days. She passed her nights alone on the sofa, crying herself into a loneliness John could not have understood no matter how much he might have tried. If he was in love with her before that night, he certainly wasn't afterward, she was certain.

She wiped a tear from her eyes as she watched her reflection in the Laundromat windows. She could still see the other woman on the same reflection. She was still crying over her clean sheets, wishing they were soiled.

Alison loaded the cleaned things into the basket and pressing her body against the hard door, pushed it open enough to squeeze out into the wintry evening. The tires spun a bit when she touched the pedal, and the wipers cleared an arc across the snowy windshield. As she drove, the lights mingled with the coiling veils of snow and gathered up about her as winter things seem to do. She was missing John. She needed him to help her out of her sadness. She left the laundry in the car and rushed to the front door. John's tracks still showed in the snow. They pointed away from the house and toward the shore below. He often walked in the evenings when writing. Even in winter. And it was quiet. Snowstorms do that; they bring silence. She sat on the stoop, huddling herself against the cold. Snow settled gently on her shoulders.

When John returned, maybe he'd find her frozen dead and covered with snow. Maybe he'd care. Maybe he wouldn't. She went inside.

3

The music had stopped, and Alison looked about her in surprise. The old man was getting up from the piano and talking with other people. Cutler was nowhere in sight. As she stood, she saw him in the doorway, her coat in his hand.

"Going so soon?" she wondered.

"You didn't seem to be having a very good time."

"He plays beautifully."

"My mother's lover."

"Have I met her?"

Cutler hadn't heard her. He was ushering her toward the foyer. "It's started to snow. I'd better get you home before the roads turn bad."

"Snow?" she wondered, as the door opened to a gust of wind.

They rushed through the rising gale to the car, each to his own door. In silence, they drove out of the settlement and into the woods. The storm was intensifying. Great curtains of snow swept in from the lake. The world went white beyond the windows. Alison kept her eyes from his.

"I'm sorry you think I wasn't much fun, Cutler."

"I didn't expect much," he returned.

"What's that supposed to mean?"

"John is between us. I suppose he always will be."

"You love him as much as I do, don't you?"

"I suppose."

"Funny."

"Why."

"He hardly knows you and I exist."

"Funny," Cutler agreed.

They pulled up to John's house. All the lights were on. His little Fiat was nowhere to be seen. A late model Cadillac was parked nearby. They sat in silence for a while.

"He must have gone back to the party," Cutler said.

She was shaking her head. No.

"Uh-huh. Well. Good night, Alison." She got from the car and walked toward the front door. Cutler was driving away. She waited outside the door for a while, then, she went in. John and Lizzie Tifgat were sitting on the sofa sipping at glasses of wine. They were not surprised at seeing her. Nor was she at seeing them.

"I'm going to bed," she said. She passed through the small room, pausing before the door to the bedroom. "Tomorrow night, you can have the bed," she said simply, closing the door behind her.

"What did she mean by that?" the woman had asked. "Just words," John had said.

Ten

"You must leave me!" said Miriam to Donatello, more imperatively than before. "Have I not said it? Go, and look not behind you!"

"Miriam," whispered Donatello, grasping her hand forcibly, "who is it that stands in the shadow, yonder, beckoning you to follow him?"

"Hush, leave me," repeated Miriam. "Your hour is past; his hour has come."

Hawthorne; *The Marble Faun*

They stood on the brow of the *Campidoglio* taking in the view, Caleb and Michael. Michael was talking, as, indeed, he had been since their meeting in front of the Church of Jesus. They had walked then through a bitterly bright January day from the cold shade of the broad thoroughfare to the sunny Piazza Venezia and its whirl of traffic and, from thence, to the icy white steps of the Victor Emanuel Monument. Behind it was the broad flight that rose in marble-edged stairs to the top of the hill. Pausing to catch their breaths, which hung like smoke about them as Michael talked, they turned to look out over the old city.

"I love this place. I think it is my favorite in Rome." He stopped talking then. Turning to face the square. Caleb wondered at what seemed then like a change of mood in the man.

"You like Michelangelo," he observed, softly, warming his hands with his words. "You talk of him a lot."

"His was a troubled genius. That combination intrigues me, I guess."

"Tell me about him."

"Tell me, instead, about your holiday."

He lifted his shoulders. "Not much to tell. Christmas away from home. I spent most of the day writing." He went on to explain that he was having difficulty with one of his characters. "The main character, in fact."

"What's wrong?"

They stood facing the low wintering sun. "I mean, it's kind of autobiographical but he seems to have a lot more hang ups than I ever had. I can't quite figure him out."

Michael laughed lightly. He reminded him that it was he, the author, who had invented the character in the first place. "Seems to me, you should be able to control him."

Caleb shared the laugh. "I'll keep that in mind." Then he asked again about Michelangelo.

He was born into a family that did not want him. Given away at birth, he was called back home at five, upon the death of his mother, to help care for his two younger siblings. He was later sold into apprenticeship by a father who could not understand the child's odd behavior. He worked in the studio of the artist Ghirlandaio and carved his first crucifix at age thirteen. He soon gained the support of Italy's most influential family, the Medici, and went on to work for the only Platonic Pope, Julius II, painting the ceiling of Sixtus' chapel and carving in Carrera marble some of the world's most astonishing sculptures. Then his estranged father sued him for financial support, and he spent most of the rest of his life caring for a man he barely knew.

In designing the square at the top of the Capitoline Hill where Caleb and Michael now stood, the *Caput Mundi*, the center of the world, as far as Romans are concerned, the artist chose a radical idea. It may have been intended as a snub to the memory of his one-time rival for papal attention, Leonardo of Vinci, whose attempt to associate human proportions with Divine, employing cosmological measurements in his famous drawing of the Vitruvian Man. There, the figure is rendered spread-eagle within both a square and a circle, the two basic building blocks of classical architecture and Humanist theory. Michelangelo chose to alter those two perfect geometrical figures, to distort them, bulge them and exaggerate them, as if something inside them were trying to get out. The square becomes an imperfect trapezoid, the circle an impossible ellipse, one inside the other. These odd shapes are difficult for the human mind to comprehend, thus irrational, suggesting confusion and lack of direction to anyone who finds himself wandering about in the square-less square.

"Michelangelo's three-dimensional concept here has found fifth-dimensional being in the intersection of time, space and proportion," Michael was saying, in reference to the design of the *Campidoglio*. "Energy, concentrated in the center, spirals outwardly in ever increasing but nonetheless infinite waves, marked in white marble on the pavement. They touch all things in their path, those waves of energy, and set them in motion."

Caleb was not looking at the marble stones of the piazza but at the man who walked upon them, gesturing this way and that. He was a hard and rugged looking man. His marble like muscles pushed at the seams of his dark wool sport coat. They seemed to be always flexed about his bones so that his solidness seemed out of place with the delicate harmony of the setting, his soft-spoken voice notwithstanding. He moved with grace, deliberate and practiced, like an athlete. Only the subtlest movements turned his shoulders as he traced with his toe the spirals on the pavement. His light features, further whitened by the sun, lay etched upon the gray stone facades behind him with a line drawn by the eye rather than the hand. His strength was evident in the pull of worsted across his back as he bent to touch the ground. His face showed age when he looked back to catch Caleb's attention, though his expressions were those of a child. He stopped expounding and asked with a smile what Caleb had been staring at.

"You," he said. "You really get into this, don't you?"

Michael stood up. "I guess I do."

He seemed to have been annoyed by Caleb's comment.

He was trying to explain. "They're just words, Michael. The dictionary's full of them."

"Yeah. Most of them as useless as those." Then: "Here's the National Museum. You want to go in? Or pass on it?"

"Let's go in. I like your lectures, even if I do complain about them."

"Thank you. I think." He stood a moment staring at him strangely. Then he started toward the gallery's marble portico.

Caleb stopped him. "Afterward," he said, with a slight but affectionate smile, "I'll buy you a beer."

"It's a deal."

"Careful, Padre," Caleb added. "I might be the Tempter."

Michael smiled. "I always knew Satan would be handsome."

Once again, Caleb had been left speechless by the other man's words. He merely shook his head and followed him into the portico of the travertine palace. They paid the entry fees and ascended a dark stair to rooms lined with bright statuary. Oddly, though the chambers were overflowing with artifacts, Michael was, for the first time that afternoon, silent. They paused before a bust of one of the Caesars. Caleb studied the crystalline eyes in silence. He marveled casually at the stillness in the ancient expression, and silently, at the repose in Michael's. Had he hurt his feelings with his flippant remarks in the piazza? He moved on to the next portrait, hoping something would inspire Michael to speak anew, as before, in fluid tones and beguiling words, on the perfect beauty of the imperfect world. But Michael remained nearly silent until they came at last to the place of rest of the Dying Slave.

Michael was not looking at the pathos of the stone face but at the softer, slightly bearded one of the writer when he said in *sotto voce*, "Let's go, shall we?"

Caleb stood near the Faun of Praxiteles, and in a similar pose, hand on hip. "We just got here."

"I know, but—" He looked about furtively. "These stone faces leave me cold." He fixed his eyes on Caleb's and added, "Your presence here puts these homely gravestones to shame."

Michael had started away, but Caleb called him back. He asked him succinctly, "Why did you say that?"

Michael's expression was almost one of anger. "Look," he said, gesturing toward the clenched face of the Gaul. "It has been praised since its discovery for its reserved ethos, its perfect pathos, and yet, it is nothing other than stone. But you: you are a living corpse, my friend, more alive than ever I believed could be possible." He paused, searching the palms of his hands for words. "My life is too much like these statues; it has been passed thus far in an embalmed state, always sealed behind walls, the very murals I paint furthering immuring me."

He had wandered to one of the draped windows and a frayed light fell across him as he went on. "After years of obedience to my vows, my bishop, well—" He turned yet farther away.

The bishop had suggested Michael take a sabbatical, a time away from his parish. "I don't know why. He's never been sure of the truth of my faith, I guess. I'm nearly seventy years old, Caleb, and I don't know what real life is.

Like this man here, I have remained, suspended in a state of dying since my youth."

His words sounded too familiar. Why? Was Caleb writing them? "I don't want to hear this," he said. Michael turned to him with a little laugh, the uncomfortable kind. "My confession?" He had turned his eyes—just his eyes—back toward where Caleb stood near the Dying Gaul. "This is why I have attached myself to you, Caleb." He was hesitant to ask. "Why, exactly?"

"I want for once to actually have something to confess."

"Again, please."

"I want to have sex with you."

They stared at each other for some time across the space of the gallery. Meanwhile, in the real world, the sun moved, and the room darkened.

"You can't," Caleb said simply, the faun smirking from behind him.

"Is that all there is you can say to me?"

His heart was breaking. "It is too big for me."

"Big?"

"Your story—" He stopped mid-sentence, short of the words necessary to finish.

Michael, who had stood with arms expanded, now let them drop to his side. He backed up to the window so that he existed in Caleb's view as a ragged silhouette. "Of course," he said, his head lowering. "What am I thinking? I've left my reason behind. I'm sorry. I only thought—"

"Two people," he went on, lifting his eyes to the level of Caleb's. "I mistook you for a species of my own self. My lost twin returned at last to my side."

"We are *not* alike, are we? It is only I who has taken refuge behind the walls of my own body like some misplaced hermit, walls that eventually crush all imagination and individuality. Like any simple pilgrim, I have mistaken the gold of the reliquary for value, apart from the gray bones inside."

"Such words," Caleb was saying, turning away, and mostly to himself.

Michael turned again toward the light of the windows and went on. "I have passed my life in endless circumambulation around an empty table. There is nothing left for me. The cross is bare, stripped of its *transubstantiated* flesh. Only the wood remains."

"You talk in parables," Caleb complained. "I don't understand you half the time."

He was reminded that Michael was not accustomed to talking to people on any subject, much less, on the topic of himself. "I even lie to my confessor."

"You sound like a man riddled with guilt and yet, so you have claimed, you have done nothing to feel guilty of."

"Except for the lie," he started to say.

"Don't talk like that," Caleb demanded. "I've come to find in you a person of greater honesty then anyone I've ever known. Don't you dare talk of lies to me, Michael!"

Michael had his back to him. He took a great breath. Shook his head and turned back, smiling with some embarrassment. "All right," he said. "How should I talk, then?"

"Your life might seem closed up to you but to me it is vast and shining," Caleb said, "like a meadow seen amidst the dark forest. You see things that I never felt possible, in art, in people, and in other ordinary objects. Michael! Talk to me about art," he pleaded. "Help me to understand what it is you see that I do not."

He was nodding slightly, smiling strangely. "I will do this for you but only in exchange for something of equal value. My request remains a condition of our friendship."

"It isn't fair, nor is it natural to put conditions on friendship, Michael."

"I know that. Nevertheless."

"In other words, if I want your friendship, I have to render something unto you in return."

"Life," Michael said, his eyes bright with anticipation. Caleb studied the patterns in the parquet flooring beneath his tennis shoes. "I can't do that," he said simply.

"Talk to me of sensual things and I will teach you how to love art."

"Sensual things?"

"The things you write about." He was suddenly embarrassed. "I write about me and my twisted life, the women I've rolled over, the friends I've thrown away." He paused, turning away. "I've started ten different novels over the last forty years or so, Michael. Finally managed to get one of them acknowledged a few months ago." He laughed mockingly. "I got a prize for that. That's what you want to learn about?"

"Your life may be as unfulfilled as mine, but in different ways," Michael was saying from his place in the dark corner of the gallery. "Together we might be able to make sense out of at least one of them, don't you suppose?"

Caleb merely shrugged. Michael reminded him of the beer he had promised him. The other was silent for a while. (Caleb was writing.) He turned back with a small smile then, and Michael reached out his hand.

Caleb hesitated but a moment then took the hand. "Beer," he said. They remained, hand in hand, for a long time in the Gallery of the Faun.

"Forgive me, Father, for I have—" He hesitated.

"Yes, my son?"

He stared a moment at the shadowy figure behind the screen, then concluded, "changed my mind."

Michael fled the confessional. The hall of St. Peter's was crisscrossed with shafts of sunlight from clerestory windows and with lines of pilgrims from different countries. The nave echoed with the din and clatter of foreign tongues. Burnished arches reflected the flash and afterglow of cameras and candles. In his haste, even through his guilt, he noted these things and pondered them in his gut. It was then, in the doorway, the great bronze portal, it hit him! Another man of equal bulk and strength collided with him, head on, face to face, shoulder to shoulder.

There was a flourish of apologies in foreign tongues, then each continued upon his individual journey, one into and one out of the cathedral. It was only then, after the encounter, but a split-second later, it hit him. He glanced over his shoulder to catch a glimpse of one met so briefly; of the one merged if only for a moment with him, on the same step. The other glanced back as well and both paused for but an instant in time.

They were one and the same person, or so it would have seemed. They looked alike, one going in and one going out, like celestial twins, one mortal the other eternal. One immortal, the other growing older. Then, they parted company a second time, turning away as if nothing out of the ordinary had occurred. Michael stepped into the cool, dry sunshine of wintry Rome and it hit him.

"Was I still intact? All in one piece? Had the look-alike stranger stolen something of me to carry with him into the basilica? Was it possible?"

"Wasn't it all your imagination?" Caleb wondered, savoring a sip of Marsala.

Michael shrugged. "I decided to wait for his return, just to see for myself, but then I began to wonder: if he comes back out, should I go back in, in order to aright the cosmic clock, or something like that?" He laughed good-naturedly. "I swear, Caleb, the longer I waited, the more confused I became."

"Did he ever come out?"

He admitted he didn't know. "After twenty minutes or so, I gave up and came to look for you at the Church of Jesus. It was warm sitting there on the steps. I dosed. That's why I was late that day. I don't know. Maybe I missed him altogether."

"It was guilt, wasn't it? That entity you ran into?"

"How do you mean?"

Caleb leaned across the white draped table, a blue-green reflection of the Trevi Fountain on the opalescent window behind him. "You personified your guilt for missing confession in the form of a look-alike stranger; don't you suppose that's what happened?"

He shook his head. "I'm not a mystic, Caleb. I don't have visions."

"I'm not talking about visions. I'm talking about psychology."

"Same thing, don't you think?" Caleb sat back again, savoring the thought. "I'm not sure."

Michael turned his eyes down toward the empty glass he held. "I am a devout Catholic," he said, as if confessing, "but I am angry. And I don't know why."

"You don't?"

He heaved a sigh. "Maybe. Angry at having been told how to live and how to believe and even how to act a certain way; a different way than my inner self would have chosen to live—or act. Every time I humbly comply, I feel I am somehow betraying myself." Caleb let out a whistle of surprise. "That's a burden, I'd guess."

"Yeah. My cross, as they say. And you?" he asked with a change of tone in his voice. "What did you do this morning?"

"After fucking Jo, I sat in the garden to do some writing."

Michael sort of smiled. "Which was more pleasurable for you, I wonder?"

He had turned sideways in the chair in order to peer out the window into the lighted piazza. "Neither, actually. She was uninspiring and so was the garden."

"So, you didn't write this morning?"

"Like you," he said, glancing back momentarily, "I sat in the sunshine waiting for—something."

"Forgive me for saying so," Michael said, a quizzical smile on his face, "but you speak of your relationship with Jo with the same lack of enthusiasm as you do your writing. I get the feeling you're not taking either one of them very seriously."

"Perhaps I'm not," he said very softly. "Like you and your faith?"

"Not quite," Michael returned. "I might have missed confession the other day, for reasons not especially clear to me, but that is not my normal behavior."

"So," Caleb said, his voice stronger, "You practice your faith faithfully despite your anger over it? That seems hypocritical to me."

Michael was pouring them the last of the wine. "Not angry at being a Catholic," he said. "More like being angry that life seems to have passed me by. Not unlike your relationships with what you hold dear, I should venture."

Those sounded like Caleb's words coming back at him. The two men were quiet for a while. Michael staring into his empty glass. Caleb at his reflection on the window. He poured more wine.

"*Cin-cin,*" he said, toasting. "Here's to us."

"To Caleb, the servant of God."

"To Michael, His Archangel."

But Michael did not drink. "No," he said. "Not to the Archangel; least of all, to him."

Caleb reminded him that he was the Messenger's namesake. Michael was nodding. "A messenger who seems to have forgotten the message." Having paid the bill, he was making ready to leave. Caleb watched after him a while, until he had exited the cafe altogether. He was growing tired of the little verbal games Michael seemed so fond of. He asked the waiter if there was a Metro station nearby. The young man looked at his watch and shrugged. The Metro had finished for the night.

"Autobus?"

"Taxi."

"Is it that late?" he wondered as he stepped into the cool night air. He glanced about quickly for sign of Michael. Only a few pilgrims remained in the glow of the illuminated fountain. They were gathered in small groups, speaking in the low tones appropriate to monuments of beauty and mystery. Their words were lost behind the sounds of tumbling water. A man stood alone, silhouetted against the azure glow. It was Michael. Caleb smiled automatically at sight of him and started toward him. Then he paused. No. Michael was not alone. Another man, smaller, having easily hidden himself behind Michael's athletic presence, had stepped into the shimmering limelight. He was gesturing energetically, like an Italian, especially one of those shorter, darker Italians of the southern coasts. Caleb started toward the two men once more, and once more, the smaller man stepped into the shadow of the larger and disappeared. When Caleb arrived at Michael's side, the stranger was nowhere to be seen. When he asked about him, Michael eyed him strangely.

What man?

He was sure he'd seen a man talking with him. An Italian.

"Perhaps my double has returned to haunt me," Michael laughed.

"You said yourself that the so-called double looked like you. This man was smaller, thinner, animated."

"It's this night," Michael said simply, starting away.

Caleb watched after him. He half expected to see the shadow return, but Michael had walked into a side street and had himself disappeared into the darkness. Caleb followed. Caught up with him. Asked casually why he did not like his namesake.

"He betrayed me, that's why."

They walked slowly. The street was very dark, the lamps hanging as black holes in the nighttime sky.

"He ignored my prayers, no matter how desperately I prayed. He remained silent. 'Pray to Him,' papa would say. 'He will make it right.' But He did no such thing." Michael's voice had become as dark as the nighttime. Caleb asked carefully, a hand on his shoulder, "Make what right?"

"My bed," Michael said, as if the answer should have been obvious. He had glanced back at Caleb but briefly, just long enough for a bit of dark light to reflect off the steel in his eyes.

"Your bed?"

Michael strode on ahead, walking at a good clip, as if in flight. Caleb caught him by the sleeve and slowed him but a little. He was a powerful man, one not so easily dissuaded. Caleb asked again, "Your bed, Michael?"

He paused at last. He spoke not to Caleb but to the encompassing darkness. "Yes. My sheets. I never could get them clean after that."

He was afraid to ask. "After what?"

"I'd dream of him," he said. "Each night. And each night he'd be there, attending me, hovering over me; his smell, his breath, his wings moving about in the pungent air." He shuddered. "It was almost unbearable."

"What was?"

"I thought I would die; each night I hoped I would die rather than to have to endure—" His voice had broken off like a dry stick.

"What," Caleb asked carefully.

Michael went on as if Caleb weren't even there, as if he was talking to himself. "It was a dream, wasn't it? I wanted it to be a dream. I pretended it was a dream." His eyes were wide with remembering. His body rigid. His hands poised in space as if awaiting some gift. "I was very young when it started—I don't know, eight or ten—I guess."

Caleb placed a hesitant hand on the other's shoulder. They stood side by side in the square of light from a restaurant window, which was laid sort of hesitantly across the paving cobbles. Caleb asked a third time, "What? When what started?"

Michael turned to him, again as if the answer to his question should have been clear. "Papa," he said simply. Caleb closed his eyes. "Your father? Michael? When you were a child?"

"He's drunk," Michael said clearly. "He never remembers in the morning. It's always the same story. I'm so sick of it!"

He opened his eyes and put them directly on Caleb's. "I was eleven or twelve the last time I—He laughed at me. He laughed so loud it awoke the household. My mother came to my door to see what had happened. It was all over the bed. It was all over the sheets, my pajamas, everything. Mother left without saying a word."

His eyes glistened in the bit of light that accompanied them, as if they had stolen some from the bright piazza they'd just left.

"I don't want to hear this," Caleb had started away.

"He never remembers the next day," Michael said again. "He goes off to work as if nothing has happened."

Then. One day. He didn't come home. Momma was worried.

"I never saw him again."

Caleb had paused in the dark alley. He waited. It seems Michael's father had died in a work-related accident. He fell from a ladder.

"And you felt responsible?"

"No," was his terse reply. "I felt cheated."

"Jesus," Caleb whispered.

He whispered the same words in return, turning his eyes away at last. Then he sort of laughed and said, "Everyone has a story, I guess."

They stood there for a long time, looking in opposite directions, into the darkness of the alleyway. Then, they started to walk again, slowly at first. They said nothing more. They quickened the pace. In a few moments, they were on the busy Corso. Even on a mid-winter evening, cars, motos, and taxis were coming and going in endless parade. As the two men parted, the taxi door ajar, Michael apologized for leaving Caleb on such a negative note.

"It's all right," Caleb had said. "I doubt we'll ever see each other again after tonight, so what's it matter?"

"Why do you say that?"

"Everyone has a story, you say, but Michael; your story is all mixed up." He concluded, frustration in his tone, "I'm not sure what parts of it to believe."

Michael nodded, smiling slightly. "You're probably right. I seem to have got real memories mixed up with false confessions, haven't I?"

"False confessions?"

"The kind innocent children make up in order to make the priests think they have a job to do."

Caleb heaved a sigh. "Trastevere," he said to the cabby. As he was closing the door, he heard Michael remind him that he knew where he lived should he care to spend another afternoon together. The door closed on his words and the cab did an about face, sloshing sideways in the slush that lay heaped against the curbs. Thus, Caleb found himself face to face with Michael once more. He stood on the far side of the street, waving cordially. Caleb nodded then looked away, but after a few seconds he glanced back through the rear window. Michael was not alone. A shorter man was standing with him. They both watched as the taxi sped down the Corso toward Trastevere. Caleb watched as well, until the view of the two men was obliterated by the rush of traffic and the spray of rain.

As they drove for a while along the river, the opalescent dome of St. Peters aglow beyond the smear of rain, Caleb sighed. He couldn't get the image of the man out of his mind. His warmth, his knowledge, his good looks, his melancholy. What was it about him? Why was he anxiously awaiting their next time together? What did it all mean?

"Poor Donatello," said Miriam in a changed tone, and rather to herself than him. "Is there no other that seeks me out, follows me, is obstinate to share my affliction and my doom—but only you! They call me beautiful; and I used to fancy that, at my need, I could bring the whole world to my feet. And, Lo! Here in my utmost need; and my beauty and my gifts have brought me only this poor, simple boy. Half-witted, they call him; and surely fit for nothing but to be happy! And I accept his aid! Tomorrow—tomorrow—I will tell him all. Ah, what a sin, to stain his joyous nature with the blackness of a woe like mine!"

Hawthorne, *The Marble Faun*

Eleven

1

Alison sat sewing. The white day outside the window was gray inside. She didn't mind the gray. It suited her mood. She sat poised among the other delicate articles of the small room in precarious splendor, her jewelry box hair and ruby lips blanched by the window light. She paused in her travail and twisted in place, striking a profile upon the steamy glass. Twisting further, she turned to gaze through the glass to the lake beyond. Her view was framed by two prickly cedar trees and low eaves. She turned back to the room. The vista was too bland for her taste. She preferred the carefully arranged clutter of the small interior; a cabinet combination radio and record player, a fireplace of charred logs and a mantel lined with half burned candles. There was a goatskin rug that had belonged to John's grandfather and an empty magazine rack that had been her mom's. They were changeless things of ancient beauty as dull as memories. There was also a full-length mirror on the bathroom door. It reflected the entire room, including herself. She looked at herself, looking into herself.

Her breasts, she could see them, just beneath the soft cloth of her sweatshirt. She knew how they must have looked, pointing up in defiance of the flannel. She pulled the shirt over her head and dropped it in her lap. Folding her arms beneath her breasts, she lifted them up to the light of the window then glanced across the room to see how the mirror had reacted. They were white and pink and bulging, young and strong and soft to the touch, like some exotic blond fruit gathered in the fold of her arms. She bowed her head low and pressed her mouth to one of them, her eyes wide and childlike. She was trying to imagine how they looked inside. Were they like fruit, luscious, veined and filled with seeds? Pressing further, she touched them cheek to cheek and breathed in to fill her folded lungs.

"Why are they there?" she wondered. What good were they to her? To Alison? To her non-existent children?

Her hands were in her lap, seeking warmth there in the folds of her sweatshirt. She took up the shirt and held it up to view, like Veronica's scarf, and studied the imprinted face that stared back at her from the woven threads. She unbuttoned her Levi's and opened the fly to reveal an opal shaped jewel of pink-flowered silk that complimented the texture of her paper white flesh. She pushed at the stiff denim and with barely a movement, slid it out from under her and lifted her legs one by one to extract them. She placed her bare feet on the pile of still-warm cotton. She touched her thighs with darker fingers. Bending until her nipples hovered at her kneecaps, she brought her tingling fingers up the stubbled shore of her calves, under her knees and along her thighs to the bulge of moist flesh that emerged from the soft fluff of pale fur. She bent further into herself, cupping her labia in her hands like a strange, fleshy poppy flower bristling with hairy sepals. The opiate scent of the dew kissed petals rose into her nostrils. She dipped her fingers into the flower's center, spreading its parts.

"Why is it there?" she asked in a breath.

She looked up and studied her bent pose in the bathroom door mirror. She stood, hands at her sides. She turned her back on the mirror and glanced at it over her shoulder. Then she ran to the bedroom and began rummaging through the bottom drawers, where she kept the lacy things.

She stood again before the full-length mirror on the back of the bathroom door, which reflected both her and the room behind her. She had propped another, smaller mirror against a chair so she could see herself up and down and all the way around all at the same time. She wore a long, pale dress and had pushed her fine hair up into the bowl of a broad-brimmed summer hat, having left a colorless wisp of curl trailing across her sad face. She put on lace antique gloves and carefully draped a knitted Angora shawl about her narrow shoulders. Then she surveyed the costume she'd chosen from all around and up and down before going out. At the front door, her hand on the latch, she paused again. The sun showed brilliantly beyond though the wind off the lake was undoubtedly cool. She turned to the coat closet just behind her. Her winter coat was too heavy for a spring day. She caressed its empty sleeve with her gloved fingertips. She opened the front door and stepped into the sunshine. She shuddered. Indeed, the wind was very cold for the lake still held winter in its bosom. It was nearly black in color and crusted with icy froth where the cold water was whipped up by the winds. A crystal-clear blue sky rested behind it. A lone figure stood on the white beach before it.

"John," she said.

She stepped back inside, pressing the door shut against the wind. She had been hoping for a fine spring day. She had wanted to take a walk, to leave the house that belonged to John and the things in it that were his too: the combination radio and record player, and the goat skin rug. She had wanted a little peace away from him. But the day was cold, and John was on the beach below like a guardian to keep watch over her lest she attempt to leave her tower. She had wanted time and a place to think, as John must have been doing, away from reminders of their less than happy life together.

She went back in and dropped into the armchair near the window so that the sunlight might warm her up. She could hear the wind banging at the front door. She could see John wandering on the sandy shore. She could almost hear him thinking. "What should I do about Alison?"

He knew he couldn't ask her to leave no matter how unhappy she might have become with their situation since she had no place to go. She knew he knew that. Having left her home to move in with him much against her old-fashioned parents' wishes, she would not be able to go back there, even if they were to invite her. She knew that, and she knew he did too. She had no job. John had never wanted her to work. He liked the thought that someone was always there at home while he was away. That was why he called home from work every day, she was certain. Not just to break up the monotony of her day but to make sure she really was there as he was expecting her to be. And, until recently, she always was there. It was after the third day in a row he'd called home to no answer they'd had an argument. He wanted her to be like a wife, but he didn't want her for a wife. That's what Alison found most difficult to understand. He'd tried to explain it to her, and she had cried, and he had shouted at her and stormed out of the house. She did not know where he'd gone. He didn't come home last night but now he was standing on the beach below the red stairs as if trying to find the courage to climb them and face her.

What should she do? Should she wait for him or go and meet him on the common ground of the lakeshore? She went to the closet and reached for her winter coat. She noticed a hatch in the closet ceiling she'd not paid attention to before. John had said something about a box of keepsakes in the attic, if they had an attic. Throwing the coat aside, she pulled the armchair over to the closet, and, standing on it, reached over her head for the hatch. It lifted up and she slid it aside. Dust and the musty smell of closed up places sifted down upon her, powdering her face and shoulders. She coughed, sneezed, and then, blew her nose on a hankie retrieved from her bosom. She stretched up into the small opening. The attic was dark, the only light coming up with her from the front room. There was a shoebox in sight and just within reach. There did not seem to be anything else up there. She pulled the box her way and carefully, as if it were as precious as a baby, she lowered it into her arms and slid down into the chair, the dusty box in her lap. She studied it a moment. There was a date written on the cover, but she could not read it. When she tried to wipe the dust away, she further obliterated the writing. She sneezed again.

She lifted the cover. Inside were envelopes stacked neatly one after the other. In one were receipts from the 1940s, in the next from the 50s. In another were Christmas cards from people with names she did not recognize, and in yet another, birthday cards from the same people. There were folders of sheet music and a few photographs. She smiled as she took them out, bringing them to light for the first time in years. There were only a few, some in black and white and some in faded color. She thumbed through them.

The first was of an old house. There were barns behind, and draft horses posed out front but there were no people in the picture. Disappointed, she went to the next, which was of an ancient couple sitting in rocking chairs on a porch. The third was of a dog. The fourth, very dark, of a young boy silhouetted against a sunny window. The name "Johnny" was scribbled across the top in ballpoint pen. There was a color photograph of a woman working in a garden, bending among tall leafy plants, her face half hidden by the leaves. Alison replaced the photographs in confusion. Now, what should she do? Return the box to the attic and let John find it? Keep it out for him as a gesture of good will or not tell him about it at all?

"Damn it," she said. "I hate domestic dilemmas!" She replaced the cover and left the box resting in the chair as she pulled on her coat and went out the front door. The wind had stiffened, and she pulled the coat tightly about her as she made her way to the red stairway. She had descended a few steps when she noticed that John was not in sight. She heaved a sigh and sat on the step. The sun warmed her a little and the wind was less raw where she sat, so she decided to wait a while.

The lake had gone wild and ragged. It spilled onto the shores with a vengeance and lashed up at the sky as if trying to undo its purity. Low hanging clouds were beginning to darken the horizon, pushed by the winds into the path of the sun. Alison watched, fascinated.

John was walking below, looking at the sand, seeing nothing but his inner turmoil. Alison had to go, and he knew she knew it. Her staying was causing them both too much unhappiness. He felt guilty for not being the attentive lover he once was. In the absence of marriage vows, he knew, affection was the only real bond between a man and a woman: especially for a woman. He didn't really want her to go. He kind of liked knowing there was someone in his house while he was away, but she was growing bored. That was her excuse. John was bored too, but he had assumed it was a normal trait for a twenty-something year old man and had not let it get to him like she was doing. How long had they been together? Three years? More?

He kicked at the sand and started up the red stairway. Pausing, something in the corner of his vision caught his attention. It was the way the sky was filling with storm clouds, like ragged shawls of dark gray fluttering in the wind about the pale shoulders of a woman. The sky was a beautiful panorama of swirling cloud and glistening cerulean counterpoints. Dark cumulus embraced the darker lake at the horizon and farther up, tattered fir trees pierced the churning firmament, and in between, perched precariously on a red ladder to the heavens, floated Alison. She had paused a few steps from the top of the red stair and was watching the sky. Her hair blew about her on the winds and she pulled her winter coat tighter about her, a royal purple pillar that defied the breeze. Then she saw him, and she smiled, automatically. How beautifully she smiled. It was one of the things he loved most about her.

He smiled in return, but not so warmly. He climbed the stairs and stopped just below her. They said nothing. She turned, and he followed her to the house. She waited for him to open the door for her. The chair still waited by the opened door to the coat closet. John said nothing. He merely stopped, just inside the front door, and stared at the box.

"I was looking for my tennis—"

"You found it."

"Yes. In the attic." She laughed a little. "It seems we do have an attic, after all."

"What's in it?" He seemed hesitant to pick it up.

She shook her head. He lifted the cover and peered carefully into the box. "Sheet music," he said.

"That all?"

He was thumbing through the music folders as if he expected something to be hidden among the leaves. Alison said his name. He set the music aside and lifted a few glossy black and white photographs, his eyes wide with expectation.

"John?"

He looked up, puzzled at the sound of her voice.

"I'd like to read your manuscript," Alison said. "I never have, you know. I'd like to."

"Oh." He kept his eyes on her for only a moment. "Lizzie Tifgat has it. She's proofing it for me."

"Oh."

He held one photograph up and smiled at it. Alison went to look at it with him. It was of the woman in the garden of tall plants. It was a very old photograph.

"But that must be your grandmother, John, not your mother."

He turned it over. There was a scrawl of inked letters on the back. "Aunt Ellie," he said, disappointment in his voice, "whoever she is." Alison started pawing through the box. "Are there anymore?"

"Nothing important," John said, dropping the box to the floor and walking to the bathroom. The shoebox had split apart on impact, spilling its fragile contents across the throw rug. Alison looked at the debris and sighed. "Maybe you didn't have a mother," she said toward the bathroom, attempting to make a joke. "Maybe, like Athena, you were born from the sea."

"Venus," he called from the bathroom. "Venus was born from the sea foam." He stuck his head out the half-opened door. "I was born of a woman, like everybody else."

"Yeah," she said to herself, "too bad." She dropped noisily into the settee as John came into the front room. He didn't look at her but placed himself before the window to watch the sunset. She kept her eyes on the interior of the house, on the deeper reflections of the blond glow that poured into the room as the sun slipped itself in and out of the horizon's fingers. As the room darkened, she closed her eyes but remained in place, as did John, standing on the edge of her memory, staring into the nothingness of night.

"I'm leaving tomorrow, John."

"Where will you go?"

"I've always wanted to go to Europe. I might stay a while in Constantinople."

"That's Istanbul. And it's not in Europe."

She sighed. "It doesn't matter where it is or what it's called, I'm going there."

"How will you get there?"

"I'll call Cutler Insbroek."

"I've got to be to work early," he said. "I'll try not to wake you. Want to meet me for lunch, like you're always asking?"

"I'll be out of town, John."

"You know? I remember now. Aunt Ellie. I stayed with her until I was almost seven. I don't think she was really an aunt; perhaps a cousin. A distant cousin. She barely knew my mother. She didn't even know how she'd died, though I must have asked her a thousand times if I asked her once."

"Your mother is still alive, John."

"Whatever—"

"John."

"Yes, Alison."

"I really am leaving tomorrow, you know." He was silent a moment. His voice came from the dark presence nearby, a darker shadow in the unlighted room. "Packed yet?"

"Not much to pack. I'll do it in the morning. After you've left for school."

"All right. Can we sleep in the same bed tonight?" She had left the room and hadn't heard his question.

2

Alison sat sideways on the sofa staring out the window. The house had been open when Cutler dropped her off. He hadn't asked why she wanted to stop there; he'd simply let her off without a fuss. She'd had an answer ready should he have asked.

"I need to pick up some things I left in John's closet." Or: "I just want to have a little talk with John." After all, she'd not seen John in nearly a month. Not since—

"Damn," she said, slamming her fist against the sofa back. "He isn't here!" With the same hand she touched her abdomen. She drew a circle on the sweatshirt she wore as if tracing the shape of her uterus. Then she turned to face the familiar little room. How she loved this little house.

"My first house."

And John? Did she love him? She shrugged as if having a conversation with herself. "That isn't the issue here," she said. "Does he love me? That is the question." Or rather, "Could he love me? Now that—"

She drew another circle on her abdomen and sighed pathetically.

"Now that: Nothin'." She stood to leave. She'd have to walk into town and find Cutler's car. He was fussing with his plants, she figured. His Winter Garden. It was a long walk.

"What if John drives by while I'm—" She decided to call Cutler. The office girl didn't know where he was. Alison suggested the girl send someone to look for him. "At least, see that he gets the message that I called. Tell him I need a ride home this instant. I'm not feeling well. He knows where I am."

She hung up without even saying goodbye. It wasn't a nice thing to do. She started to call back with an apology. She was studying John's manuscript as she dialed. The phone was next to his typewriter on a side table near the fireplace. She lowered the handset into its cradle with one hand as she picked up the stack of pages with the other. Standing in place, in the center of the small, cluttered room, she began to read.

White. Fluttering. Something like the memory of a woman running in the fog. Or of blood that should have been white, scattered on linen, and flashing. Like a sign.

It was as if all light had been shut out of the small room except that which found a perch on the edge of the steel blade, deftly wielded. It dropped in slow silence, finding the floor, mating with the wood of the floor since all the world had stopped to watch, turning a cold eye, stopped and glazed, dark and crusted over with a kind of knowing terror that none can ever recall, given the end of time to recall it. The fact was: she was gone.

And one thing more: Bright with dread, hot water withheld, never to escape these eyes, I weep only on the inside; in slow silence. She's gone. Escaped from my bed as if she'd never been violated. I watch her through the fog-gauze of curtains that hang like faded memories, clogging my vision. I didn't mean to threaten her with so sharp a blade as this indifference.

There was music in the house then. She always left the radio on even when going into town. Didn't like coming home to a quiet house, she'd say. There's truth in that. But there were others, too. Standing about talking as if we were the only topic of conversation. How they sniggered behind their glasses of rum punch held just so, as if to hide their vulgar, chewing mouths filled with teeth. How they loved to expose their innards, the flesh and blood of their mouths!

She smiled too. With other parts of her body. She opened her flesh like a handbag and let me toy with the secret things she kept there. She offered me a smile like no other though others have tried to steal even that from my memory of her. That smile has changed the face of every other woman I have ever met as if every one of that other sex has conspired against me by pretending to be her.

How we danced: a flashing, a fluttering of gauze curtains, feet above the ground. There was a sharing of flesh, like children exchanging clothes, with laughter. There was a sharing of something else, but I don't remember what it was. It was a brief dance: a passion dance among the dunes of my indifference; something like the memory of a woman running in the fog.

I open my eyes at last only to close them again to keep that image with me. I'll not let her escape my dark touch but I'm too late. She is gone; fluttering, white, and in the mornings, day on day, as I have taught myself so well to do, waking from my dreams, caressing the linens with a dark touch, smoothing them to the sleepy eye, bending closer, seeking signs I know are not there and I wonder; was she ever here at all?

And in the mornings, I watch while she bathes. And in the evenings, I retire to that all-too-full-half-empty-double bed. I feel her moving under the sheets nearby. I await the touch of her warmth even as I drift off at last in blessed assurance that she must be there. And in the mornings, I await her waking from sleep as I search the sheets for signs that she was ever here at all.

Fog has persisted into autumn. It lasts the winter long and tints the pre-green trees of spring with a pallid cast, casting a pastel pall across the dooryard where once she'd sat. A veil of half tones has settled upon my eyes. The land, the fields, the sky are steeped in beige. Nor are nights as dark as once they were, nor days bright. Nothing remains but the memory of a woman running in the fog. What happened to that pre-green brilliance of my youth, the clear-eyed days of innocence, the unobstructed vision of the child's eye that once stared at me playfully from across the expanse of bedclothes?

No scent. No lingering stain. No prints in the sand. No trace of her has endured these many years but for the one gift she left me: an abiding emptiness so deep that I stumble about in its mire like some prehistoric beast caught in the mud; an emptiness that has taken up residence where my heart used to live.

"Small heart that it is," she read, "as she might remind me. Nonetheless beating. Nonetheless, my heart."

Alison dropped the pages to the floor and standing in place in the center of the small, cluttered room, she wept as she had never wept before.

3

She awoke to the sound of a car engine in the dooryard. She jumped in place, then smiled, having remembered where she was. She got to her feet, trying to contain her excitement. She bent to gather up the scattered pages of the manuscript to be placed carefully back in its folder on the side table near the fireplace. Then she paused in her happy labor. She had heard a woman's voice. Funny how women's voices carry, she thought casually. She stood up. Lizzie Tifgat.

Instinctively, she ran to the bedroom, closing the door behind her. The voices grew louder as the couple entered the house. She glanced about, seeking an escape route. The room was filled with another woman's things.

"Someone's been here," John was saying.

"How do you know?"

"My manuscript."

Lizzie laughed. "Your paranoia used to be amusing, John."

"And now?"

"Boring."

"You said it," he said, just inches away from the closed bedroom door. He opened it and went in, throwing something on the bed. Alison pulled herself yet farther under it. She could peer out into the front room to where Lizzie Tifgat was lighting up a cigarette.

"What a dreary day," she sighed, though it was brilliantly sunny beyond the window. "Want a drink?"

John left the bedroom. "Sure."

"You sure it was Alison again?"

"Who else?"

Lizzie was puttering at the sink. Alison couldn't see her, but she could hear her as she dropped ice cubes into glasses. "Considering how much she wanted to leave you," Lizzie was saying, "she sure finds enough excuses to come back here, doesn't she?"

"Leave the kid alone, will you?"

"Sure. Here's your drink. Cheers."

They were quiet for a while. "She doesn't know I moved in with you, does she?"

"Lizzie—"

"Sorry."

They strolled into view, and into the front room. John paused at his typewriter. Lizzie was asking how his writing was coming.

"It's shit," he said.

She had sat on the sofa as if she cared to be in full view of where Alison lay, crouched under John's bed. "That's no way to talk about your baby, John," she scolded.

"It's a motherless baby," he said, flopping down next to her.

"Let me read it, will you?"

He was shaking his head. "Not yet. I want Alison to read it first."

Lizzie seemed surprised. "Why?"

He shrugged. "It's sort of about her, I guess."

Lizzie reminded him Alison had gone to live with Cutler Insbroek.

"Only because she had no place else to go."

"She has a family, doesn't she?"

"Not close. No, Liz. She's pretty much alone in this world."

"Don't," she said gently, placing a hand on his cheek.

"What?"

She bowed her head. "It hurts me when you talk about Alison, John."

"Why?"

"Because she reminds me of myself; once."

"Really. I never would have—"

She had laid her head on his shoulder. "Haven't you figured it out yet? She and I are two of a kind. We are the kind of women you are attracted to, and we depend on you, or others like you, for our very survival."

"You're talking nonsense."

"That sounds like something you'd say to her," Lizzie sighed.

"No," he said. "To her I'd say she was nonsensical. I was crueler with her, Lizzie."

Lizzie looked up as if aware they were being listened to. "It's what she needed from you, don't you see? She needed you to treat her badly in order for her to confirm to herself her own self-pity, don't you think?"

He tried to contradict her, but she added, "I know, John, because she's just like me."

"No," he said. "She isn't that pathetic, Lizzie."

She stood up. "Thank you, Mr. Freud." He laughed lightly and after a time, she laughed with him. She sat back down, and they drank for a while in silence. Meanwhile, Alison fell asleep. She didn't see John get to his feet to retrieve his manuscript. She didn't see him hand it to Lizzie Tifgat. She didn't hear Lizzie ask, "Are you sure?"

"Why not? I'll never see Alison again and I know that."

He sat next to her on the sofa as she read. He pulled his feet up and hugged his knees, watching her. She finished the first page, saying as she put it aside, "Not bad."

"Not bad?" John wondered. "You read one page and you say, 'not bad'?"

"What do you expect me to say?" she asked, still reading.

John started to pout and after a time she dropped the manuscript into her lap. "I'm sorry," she said. "I can't read it with you watching me like this. Let me take it home with me."

"Home?"

"My place," she corrected. "Let me read it there, okay?"

"You don't like it, do you? You don't like it because it's about Alison."

"I don't know what it's about." She said. "I haven't got very far into it yet. Give me a chance, will you?"

He bowed his head to his knees. "You had your chance, as I recall."

"Oh, John," she said softly. "That wasn't very nice."

"You took advantage of me, Liz. Didn't you?"

She lowered her head as well. "Perhaps I did," she admitted, keeping her distance. "You were very naive, and I was a desperate woman." She sighed deeply. "Nothing more pathetic, John, than a desperate, middle-aged woman." Then she turned to him, "Excepting, maybe, a self-pitying man?"

"Stop it," he said, turning to look out the window behind them. "I'm not feeling sorry for myself."

"What would you call it, then?"

"Anger, I guess. I'm angry at myself."

"Ah, yes," she said, leaning back and staring at the ceiling. "I remember it well. Only I blamed everyone else for my anger. It's the woman's way, I suppose. Funny."

"What's funny?"

"I know the truth now about anger, but nothing's really changed. I'm still alone, aren't I?"

He looked to her, asking plaintively, "What about me?" She smiled and caressed his forehead. "We're not really a couple, John, and you know it as well as I. Christ! Why can't I get it right?"

John sat up, stunned. "What?"

She threw her hands into her lap. "My life!" The manuscript fell to the floor in a fluttering of pages. Lizzie bent to scoop them up, apologizing profusely. He bent alongside her and stopped her. "They're just words on paper," he said.

"But they're your words." He pulled her back to nestle beside him on the sofa, the manuscript scattered at their feet. He embraced her and kissed her. Then they were silent for a while.

"I remember the day he left," Lizzie said at length.

"Who?"

"Larry. Lawrence W. Tifgat. My husband."

"Oh," he said, disinterested, "him."

"I remember that day better than any other memory of any other event in my life. Isn't that strange? I was in the bedroom of our apartment, in Chicago. God, I loved that apartment! He was near the window. I was looking the other way, but I knew where he was and what he was doing. It was our customary position, paced off like duelers, only I was curled up on the bed. He was standing firmly, as was his custom, aggressively facing the light of day but not really looking at it. His arms were folded, one hand raised, his face buried in his palm. That was not customary. 'Why did we ever get married, I wonder,' I asked him.

'It was the only way I could get you to sleep with me,' he said.

'Was that all there was to it?' I asked."

"He didn't answer as he'd left the room. I didn't realize he'd left, and I remember asking what he wanted to do that evening. 'Go out and fight in public or just duke it out here at home for a change?'"

"Then I heard him at the closet in the other room. I didn't move. I just lay there watching the light patterns change on the far wall. It was a shifting sort of light, typical of late afternoons. Hues were deepening, colors fading. I heard things occasionally from within the apartment, the bathroom, the music room, but I concentrated all my attention on the failing light in the bedroom. Soon, it was too dark to see though there was still light behind me, elsewhere in the house. There were door sounds, and something crossed my mind. It was something I wanted to remember though it was never clear to me exactly what it was."

She paused to take a breath. When she started speaking again, it was in a voice distant and blurred, more like an echo.

"It is cold and distant, never hot or close, yet always with me, the memory of that memory. The hall lamp cast a shadow of him briefly on the far wall, then everything went black. Or was it all an image in my mind, like some specimen floating in some glass bottle?"

"Something gripping had crossed my mind, passing through me like a winter wind across the eyes as a door closes against a storm, shutting me into my own inner rooms at the same time."

"I never saw him again." John was very close. He held her face in his hand as he smoothed her hair with his fingers. He asked softly why she never divorced him. She shook her head without answering. He asked why she had never written that story.

"Liz?"

"Ha!" she said, composing herself. "That romantic crap? Listen, John. I promised myself years ago I'd never write like an angry woman." She laughed a little and wiped her eyes. "But I do, don't I?"

"It's why your work sells," he said. "There are lots of women who identify with your stories."

"Women," she said, as if it were a dirty word. "I would rather appeal to men. They know what good writing is because it is so damned hard for them to do it. For women, it comes easy. We were born to be storytellers. But men—"

"I don't buy that bullshit," he snapped suddenly.

She sat up straight and let out a breath. "Oh, well," she said, "neither do I." They bent to scoop up the pages of the manuscript, bumping shoulders as they did so. They laughed and bumped each other again. The pages went flying as John bumped Lizzie off the sofa and onto the floor. She was laughing as he threw himself upon her. They began squirming about, kissing and reaching their hands into each other's clothing. Her blouse came open button by button as John nibbled her ears, first one, then the other. He was making munching sounds as he chewed on the flesh of her throat. He wriggled out of his sweatshirt as Lizzie fussed with the clasp on the back of her brassier. Suddenly, she stopped him.

"Not here, John," she whispered, as if a secret.

"In my own house?"

"On top of your manuscript!"

"O, my god!" he gasped. "You're right."

He picked her up and carried her into the bedroom, falling with her onto the bed at the sound of two cries of surprise. Two cries? John and Lizzie exchanged glances. Together, they bent over the edge of the bed and peered beneath it. Alison was just pulling herself out from under the other side. She paused and looked back over her shoulder. She was covered with dust balls and her hair was a fright.

"Don't you ever sweep this place?" she asked, in a furor. Lizzie lay back bare breasted on the bed and laughed. Alison got to her feet and glared at John across the space occupied by the other woman. John merely turned and walked away. He left the house. He took the car and drove off.

"Just like a man," Lizzie was saying as she returned to the front room.

"Worse," Alison said.

As Lizzie got herself dressed, Alison went to the kitchen to make some tea. She explained casually as she went that she was waiting for Cutler to pick her up but, as usual, his timing was off. Lizzie followed her and leaned against the table watching her as she puttered about the stove.

"What are you doing?"

"Tidying up. Sugar?"

"Straight. Why are you tidying up? John is nowhere around to see you doing it."

"I'm not doing it for—" She paused. "Stupid, isn't it?"

"What?"

"The habits we get into because of a man."

She was lighting a cigarette. "Stupid and dangerous. Fag?"

"What? Oh. No, I don't smoke any more. Cutler doesn't like the smell of it in his house. His mother's house, actually. I'm living in the maid's quarters. Isn't that something?"

"Something else," Lizzie said with a little smile. "So, you're not actually living with Cutler."

She shook her head. "I wanted John to think that but, no. Cutler has this loyalty thing."

"Loyalty? To whom?"

"John. He's his best friend," she said, as if it should have been obvious.

Lizzie nodded. "I guess that makes sense to men." She returned to the front room and was picking up the pages of John's manuscript when Alison came in with the teapot and a couple of hand painted cups, all on a silver tray. "These are mine," she mused. "I forgot they were still here. I only used them when Mother came by; but then, she never came by all that much, so—"

"Jesus Christ, woman, don't you ever finish a sentence?" Alison had paused. "Another bad habit, I guess." Then, "You read John's story?"

"No. I don't think he wants me to."

She placed the untidy stack of pages on the table near the typewriter and sat next to Alison on the sofa. "So," she said, "whatever shall we talk about?"

"Let's not talk about John," Alison suggested, as she poured the tea. "Or me, for that matter."

"What about Cutler Insbroek?"

"What a bore," Alison sighed. "I thought John was anal!"

"So, why do you stay there?"

"It's nice there," was her answer. "Alma, Cutler's mother, dotes on me and her boyfriend plays the piano for me every afternoon when we have our tea. I walk on the beach, I read, I listen to music. It's nice there."

"But it isn't here, is it?" Alison smiled. "Not quite."

"But, you were unhappy with John, Alison. Isn't that why you left?"

She sipped her tea. "I guess. But I sort of thought he'd—"

"Come after you?" She nodded. "Sort of hoped, you know?" Lizzie was quiet for a while. She held her teacup before her, but she did not drink from it. She looked into the midst of the room as if there was something to look at. Then she stood up.

"Tell John I—I'll call him."

"Are you going someplace?"

"I need some cigarettes. I'm going down to Evelyn's Bar to get some. If John comes back, tell him I'm there."

"But Cutler will be here to pick me up."

"Yes," Lizzie said, moving toward the door. "Well, I have to go." Alison stood up. "You don't have to go because of me. I'm not staying, you know. Mrs. Tifgat?" Lizzie was nearly running down the road toward the lake. Alison watched her from the opened door. "Goodbye," she called.

Then she returned to finish her tea. She was just swallowing the last from Lizzie's cup when John's car pulled up outside. Thinking it was Cutler at last, Alison called through the screen door that she'd be right out. She returned the tea things to the kitchen and rinsed them out. She replaced the teapot on the shelf above the stove and hung the hand painted cups from hooks on the window frame. Before leaving, she paused at John's typing table and neatened up the stack of pages Lizzie had left there. Then she rushed from the house, leaving the front door wide open, and hurried to get into the car. Half in the seat, she paused.

"John?"

He picked her up in his arms and carried her into the house, pulling the door shut behind them.

Twelve

They all bent over, and saw that the cliff fell perpendicularly downward to about the depth, or rather more, at which the tall palace rose in height above their heads...

"Who were they," said he, looking earnestly in her face, "who have been flung over here, in days gone by?"

"Men that cumbered the world," she replied. "Men whose lives were the bane of their fellow-creatures. Men who poisoned the air, which is common breath of all, for their own selfish purposes. There was short work of such men, in old Roman times. Just at the moment of their triumph, a hand as of an avenging giant clutched them and dashed the wretches down this precipice!"

Hawthorne, *The Marble Faun*

They stood in the Forum, the *Forum Romanum*, the three of them, Caleb, Michael and one *other*, lurking in the shadows. It was a warm and sunny day in February. Many pilgrims had come out to walk the streets of old Rome. "It's Sunday," Caleb had insisted, waiting outside Jo's locked door earlier that day. "You need some fresh air. You haven't been out of the villa since the New Year!"

"I'm writing, Caleb. That is what I am supposed to be doing. What about you?"

"No time to write. Come on, Jo. Join the human race!" Her voice was closer to the locked door this time. "I don't care to join you and your boyfriend for an afternoon stroll," she called.

Caleb laughed. "Michael's a friend, Jo. Nothing more. And he's fun to be with. You'd like him if you'd let yourself." She opened the door. "I've no intention of—" she had paused. "You look chipper today."

He laughed again, this time at her choice of words. "He knows a lot about history and art," he added.

"Really?" she said, looking up and down the empty hallway.

"Really." He was smiling broadly.

"If he's so charming, why do you complain about him all the time?"

He insisted it wasn't complaining so much as confusion. "He's moody. Some days he's happy and energetic and others—"

"Dour and sad?" she asked, skeptically. "Are you sure you're not talking about yourself, John Caleb Wilson?"

"Pah!" He threw his hands in the air and walked away. She watched after him for a while, then returned to her room and shut her door. The sound of it echoed through the old palace as he descended the grand marble stairway. He left the villa and took the bus, then the Metro into the city of Rome.

They met at the *Colosseo* Metro station, he and Michael. The sun showed brilliantly on the crisp marble facade of the arena. It was Michael's idea they walk the forum.

"I don't much like graveyards," Caleb sighed.

"Jo didn't come with you?"

"She doesn't like them either."

The other laughed. When confronted by Caleb's skeptical and impatient expression, he demurred. "It isn't a graveyard," Michael said steadily, taking him by the arm and leading him down the street. "It is, in fact, the living heart of this city. Okay?"

"Okay."

Michael took a breath and continued. "This city is not dead, you know. Some people want to believe that myth. Hawthorne did. But I believe its heart beats still."

Caleb said something about him being a little melodramatic for so early an hour and Michael laughed, good-heartedly. He had paused and was looking intently at the writer. He asked seriously if he wanted to call it off. Caleb shook his head, so he suggested the two of them go see for themselves.

"Okay?"

He had glanced over at Caleb and he rolled his eyes. Michael merely laughed.

"No sex last night?" he asked. Caleb stepped away from him and walked on, with a purpose. It was Sunday. St. Brigid's Day. She was the Irish girl who asked God to take away her beauty so that men would not lust after her. Her day marks the beginning of lactation among cows for their calves and also the lambing season: a pagan Gaelic feast day in earlier times. Caleb did not know anything about St. Brigid, and he didn't pay much attention to Michael's discourse. Being Sunday, entrance to the Forum was free. The gates were open. Caleb strolled casually into the vast ruin, pausing just below the baroque facade of the Church of San Lorenzo, the ex-Temple of Antoninus and Faustina, there, to wait for Michael, who had lagged behind for some unknown reason. As he walked up, he was pointing out the various monuments. To the left, the *Via Sacra* meandered toward the nearly perfect Arch of Titus; to the right, it marked a straight path through the grand Arch of Septimus Severus. At the foot of the precipitous Capitoline Hill, it made an abrupt turn to the west, squeezed between the *Curia* and the Marmertine Prison and opened out into the Rome of the Caesars; Imperial Rome, Modern Rome.

Michael moved on steadily in the direction of the *domus Vestalis*, the house of Vesta and her virgin nuns, while Caleb remained. A portion of the small round temple to the virgin goddess of female functions still stood and statuary graced the garden promenade beyond it. But Michael had passed on by and now stood in silence near the Temple of Castor and Pollux, its three surviving pillars casting bony shadows across the piazza in which he stood. He was simply standing there, hands on his hips, staring into the sunshine.

"What's he doing?" Caleb wondered aloud.

Michael had heard him and turned toward him with a little laugh. "Communing, I guess"

"With whom?"

"The Celestial Twins?"

"Weird."

Michael merely sighed. The afternoon outing, though less than an hour old, was already proving tedious. Michael was not as talkative as usual, not as entertaining. A quiet tension had settled on the two of them upon entering the forum. Caleb had put it down to boredom, but it was something bigger than that. He later tried to talk to Jo about it.

"He was in an awful mood today. Like he didn't want to be with me but was doing so just to keep me happy."

"You don't think that sounds just a little sanctimonious?" she asked.

"You wouldn't know sanctimonious if you ran smack dab into it."

"Caleb," she said, her hand on his chest. "I spent my entire childhood in Christian schools. I know sanctimonious when I see it, even in its most subtle form. And one of the subtlest of all is the kind with which your friend seems to be afflicted."

"Afflicted?"

She continued talking, her voice softening, as she wandered to the window to gaze into the late afternoon twilight. "The unacknowledged form. It's there, deep inside him, but either he can't or won't acknowledge it. It's almost like a compulsion. The more he consciously suppresses it, the stronger it becomes. It doesn't always reveal itself. And when it does, it is in the subtlest of ways." Caleb was thinking. "I don't feel that about him, Jo, but—"

"Watch him," she insisted. "Listen to him. See if you don't detect just a little smugness in his tone."

"You mean, like he tries to cover it up, overcompensate, as it were."

She nodded. "He pretends, even to himself, to be humble. But he isn't, Caleb. He's self-righteous to the core!"

"You don't even know him," he started to say.

"I'm beginning to," she returned, not looking back at him.

Back in the Forum, earlier that day, Caleb had walked carefully up to where Michael was standing. He was staring as if lost in thought at the ruins of the Gemini Temple.

"I love those three columns," he was saying. "They seem so delicate and yet they have managed to survive the ages. Earthquakes, wars, bombs; yet they stand, scarred yet majestic!" He paused a moment, a marvelous expression in his eyes. "There's a lesson in them somewhere," he laughed out loud, "but, damned if I know what it is." Then: "Getting hungry?" Caleb suggested they walk a little more. In silence then, they ambled toward the Arch of Titus and the still impressive ex-temple of Venus and Rome. Odd combination, Caleb thought, Michael having named the brooding edifice in answer to his inquiry.

"The late Greeks had a custom of personifying their cities in the form of earth-mother goddesses called *tyches*," Michael explained. "I suppose the Romans picked up on the custom from them. They represented the city of Roma as a dignified and stalwart woman. How she became a counterpart to Venus is a mystery to me."

"Not to me," Caleb said, pausing to peer up at the medieval walls that incorporated the old temple. "Why not merge civic pride with love and beauty?"

"Venus was not exactly an emblem of love to the Ancients," Michael said, "That notion is more recent, since the Renaissance, maybe." The other asked him what he meant. "Venus was not loved among the Greeks, you know. They called her Aphrodite, a symbol of girlish tricks and revenge. Remember the story of the judgment of Paris? He awarded her the prize for beauty and look what happened. The Trojan War!" He sort of laughed. "She was a symbol of all that is negative in female behavior, a product of her birth, I suppose."

"Sounds to me as if you don't like women," Caleb said, starting to walk away.

"It was the Greeks I was talking about," he said cordially. "But I suppose some of that attitude toward women has survived into the twentieth century."

Caleb wondered what her birth had to do with her behavior.

"She was born of the sea foam," he stated emphatically. "The white froth that ejaculated from the severed genitals of the Titan Uranus." The other had paused to listen, but each of the two men kept their eyes from the other.

"Cronus, having castrated his own father in a sort of power play for control of the cosmos, tossed the foaming organs into the sea. From that fertile slime arose the beautiful Aphrodite." He was speaking steadily, as if delivering a medical opinion. "*Venere* is her name in Italian. It is an allusion to the diseases of which she is the patroness."

"Then," Caleb wondered confronting him at last, "why is she so beautiful?" He eyed him directly. "Temptation is always beguiling, don't you think?"

"You're a sexist," he said.

"No," he laughed. "Just reciting the facts behind the myth is all. She represents sexual desire, which, as you know, can be deadly if not tempered."

Caleb walked away as if no longer interested in Michael's soliloquy. He then paused, the great vault of Constantine's basilica yawning before him. Michael had asked if he agreed. He nodded.

"She is carnal love, Caleb. That is the vehicle that carries us from life to death. It is the reason we are here, the reason we live, and it is, in some ways, the very cause of our deaths. It is the destroyer of youthful innocence, the bringer of old age, disillusionment, and, ultimately, grief. That is what mythology tells us. That is why mythology pairs her with Mars, the custodian of war and pestilence."

"Sex and death," Caleb said. "The substance of every good novel." Then he asked, glancing back, "Was not Cupid their love child?"

"Right," Michael said, coming up close behind. "Born blind, he shoots the arrows of desire into the hearts of men and women. Sometimes it is the pleasure of love we enjoy, sometimes the pain, depending on which arrow he blindly fires our way."

He went on to marvel at how simply and logically the myths seemed to explain the complex workings of the human heart. Caleb remarked at the absurdity of it. When asked why by the other, he reminded him that the symbols of Venus and Mars have become the trademarks of human behavior in the modern world. Venus, the trickster, and Mars the punisher of all who fall for her tricks.

"That's a rather cynical way of looking at it," Michael said.

"Don't you think the story of Venus and Mars is just a little cynical?"

"No," he declared. "I think it's rather beautiful."

"It's just a story," Caleb reminded him. "A way of explaining the origins of immorality—and its relationship to mortality"

"You mean," Michael began, "by giving us someone to blame our immoral behavior on! Like some pious people I know who blame their sins on Satan while taking credit for all their accomplishments themselves."

"I think you mean people like yourself," Caleb returned carefully. Michael merely laughed, the sun glancing off his sunglasses. "Me? I have few accomplishments for which to take credit, my friend."

"And your sins?"

He smiled while turning away. "I do take credit for them, and gladly." He shook his head and swung his arm through Caleb's, surprising him. "In truth, I don't have too many, but that isn't because I haven't tried." He laughed. "I just haven't succeeded, is all!" He laughed again and started to walk them along the sunny pathway. "Food!" Michael was calling with a sweep of his free arm in the bright air. "I must have food!"

Caleb pulled away from him and paused. He watched after him from a few paces back. "How does one do this?" he asked himself, with a scratching of his forehead. "How does one find a balance between his faith and his life, I wonder?" The other had left the forum. Caleb followed at a distance. He caught up at the corner of Cavour and Imperiale. They locked arms again and crossed the busy thoroughfare. There was a small restaurant on the far corner. Michael had been talking the entire time. Caleb was again becoming bored.

"Whistler's mistress was named 'Jo'," Michael was saying as they sat down at a table near the window. "You know? Whistler? The painter?"

"Whistler's Mother," Caleb recited.

"Arrangement in Gray and Black," Michael said. "He did several paintings of Jo in Japanese settings."

"Cool," Caleb sighed, perusing the menu. "What are you going to order?"

The waiter approached slowly. He was apparently unaccustomed to serving a man who was talking to himself. Caleb looked up suddenly. Michael was gone.

On the Metro ride home, Caleb sat quietly on the nearly empty train. He got off at the Trastevere station and caught bus number 870 for the short ride to the Church of *San Giovanni in Trastevere*. From there, it was a kilometer or so walk up and down curving lanes to the academy. No sooner had he started out and it had started to rain, so he took shelter near the walls of the venerable old basilica, leaning against the cool, damp stones. He stood there for some time, huddled against the chilly wind. It was time to write Michael out of his life, he thought. He was certain Jo would have agreed. How she had ranted about him the last time they had walked the up and down lanes of Trastevere.

"I was hoping you would like him," Caleb had whined.

"I might, if I were to spend time with him as you have." It was another rainy night and they huddled together for warmth. She admitted she had thought he was a product of Caleb's imagination at first.

"And now?"

She shrugged within his embrace as they walked into the rainy wind. "The way you talk about him, Caleb, he seems to be not of this world, I mean, the world of the likes of us."

He nodded. "Maybe that's it. I like his strangeness."

"A character for your novel?"

He grimaced. "Hardly. Who'd believe in a character like that?"

"Isn't it the task of the author to make him believable?"

He was nodding, half listening. "I suppose."

Arm in arm they headed into the gentle downpour.

"We'll catch our deaths yet," Jo complained.

"At very least, we'll be soaked to the skin."

"Oh," she cooed. "We can dry each other off, then."

"Deal."

They slowed their pace. The villa was not far. The rain was not heavy. They walked ever slower as they neared the front gate. The gatekeeper nodded and smiled. He was accustomed to their late returning. And Caleb had always tossed him a handful of lire. He was an accommodating watchman.

The rain was falling more heavily. Blankets of it rippled across the lamp lit lawns like bed sheets billowing on clotheslines. The two ran into the portico and pressed the night buzzer. The less than cordial night man, having been roused from his nap in front of his little television, admitted them with a grumble. They giggled and dashed up the grand stairway.

"Your room or mine?" she wondered in a rushed whisper as they huffed up the stairs.

"Whoever has his key out first."

But that was several weeks earlier. Caleb and Jo had not spent a night together in some time. Michael's fault, he assumed. He had been occupying Caleb's time; he hadn't even been writing like he should.

"Yes," he said as he started toward the lights of the villa, "It is time to write him off."

Caleb stood naked before the mirror in Jo's room. The room was dark but for light from streetlamps that burned beyond a fringe of bare plane trees. The speckled aura filled the small room. She asked him what he was looking at. He said he was hoping he had gained some weight, considering all the pasta he had been eating lately.

"Still thin as a rail," she observed from her warm place beneath the blankets of the bed. He rejoined her, and they snuggled. He said they had to stop meeting like this and she laughed.

"No, I mean it, Jo. I told you. I can't write when I'm sexually satiated." She laughed again but he persisted. "When I'm lonely and miserable, I write beautiful things; things of value, things, *perhaps*, of lasting value."

He turned to her and kissed her forehead. "That's a great responsibility, you know. Fate seems to have dealt me a losing hand. When I'm with someone I care for, I feel guilty for not being in touch with myself. When I'm alone, with just myself, I find it isn't so much a burden after all; to be alone." He sat up suddenly. "Oh, shit. I don't know what the hell I'm talking about!"

He looked over his shoulder at her. She had deliberately laid her breasts above the sheets, her dark nipples piqued by the cool atmosphere. "You're saying you can't be both writer and lover at the same time?" She shook her head and sat up, her back to him. "That's a new one on me!"

"Is it?" he asked, reaching back and touching her cold shoulder. She recoiled at his touch. He asked again, "Is it, really?"

She let her head drop a little. "No," she said. "I've used the same excuse myself."

"Is it just an excuse? I wonder."

"It's why I left my husband," she said. "Though I blamed him for it. It's why you ignore your mother."

"And my sister. God, how they love me and how indifferent I have been to them, especially these past few years. But, damn it, Jo! Their love makes me feel safe and I can't write about that!"

"It's why you left your wife," she added but he interrupted.

"No. She left of her own accord. I had nothing to do with that. Besides, we weren't actually married."

"You what?" She was putting on her sweatshirt and turned within it as if she had no arms.

"We were just living together," he admitted. "She wasn't my wife. She was my—bed partner."

He had kept his back to her. She turned back to her dressing activities. "Then, the story of Alison is about her, isn't it? It's not a fiction, is it? It's about you and her, isn't it?"

"It is," he admitted in a soft and childlike voice.

"I read your last chapters," she said, staring at the dark window, his dark reflection upon it. "The ones about Alison. They were written by someone who seems to know what it is like to be a lonely woman. How do you know that, John Caleb Wilson? I want to know how you know that."

"Easy," he said to her reflection in the mirror opposite him, though they still sat with their backs to the other. "I just wrote about what it was like to be a lonely man and then multiplied it by a hundred."

She lowered her head. "Very touching. Did you love her as much as the book seems to say?"

He lifted his shoulder very slightly. "I don't know. The memory of her leaving overshadows every other feeling I have or may have ever had for her." He bent over to pull on his shorts as a chill was collecting in his groin, where it should have been warm. Jo watched him by way of the window glass, perhaps wondering if she was seeing his body for the last time. "I hate being lonely," he said. "I have to be a writer, I have no choice there, as well you know. Must I endure a life of loneliness to suit my passion for writing? Is this the punishment God has meted out to me for my transgressions—whatever they may have been?"

"Seems to me;" she said, walking to the window to better see him in the misty glass, "the real question is why you cannot be both writer and lover?"

"I know that," he said with a zip. "I *do* know that, but I'm not sure how to accomplish what seems at moment an impossible task."

"Is that why you've taken up with Michael?"

He heaved a sigh. "There's passion in my affection for him," he admitted. "And it doesn't seem to interfere with my creativity."

"No sex." she said. "That's why. Passion without sex! You are, after all, as you have claimed, a child of Hawthorne!" She had turned at last to face him in reality.

"What's he got to do with it," was his response.

She smiled thinly. "Attempted joke," she said. "But, listen. He believed in the power of intuition over external sources of inspiration, didn't he? That from intuition comes inspiration, which is similar to understanding; understanding the whole of reality; is that not so, Caleb?" He nodded. "So long as the individual maintains faith in his own intuitional powers, yes."

"So long as you know yourself," she said. "And if you trust your own intuition, it goes without saying that you must be able to trust other people's as well. That's a little like love, isn't it?"

"I guess."

"And evil is a product of our own failures to trust in our own selves, and not the invention of some extra-mortal power."

"But Hawthorne also believed in the independent power of sin," Caleb insisted. "He believed in its relentless self-destructive presence and in the inevitable punishment it inspires."

She agreed. "But not punishment from God in the Christian sense."

"No," he said. "We inevitably find a way to punish our own selves for the sins we believe we have committed."

"You mean guilt?" she said. She was nodding knowingly. "But he also believes, as with Hester Prynne, for instance, that guilt can eventually make a person strong. It can lead her to triumph over those who have taken it upon themselves to punish her on God's behalf."

Caleb nodded in silence. Then he added, "But that takes time, doesn't it?" She was moving closer to him by way of the mirror through which he still watched her. "Guilt is therefore the product of solitude; it is the punishment we inflict upon ourselves for having failed to meet our own self-expectations. Caleb. All this is so simple and so easy to get on top of—If you want to."

"The antidote to guilt must be love," he was saying, his eyes having glazed over. "Because love is selfless." He turned to her, smiling. "He believed that a man could achieve his personal goals without destroying the goals of others because the way to that end is through an understanding of the inner self in relationship to the outer world. That's not possible in today's 'Me first' society, Jo."

She was nodding, strangely. "Make it possible," she said. "Why not?"

"An easy philosophy," he said, reaching out to embrace her. "But one must sacrifice something before gaining and I—"

She had pulled away from him and now walked back toward the dark window. "Sacrifice? Let me talk to you about sacrifice:"

"My God, Caleb! If our culture filled men with the same kind of trauma it does women over, say, the loss of virginity, they'd have a much better understanding of what it is to sacrifice—and to be sacrificed!"

Caleb shook his head. "I love it when women confuse sex with gender-consciousness."

She interrupted. "I love it when men make inane comments like that one!" She had turned toward him, quarter-wise. A strand of her hair having slipped from its barrette, fell over her forehead and dangled casually before her right eye. Caleb took in the image and sealed it deep inside. He knelt on the cool marble floor and bowed his head into her opened hands. The pungent warmth of her body rose between her fingers.

"I never would have fallen in love with you, Jo. You know that, don't you?"

She nodded, closed eyed. "I know," she said softly. "I'm not pretty enough, am I? To suit your fantasies; am I?"

"It isn't that."

"But he is, isn't he?"

"What?" Caleb turned his eyes upward.

"Michael. He is beautiful enough to suit your fantasy, isn't he?"

He stood slowly, raising his hands and clasping her thin shoulders. "He *is* the fantasy, don't you see? I didn't invent this one. I stumbled into it; in the flesh."

She pulled away from him. "Oh," she moaned, "to be spoken of in such words!"

"But you are part of it too," Caleb insisted. "One cannot exist without the other except in fantasy!"

She was shaking her head and rattling her hands in the air as she walked away. "I do not understand you," she cried.

"Dear God," he sighed, from where he stood in the middle of the room. "I was hoping you did. Maybe then you could explain *me* to me."

She had placed herself before the window and was watching him by way of its dark reflection. After a time, he turned from her gaze and returned to the mirror. He watched her undress for bed by way of the glass. She did not look back at him. He pulled on his shirt and bent to tie his shoes. She watched him then, in secret, standing naked before the reflecting window. He was still talking as if she were still listening.

"I always want what I cannot have," he sighed. "But wanting is so important to me that, even when I discover I can have what I thought I wanted I reject it in order to keep wanting it—Isn't that absurd?"

Jo had put on her robe and was moving toward the door. "I'm going to take a shower." She paused. She did not look his way. "See if I can wash some of this absurdity off me." Door closure.

All gone; and only herself and Donatello left hanging over the brow of the ominous precipice!

Not so, however; not entirely alone! In the basement-wall of the palace, shaded from the moon, there was a deep, empty niche, that had probably once contained a statue; not empty, neither; for a figure now came forth from it, and approached Miriam.

Nathanial Hawthorne, *The Marble Faun.*

"*San Pietro*," the woman had told him.

"St. Peter's?" he wondered.

She shrugged and closed the door.

"St. Peter's?" he asked again, though the housekeeper had departed. "Why would he have gone to church so late at night?"

Caleb heaved a sigh. The mid-winter sun was already set, and the dark streets of Old Rome offered little comfort. He started walking toward the light patch of gray sky that marked the Tiber River in its course. There was snow in the air. It seemed to cluster about the few streetlamps that hung from the corners of the old palaces lining the ancient alleyway. The cold streets were empty, at least at first sight; but there were shadows afoot that moved, stiffly, like corpses in their catacomb niches. The silence was most oppressive of all. It draped itself over his shoulders like an old coat that offered no warmth. Caleb pressed on through the weather as if the very air had congealed about him.

Ahead was the river. A smear of pink steam marked the taillights of cars plying their ways along the quays. A blur of green and amber marked the location of traffic signals. The narrow way was dark and glistening and speckled with white all at the same time. He entered the eerie brilliance of the thoroughfare and crossed to the *Ponte Sant' Angelo*; the bridge dedicated to the Blessed Archangel—Michael. It was a gray path to nowhere as the far shore had been obscured by the building storm. The river flowed somewhere below, a black chasm separating the snowy See from the rest of the world. He paused halfway.

Another man stood nearby, having appeared suddenly as the shower lulled. Caleb drew himself toward the marble balustrade, resting his hands upon the snow-clad stones. The other man had done the same, his hands upon the same wall. They eyed each other darkly for a few moments, then nodded, and went their ways, passing close enough, shoulder to shoulder, that the smell of stale cigarette smoke attended him. He tightened his scarf about his throat, hunched himself into the wind, and trundled on. Walls slipped silently past, as silently as water. Bare branches slithered overhead. At last, he stood upon the Street of Conciliation; that broad road that bridges the chasm between the sacred and profane worlds of Rome. The Then and the Here-and-Now. Ahead, glistening like a movie still within the mantel of the snowstorm, St. Peter's dome hovered reassuringly.

Caleb paused, overtaken by the serene and noble beauty of the scene before him. He stood in the middle of the street, hands at his face, his mouth agape in wonder. He began to understand why Michael had come to this place in the middle of the night. But, no, that wasn't it!

A bitter chill raced through him. Lowering his eyes and dipping them below the aura of streetlamps, he saw a strange ritual unfolding. Men. Darkly dressed. Huddled against the chill. Wandering aimlessly in and out of the shadows along the sacred via. Somnambulistic pilgrims. Meandering to and fro among the obelisks, having stumbled out of the sanctified past and into a present of immorality.

"Gypsies," he thought.

Fascinated, he walked on. There were only occasional cars on the boulevard. They would move slowly along the curbs as if their occupants were searching house numbers, then they'd duck into one of the dark crossroads. He knew he should retreat, return to the safe seclusion of Trastevere, but he continued. He wasn't sure he understood what was going on.

A man in a fedora passed him by as he entered the square. Their eyes met—only their eyes—and there was anticipation in the other's. Another figure was walking just behind him, like a visible echo, more sensed than actually seen. The two men had paused together at the corner of the portico. Caleb watched them over his shoulder. They turned away and entered the shadows. He stopped. Chilled to the bone. But the great cathedral by some urge was drawing him onward.

It was snowing again, like curtains drawn one after the other between him and the great dome. St. Peter's square was absolutely quiet. The *Via Della Conciliazione* was a gray campus, pure and unsullied, unmarked by tire tracks in the snow, blemished only by the slow-motion figures that traced its lighted pathways. Caleb had entered the Ellipse. A host of dark angels awaited him there, moving slowly, silently as ghosts, darkening the square with their sinister amblings.

A little light lay at the foot of the nearest obelisk. He sought it out. The illuminated fountains sparkled like icicles, breathing a subliminal chant. The mumblings of men in canticle, a plane song of 'why?'

He pulled his white hands out of his dark jacket pockets and turned them toward St. Peter. Thumbs out, like a hitchhiker, he spread them in a gesture of resignation and dismay. His eyes closed and his mouth, like a sleeping beggar's, hung open. He waited for someone to answer in response.

His space darkened further. He opened his eyes. A man had come upon him from out of the pallid gloom. A big man. A handsome man, his face bright with excitement, his eyes dark with mystery. His lips moist with readiness.

Caleb recoiled. The man reached out for him. Caleb braced himself. Nothing.

The hand had withdrawn suddenly. The man had stepped back into the shadow from which he had emerged, his face darkening. He bowed his head as he backed away, mumbling.

"Perdona. Padre. Perdona mi!"

Forgive me, Father, for I have—

"What?"

Caleb came to. The world returned to normal time. "Why did he—?" He glanced about himself. The piazza had emptied. But for him. Snow once more settled gently and benevolently out of the firmament, dusting his shoulders. He bent to tighten his scarf, then pulled it out to stare at it. It was striped, black and white. He'd had it tucked into his jacket, tightly about his neck. Caleb started to laugh, then quickly suppressed the levity and hurried from the piazza. He had been mistaken for a priest!

But no. He had not been alone in the piazza. Two figures remained, barely visible, in the shadow of Bernini's magnificent portico. Caleb paused at sight of them. One of them was Michael. The other, his mysterious companion. Caleb waited as Michael dismissed the other and started toward him.

"I was looking for you. Your housekeeper told me—"

"My model," Michael said simply.

"Your model."

"He's a member of the Swiss Guard. I often walk him home. As you see, he's a small man. He's afraid to walk these streets alone, as well you should be, my friend."

His voice had held not a hint of mystery. It was as placid and ordinary as if he'd been talking of the weather. Then he asked with sincere concern what Caleb was doing out without an overcoat.

"What? Overcoat?" He looked down at himself. No wonder he was so cold.

Michael took him by the elbow and began to escort him back down the *Via della Conciliazione*. They walked in absolute silence, all the way back to the Tiber.

"Your model," Caleb stated, as Michael stepped into the street in search of a taxi.

"It's late. We might have to wait a while."

"Your model," Caleb repeated.

"The mural," Michael said. "He's posing for me."

"I'd like to see that mural someday," Caleb said.

"I'd love to show you my work!"

"Tomorrow, maybe."

"Yes, yes. Oh! There's one now."

Michael told the driver where to take him, bade him good night, and the adventure was over. Caleb turned to watch out the rear window, half expecting the little imp to rematerialize out of the storm but all he saw was Michael, waving, smiling, and alone.

Thirteen

1

The telephone was ringing in the bedroom as Cutler stepped from the house and into the cool morning sunshine. The lake glistened off his left shoulder as he started across the small patch of grass to the dirt road where his Triumph waited in the dappled shade of newly leafed beech trees. Their tiny chartreuse leaflets trembled on the lake breeze. The sun striped their silver boughs with gold. Cutler took but casual note of the view and folded his bulky body into the little car. As he drove out from the speckled shade, a sea gull flashed, like a white accent on the clear blue sky. It let go and spattered his windshield with a smear of glistening, white dung.

"Shit," he said, flipping on the wipers. All they did was to spread the smear across the entire glass in a gauze-like arc.

He pulled over and reached out with a towel to wipe a spot clean and continued into town. He did not take the scenic lakeside drive as he might normally do, but the maple lined avenue that curved into town from behind the dunes, passing by the cemetery, and ending at the old wrought iron gate on the east side of the campus. He parked under a tree and went into a quaint brick building opposite the gate. Cutler paused in the gothic arch of the Faculty Building noting how the stone archivolts imitated in silent admiration the living branches of the hawthorn trees (*Crataegus monogyna*) that flanked the walkway.

A strange, unnatural sound emanated from the crumbling relic next door. A quintet was practicing in the chapel. Smooth and mellow tones issued from the stone walls, rounding and softening the other sounds one hears on sunny mornings in small towns. The sliding bows on cat gut strings somehow rendered forth a sound so sweet, he had to pause and listen, and the clarinet, like a soaring bird, flitted in silhouette past the sun touched glass of the rose window in the chancel. Mozart's melancholy "A" seemed a fitting compliment to Cutler's disillusioned "I."

He turned to enter the building and encountered a student he did not recognize at first. She told him the phone in his office had been ringing all morning.

"Thank you, I—"

"Have any travel plans for the summer, Professor Insbroek?"

"Paris, maybe."

"You'll be back in the fall? We all love you, you know."

She was hurrying away. He hadn't even seen her face in the brief encounter and was wondering what class she must have been in. He did not go to his office but left the sunny street side and started across the wooded campus. Science Hall lifted its brick gables above the trees beyond. Spring finals were in session and the pine grove was dotted with lounging students in baroque fashion, their outlandish clothes like beds of flowers among the conifers. They were reading and talking softly, enjoying the good change in weather that the morning had brought. Lakeside springs were often cold, and the hardy denizens knew how to appreciate the few sunny days with relish. Cutler smiled at the sight. This was his garden; these were his tender perennials, having been carefully nurtured through a winter of indecision. Waving hands greeted him from dormitory windows. Cutler smiled and returned the salutations, walking proudly among the grave, old buildings.

Hands in pockets to warm them, he paused again, and with appropriate reverence outside the little botanical laboratory situated just behind the Chem Building on the Old Campus. A glass house, his special project, glistening with dew in the Spring sunshine; his Winter Garden. Inside, benches of exotic specimens reached for the tropics, trailing, twining, branching, ignorantly searching the glass heights for what that transparent veil would always keep from them: freedom. Beautiful. It was a shining green gem within a setting of alien pines and the rough stone hewn classrooms to either side. *Le Jardin d'Hiver*, a plaque attached to the jamb proclaimed, was the project of Cutler Aemes Insbroek. He unlocked the door and went in: a summer pest house, intensely hot and humid and smelling of earth and mold and rotting plants.

On either side, stretching in all directions to the glassy limits of the crystal gothic palace, were strange and wild savages from the tropics, patiently abiding their shining showcase, biding their time. He closed the double glass door behind him, and all went silent. The distant call of the music, the mumbling of students reading aloud in the pine grove, the ambient sounds of small towns on average days—all went silent in reverend regard for the sanctity of this place. Even the fans stopped in reverence for his presence. He walked under sprays of arching empress palms flanking the door, an arbor of flaming *bougainvillea* overhead. Beyond were birds of paradise and *bromeliads, philodendrons, sansevieria* and *schefflera*, and dark and feathery *Podocarpus. Stephanotis* and gardenias saturated the heavy air with suffocating fragrance. The broad wings of arching bananas and the lacey fringe of hanging *lianas* framed bristling succulents and *dracaenas*, while *nephthitis* and *panduraeforms* filled in the spaces between. Prehistoric sago palms and tree ferns clustered at the rear. All were poised and waiting, tied and propped, crashed together, trellised and pruned, coiling and nodding unseen, anticipating the Grower's touch. And he touched them all as he moved about them, caressing their slick leaves, fondling their trembling tendrils. He praised them and reassured them, and they leaned back comfortably and at ease. All was at peace in the Winter Garden.

Then there was a tapping at the door, an almost obsequious rattling of fingernails against the glass. Cutler ignored the sound. It could have been the rustling of twigs in the wind or the dropping of hard seeds to the fallow concrete floor. Again, the tapping sounded. He paused in his bent position, having been studying the delicate skin of a potted succulent, and looked up through the fringed tunnel of arching fronds. A face showed through the wet glass; a face with plaintive eyes. Cutler sighed and turned away. He did not want to have to talk to Alison this day. He was enjoying his moments of peaceful solitude. But the face was persistent. It still hung there like a ghost, or a memory, caught like an ancient insect in amber glass. Cutler started toward the door.

It wasn't the sad and childlike face of Alison he'd seen. It was the soft but handsome face of Joseph Agnus.

Cutler motioned him in and a cool breeze invaded the place along with him. He was a small man with refined features, perfectly proportioned and carefully groomed. His hair was almost white with Nordic luster and his eyes the deep blue of cold oceans. He was fair, but the hue seemed appropriate to his nature. His arms and hands were strong and his face smooth as ivory. Having hesitated among the greenery, he could have been taken for a statue, a term of pan, a marble fawn exquisitely carved and radiant with recently endowed vitality. He was smiling, and his smile dispelled the cool breeze he'd brought in with him. Nonetheless, despite the touch of beauty he lent to the winter garden, Cutler was not happy to see him.

"I thought the door was locked," Joey was saying in his surprisingly resonant voice. "I know how you love to abide in this place."

Cutler smiled at last. Joey knew how to endear himself to those he cared for.

"The Mozart piece sounded wonderful," Cutler said.

"I thought it was you I saw through the window. We're practicing for commencement."

Beads of sweat were beginning to form on his forehead. "How's your garden growing?"

"Wonderful. I'm glad you stopped by."

"I've never been in here."

Cutler indicated a wooden bench nearby and Joey sat and watched as Cutler went about his mystical chores. "You know they've not renewed my contract," Joey was saying.

Cutler did not look at him. "I know. I'm sorry. I know how much you've liked it here."

"One more year and I'd have been tenured."

"I know, Joey."

He let out a reedy breath. "Well. I can always go back to playing clubs, I guess."

Cutler paused in his labor. He turned to face the other man. "Did they give you a reason?"

He shook his head, his eyes on the damp pavement. Cutler noticed that his gestures were not effeminate. How would anybody know, that didn't know him personally, he wondered. But someone did know, as Joey was explaining: a student complained to a parent. There was an exchange of telephone calls between the concerned parent and the chancellor. Then there was the short and tense meeting with the tenure committee.

Joey dropped his hands and turned his wet face upward. "I never touched him, Cutler. I considered him my friend. I thought he felt the same toward me."

Cutler placed a hand on his shoulder, but he shrugged it off.

"I'm not into sympathetic displays," Joey said, half-smiling. "Thanks, anyway."

Cutler observed, "They'd think nothing of it if it were a female student. Remember when John was first dating Alison and her parents threatened a lawsuit. The chancellor actually said he'd stand by his faculty no matter what."

"I understand Lewis won't be back either," Joey was saying.

Cutler nodded. Said something about the college becoming whiter and more conventional.

Joey merely nodded, then said, carefully, "I understand you've been dating her."

Cutler shook his head, having turned his back and gone back to puttering among the potted plants. He wasn't certain why he'd shaken his head. He explained that it wasn't exactly true. That Alison had been staying in his mother's house while she looked for a place of her own. She'd been depending on Cutler lately for companionship. Nothing more.

"Slept with her?"

"What?"

"Cutler?"

Cutler paused, keeping his back to the other man, then went back to work. Joey was quiet for a while. He was perhaps curious what Cutler was doing with all these exotic creatures. He had come up behind him to watch more closely. Cutler began explaining why he was pruning one plant but merely tying the other to a stake. He pointed out the tufts of fungus on the bark of the tree fern. The two of them leaned together into the damp foliage to search for hidden fruits. They reached together into the thick cloak of bougainvillea to touch the brilliant clusters of flowers wet with water from the glass they caressed in search of the sun. And then Joey said, "I never thought you were a man who cared that much for women's company, Cutler."

He had spoken in a soft and comfortable voice, neither one of accusation nor curiosity. They were very close, the two of them, shoulder-to-shoulder in the steam bath atmosphere of the little hothouse. Cutler ignored the comment and pointed at something among the tattered leaves of the *monstera deliciosa*.

"It's coming into fruit—"

Joey went on. "I mean: you're such an independent man. You're a true individual on this campus of paper doll cutouts. Like these plants, Cutler, you're a rare beauty, an exotic prisoner of the frigid north." He reached in front of him to caress the monstera's phallic flower sprout. "This is your real love, Cutler, isn't it? As my sonatas are for me?"

Cutler turned to him, face to face, nearly touching, and pushed him away. Joey's eyes were bright with mischief. Running water had limned the features of his face in lacy patterns that sparkled in the speckled sunlight. His hair was wet and curling about his ears, his shirt darkened at the shoulders and across his chest. His nipples had pursed themselves against the wet fabric. Cutler stepped back a bit.

"You're right to some degree," he admitted, in a throaty voice. "I cherish this place, these growing things, but not to the exclusion of real people, Joey."

"You spend hours in here, Cutler," Joey chided softly. "I know. I've stood long hours myself watching you through the glass."

"I know," Cutler said glancing about. "But they depend on me. I provide them with everything they require."

"And what do they do for you?"

"They grow," he said, barely above a whisper. "They prosper. They become even more beautiful."

"You can't do that with a person, can you?"

He did not respond so Joey added, "But it isn't in the nature of people like you and I to leave well enough alone, is it, Cutler?"

"What do you mean, like you and I?"

"Creative people," he said simply. "Sensitive people. People who are constantly seeking some kind of perfection in our lives."

Cutler took another step back into the greenery. He was sweating profusely. Joey had moved closer once more. Cutler pushed him aside and swiped his arm across his forehead, muttering some complaint about the ventilation system.

"What?"

"The fans aren't working lately. It shouldn't be this hot in here."

"It's the Garden of Eden." Joey smiled. "It's supposed to be hot for men like us."

"What do you fucking mean, like us?" Cutler suddenly shouted.

Joey stepped back, surprised. "What's wrong with you today, Cutler?"

Joey was right. Such behavior was very much unlike Cutler's normally reserved demeanor. He shook his head in embarrassment. "I don't know, maybe it's—"

"Alison?" Cutler turned and walked toward the other end of the small house. He momentarily disappeared among the fronds and tendrils. "Why do you suddenly seem so insistent on finding some fault in me, Joey?" he asked from somewhere in the thicket. "Is it because of your own misfortune?"

"Don't be an ass," Joey said steadily. The confident tenor of his voice caused Cutler to pause.

"Why, then?" He had pushed the vines out of his way and was peering back at where Joey stood. He was dowsed in sweat, glistening, as if he'd just stepped from the sea. Cutler asked again, "Why?"

"It is because I care about you," Joey returned steadily, coming forward. "I care about what happens to you, especially after what has happened to me, and it is pretty obvious to me this past few weeks, since Alison has inserted herself into your life, that you have become a man troubled and as you are my friend, that concerns me very much."

"Troubled? Nonsense." He released the handful of leafy vines and they fell again into place, cloaking him from view.

"Troubled!" Joey said, for the first time raising his voice, and pushing the greenery aside. "You're not the kind of person who can live a lie comfortably for very long."

"My relationship with Alison is not a lie." He had his back to him. He was trimming dead spikes off the *dracaena*.

"The relationship may not be, but the public image is. Isn't it?"

Cutler turned to face him. "How? How can you say that?"

Joey clasped his shoulders with both hands. "Because, my friend, I'm an expert at lying for sake of a public image."

He dropped his hands and relaxed a bit, asking as if out of context, "How old are you, Cutler? Oh, it doesn't matter. You're single, aren't you?" He raised his eyebrows. "A single man in his thirties who spends most of his time in his Winter Garden? Is that an apt description of you, Cutler Aemes Insbroek?"

Cutler had dropped onto a wooden bench with a great sigh. He was staring into his dirty hands. "What of it?"

Joey knelt on the floor before him and took hold of his hands. "Nothing. Nothing of it, as far as I'm concerned; but haven't you ever thought about what others in this exclusive, little community might be thinking?"

"Of course not. I—" He looked Joey in the eyes. "I know all that," he said. "I try not to worry about what other people think, Joey. I know myself better than you give me credit for, I think. I know my limitations."

"Limitations?" Joey interrupted.

"Let me finish. I know my limitations, but I've learned that limits can be extended, even overcome. I believe that."

"What do you think of me?" Joey asked, standing. Cutler seemed surprised at the apparent change in topic. "I'm serious, Cutler. I'm leaving at the end of the semester. You may never see me again. Now's your chance. What do you think of me? Why, for instance, do you think I'm single?"

Cutler answered softly, intentionally. "I suppose, like me, you haven't found the right person yet."

"You mean," Joey began softly, "the right kind of person?"

Cutler closed his mouth. "Yes."

He picked up a potted succulent that and gone yellow. Joey asked what was wrong with it. "Too much humidity. This isn't a very healthy place for some living things."

"How metaphorical of you," Joey said.

Cutler was looking at the wilted plant. "It isn't me you're in love with, is it?"

"Why don't you put the plant out in the sun and let it dry out for a while?" Joey suggested. "Would that help?"

"Might. Maybe it simply has a death wish. Maybe it wouldn't survive anyplace."

"So, what are you going to do with it?"

Cutler spread his hands and the pot dropped to the pavement with the sound bodies make when they fall. Joey jumped back in surprise.

"Why did you do that?"

"It didn't like it here."

"So, you killed it?"

"I'm the Grower. I gave it life."

Joey shuddered noticeably though it was sweltering in the place. "Why aren't the fans running?" he whined, ringing his hands.

"Timer switch, or something," Cutler was saying. "Let's get out of here."

"What about the—"

"My students will clean it up."

He had started for the door, but Joey had grabbed him by the arm and pulled him back. "Cutler," he said sternly. "Why are you pretending to have a sexual relationship with Alison?"

"Because I want to," was his answer. "Why are you still alone, Joey?"

"Because I love someone I cannot have."

Cutler heaved a great sigh, filling his body with what the plants breathed out. "I know, Joey. I know." Then he broke free of the other's grasp and strode to the door.

Joey said after him, "There is a great difference, you know, between what you want to be and what you really are, Cutler Insbroek."

Cutler opened the door and left the Winter Garden. The fans came on as he left, rustling the greenery. Joey glanced about and smiled at the rush of fresh air. "Cutler. Look. The fans."

Cutler had paused at the sound. He was standing just beyond the glass looking back as Joey came forth. The door closed behind him and he paused to say one last word to his friend. "I just wanted to say these things to you while there was still time."

Tears were escaping Cutler's eyes, mingling with the sweat on his cheeks. He smiled slightly, with a little embarrassment. The expression on Joey's face was of both wonder and surprise. They continued to stare at each other for some time.

As they walked away from the Winter Garden, the cool breeze puckering the damp skin under their clothes, Cutler was asking if there was anyone in Joey's life. He was shaking his head. Never had been, but for those occasional lapses in upright moral conduct. He laughed with the words. "Otherwise, mostly celibate, Cutler. Easier that way."

Cutler sighed that maybe, someday, growing up and mixing in with the rest of us will be easier for men like him. Joey had come to a stop at the sound of his words. "Yes," he said, a note of sarcasm in his voice, "for men like me."

He started to walk away, whistling, and may not have heard Cutler saying something, mostly to himself. Joey stopped, then continued on his way, whistling.

Cutler smiled and watched him walk away. He stood for some time in a sunny spot at the edge of the Pine Grove, then, he started for the car. He was soaked to the skin. He shrugged his body out of his tee shirt and flung it over his shoulder. As he walked back toward the street beyond the gothic gateway, he could hear Joey whistling the clarinet part from the *adagio* of Mozart's Quintet in A minor. He stood by the car until the tune had faded behind the gentle cacophony common to small towns on sunny days and then he slid into the warm interior, and he drove away.

The little glass house, its panes cracked and shattered, its shelves scattered with broken crockery and a compost of decaying botanicals still stands behind the Chem Building on the Old Campus, a crumbling relic of the past, barely visible today within its thick cloak of Virginia creeper vines. *Parthenocissus quinquefolia.*

2

Naked on top of the sheets, Cutler lay spread-eagled, eyes wide open. It was a hot night with no wind. The windows of his room were open, the sound of waves turning on the beach below providing little distraction from the heat. Distant thunder trembled in the west and a flickering red glow occasionally slithered across the ceiling. The waves were building. They sounded as if they were at the very sill of the casements. The curtains lifted on a breeze, but it was a warm one. Then they retreated and pressed themselves against the screens. He flung himself over, burying his face in the damp pillow. A flash of light dashed about the room and a thud of thunder shook the rafters. Cutler rolled over and sat up.

The drapes jumped into the air on the hot breath of the night wind. They stretched and fluttered like magicians' hands reaching for the bed. Then they slapped back against the screens with a racket. The sky went yellow behind them then blackened at the call of the thunder. The storm was nearing. Waves were crashing almost on top of each other at the fragile beaches below. Rain was pelting against the walls, spattering through the screens.

Cutler went to close the windows. The splash of rain over his body was soothing and he paused before latching the panels shut. Water poured down the panes of glass as if they were melting. Lights flashed and lingered in the running rain. Trees danced and bowed at the behest of the wind, then struck against the house with a vengeance. Cutler stood back a bit.

The storm was raging all about him now, on all sides. He turned his back on it and quietly left the room, slipping on his robe as he crossed the threshold into the upper hall. He found his way to the open landing, half illuminated by the almost constant flashing of lightning. Wind whistled through the old house like a pipe organ, different pitches at each corner. He descended into the house and, guided by the phantom light, found the double glass doors that led to the sunroom. This room, just beneath his, was likewise walled with windows on the three sides that faced the lake. He sat in the old wicker swing and sighed pathetically.

"Beautiful night, huh?" Alison's voice. He closed his eyes, wishing to shut her out of his present existence.

"Depends on your point of view, I suppose."

"I like this room," she said. "I quite often sit here the whole night long."

He turned toward her, or, that is, toward the sound that came from the blur of white in the armchair nearby. "All night?"

She laughed lightly. "I haven't been sleeping much lately, it seems. Not like me at all."

"I'm glad you're enjoying your stay with us," he started to say, with as little emotion in his tone as he could manage.

"I'll miss this room," she was saying, over top of his words.

"What?" He sat up; a dark silhouette against the flashing lights. "You going someplace?"

"I can't stay here forever, Cutler, now can I?" Her voice was soft and whiney, like the wind at the windows.

He sat back and asked, as if bored with the topic, "Where will you go?"

"Back to John I suspect."

It was quiet for a while—silent of words though the storm continued its noisy assault on the old house. Cutler was sort of mumbling and Alison asked him to speak up. "John?" he asked, louder. "I kind of thought he was out of the picture."

"Was. For a while. But, well. Who else?" He mentioned causally that he thought she was looking for a job and a place to stay in town.

"Not in my condition," she returned all too quickly. "I mean, it wouldn't be healthy, I shouldn't think."

"Whatever you say," he said, clearly weary of the small conversation.

Thunder cracked overhead, shaking the house to its crumbling foundations. Wind slapped at the clapboarding and rain and hail pelted against the windows. Then it was quiet for a while, but for Alison's rambling.

"I'm getting along famously with your mom," she was saying. "I can see why she has so many friends. I can talk to her about things I'd never be able to say to my mother."

"Have you told her about—"

"No. I don't want her to think badly of me."

"Why should she think badly of you? Having a baby is a nice thing."

"For a married woman, it is."

"Oh." He stood and walked to the window. The storm had already vented its anger and the wind was calming. Thunder still pounded the inland hills behind the house. There was still a grumbling in the floors and rain still pattered across the roofs like running feet. Cutler had opened the window and a fresh breeze blew in from the lake. "Oh, that feels good," he sighed.

"Besides;" Alison was still talking, though he had stopped listening. "Nobody knows but you, you know—"

He turned to her. "You haven't told John?"

"My god, Cutler! He didn't want to marry me. He surely isn't going to want me to have his child."

"What do you intend to do?" he asked carefully.

She let out a big sigh and came up next to him. "I thought I might say it's yours. If that's all right with you."

"It certainly is not. I have a reputation to maintain, too, you know." Cutler started from the room, but Alison kept talking from her place by the opened window. "You're right, Cutler. And that reputation could use a little boost if you ask me." He paused. "I thought you'd be glad about it."

He was shaking his head as he turned a third time to face her. "What do you mean by that?"

"Well, people wouldn't be going around asking questions about your relationship with women anymore."

"My relationship with—" He dropped again into the swing. "You mean to tell me that some people have nothing better to do than to talk about the fact that Cutler Insbroek doesn't date?"

"Not just some people," Alison said cheerily. "Most everybody talks about it. Even your mom."

"My mother!" He stood once more and started again from the room.

Alison was laughing. Again, he paused. "Cutler," she chided. "You didn't believe all that bullshit, did you?"

He paused, and she came up behind him. "Come on. You know better than that. I made it all up."

"Even the baby?"

She merely shrugged.

"And what are you going to do about it?" He had inquired over his shoulder.

"I told you," she said, passing him and starting up the stairs. "I'm going to tell John it's yours."

"It could be, you know." She stopped and spun about on the third tread. "How? Osmosis?"

"If you hadn't been John's girl, I'd have gone to bed with you," he said.

"Really?" She adjusted her fists to her hips. A soft and almost flattering light fell upon her from the landing above. "Well," she said, "I'm not his girl anymore. I haven't been for almost two months and we're living in the same house and you haven't even looked at me since I've been here. Really, Cutler, get real!"

"I knew about the baby. I know you love John."

"Then you know too much."

"What?"

She had started up again and he pursued her, stopping her on the sixth stair. "What is it you want, Alison?" he asked. "What is it you really want?"

She struggled to be free of his grasp then relaxed. "Want? Easy, Cut. I want to be John's wife and the mother of his child."

"But, why?"

She shrugged. "I don't know, I just do. Is that too much to ask?"

"I guess not. Why don't you try and make it happen?"

"I did try," she said sharply, pulling her arms away. "I failed."

"Try again. Try harder. Seems to me someone who knows so certainly what they want ought to go after it at any cost."

"Yeah? And what about you," she asked. "You seem to be content with less than I have. What do you want, Cutler Insbroek?"

"Me?" He drew his hand to his chest. Then he sort of laughed and shrugged at the same time. "Good question."

She put her hands to her hips again, hiking up her nightgown. "Here you are a man of wealth and education, a Ph. Something or other, a professor, world traveler and a socialite and you don't know what you want out of this life?"

"I never really asked the question, I guess."

"Boy, I did," she said pouting, and sitting on the step. Her voice took on a distance associated with unpleasant memories. "As long as I can remember, I've been asking the question."

Cutler sat next to her. "How did you discover the answer?"

"It was easy," she said, a hint of bitterness in her tone. "I simply decided I wanted everything I didn't have as a child. Love."

He stood up suddenly. "And you chose to go with John Caleb Wilson?"

She bowed her head. "He was the first man in my life. He was the only one I ever knew aside from my father. He is a lot like my father. I guess I didn't think there was any other kind of man, so I stayed. Until I met you."

"Me? You never told me that."

"No," she said, peering up at him out of the darkness that attended her, just her eyes mostly. "It wasn't that I was attracted to you, Cutler, it's just that—I discovered you to be another kind of man. Thoughtful, gentle, soft spoken, refined—and not the least bit interested in me."

He laughed lightly. "I guess I am all those things, aren't I?"

She reached out her hand for assistance in standing. As he lifted her up, she pressed herself against his body. He let out a heavy breath. "You're the first man I've ever known—including my father—who didn't touch me with lustful intentions."

They stood close together on the sixth step. Cutler took another breath, swelling his chest against her, and breathed an almost subliminal, "Christ!"

She rested her hand on his shoulder, whining, "Life sucks, doesn't it, Cutler?"

He threw his arm around her, pulled her to him gruffly, and they embraced. Outside, the wind was picking up again. Another storm was brewing in the west.

3

It was raining again. Had he cared to look up from where he lay on the bed, he might have seen the sky flashing on and off. He might have seen the branches beyond the windows swaying in the wind. Had he even cared to open his eyes he might have seen his naked body stretching away from his shoulders and the knot of arms about his chest. He might have noticed how the wet sheets seemed to make a white hole in the dark room; the tangle of legs, a darker hole in them. Knees touching knees and toes interlocked. He might have seen the swollen abdomen and the bulging breasts like melons cradled in crossed arms. He might have seen her face so close to his, not fair and glowing as in daylight, but dark and angular, hard and hurt somewhere deep inside. Alison kissed him, and he opened his eyes but saw only a net of hair that lay like a snare across his face.

"It's raining again," she said at his ear.
"I know. I can hear it on the roof."
"It's a nice sound. You comfortable?"
"Very."
"Want to try again?"
"A little while," he said.

She sighed into his cheek. Her hand was moving over his hand and along his wrist, gripping and stroking. His eyes were blinking in the nest of her hair. He could see the contour of her face but in the non-light her features were indistinct. Try as he might as he lay there in her embrace, he could not remember what she looked like. He could feel the press of her hand, the moist softness of her mouth, the bulge of her body, but he could not see her.

She had taken hold of his hand and moved it to her breast. He began to press his fingers into it, full of milk, he supposed. He toyed with the large and erect nipple.

"Put it in your mouth," she whispered. "It will make us both feel good." She slid down a bit and pressed his face against the breast. He could sense its fullness and milk-like taste. Alison was breathing very deeply, and it rose and fell away from him. He had to stretch his chin out to reach the nipple and she laughed. He opened his mouth wide. He felt the night air touch his tongue and his teeth. He pushed his face into the breast, his mouth enclosing the nipple, and he sucked as deeply as Alison had sighed—but there was no taste.

Alison was massaging him somewhere, but he couldn't tell where. He was relaxing in some places, tensing in others. He was dry and cool in some parts, hot and sweaty in others. He felt confident and embarrassed, sensuous and clumsy, ignorant and knowing all at once. He tightened his arms about her. She slid her body over his in a slow damp spiral. He spread her legs with his knees and vivisected her with the fingers of his left hand. With the right, he was scratching his thigh.

Her mouth was at his throat. She was biting him. His mouth was in her thick hair. It caught in his teeth. He pressed himself into her but had to arch over the promontory of her belly.

"Careful," she cautioned.

He pulled back. "It's okay. I think I'm finished."

She was pulling him back. "You haven't started yet, she said."

She squirmed herself into place, using her hand to guide him.

"There," she breathed. "Isn't that better?"

"It's so strange," he started to say.

"Analyze it later," she cried in a breath.

She flipped him over, settled upon him and began to ride him like a rodeo bull. He flung his arms aside with the force of her thrust and his mouth broke open in a silent shout. His air burst out in rhythms timed to her movements and to the building storm beyond the windows. He clasped her arms and rolled her over, using his own power to force himself deeper and deeper into her. They both burst forth with a gasp akin to that of the soul when it leaves the body.

They did not part for some time. They did nothing at all. Nor did they speak. Rain was pouring in upon them. It spattered against their shoulders and trickled down their arms. It caught in their hair and flowed in delicate trails about their eyes. It touched the corners of their mouths and they smiled.

"You did it," Alison said.

"Did I?"

"Did you like it?"

"Analyze it later," he said, nestling himself down beside her. Then, "Did you?"

She nodded within his embrace. "You're right."

"About what?"

"You could have been the father."

"I will be, if you want me to be."

She kissed him gently. "Thank you, Cutler. The baby already has a father."

"But you don't have a husband."

"I know," she said softly. "But that's not for you and both you and I know it."

He breathed out slowly. "I suppose you're right."

"But I thank you from the bottom of my heart for asking."

"It felt right," he said, "at the time."

Naked on top of the sheets, they drifted off into a kind of sleep, each into his own kind of sleep; Alison into a fretful twitching and moaning slumber filled with images of empty rooms and stairways to nowhere, Cutler into a waking kind, his eyes on the ghostly patterns that swirled and slithered across the walls and ceiling.

The night had cooled. The windows let in a comfortable breeze and the reassuring sound of waves gently turning themselves over on the beaches below. Just before dawn, Alison got up and wrapped herself in her nightly. She paused a while before the windows, on the rim of Cutler's frayed vision, then she left the room.

4

Thunder shook the little house to its foundations and Lizzie blinked her eyes open in rhythm with the flashing lights. She found herself lying across John's body, her head on his chest. The bedside lamp was yet burning as she turned her eyes upward to see if he was asleep. He was reading, the book resting on her shoulder.

"It's the middle of the night, John," she said in a cracked voice. "Can't you sleep?"

"I want to finish this book," he said, as if from a distance.

"Oh" she said. She nestled herself into him a bit, seeking the comforting sound of his heart but it had gone silent. Even storm sounds were softening as the thunder had retreated into the eastern heavens. She let her eyes take in what they could, given the dim interior and the heap of sheets that engirdled their hips. The mirror on the bathroom door, Alison's mirror, reflected the scene back to her. She spoke to John's indifferent reflection. "We're just about finished, you and I, aren't we, John?"

"Don't be silly," he said with the turn of a page.

"No," she said. "It's time. We never seem to last very long together. Our passion for each other comes with an expiration date already affixed at the factory." He turned another page. "Bad metaphor."

"I'm a romance writer, remember?"

"Maybe that's why."

"Why, what?"

"Why we never last very long." He put down the book and rested a warm hand on her shoulder.

She lifted her head a little to better see him by way of the mirror. "My stories always end happily," she insisted.

"For the heroine," he said. "Not necessarily for the hero."

"Marriage," she sighed. "You're right. I guess that is why most of my readers are women."

"You always justify the lover's relationships, no matter how lewd, with that ultimate benediction," John said, "as if the marriage in the last chapter absolves the preceding two hundred pages of any sexual promiscuity."

"My god," she said, sitting up, "you make me sound like a pornographer!"

"In a way, you are. Me too, I suppose. We take the very best virtues our species is able to muster and turn them upon themselves like the monster Scylla. So disgusted have we become with our own blighted beauty we feed upon ourselves as if to rid the stinking world of any trace of us. And then, we write our memoirs for others to read that they too would have reason to hate what they helped us to become."

"We have become a race of Scyllas," he said, "each of us intent on devouring our own rotting carcasses."

"Stop it," she cried. "You're being ridiculous!"

He smiled strangely. "Must be the Poe I just ate," he said, holding up the book.

Lizzie shuddered and lay back down, smoothing her nightshirt about her as she did. "I know what it is. It's autumn. Winter is upon us. We can't seem to abide each other during the holidays."

"What do you mean?"

"Last time, we parted on Christmas Eve. I remember because it was the most horrible day I've ever had to endure."

"Yes," he said. "I remember. I had bought you a gift I never got around to giving you."

She caught his attention by way of the mirror. "You did? How sweet. What was it?"

"A silk nightgown."

She smiled. "You still have it?"

He shrugged. "I probably gave it to Alison."

"Oh. Well. I'm sure she loved it."

"She still wears it."

Lizzie closed her eyes at the sound of the emotion in his voice. "Can we agree on something, John?"

"What's that?"

"Can we wait until after the holidays to part this time?"

He nodded. "I suppose."

"Can we exchange presents?"

He nodded again.

"And could we have a little party? Like married couples do?"

She didn't wait for his answer. She closed her eyes and snuggled herself against him. He took up the book and rested it on her shoulder. She said his name very softly.

"Umm?"

"What will you do afterwards?"

"Another Poe, I suppose."

She had meant, "after us!"

"I don't know." He turned a page. "I haven't really thought about it."

"Will you go back to Alison?"

He closed the book and set it aside. "Probably." He switched off the light and the room settled back at last into the arms of the night.

"Will you marry her?"

"Hmm?"

"Will you—"

He sighed. "I suppose. It seems the right thing to do, somehow."

Lizzie opened her eyes but this time they saw nothing as the room had gone black. "Yes," she said very softly. "It does seem the right thing to do, doesn't it?"

"Does that hurt you, Liz?"

"A little. But I knew it was coming."

He breathed out a heavy breath. "Like you say; we seem to have a predetermined expiration date. Alison and I; oh, I don't know, despite everything, we just seem to keep going on and on."

"How lucky for you," she said flatly.

"Yeah. Funny how separation brings out the realist in a man."

"In a woman, too," she said. "My next novel isn't going to be so womanly."

"Lizzie. You are, if nothing else on this planet, a woman! Don't ever slight yourself on that one."

"Okay," she said, as he slid down close to her. They embraced. "But it takes a man to bring out the woman in me. That is my problem, it seems. I never seemed to learn how to do it myself."

"Well," he said at her ear, "since you are a woman at the moment, and I am a man, let's do what men and women do."

"You mean, besides quarrel?"

"There are all manner of words for it," he said into the hollow of her throat. "It's all in the interpretation."

"Analyze it later," she said, throwing her arms about him.

Beyond the windows, the sky was clearing. September thunderstorms were giving over to frosty nights as regularly as leaves fall and the stars turn upon their northern spindle until the Pleiades rest in the east and the giant Orion marches to his annual death by drowning in the southern oceans.

Part III
This Strange Persecution

Fourteen

Hereupon, a whole host of absurd figures surrounded him, pretending to sympathize in his mishap. Clowns and parti-coloured harlequins; orang-outangs; bear-headed, bull-headed, and dog-headed individuals; faces that would have been human, but for their enormous noses; one terrific creature, with a visage right in the centre of his breast; and all other imaginable kinds of monstrosity and exaggeration…

Hawthorne, *The Marble Faun*

Jo was a blaze of color. She pirouetted in the doorway laughing. She wore lipstick and painted nails, a brilliant red, and she had silk flowers laced among the curls of her wig. She wore a seventeenth century styled day dress of red silk, somewhat tattered, having been purchased at one of the smaller costume shops in Dorsoduro. She had had to take it in at the waist and had covered her less than accurate sewing job with a sash of pink velvet, draped over her hip and fronted at the abdomen with a great bow. More silk flowers embellished the tattered hems of the old theatre gown and she had sewn some onto the yellow gloves she carried in her left hand. Caleb was sitting on the edge of his bed in his under shorts watching her. He was quiet compared to her sudden burst of levity. He had been preoccupied ever since they'd alighted in Venice the night before. She was trying to be conciliatory.

"What do you think? I had so much fun shopping this morning! I found a real bargain. Caleb? What do you think?"

He grinned. "I doubt it's very authentic, but it's great, Jo. You will definitely catch their attention."

She was looking over her shoulder at herself in his mirror. Her room across the hall didn't have one as big. She had been talking nonstop since arriving at his door in her newfound persona. "It was so nice of Michael to get us these rooms, Caleb. I don't know how he did it, being Carnival, and all."

"He knew some people who had to cancel. Least wise, that's what he told me."

"One of the rooms was in his name, did you notice that? Who was the other one reserved for?" She had paused in her primping to kneel with her back to him. "Undo me, will you? This thing weighs a ton!"

"You'll be exhausted by midnight."

"I don't care! I've always wanted to come to Carnival in Venice." She turned and kissed him quickly, before he had the chance to turn aside; "and here I am."

"Actually, I think he still plans on using one of these rooms," Caleb said, in response to her earlier question.

She stood up, the dress settling with a rustle about her feet. She was wearing a black leotard underneath. "He's coming here?" He shrugged. "I'm not sure. We've not been communicating very well lately."

"Likewise," she interjected, stepping out of her dress, her hand resting casually on Caleb's shoulder. He went on. "I mean; when he called to give me the name of the hotel, he said, 'see you there.' I think that means he plans on joining us." Jo had started fidgeting with the silk flowers caught in her hair. "Which room do you suppose he'll want?"

"The one with the single bed, I suppose."

"Mine."

"What's the matter, Jo?" he asked, with sarcasm in his voice, "don't you want to sleep with me anymore?"

She looked to him, hands on hips. "I do sleep with you, Caleb, on a regular basis; but lately, that's all it's been—sleep!"

He smiled with some embarrassment, lowering his eyes. "I told you; I'm stressed. I'm having problems with one of my characters. I told you that. It's why I accepted Michael's offer for the rooms. I thought it might be good for us—you and I—to get away from Rome for a while."

She softened, taking his hand in hers and sitting next to him. "I know, Cabby. I'm sorry." Then she changed both her mood and the subject with an adroit snap of her head. "So! What are you going to wear tonight?"

He stood slowly. "We'll, I've been shopping, too." He went to the *guardaroba* and opened the mirrored doors. He retrieved a *Mefisto* costume complete with a long pheasant's feather in the cap. "If you can go as Columbine," he said, "I can go as Scaramouche!"

"You devil," she laughed, apparently pleased he was beginning to get into the Carnival spirit. They embraced.

"Sex?" he asked.

"What should we do about the other room?"

He was unzipping her leotard, a gentle rippling down her back. "We'll think about it later."

"I'd better lock the door."

"Later."

"Wait a minute!" She stood back, pulling herself back into her leotard. "What if Michael shows up! Jesus, Caleb, can't you concentrate on more than one thing at a time?"

He watched her bundling up the dress and hurrying to the door. He watched her stumble across the hall to the other room and he watched the door shut behind her. He stood for some time in the center of the modestly furnished little room and stared out his opened door at her closed one. Then he pulled on his pants and crossed the hall. He tried the handle. The door was latched. He called her name.

"Jo? Lunch?"

He knocked and called her again. Her door opened. She was sullen. Apologized. He said it didn't matter. She suggested that it should matter but agreed it probably didn't. He asked again, "Lunch?"

"I'm starved," she said, softly, keeping her eyes away from his.

"We both are," he said. He returned to his room for his pea coat. "Is it still raining?" he asked over his shoulder.

She checked the gray view out her window. "Stopped." They paused then, in their respective doorways, and stared at each other from across the space of the narrow hall. "Ready?" she wondered. He nodded. "Should we leave a note for Michael?"

"At the desk."

She nodded. They pulled their doors shut behind them as they filed into the dark corridor, she behind him. As they neared the open stair, the musky scent of the winter canals touched them, and they pulled their scarves about their throats as they entered upon the overcast afternoon. They walked in silence up the narrow alleyway to the misshapen *Campo Diagonale*. Its narrow side fronted a juncture of canals and there were two small trattorias there, one at each quay. Though the weather was wintry, the place on the right had a few outdoor tables set under canopies, radiant heaters tucked up under the lips of the canvas umbrellas. One intrepid couple sat huddled together at the nearest table. Without hesitation, Jo and Caleb chose the other table: at quayside. The seats were wet and the *cameriere* wiped them vigorously. He watched them as he worked, then motioned with a smile for them to sit. He was a boy of about sixteen with the mannerisms of a lecherous old roué. His smile was almost a leer. His voice annoyingly sensuous. Jo was enthralled. Caleb was bored. They sat in silence and watched the grey-green canal water slip casually by on its way to the lagoon and the rolling Adriatic Sea beyond.

A gentle but chilly rain was falling. It dimpled the placid canal with pox marks. A banner of haze lay suspended a few yards above the water and the old palaces beyond seemed to rise out of it as if they were just getting out of bed. The view was entirely colorless, but for a blue plastic bag that was floating down the canal in its course.

Jo was eying the other outdoor couple nearby. They were both annoyingly handsome people, she with her dark hair tied up in a stylish silk bandana, he, balding, wearing a camel-colored cashmere scarf. They were leaning against each other, talking quietly.

"I wonder what they're talking about so softly?" Caleb was perusing the menu. He merely shrugged.

"I think we should wait until spring," Ireni was saying, in Italian and in a very soft tone. She spoke in a round voice, held in suspended animation just above a whisper.

"No-o," Massimo mused, his voice almost the color of the dark wine he sipped as he talked. "I want not to wait, *carina*."

"But your mother! She won't be back from Calabria until then." He pursed his lips sensuously. "My mother doesn't like you, so what does it matter?" She assumed a playful pout, sitting back slightly in her chair, apparently mindless of others in the small piazza. "And Maria Pia? What of her?"

"Pia?" He too sat back, but just a little. "My wife? Ireni," he scolded, "you know she has no head for business. That's why she lives in the country." Ireni snuggled up next to him. "I'm cold. Let's go in." They started to collect their glasses, their purses and their umbrellas. She noticed the Americans then and whispered near Massimo's ear, "Look. How cute. They brave this horrible weather like lovers. How I envy them."

"Why?" he wondered casually. "You have had your romantic days, I'm certain."

"Ye-s," she said, loud enough for the American woman to have heard her. "But so long ago, Massimo. I miss it."

"Isn't your Mario attentive enough to suit you?" There was just a hint of sarcasm in his tone and she smiled slightly at the sound of his voice, her eyes on the table, where she traced the designs on the tablecloth with her lacquered fingernails.

"But, yes," she insisted. "His appetite is wonderful. You know how much I love him, but—The mystery is gone."

He glanced over his shoulder at the Americans as he ducked out from under the canopy. "They don't look very romantic to me," he laughed lightly.

"Oh," she exclaimed, in the Italian manner. "You know the Americans!"

They were laughing as they passed near the Americans' table and went into the cafe. They took seats near the front window so that Ireni could continue to watch the young couple at the canal side table.

"So," Massimo began, "you would rather wait until April to open the branch office?"

She nodded from her place across from him. She didn't have to hug him for protection against the cold now since the cafe was brimming with kitchen warmth. "Do you still want me to manage it, or should I stay in Florence? I know your mother owns the business and she might not want me running the Lido branch."

He was rubbing his chin. "Ye-s," he mused. "We shall have to plan this very carefully." Then, "In the meanwhile, why don't you and Mario join Pia and me for the weekend. The children would love to see you."

"They talk so softly," Jo observed, her eyes on the couple just getting up from the nearby table, "the Italians; especially when being intimate. It bothers me I can't eavesdrop on their conversations. How wonderfully romantic their talk must be."

"What"? Caleb hadn't been paying attention. "You don't know their story. For all we know, they're brother and sister. You know how affectionate the Italians can be."

She glared at him. "Were you ever romantic, Caleb?"

He answered without hesitation, "No. Never. Sorry." She sighed again and sipped at her wine. "It's all right. Funny," she added, in footnote, "when I got the invitation to come to Rome, all I could think about was how wonderful it would be to have a place to write my poetry unencumbered by the real world. I never once fantasized about the possibility of meeting a dashing Italian man and running off to Carnival in Venice with him—Or something like that." She let out a heavy sigh. "And yet, I realize now that the fantasy was actually always there, somewhere in the back of my mind, and now I suddenly feel irreconcilably sad."

He looked up at her at last, taking her gloved hand in his. "Sad? Why?" he wondered, "Because I'm not a dashing Italian?"

"Silly!" she said, sort of looking away, but still keeping the Italian couple in her line of sight. "No. My time in Italy is nearly over," she whined. "Come Spring Term and I'm back at my teaching job in Ohio. (Ohio, she repeated to herself, just a motion of the lips.) My time is nearly over here, and the fantasy is unfulfilled." Tears had collected in the corners of her pale eyes. She was suddenly embarrassed as she wiped her face on her napkin. "I don't know what's come over me!"

Caleb started talking, almost as if she were not there at all. Something she had said had awakened him, had stirred his own fantasies to rise out of the haze of his present boredom. At first Jo refused to listen, but Caleb was an accomplished storyteller. Soon she was sitting back in her chair, her wine glass poised before her, staring into the mists of Caleb's dark mind, enthralled.

"Having alighted in Italy," he said, "a land in which physical beauty is pandemic, I found myself feeling suddenly ordinary. Isn't that odd? I'd never felt ordinary before."

She might have been thinking that it was usual for her to feel that way, but she let him ramble on, anyway.

"The feeling was, I suppose, a necessary adjustment to my character; the kind of adjustment I'd been told by others of lesser character that was required if I was ever expected to have a decent relationship with another person—especially a woman. My arrogance. Is that what it was they complained of, Jo? You must have an opinion on that subject."

"Don't get me involved in your little debate, Caleb." She laughed lightly, but it was a forced laugh.

He went on. "Hawthorne would have described that adjustment as a natural and important change of course in my Life's Journey. Remember? He saw life as a pilgrimage, not from a birth stained with the mark of Original Sin, to a death sweetened by Divine Salvation; but from a birth divinely inspired toward an end blessed with fulfillment." His voice faded a bit then. He was staring blankly at the canal, or what could be seen of it through the ruddy mist that floated just above its grey skin.

"Life is not merely a means to an end but a process in and of itself, a process of self-realization and inner contentment—"

He turned back to her momentarily as if seeking some kind of affirmation on her part. She merely nodded.

"You see, Jo—" He seemed to be having difficulty finding the words. "It's like the Soul of the Creator is overreaching, encompassing all things, both external—the substance of God—and internal; that individual core of divine wisdom inherent in each created being, that nugget of common sense with which each of us is born. Is that it?"

Jo asked, "You mean that all creations of God are endowed with Divinity because they were divinely ordained?"

"Uh huh. But, since humans were also given an intellect, we enjoy special privileges: guilt, sorrow, anger and intelligence. The first three are selfish. Only intelligence is generous." She was saying that it sounded a bit arrogant. That only intelligent people could be generous. He was shaking his head and laughing lightly.

"You don't get my point," he exclaimed. "By intelligence, I mean common sense, self-knowledge, which we all have—if we choose to use it."

"Most of us have forgotten how to think for ourselves," he explained. "We let others speak for us, preachers and politicians. We've forgotten how to trust in our own judgement."

They were served their steaming plates of lasagna and they started to eat in silence. Jo admitted after a few moments that he was right about that last statement. She looked up, red sauce on her chin. He reached over with his napkin to wipe her mouth as she was saying, "It's time we started listening to the voice of our own consciousness." He nodded but apparently had not considered the seriousness of her words. Nor had he noticed the intensity of her expression. Without realizing it, so caught up with his own inner turmoil as he was, he had given her just the advice she needed.

"It's time I start listening to my own music," she said, absently, her eyes on the couple departing from the nearby table.

They went back to their meals and continued to sit in silence for some time, long after the other couple had left. She leaned over to embrace him and then, she kissed him on the cheek. "Let's go, shall we?" she suggested at his ear. "I have a lot of work to do on that stupid costume."

He nodded in silence and went to the doorway, motioning for the young man. He came out, but only as far as the canopy over the door and handed Caleb a sheet of paper. Then, having paid the bill, having tipped the *cameriere*, the two started off into the misty rain, hunching into their clothing and hugging each other for warmth, after a fashion.

From inside the warm trattoria, the Italian couple watched them by way of the steamy windows.

"How I envy them," Ireni sighed. "Look how much in love they are."

Massimo agreed. "I envy him what's going to happen next."

"Massimo!" she cried with a laugh. "Don't be naughty. We have too much business to talk about to think of pleasure."

"Could you ever go to bed with me?" he asked casually. "Just out of curiosity, of course."

She leaned her chin in the palm of her red-gloved hand. "How sweet you are, Massimo. Of course, I could not, my love! You are much too old for me."

"Ah," he said, playfully. "And you are far to vain for me."

"Good," she smiled. "Then we should have no trouble working together as business partners."

And they went back to studying the charts she had taken from her valise.

Caleb and Jo wandered arm in arm down the narrow walkways of Dorsoduro. It was one of the older sections of Venice, a collection of islands stitched together by a web of canals that glistened like silk banners in the afternoon ambience. Caleb spoke of a favorite church, the family church of the painter Tintoretto. It is off the tourist route, on the other side of the Grand Canal and it is nearly empty of pilgrims this time of day. It is a huge barn of a place, gothic vaulted and brick walled, its massive nave larger than most of the piazzas of Venice. He asked Jo if she would like to visit the place before going home to dress for Carnival. It was a bit of a walk, he explained, since it was located in Cannaregio, beyond the Ghetto. Without awaiting her answer, he started off.

They walked at a good clip, their hard shoes sounding on the damp stones of the walkways. They walked hand in hand, but Caleb was clearly way ahead of her, his eyes already on the magnificent paintings of the apse, his breathing already hushed by the luminous presence of the artist. He was walking nearly at a march. Jo watched him as they went, as he led her around corners and over ornate marble bridges. She had fallen in love with him, she knew, and she was not happy about it.

They came to the Grand Canal at *Ponte Santa Lucia*. The quays were alive with people, coming and going, hawking their wares, studying their maps, adjusting their elaborate costumes. A gentle mist contributed to the atmosphere of peaceful gloom, of impending doom, of the slow dyeing of an ancient city.

They paused at the top of the bridge. The canal was filled with gondolas, each in turn filled with women in rococo gowns and high powdered wigs and men in black velvet waistcoats and tricorns. The world had been rendered into black and white at the behest of the revelers. Only an occasional red scarf or banner interrupted the otherwise perfect dichromatic symmetry. Jo turned from the gaudy scene toward the bridge itself. A prostitute in a bridal gown was parading up the bridge from Cannaregio. She was immense, wore her yellow hair atop her head and her gown décolleté, so that her nipples peaked over top of the lacy bodice. She had hiked her skirts up to her thighs, as if traversing puddles, and her unshaved vagina shouted in black and red amongst the subtler colors of that rainy afternoon. Jo turned back to watch the spectacle on the canal below. Caleb had not seen the little episode behind him, and she smiled secretly.

"My God in heaven," she mused.

"What?"

"All this pageantry. Isn't it marvelous?"

"Everyone likes a parade," he replied as casually as he could.

They turned off the loud and crowded *Lista di Spagna* into a dark alleyway. Caleb insisted he knew a shortcut to the church of *Santa Maria del' Orto*.

"Holy Mary of the Garden." Jo said. "Isn't it a lovely name?"

"It's a veiled reference to her body," Caleb said. "The secret garden of heavenly bliss, and all that rubbish."

Jo stopped him. She wondered how he could speak so irreverently about a place he had called his favorite church. It wasn't the building he was railing against, he explained, but the dogmatic religion behind it.

"Oh," she said, lowering her eyes. "*That*, again."

"Well?" he asked, his arms spread in anticipation of her reply.

"I am Catholic," was all she said as she turned her back on him and walked away.

"Then you know whereof I speak, I shouldn't wonder."

She stopped, spun about on the spot and glared at him. "Such words!" she cried with a sweep of her hand, as if she were trying to keep evil demons away from her. "Such words, Caleb. Aren't you gifted, though, to be able to find just the right words to express your own irrational bigotries in such poetical verbiage! I don't wonder that you're on your way to becoming a famous writer. Nor do I wonder from where the twisted, half-hearted characters who people your gloomy stories arise. They seem to come from your own winter garden, Caleb. A garden of thorns and brambles!"

"My God! Don't you like anybody or anything on this dark earth?"

He had stood quietly in the dark alley as she spoke. His hands rested at his sides, but the palms faced outwardly as if in expectation of the stigmata of St. Francis. "Jo!" he said, with somewhat of a smile on his face. "You do have a passionate nature, after all."

"It's called outrage," she explained. "The kind of sentiment that erupts when too many lines of social decorum have been crossed too many times. And don't get me wrong," she declared before he had time to interrupt. "It isn't the Church I'm defending but the rights of those people who choose to embrace it."

He bowed with a flourish of his make-believe tricorn. "Brava, Signorina." Jo could not restrain a chuckle at his antics. "Oh, you," she said, for lack of better words. "You—monster, you!"

"*Io?*" he asked, gesturing humbly toward the region of his heart. "*Ma, di mi,*" he continued in the Italian language, "*Perché un mostro, Io?*"

She was giggling at his carnivalesque mannerism. "Why? First off, you defame the Blessed Mother of God." She became serious then. "Second, you ridicule and belittle your own person in a way verging on the goddamned pathetic."

His smiled dropped and he righted himself to listen. His expression was one of deep concern. "And thirdly?"

"Thirdly—" She took a breath. "And third, you endear yourself to people to the point that they cannot get through a day without you and then you close all your doors as if having retired into your own self-deprecating cloister."

"Really?" he asked, as if stunned, but cool-voiced, nonetheless.

"Really," She said, lowering her eyes to the wet paving stones. "I might have exaggerated a bit on the endearing part."

"The endearing part?" he wondered soft voiced. "I always thought that was my best trait."

She looked up at him. "It worked for me," she said, barely above a whisper.

He smiled very slightly. "Did it, Jo?" She smiled in return. "Like a charm." They had paused at a swelling in the corridor, an expanse of lighted piazza spreading out before them. The Old Ghetto. No, Caleb mumbled. I don't want to be here.

"What?" She had taken a few steps into the piazza, but he was pulling her back. He said something about not being able to go there. She was shaking her head in confusion. Asked him why not.

"Too many horrible memories," he said. Why should he have said such a thing, she was wondering.

"I died here," he said, pulling her back into the dark alley way. She did not ask for an explanation and he did not offer one. He did not tell her of his dreams. Of this place, though he had never been there in his life that he could recall. Of the cries and screams of terror. Of the awful sounds of machine guns. Of bodies falling to the ground.

All that had happened before John Caleb Wilson was born. A history of which he knew nothing. A memory he could not shake. He had never tried to explain it away, even to himself. Such memories. They were too real, too familiar to be dismissed.

He had strong hold of Jo's arm and was leading her into the dark corridor. He was breathing heavily. She was struggling to keep up. He slowed his pace somewhat. Paused and looked back at her.

"Do you think you could stand being loved by a man like me?" he asked. They were alone in the dim lit passageway. Jo took a breath. She swallowed a "yes," and said, "I could try. Could you stand being loved by me?"

He also took a breath. "That's the really big question, isn't it?" She nodded. He took her hand. "It's getting dark," he said. "They close the church at five." They walked on in silence, slowly.

"You didn't answer my question, Caleb," Jo said, her eyes on the bright piazza at the end of the dark corridor.

"What question was that?" he asked. She was not about to let it lie. It had to come out now or never. "You asked if I could stand you loving me. I answered. I asked you the same question and you evaded it."

"Don't be silly," he said, hugging her. "It was just a little word game, after all, wasn't it?"

"I'm not being silly," she persisted. "Contrary to your world view of the human race, not every woman is silly. I for one am rational—in the extreme, I fear."

"And yet, you call yourself a poet," he said.

She stopped walking and waited for him to look back at her. The houses were close on either side, barely a yard between them. Light from half-shuttered windows illuminated her plane face. "What," he asked, his face obscured by darkness.

"So; could you?"

"Could I what?"

They stood at the opening to a small irregular piazza. Light had gathered there as it does on certain Venetian evenings, in front of them, though they yet stood in the darkness, as if everything luminous had been drained from the rest of the world. She let out a small sigh.

"Could you let me fall in love with you?"

"I don't suppose I could stop you, now, could I?" He was staring straight ahead, then turned his back on her. "I always get confused here."

"That's an understatement," she started to say.

"No," he said, his voice in his gut. "I mean; as regards the most direct route to the church. There's really only one way to get there from here."

"Caleb?"

"Wait a minute."

They stepped into the small piazza. At the far end were two narrow alleyways. He gestured to them both and asked which one she thought they should take. "The left one or the right one?"

"I?" she asked. "You're letting me choose?"

He shrugged. "Does that not answer your question, Jo?"

"My question? Oh." She lowered her eyes and snuggled a little closer to him. "Yes," she said. "I guess it does."

"So?" he wondered. "Which one?"

"The lady or the tiger?" she mused. Her eyes had widened, alive with a kind of delight, as she glanced from one opening to the other, the kind of delight one uses to replace other, less easily defined emotions. Then she closed her eyes and pointed. "That one."

"The one on the left?"

"The one on the left."

"Brava!"

And off they went. They strode hand in hand into the alley. It was darker than the other, the sun having moved closer to its demise in the western oceans; here, there were neither lights nor shadows. Only moving things caught the eye's attention: laundry lifting on the breeze that rose from the alley floor to the third story clothes lines, cats yawning on the cornices above the doorways, an occasional pigeon, having arrived too late to find its favorite perch on the windowsill. Sounds, too, had settled down for the evening. Apart from the scuffling of feet on damp pavers, there was the always present drip-dripping of water off unseen eaves, the far away moan of boat motors in the distant lagoons, the subtle creaking and sighing of a city gently sinking into the remains of its own luxurious past.

There was a canal ahead, glistening in the light that had collected earlier in the piazzas. Caleb explained that there was no bridge, they'd have to return to the piazza and take the other alley.

"There has to be a bridge," Jo said. "I know it in my heart." They paused at water's edge. The tower of *Santa Maria Dell-Orto* stood above the mists in the near distance. There was no bridge.

"There's the one we need." Caleb pointed—then, stopped.

"What?"

She turned to see what he was staring at. Two men had come upon the next bridge. It lay about thirty meters away, lifting out of the water hugging mists in gray silhouette against the grayer buildings beyond. The two men had also paused, as if to find their bearings by counting the church towers that serve as beacons for the lost and the faint at heart.

"Michael?" Caleb asked involuntarily. The two men were in costume but only one wore a mask. The other, handsome and blond, stood in clear profile against the bright haze of the canal. Jo was about to call to him, but Caleb stopped her. She asked what was wrong. "The model," was all he said. "The model is with him."

"The model?"

"The young Swiss Guardsman he's been drawing for his mural. He's got some kind of weird obsession with Michael. He's been trying to shake him. I think it's why he came to Venice."

The smaller man was dressed in capes and pantaloons. He wore a mask and a cap with a long pheasant's feather in it. His hump-backed form stood at odds with the tall American with whom he was speaking in hushed tones and animated gestures.

Jo suggested they should go to Michael's rescue. "Maybe he's looking for the same church. Maybe he's looking for us."

Sounds of voices spoken in anger reached their ears. The two men were arguing, oblivious of the two watchers a few hundred steps away. In between, the fog lay in irregular banners just above the canal so that the bridge and the nearby quays seemed to be floating, as in a dream. Even the view of the two men shifted from place to place as the mists rose in fluttering layers to meet with the low hanging clouds that now obscured the tower of *Santa Maria dell' Orto*. The sun had set, and night was rising out of the canals to reclaim its share of winter's hours.

Tense voices rumbled like soft thunder through the thick atmosphere, now loud, now silent, though their mouths were moving, and their hands gesticulated nervously. Sounds of their voices rose but without form, more like the muffled sounds one makes when being suffocated.

They were struggling. Jo had become extremely agitated. The two men were wrestling against the railing of the old wooden bridge. The sounds of their expletives filled the small arena. The boards of the bridge resounded with the trampling of their feet and the banging of their elbows.

"Michael!" Jo cried at last, and she darted back into the alleyway toward the irregular piazza.

Caleb had remained but a second, just long enough to see the two men pause in their struggle and glance his way. Then he took off after Jo. His hard shoes pounded down the corridor. His quick breathing filled the small space with energy. He caught hold of Jo's sleeve as she was rounding the corner into the other alley.

"Wait," he huffed.

They were both panting heavily. He was having difficulty getting his words out.

"Let him be. It's his problem. He can handle it."

"What?" she gasped. "It didn't look to me—like he was handling it—"

"I mean. Give him a moment to resolve it. I don't want to embarrass him."

"Embarrass? What is it with you men? You would rather he lose his life than his dignity?"

He let out a ragged breath. "Something like that."

"Well, I—" She calmed. She took a breath. "You're right. We're being way too melodramatic here, aren't we? After all, what do we expect, a murder?"

Her eyes sprang up suddenly to Caleb's. His too had widened with sudden fear. He grabbed her arm and pulled her, running behind him, into the other dark alley.

Though the alley was nearly pitch dark, the canal showed softly ahead within its raiment of misty light. As the two of them neared it, they slowed their pace. From the alley, they could see only the corner of the ramp that led to the bridge. They paused and listened. There were no sounds. The sun had died as it does in northern climes in winter without ceremony and the lagoons had begun to give up the light they had stolen from the bright afternoon now ending. Light came from below, from the water, not from the sky or the meager streetlamps that sprang from the corners of buildings closest to the waterfront. Everything above the water line was gray and formless. Buildings, bridges and people.

Caleb and Jo stepped from the alley and into the gloaming. The bridge sprang from their feet into a tattered banner of canal fog and disappeared. The only sound was that of water drip-dripping from the eaves, and in the background, little more than a subliminal flutter, the sounds of running feet growing fainter.

"Michael?" Jo wondered, in *sotto voce*. Silence. "Michael?"

She started up the steep incline, but Caleb pulled her back. He asked if Michael were there. There was no reply. Once again Jo started up the bridge and once again Caleb pulled her back. She turned to him in frustration only to be confronted by an expression she had certainly never seen cross his face before. It was one of horror.

He was looking toward the dark and placid waters of the canal at high tide. He was pointing with his fingers as well as with his eyes. Jo took a breath of courage and looked toward the place at which he was staring. Like a blemish on the dark water, floating up against the marble steps that led to the quay, was the body of a man. He floated face down, the ruffles of his costume flattened out and covering his head, billowing about him in the water, like gossamer wings.

She clasped Caleb's hand. Their eyes locked, they glanced together down the alley they'd just left. There was no one in sight. The buildings that flanked the canal here were mostly warehouses and boat works. Caleb and Jo were alone on the quay. They stepped into the cold water, descending the three steps that made their way into the invisible depths of the canal. Reaching together, they grabbed the folds of the man's costume and pulled them toward them. Together, they lifted the sopped ruffles away from the Pulcinella mask, its long-hooked nose disappearing into the black water. They hoisted the heavy costume up onto the quay, just far enough to roll it over. The cloth fell away of its own accord. It was not Michael. It was not, in fact, *anyone*. The costume was empty.

Jo jumped back suddenly, shaking her hands in the air as if trying to rid them of the touch of a dead man. Caleb stood, shaking his head.

"The model?" Jo wondered, her voice trembling. "What happened to him?"

He was still shaking his head in confusion. He eyed her oddly, then, standing and with the toe of his foot against the heavy wad of sopped ruffles and folds, and with a furtive glance this way and that, he nudged the costume back into the current.

"Do you suppose he's at the bottom of the canal?" Her voice was as flat and opaque as the surface of the dark waters.

They stood and watched for a time as the costume floated away, held adrift by its voluminous yards of fabric. It slipped under the lip of the bridge and out of sight.

"I don't know," was all he said. Then he heaved a breath. Once again, they turned their eyes upon each other. Jo was backing away, toward the comfort of the dark alley.

"I want to go home," she said, in a small voice.

"You mean; back to Rome?"

"Ohio," she said. "Where I belong."

He slipped his arm about her and hugged her. Behind them, lamps were flickering to life in the alley. "Is that where you belong?" he asked.

"Not really," she said, into his collar. "But it's someplace."

"Someplace?"

She let out a breath. "Someplace better than here—And now."

"What about carnival?"

She was shaking her head. "I've had enough carnival." They started back down the dim-lit alleyway toward the irregularly shaped little piazza, now aglow with lamplight.

"I've never been to Ohio," Caleb said. "Is it pleasant there?"

"The lake side is nice," she said. "But I like the hills along the river best. Just south of Columbus, it gets into rolling forestlands. There are lots of fine little villages nestled in the valleys where everyone knows everyone, and nobody locks their houses. Kids ride horses bareback to summer school and women gossip over the backyard fences while hanging up their laundry."

"Is that where you want to go?" he asked.

They had paused just before entering the bright piazza. "It's a start," she said. "I mean, it's a good place to start, I suppose."

"Start what, Jo?"

They walked into the center of the small piazza, glancing back at the two alleyways, the right one and the wrong one. "My life's journey," she said. "What better place to start than a place steeped in peace and beauty?"

"Don't kid yourself," he said dryly, eyes on hers. They were sharing a few silent tears. "I started out in a place like that," he added, soft voiced. "Problem is, no place is better than any other, so each place you go is a step farther from the paradise you are seeking; the paradise you left, the one you didn't know you had until you had given it up."

She was shaking her head. "You, my friend," she smiled, "are a master at mixing metaphors."

"Oh," he sighed, "is that what's wrong with me?"

They walked on. She agreed it was a fantasy to think that any place was any better than any other. But, escaping into fantasy could be just as beneficial as traveling the globe, seeing new sights, experiencing new adventures. She stopped talking and held him back as they were about to leave the piazza. She asked with emotion in her voice, "What do you suppose happened back there, Caleb?"

He shrugged. "I don't know."

"Is Michael gone from your life now?"

"Michael has served his literary purpose," he said. She was nodding, smiling slightly. "Yeah. So have you." He grinned. "So. Does that mean our story's over? Has it no ending, Jo?" She didn't answer but she may have been thinking that the answer to that question was up to him.

"You're the writer," she said at length. "I'm just a poet."

Fifteen

The Gentle Reader, we trust, would not thank us for one of those minute elucidations, which are so tedious, and, after all, so unsatisfactory, in clearing up the romantic mysteries of a story.

He is too wise to insist upon looking closely at the wrong side of the tapestry, after the right one has been sufficiently displayed to him, woven with the best of the artist's skill, and cunningly arranged with a view to the harmonious exhibition of its colours. If any brilliant or beautiful, or even tolerable, effect have been produced, this pattern of kindly Readers will accept it at its worth, without tearing the web apart, with the idle purpose of discovering how its threads have been knit together; for the sagacity, by which he is distinguished, will long ago have taught him that any narrative of human action and adventure—whether we call it history or romance—is certain to be a fragile handiwork, more easily rent than mended. The actual experience of even the most ordinary life is full of events that never explain themselves, either as regards their original tendency.

Hawthorne, *The Marble Faun*

Having left their fancy dress costumes hanging in the hotel armoire, they packed quickly and were able to get to the station in time to catch a late train to Roma Termini, via Firenze Santa Maria Novella. The train was nearly empty. It was, after all, a Tuesday evening, on the cusp of lent. They found a compartment in the first car they got themselves into and settled into opposite window seats, their faces turned to the glass. At first, they saw only themselves reflected on the windows by virtue of the lights in the station. But as the great steel monster lumbered onto the fragile causeway connecting Venice to the mainland, light receded, and the compartment went dark. For a while, they could see the towers of the mist-shrouded city floating like a dream beyond the black lagoon. Then. Nothing.

Caleb switched on the reading light and opened his notebook. He hadn't spoken a word since they'd sat down, when he had observed that it would be after midnight before they got home.

"Sorry," she had said. "I just didn't feel like partying, is all. Ironical, isn't it?" she added, as the train had begun to move. "It was Michael who provided me with an opportunity to fulfill my dream of Carnival in Venice. It was Michael who denied me that very dream."

"There is no Michael," she was reminded. Jo had turned her eyes from the dark window to the soft circle of light that had settled about him as he studied his notes. She watched him for some time; the slow ride into Mestre, the noisy stop at the station there, and then racing across the plains of the Veneto toward Padova. He paused to turn a page and she spoke.

"Writing?"

"Sort of—" He stopped, put the pad down and looked her way. "I'm getting into the last few chapters. It's difficult going. There seem to be so many loose ends I have to tie off before concluding it."

"A good story always leaves a few loose ends untied," she said. He nodded. "I'm having a problem with Alison's character." She wondered casually what it was. "She's in love with two men though neither of them love her."

"I thought John loved her, I mean, down deep inside."

"I don't know," he admitted. "I don't know him very well."

"But he's you, isn't he? I thought this was an autobiographical story."

"Vaguely, I suppose."

"You call him by your own name, after all."

"John is a common enough name," he insisted.

She hesitated then asked, "What about Cutler? What about Alison? Aren't they real people too?"

"I gave them different names, but—Actually, I made him up. There is no Cutler Insbroek. Never was." He closed his notebook and turned toward the dark window glass as if talking to someone who never was. "Never was," he repeated, mostly to himself. Then he turned to her and grinned. Indicated it wasn't a good time to be writing. She disagreed. What better time, she suggested, when in a period of heightened emotions?

He turned back to the dark glass. It made no reflection.

"Where are you in the story?" Jo wondered, perhaps uncomfortable with the silence.

He started reciting. "Alison and Cutler are about to go their separate ways. It starts out in autumn. She's still living in his house, but their relationship has not gone as she had hoped. He's beginning to understand and accept his lack of interest in women, but he doesn't quite get it yet. Remember. This takes place several years ago. She keeps trying to seduce him like she did during the summer, but nothing happens. She decides without telling him that she's going to leave."

"Where will she go, I wonder," Jo mused.

"Home, I guess. To face her mother. Where else?"

"Poor thing. It must be awful not having a family you can count on in times of trouble."

"It is," he said.

She asked him to read some of it to her. "It'll help pass the time."

Alison lay beside him. As usual, she had come into his room in the middle of the night and had crawled in next to him. As usual he had pretended to be asleep. Now it was morning and he had to do something. He sat up and turned toward the windows. A delicate fringe of snow decorated the branches of the beech tree beyond the glass. He smiled. "First snow," he said involuntarily.

She did not move but he was certain she must have been awakened by his movements. He sat on the edge of the bed for some time watching the snow fall, perching as it does on the smallest twigs. Cutler said her name. "Alison." She grunted. "It's snowing," he said. "The first snow."

"What of it?" she asked into the fold of comforters she held onto.

He stood up and the bed reclaimed her. She returned to her mantle of sleep and dreamed on. In like fashion, though standing, he turned his back on her. He bent to put on his slippers; paused. His toenails needed clipping. He walked barefoot to the bathroom, pulling the door closed behind him. He turned on the shower and steam began to fill the small painted room. He stared at his reflection in the mirror until it faded. He pulled himself out of his pajamas and stepped into the shower. Barely aware of his actions, he went through his morning routines like a robot. His conscious mind was preoccupied with one simple question. "What am I going to do about Alison?"

He shaved and wrapped a towel about him before returning to the cool bedroom. Alison was gone. The bed was empty but for the heap of sheets and blankets she'd left behind. He dropped the towel and walked naked to the window. It was still snowing. The view was immaculately white. The house dead quiet. Waves lapped softly on the silent beach below and there was no wind. The world seemed, at least for the moment, to have settled into a state of absolute peace.

He dressed and went downstairs. He could hear his mother and her friend talking softly in the kitchen as they sipped their coffee. Cutler was not a coffee drinker. He merely paused in the doorway to wish them good morning and was off to work.

He paused on the front stoop and surveyed the idyllic scene of Lakeside Grove and its cluster of cottages scattered randomly among the beeches that clustered in the hollows of the dunes. The streets were yet bare. Though snowing, the air off the lake was mild. It was a light, wet snow, sponsored more by the presence of the lake than by the encroaching winter. He put on his leather coat, one which would not be too warm, and a soft cotton knit scarf. He stepped onto the brick walkway, leaving dark prints where his feet crushed the delicate frosting. He car was festooned with tufts of snow, especially on the fenders and ragtop. He brushed off the windows with his gloved hand, having forgotten to buy a scraper. He slipped into the cold interior with a squeaking of leather against leather and turned the key. It started and stalled. He started it again and pulled out onto the narrow lane. The wipers click-clacked on the slick window, dashing globs of wet snow about. His headlamps yellowed the scallops of ice that fringed the dunes along the water. The sky was speckled with bits of its own stuffing.

Little by little, and without realizing it, it began to happen, as it had happened every day before: The passing scenes were bringing back his joy. The cottage tensions were fading as the bright vistas of lake and farmland drifted by. When he turned onto Lake Street and its long line of big old Victorian homes, he was actually smiling. He passed white, clapboarded churches and two-story storefronts already swagged with Christmas lights. There were parks of pruned shrubbery that cut the snowscape into geometric patterns and playgrounds were already mud stained where children had rolled the snow into big balls for their snowmen. Recent memories slipped away in favor of more distant ones: sledding and skating and rolling about in the drifts that used to pile up against the house. He pulled into a parking space on Lake Place and got out of the car. He could hear the sounds of snow shovels down the street, the muffled grunts of shovelers. He could hear the choir practicing in the chapel as he walked under the cast iron archway and onto the campus.

The commons were empty. Morning classes had already begun. He crossed the sacred little space in silence and entered the science building. Insbroek Hall was named for his grandfather, one of the college's founders.

He replaced his leather jacket with a lab coat, which he'd taken from a hook on the inside of the door to his office. He stepped into the small reception room to greet the secretary. She was an older woman, a widow who had come back to work after her husband's death. She was pretty, well dressed and very personable. Her name was Verna. Even before he had spoken, she was going through her daily routine of messages, reminders and suggestions. Her tailored suit and beauty-shop hair seemed a strange compliment to the disarray on her desk and the shelves behind her. "Now where did I put that—"

She was looking for a note she'd written him. He waited patiently while she rummaged through piles of papers and folders. She found it. Alison had called. She wanted to meet for lunch. "At the Brownstone. They have a pretty nice buffet, I understand."

"Thank you, Verna." She was still talking. "Mail's late. Probably because of the snow. The first one always seems to catch us unawares even though we know it's coming," she observed. "Pretty, though."

Then she paused is if she was expecting him to agree with her. "You all right?" she asked.

"What? Sure."

"Cutler," she said, carefully, "Maybe it's time to get that girl out of your mother's house?"

"Oh, she's no problem."

"Not according to Alma."

Cutler had forgotten that Verna and his mother were long time bridge players together. He wondered casually if his mother had said something to her. She shrugged and admitted it wasn't what she had said but what she had not said.

"That doesn't make sense," Cutler said. She was smiling warmly. "Of course, it does, Cutler. You know Alma." He smiled as well. "Yes," he said. "I know my mother. She won't talk to me, you know. But she knows you will."

Verna nodded. "We don't like to see you unhappy, Cutler." He had started to leave but paused in the doorway. "As long as I'm happy, you'll be happy? Even if my happiness is not what you would feel was the right way to find it?"

"Cutler," she said, as if she knew something he didn't. "We love you," she said. "You couldn't possibly do anything that we didn't like—if it was the right thing for you."

Cutler stepped into his office and the lights went out. He sighed and dropped into the chair at his desk. The lights still glowed in Verna's office. She assured him the janitor would have his lights replaced within a few minutes.

"No matter," he said from the doorway. He was slipping out of his lab coat. "I'm not staying."

As he left his office, the lights went back on. He hung the lab coat on the hook from which he retrieved his leather jacket and scarf. He mentioned as he left that he was going to the Winter Garden and then to the lab in the horticulture annex.

He didn't go to the Winter Garden. The last time he'd gone in, all the blowers had gone off and the temperature had begun to drop. He stood instead outside the crystal treasure house and peered in through the frosty glass. For some reason, he was blaming Alison for his not being able even to enjoy his favorite hiding place. How he wished he could walk among the heavy fronds, smell their earthy bodies, touch their glossy skin. He stood for some time in the snow and stared at the glass walls, his own reflection pinioned upon the view of greenery in an otherwise white world. It occurred to him then what a thin and fragile barrier there was at times between reality and fantasy.

He started to walk. He had no classes until afternoon. There was lab work that could be done but it could wait. He left the campus, slipping out between the music building and the Gym. He could hear someone practicing the oboe and he thought of Joey Agnus. He was still teaching but only private students since the college had not renewed his contract. Cutler quickened his pace lest the oboe player prove to be Joey and he'd come running in pursuit—though, in truth, they'd not seen each other since last spring when they had talked for some time in the Winter Garden.

Just the pronouncing of those words brought melancholy for some reason: Winter Garden. Cutler paused and glanced over his shoulder. The little crystal palace glowed softly against the bland background of its snowy courtyard. He pulled out his wallet, opened the center section and found tucked among the bills a fold of paper. He didn't open it and read it. He knew it was Joey's address and phone number. He'd kept it in his wallet for reasons he did not fully understand, or rather, was not letting himself understand. He slipped the wallet back into his rear pocket and started out again, walking briskly up College Avenue.

Tattered clouds were moving up the street from the lake. Snow spiraled in slow motion about the trees on the grey-green lawns. Walkways and drives crisscrossed the sheeting with darker stripes. There is something almost sacred about a first snowfall. Folks are less apt to walk across the newly blanketed lawns out of respect for the purity of form and color that only a layer of snow can bring to the landscape. But the day was warming, and clumps of snow were beginning to drop from the trees, pox-marking the blanket until it resembled chenille. The wind was rising and blowing wet snow into Cutler's face. He turned at the corner and slowed his pace. Alison was meeting him at eleven. It was only nine. He'd be cold and tired by then, but he didn't feel like doing anything else. So: he walked.

Caleb paused and looked up. "Sleepy?"

"No," Jo said.

"Bored, then," he grinned.

"Sad."

"Why sad?"

"Cutler. I feel sorry for him."

"He's just a character in a book, Jo." He lay back and closed his eyes. "He's based on a guy I used to know, but I never knew him well. I always thought he might be a latent homosexual, but I heard a few years ago that he was married and had three kids. A Ferrier."

"A what?"

"An iron worker. He builds bridges and the like. Isn't that an odd profession?"

"And writing isn't?"

He sort of laughed. "Yeah." He wondered how she was coming on her collection of new poems. Not well, it seemed. She'd not been miserable enough, he ventured. She was not amused. He looked directly at her. "I do like you, you know. That's something, isn't it?"

"Oh, god," she said suddenly, shedding tears and turning her face toward the window. "I wish you hadn't said that."

Caleb's heart reached out to her, but he remained as he was, sitting opposite her in the second-class compartment on the train to Rome. "I can't admit to any more than that, Jo," he tried to explain. "I'm sorry. I wish I could."

Jo wept quietly for a long while. Caleb collected her grief like a trophy and stored it in his soul as if it could take the place of the immortality he'd so long ago lost during the confusion of a prolonged adolescence. How could he explain it to her? How could he explain it to anyone? His need to be alone. His obsession with loneliness.

"Some people there are, I've heard, who learn how to survive this life by themselves. They try at relationships and fail—time after time until, if they're smart, they stop it altogether. Who knows why they fail? If it even *is* failure?"

"I don't know. I've been thinking about this for most of my life and I haven't figured it out yet. There are some of us, it seems, who thrive on isolation."

She turned her tear-streaked face to his. "Then all three of your characters are you, aren't they?"

"Huh?"

"Alison. John. Cutler. None of them knows how to interact with other people, least of all with each other. That's how it seems to me, Caleb."

"I suppose so."

She sat forward and spread her hands. "But why?"

He shrugged slightly, surprised at her outburst. "I don't know, Jo. That's why I'm writing this novel. I'm trying to find answers."

"Stop!" she said, coming over to his side of the cabin. She placed her hands on his two shoulders and looked him directly in the eyes. "Art does not provide answers, Caleb. You know that, as well as I do. It asks questions to which there are no answers. Doesn't it?"

"Is that all it—"

"Listen to me." She held him tightly and said to him, "I love you, Caleb. But that does not mean I want to be with you. I almost forgot the same thing you forgot. Love is like art."

"It does not answer questions?"

"It only poses them." She was smiling warmly. "You see; once you stop waiting for your books to answer your questions, once you realize that some questions simply have no answers, you will stop asking the questions and, by god, Caleb, you will be one hell of a happier person than you are now. I guarantee it!"

He took on an air of obstinacy, but only slightly. "What's happiness got to do with it?" Then, before she could answer, he asked another question. "Besides, I have to wonder what makes you the expert all of a sudden?"

"Michael," she answered.

"There is no Michael."

"Will you stop saying that? I saw him. We both did."

"Maybe," he started to say but she was still talking.

"I've been thinking about him all evening. According to you, he came to Rome to seek answers to questions the answers of which he already knew, deep down inside himself. He wanted you to be the answer, but you were troubling with your own questions." She paused, then added, "He had to kill his model, Caleb—if he did kill him—don't you see? The young man *was* the enigma; the question in Michael's own soul, the reality he refused to face. Don't you see?"

"There is no—"

She tightened her grip on his shoulders. "Caleb. We saw him push a man into the canal. We saw him murder someone. It was not a fantasy." Caleb pulled away from her and moved to the opposite corner of the small compartment. "We saw nothing, Jo. Except what we thought we wanted to see."

"There was a body."

"There was no body."

"Then where did it go?"

He suddenly stood and said loudly, "I do not know where it went, if it was ever there at all! Neither do you. I'm not even so certain it was Michael we saw struggling with the man in costume."

"But," she said, bowing her head, retreating a little. "What if it *was* him?"

"What, then?"

She peered carefully up at him. He stared at her for a while and then, he sat down. He took hold of her hands. He spoke softly and soothingly. "So. What do you think we should do? The police?"

She shook her head. "I think we need to talk to Michael. Let's hear from him what happened. Then, we'll decide what to do."

"I doubt I will ever see him again."

He added that, knowing Michael, he had probably already turned himself in. Then, for some reason, he reminded her she was scheduled to return to the states in three weeks. She nodded and admitted she could not return before knowing the real story.

"Real story?" he wondered.

"You'll let me know what you find out?"

He nodded. Promised. They both took very deep breaths and smiled with a little embarrassment at their behavior. She settled back once again leaning her head against the window and closing her eyes. She asked in soft words if he would read the remainder of the chapter to her while she dozed. After a moment, he picked up the notepad.

Alison was waiting out front of the old hotel and Cutler waved to her as he rounded the corner. He was wondering what odd outfit she might have on that day, under the full-length second-hand fur coat, and he smiled in spite of himself. She was smiling, too. He could see her petty face clearly through the swish of traffic and the wet, glistening colors of the snowy street. Christmas music trailed intermittently along the festooned walks. She had colored her hair in recent weeks. It was flame red. And she wore bright orange lipstick. She reached out to him, a wrist full of jangling bracelets stretching from the oversized sleeves.

"I'm glad you're here," she said. "I've something important to talk to you about."

"Oh?" he responded with hesitation. "Me, too," he added.

She stood away from him and smiled. "Me, first." Then her smile quickly faded. "I talked to my mother this morning."

"She called the house?"

She raised her hand to quiet him. "I called her." He nodded. They were standing on the very edge of the walk, and cars were sloshing past them, spattering them with slush. They were unmindful of it as she added with a strange timbre to her voice. "She said Jesus would make a better bed-partner than you. Isn't that a silly thing to say?"

"What did you say to that?"

"I told her Jesus wasn't as much fun as you were. She said I wouldn't be in this condition if I had thought of Jesus first." She bowed her head. "I suppose she's right, there."

"Why did you call her? You knew she'd do that to you."

"She's my mother," was her answer.

The lobby of the Brownstone was packed with holiday shoppers waiting for tables. The old-fashioned buffet lunches were always popular during the holidays. Cutler hung his jacket in the rack, but Alison merely hefted her coat back on her shoulders. "I seem to get cold easily, lately," she explained.

They were led to a table near the front windows so that they could watch the passersby on the wintry street. Alison threw her heavy coat over the back of her chair and Cutler smiled. She wore purple maternity pants with an orange top. Aware of his scrutiny, she glanced down at herself. "Colorful, aren't I?"

"Alison," he said, "you're colorful even when you're naked."

She grinned and took the chair he offered her.

"Alison," he said again. "Are you going to keep it? The child?"

"I can't, Cutler."

"Your mother convinced you?"

"She and Jesus."

"Oh."

He suggested they get in the buffet line. He had to be back for an afternoon class. She followed him to the buffet, and he handed her a tray. Their voices entered into a chant like clatter of dishes and flatware, the pulsing antiphon of talking people and the tenor of piped-in music. They placed their plastic trays on the steel counter and began to slide them along in a kind of slow-motion ritual.

"So, why did you call her?"

"I gotta have someplace to go, Cutler. We both know I've outstayed my welcome in Lakeside Grove."

He bowed his head. "It isn't that, exactly—" They returned to their table. They were quiet for a while. Cutler was watching her, sipping at his drink, wondering what to say to her. She had paused to stare out the window at the passers-by on the snowy street. "I'm sorry I didn't fall in love with you," he said. Softly.

She smiled genuinely. "I know." She had paused and they stared at each other for a while. "I do like you, you know. It *is* something."

"Me, too," he admitted. Then he asked her very carefully why she had allowed herself to get pregnant. "Did you think it would make John love you more?"

She turned to gaze out the window again. The soft light of the snowy street settled about her, softened her harsh colors and imparted a Madonna-like grace to her. Cutler immediately wished he hadn't asked the question, but she seemed to have been unmoved by it. "Something like that," she admitted. "I thought I'd at least have something of his he couldn't take back, I guess."

"And now you're going to give it up?" She smiled slightly. "Something like that—"

He told her she could stay until the baby was born and she said she knew that. She didn't want him to be part of it. She knew his sympathetic nature. She didn't want him to feel somehow responsible for her and the baby. She smiled graciously. "You've done so much for me already, Cutler."

"You are a friend of mine," was all he said.

She returned to the buffet line, and Cutler glanced at his watch.

Jo rested her head on Caleb's shoulder. He had paused in his reading, and she let out a breath. She observed that Alison and Cutler reminded her of herself and Caleb. "Is that who they are?" she wondered.

"No," Caleb said. "They aren't as honest about their true feelings as we are."

"Why isn't Cutler able to make love to her?" she asked.

"He's John's alter-ego," he explained. "He knows she loves John more than life itself and he's unable to break that bond. The very presence of it makes him impotent."

"And who are *you*?" she asked, tightening her embrace about him.

"I'm both of them, I guess, like you said."

"And I?"

"You are a friend of mine," he answered.

Sixteen

1

Lizzie Tifgat sat on the sofa near the fireplace. She had her feet tucked under her and she was reading a magazine, thumbing through it slowly. She looked up once to see John as he came in from the kitchen with two drinks. He handed her one and she thanked him with a nod and a small smile. She went back to her reading and he took a chair near the Christmas tree, which they had put in the front window. He was correcting papers. They were scattered across the floor at his feet. The house was quiet. A thin line of chamber music meandered above the subtle sounds of turning pages and ice cubes in glasses. A heavy snow was falling beyond the windows and the world lay in a deadly silence.

Lizzie and John and the tree were arranged like other Christmas trappings within the small space of the living room. She was in pink, a floor length velveteen robe wrapped about her. Her glass of bourbon complimented the pastels she'd been given to wearing since the weather had turned cold in the little house. John wore black: dungarees and a sweatshirt.

There were spruce boughs on the mantle and candles sputtered in glass bowls in amongst them. A cluster of satin fruit formed a wreath above the mantle and the backs of the chairs were draped with red-embroidered doilies. The tree was decorated with red satin ornaments and blue twinkle lights. The whole atmosphere was one of warmth and color.

John dropped one of the test papers in his lap and glanced at the tree, looking past its decorations and into the heart of it; the way its branches spread out from the trunk, bristling with pungent needles. Sensing Lizzie's gaze, he turned toward her.

Silence prevailed. They went back to their reading, turning pages, sipping their iced drinks. He dropped the paper again and took off his glasses, rubbing his eyes until they were red. He watched Lizzie for a while. She turned a page, and he pulled his eyes back to his own lap. Wing like darts of light were wriggling across the papers. He spread his hands to catch them. At his elbow, on the small side table, a couple of books lay. He reached over and patted them as if they were pets. He shuffled through the papers he had yet to read, then set them atop the books and got to his feet. He could feel Lizzie's eyes upon him as he returned to the kitchen for another drink. At the sink, he turned on the water and let it run, if for no other reason than to change the timbre of sounds in the house. He turned it off, took the bottle by its neck and returned to the front room. He splashed a little more bourbon in Lizzie's glass as he passed, then sat again in his chair next to the Christmas tree. He emptied the bottle into his glass. He set the empty bottle on the floor next to the papers he'd already corrected. He raised the glass toward Lizzie, but she was involved in her reading and did not return the toast. He looked at the test he'd picked up but saw only a blank page; a page on which the tree lights flashed in random display.

Lizzie finally put down her magazine and turned toward him. "Having trouble concentrating?" she wondered. "It's this snowstorm," he responded. "Makes me feel trapped." She said she kind of liked the feeling. "Makes me feel cozy." Then she added that school might be called off the next day. "Maybe you don't have to have these things corrected after all."

He took a breath. "They have to be finished sometime." She suggested he get up early in the morning and finish them then. "When you're refreshed." She pointed to a stack of Christmas cards that had come that afternoon. They were slipped in among the boughs on the mantel. He admitted that he hadn't looked at them yet. She went back to her reading and he got to his feet once more and went to the fireplace. The smoldering logs cast shimmering shadows across the floor. The carpets were warm to his bare feet. He took the cards back to his chair and sat down. With his toe, he pushed the test paper under the lip of the chair and out of sight. Lizzie chuckled at his antics and he smiled at her. He began shuffling through the cards.

Most were from colleagues he barely knew. Most were religious scenes: Nativities, Adorations, Presentations. Some showed angels in glory descending upon the unsuspecting village of Bethlehem. Some depicted scenes of the Holy Land in better days. Some revealed the Word of the Lord. There were primitive landscapes of New England, UNESCO portraits of children, non-denominational proverbs and even a card in Hebrew celebrating the Feast of Lights. Some of the signatures were illegible but John was able to recognize the unmistakable scrawls of his colleagues in the English Department.

Lizzie had arranged the cards by subject matter. After the religious and primitive landscape scenes were wintry scenes and then, contemporary designs: odd shapes in day-glow colors. Finally, there were cards from students with pictures of purple reindeer and mod angels and epithets like "Cool Yule," and "Krazy Kristmas," on them. He smiled though he didn't really consider them very humorous.

She had also taped the corners of the envelopes to the back of each card so that the addresses could be confirmed when she and John got around to sending out their own cards. Her care was to prove idle, however, since they were not destined to mail cards that winter. John didn't know that then, as he casually thumbed through the paper missiles. He returned them to the mantle. Back in his chair, he pulled the tests out from under it and began once more to read them.

The telephone rang. The two glanced at each other, neither one ready to get up from comfortable seats. It rang again, the sound of it shattering the quietude. Lizzie unfolded herself and got to her feet and crossed to the small table near the front door. The phone rang a third time and she answered it.

"Hello?"

John was watching her. She drew her forehead into a scowl. She turned toward him and extended the receiver toward him at arm's length. He asked who it was.

"It's Verna. She's trying to get Cutler."

"His phone hasn't been working the last few days," he said.

"She said it's an emergency. She wants you to go to his house after him." John glanced out the window behind him. "In this shit?" Lizzie was shaking the receiver in the air impatiently. He let out a breath and got to his feet. The test papers fell in disarray to the floor. He'd forgotten they were resting in his lap.

"Damn."

He took the receiver from her cool hand. She remained nearby as he talked softly. Something in the tone of Verna's voice had apparently touched her. She took hold of his arm. His eyes had locked with hers as he slipped the receiver into its cradle.

"What?"

"She wants me to bring him into town."

"Where is he?"

"His place."

"Why now? In this storm?"

"The Winter Garden—"

Her voice dropped to almost nothing. "What about it?"

"Someone's broken into it. Shattered all the glass." She posed a silent question, "Who?" He shrugged. He was dialing the phone.

"Oh," she said with tears in her voice, her eyes still directly on his. "Poor Cutler." Then she asked who he was calling.

"Hello? Joey?"

She nodded. Joey lived close to Cutler. John was asking him to bring him into town. "His car isn't working," he added. He took a breath as he hung up the receiver. They remained there, near the small table, for some time. She asked if he wanted to go into campus. He nodded.

"Would you drive? You know how I hate—"

"Of course," she said.

She rushed into the bedroom to change. John turned toward the hooks near the front door where his heavy coat was hung. He was slipping it on when Lizzie returned. She'd simply pulled on a pair of pants and a sweater over her pajamas. He reminded her that she was barefoot. She laughed, sort of, and returned to the bedroom to find her boots. He called that he was going out to warm up the car.

2

The snow was falling heavily, and a wind roared in from the lake. It carried the sounds of waves pounding the hard beaches below the dunes, and of the cedars whistling in harmony to the heavy percussion. John bowed into the wind as he fumbled with the key to open the car door. Despite the blizzard and the night, as often happens in winter, a glow of light permeated the storm. Trees stood in clear contrast against the white sky. The windows of distant cottages glimmered like ornaments among the bare branches.

The car waited ominously, kept clean of snow by the winds that howled up the street, which seemed to unroll like paper tape down the gray dunes toward the black water. John slipped into Lizzie's Cadillac, leather and metal squawking with having been disturbed on too cold a night for a vehicle such as this. It started first time, trembling with renewed energy. He was sweeping a brush over the windshield to clear it of ice when the porch light burst on above him. Lizzie had come out, slipping on her red calfskin gloves as she came. It was the only color available to the eye at that moment. John called to her to be careful.

"The roads might be icy."

"Verna called again. I told her that Cutler was on his way."

They faced each other for a moment or two. They agreed they should go. It was only a few treacherous miles into town. Cutler might need moral support.

John took her hand and guided her to the driver's side door. She ducked into the seat, her dark coat making a hole in the light from the dashboard. He got in next to her as the vehicle began to move, sort of sideways, onto the street. The roadway had also been cleared of snow by the wind and had been buffed to an icy sheen. Lizzie switched on the headlamps, which played across the front of the house with eye-stunning precision as she spun the car about to face the water. John grabbed the dash for support as they descended into the storm.

The tires crunched the ridges of ice that marked the diagonal path of the winds across the paving. Below, the harbor lights plied the hazardous straits between the land and the storm as they swept the crests of the waves and moved like a tracing finger across the tall pines that slanted landward along the rows of sand hills. The car dropped into the valley, momentarily out of the wind, and then, turning its back on the lake, it ascended again toward the line of streetlights that pointed the way to town. The blizzard was now at their backs and the snow fell more steadily, charging the headlights like banks of icy arrows. The road here was deeply rutted with drifts and the car, big as it was, struggled to keep pace with the wind. Lizzie was an intrepid driver and took the curves and hills with the ease of a skater. John was petrified.

Having topped the dune and descending into town, the winds once more subsided and the snow fell in great heaps, blocking the view, piling up on the windshield. She turned on the wipers. All they did was to slap the slush back and forward across the frosty glass. The streetlamps here wore tufted caps of snow and were fringed with crystal pendants of icicles. They floated in the haze of the night, each surrounded by a delicate halo.

The quality of the storm caused light to disperse itself so that areas of gray darkness lay interspersed with the lamps, creating a strobe-effect as they drove. The light did not remain where it should have been, clustered about the lamps that engendered it, but instead it seeped away into the remotest corners. As if floodlit by an unseen moon, the storm illuminated itself. The subtle ambience was to become one of the most persistent elements of John's memory. From that day forward, every thought, every recollection, every discovery, whether natural or induced would share his brain's quarters with the memory of that night's luminous presence.

The Caddie came at last to a sliding stop at a curb, in a tight space illuminated by a streetlight. The winds had let up a bit, but the snow continued to fall heavily, obscuring the view. Two large edifices loomed to either side, Insbroek Hall and the Horticulture Annex, faintly silhouetted and pox-marked with dark windows. The scene was accompanied by a shrill sound as the wind coiled about the buildings, squeezing between them, and pouring into the street, shaking the parked car. There was also a cluster of feeble lights between the two structures that marked the final resting place of the Winter Garden. Dark figures moved ceremoniously amongst them. John heaved a sigh and got out of the car.

"Next time," he said. "I'll drive."

She reached for his hand and he led her around to the curb. They bowed into the gale as they walked, searching the snowy ground for the walkway with their boots. Drifts abutted the walls to either side of them so that the passage resembled a gentle valley rather than an architectural alleyway. The tall trees that stood beyond contributed to the illusion. As the couple neared the circle of light, other sounds came their way: muffled voices, electronic noises and pagers. But everything sensual—whether visible or audial—was muted and flattened. Indeed, the world seemed to have retreated into a two-dimensional state.

The small courtyard was quieter. It was better sheltered from the winds and the snow settled gently there as if in reverence for some sacred act. The shattered crystal vault was backlighted by the lamps of searchers among the ruins. Its door was open to the storm, its fragile skin shattered.

"Oh," Lizzie gasped softly. "No!" She had paused just at the opened door. Her red gloves provided the only color. Everything else was white, including the interior of the Winter Garden. A single naked bulb still burned just inside, dangling from a cord. A few students knelt in the opening, picking up shining slivers of glass and displaying them in their mitten-clad hands as if they were hallowed relics.

Cutler was just coming into the courtyard from the science building, Joey Agnus just behind him. They stopped on the rim of the light and Cutler dropped his head. John went to him. Lizzie watched them embrace. Then Cutler continued on to the shattered door of the hot house. There he paused, his hands in his coat pockets, staring at the snow banked piles of blasted tropical plants. Lizzie and John joined him though Joey remained apart.

"It's absurd," Lizzie was saying. "It makes no sense."

Cutler asked one of the students in a steady voice what had happened. She said she was on her way back from a party. "Freshmen have to be in by midnight, you know, Dr. Insbroek."

"You discovered this?"

"I saw that the door was open," she said, her face hidden in the shadow of her parka. "I saw that some of the windows were broken. I called the security guy—"

"Security guy?"

One of the men with the flashlights came out of the Winter Garden. Cutler started in, but the man stopped him with a hand on his shoulder. "Everything's dead," he said. "It's been at least several hours. Look how much snow has piled up in there."

Cutler started again but this time it was John who stopped him. "You can't do anything about it," he said. "Let's go for a beer, just you and I. We'll clean it up tomorrow—after the storm."

"We'll tape it," the guard said. "It'll be all right, Dr. Insbroek. Sorry about it."

Cutler took a breath and turned his eyes to the ground. It was packed hard from the activity, and it sparkled from the shards of glass that lay scattered about. He turned his eyes toward the shattered house. There were broken pots everywhere, as if they'd been deliberately thrown to the brick floor. But most of the exotic flora had been left to die in place, blasted by icy winds, melted to mush by the cold, snapped and stiffened by the snow. Graceful fronds still arched over the walkway, now crusted with hoar. Delicacies of the tropics lay in blackened and formless heaps.

"It's all over," John was saying at his ear. "You can't save them. Not even you."

"I know that, John," he said at last. "I know that, my friend."

His voice had cracked, and John turned him away from the sight to save his dignity in front of the students. The two young girls were standing nearby watching in silence. John thanked them for their help and began to guide Cutler toward the curb where the car awaited. Lizzie followed but Joey went to the Winter Garden.

"We found this," one of the girls said to him.

She held out an envelope at arm's length.

"It's for Dr. Insbroek."

Joey had taken the letter and was looking at it. He called to the others. They ambled back, and he displayed the note to Cutler. He bent close to see it more clearly in the soft light of the courtyard. The writing was blurred. A curl of adhesive tape was attached to one corner. "It must have been taped to the front door," Joey said.

Cutler admitted he couldn't read it. "What does it say?"

"Your name, as near as I can tell."

"Cutler Insbroek," he read as if it was a name with which he was unfamiliar. Cutler glanced again into the cold heart of the Winter Garden. Its walls were arrayed with rotting plants, piled against the cold glass like garbage, weighed down with mounting snow, flopped over and hanging from their boughs, great melting leaves and trailing vines. He took the envelope and opened it. He read it. "No," he said, handing the note to John. "It's for you."

"Me?"

"John?" Lizzie wondered. John refused to take the letter. Cutler had let it drop as he started off. Lizzie retrieved it and opened it. "No," she said. "It's for all of us." Cutler paused. John turned his back and started toward the car. Lizzie read aloud, and he stopped walking.

"I wanted to leave you a message, as cruel as it may seem. It's the only way I know how to get your attention. Please don't hate me for it. Think about what this message means, and you will learn something about life I was too stupid to realize, until it was too late. Love. Alison."

"Too late?" Joey wondered.

"Too late for what," John asked, coming nearer.

"But why?" Lizzie asked, turning toward the scene of carnage. The two students were once again bending in the doorway, searching for signs of life. "Why direct her frustration at Cutler?"

"It was meant for me," John said. "I know Alison. I know how she thinks." Lizzie still didn't understand. John went on. "She knows how much I cherish my friendship with Cutler. She knows that I will feel greater hurt because of this than he will because I will blame myself for it."

"And do you?" Lizzie wondered. Cutler had turned back to hear his response. He nodded. "Yes," he said, softly. "I do."

"No need for that," Cutler assured him.

"Nevertheless," he said, barely audibly.

"She went home to her mother's, you know."

He nodded. Then Cutler asked him if he knew about the baby. Again, without looking up, his eyes on the frozen ground, he nodded.

"How long?"

"Almost from the very beginning," Lizzie answered, since John had started to cry.

Cutler embraced him. Told him it was all right. "They're just plants, you know. Easily replaced."

"I know," he managed to say. "It's not what happened that hurts me; it's why—"

"I know—"

Lizzie had started back to the car; said she was cold. She took a few steps, then paused to glance back at the two friends. The wind had finally let up and even the snow was settling more gently than before. The cluster of lights, the reflecting panes of broken glass, the shadowy figures—the scene might have been a Christmas card. She shuddered with a chill and turned once again toward the car.

There was a scream. It split the soft air like a blade. It startled everyone. The four turned back to see one of the students standing in the midst of the green house with her hands waving about in the air. Cutler dashed to the Winter Garden. He broke past other on-lookers and came to the student's side. The other girl was bending over something near the rear bench. Cutler extended an arm to push the frozen branches aside. He stepped into the circle of flashlights. Snow was settling very gently on the curling foliage, standing in puffs on the rims of the terra cotta pots. There was a mound of snow more solid than the rest, heaped against the glass between the heavy buckets in which the dead palms were planted. The student had brushed some of the snow away to reveal a bit of fur. Red hair showed through the snow, a white skinned face and bright lipstick, a ruby among pearls of ice.

Cutler glanced back to the opened door where John stood, as if afraid to enter.

"Stay back," Cutler said. He took off his glove and caressed the frozen face, moving the stiff curls aside. Snowflakes of incredibly delicate beauty fluttered like tiny wings about her lashes. He smoothed her hair back into place behind her ear, as she preferred it, stood, and turned toward the others. John had fallen into a heap on the ground in a convulsion of sobs. Lizzie and Joey were bending over him.

Cutler asked one of the guards to call the police. "There's a dead woman here," he said. The student in the parka took hold of his arm. He turned to her with a consoling smile, but she was crying as well. "There's a baby in her arms," she said.

The other student still knelt in the snow. "No," she said, steadily. "It's just a doll."

Caleb stopped reading. Jo was holding onto him as hard as she could, rocking back and forth in the small space of the second-class cabin. The manuscript pages lay scattered about, having fallen from his lap as he had finished reading. He held her head close to him and rocked her like a baby. He patted her on the temple and rocked her gently.

"It isn't fiction, is it Caleb?" she gently posed. "It is real, isn't it? It is the cry of your breaking heart, isn't it? It is the confession of guilt that you have been trying so desperately to rid yourself of these past thirty years or so."

"Isn't it?"

He did not answer her. He simply sat in silence, his face to the glass. There they remained for a very long time. The lights of Rome were beginning to trundle past. Soon they'd be in the bright station. Then, Trastevere. They stood to gather their things.

"That's why you can't finish it, isn't it?" she asked from just behind him. "Because the remorse is still there, as big and bold and destructive as it was then, isn't it?" She bent to pick up the scattered pages, taking care to keep them in numerical order. She paused a moment and added, "My god, Caleb." She glanced up at him though he had his back to her. "Why are you doing this to yourself?"

"My cross," was all he said. It was a clue that he was not in the mood for talk. She gathered up the remainder of the pages and handed them to him. Then, she ambled into the corridor and waited, her face to the dark window, watching the lights of Rome moving by. The church bells were ringing. It was midnight. Carnival was over.

Seventeen

There comes to the Author, from many readers of the foregoing pages, a demand for further elucidations respecting the mysteries of the story...On that point, at all events, there shall be not one word of explanation.

Nathanial Hawthorne, *The Marble Faun*

"I grew up in a small town," Caleb had said. There it was again, that small town with its aging mother and dying elms; and especially, that one elm on the corner, where Elm Street lost its asphalt frosting and ran on into the cornfields like a shadowy confection. Gooey molasses in rainy weather, powdered sugar in dry. The smell of holiday baking this side of the tree and get-it-in-by-the-fourth haying on the other. God, it was tall to his small-boy eyes, that tree. How it arched, like a great fountain of green, up, over, and out: down, trailing in heavy-scented heaps its long twigs of fingers almost to the ground and, God, how it arched! But that was then, small boy eyes and all. Now gone, along with the cornfields, the bakery smells, the brown sugar road.

Caleb was in college when the fist elm on Elm Street turned yellow in mid-summer and died by autumn. Yet it stood for some time longer, a bent and blighted shadow, a crippled hand when seen against the grey smear of autumn. Why didn't they cut it down? Why make me look at it every day to remind me of its once elegant beauty? Perhaps they could not believe it was really dead, so long had it stood there. The shock of its untimely death at the hand of a violent suitor had left them baffled and wondering what could be done about that one elm on Elm Street. Their bafflement notwithstanding, another elm died. One by one, they each fell, first to the blight and then to the saw and the chipper. Each year the street grew brighter and the future in elms darker. Trailer parks and retirement villages replaced the cornfields; asphalt replaced shady tree-sides. The small town became a big town.

A wet wind cut between them, lifting Jo's coat collar so that only one shining, blue eye showed, and it blazed in an almost ethereal way. Caleb paused, for when the collar fell away again, he saw that her eyes were closed, as if she were thoroughly engrossed in his tale. Sensing his scrutiny, she blinked her eyes open and asked why the tree had been so important to him. He frowned again, this time at Jo's wide-open eyes.

"Don't you know?" he was about to ask, but, instead, he simply shrugged. They sat in the late winter garden of the Academia San Marco. A light rain darkened their shoulders, but the air was mild and fresh, especially when compared to the musty ambience of their third-floor rooms.

"Hell, I don't know," he added with a laugh. "My lost innocence, I guess; or something like that—"

He could not have told her the real reason for his nostalgia; that lost little episode in the tall grass that flourished beneath those arching boughs. He could not have talked about that child of a woman pleading with him to stop. The torn underclothes; the torn filament of flesh. How could he have explained to her that it was not exactly *his* lost innocence he grieved. For one thing, Caleb had never quite been innocent, so he had had nothing much to lose in the first place. In the second place was that child of a women-yet-to-be and the blighting of that sacred tree. The girl was soon forgotten along with other adolescent nightmares, but the last American elm remained, on the corner of his memory, deformed, empty of life, filled with contempt for all humanity.

How he hated that tree as the years accumulated and flourished in the arching memories of its finger-like branches. How he had wished it gone; and every other like it! Jo had been contemplating his words. "But why does the memory of it make you so sad?"

"I'm a storyteller," he snapped, standing and walking away, "and a damned good one!"

The small late winter sun had faded and a cold chill, steel-gray and knife-like, had fallen like a blade between them. Caleb moved about the garden statuary in successive scenes, like one viewed walking past a row of windows or as if pieces of his progress had been missed by the blinking of one's eyes; a story board with some of the pages gone, some of the figures erased. Only fragments of Caleb's physical self were ever visible at any one time; depending upon the angle of vision or the placement of a foot. Jo watched him stride away, in slow motion, flickering into and out of view among the cypresses as a fog drew itself between them in torn curtains. She drew her fingers to her lips. She tapped her lower lip three times, pulled it out, striking her teeth with her nail, then she dropped her hands in despair.

"I've been seeking something to fill the empty panels of my own story board," she was thinking, "but, there it is: a story with even more pieces missing." She had been sacrificing pieces of her own self to fill the holes left in other's lives for too long already. This was it; this was going to be it. She had no more spare pieces left. She shed a furtive tear. How beautiful he was in his incompleteness. She wiped her eyes and bent to retrieve the bottle of Pino Grigio from the pavers at her feet. She refilled their glasses and called to Caleb. "More wine, dear heart?"

That was it: a glass of wine, a bit of talk, and 'ciao.' He returned at length and sat in silence. "Storyteller or not," Jo mused, mostly to herself, "that tree means something to you."

He merely shrugged and toasted her. They touched glasses silently.

"I have a tree memory, too," she admitted. "Maybe everybody does." He was suddenly interested. He perked up and even smiled her way. "Tell me about your tree," he said.

Jo's grandfather had planted a garden. It was behind the old family house on Church Street. Little by little, over the years, it grew in height and width as phlox and peonies spread into thick clumps and spring bulbs stretched out their sprouting fingers into the surrounding lawns. He dug it and tilled it and piled it and hilled it into stone walled terraces for small plants and neatly edged beds for tall ones: the scillas, and the squills, the pansies and primulas, the roses and the chrysanthemums, the iris and the delphiniums. It was a place of rockeries and brick walks. The arbor vitae pillars grew into open colonnades and the carpet spreaders tumbled in silent cascades over the lichen-crusted rocks, softening their hard corners and cushioning the footsteps of intruders. By the time he died, a small victim of the Great Depression, the garden had taken on the comfortable air of an aged matriarch awaiting the return of her youthful suitor.

But the suitor came no more. She waited, ever-aging, slowly and gracefully ever softer; ever more serene. "Grandfather died before I was born," Jo sighed. "I never knew him." Then she brightened. "But I knew his garden." So well planted was she, even after years of neglect, she thrived, with a kind of shabby dignity. Spring still brought forth a blaze of bulb flowers, star-scattered on the grass. Despite the height and breadth of the cedars, iris and roses flourished in the dappled shadows. Delphiniums and phlox and then mums each in turn stretched the blooming season into fall and beyond even to the first snows of winter. Only the heavy drifts from blizzards stopped her from blooming.

"I'd stop each day on my way home from school, certain she had finally died. I would walk out of my way as the days lengthened to visit my grandfather's garden and search for signs of life. A breath. A heartbeat. The house was gone by then and the small patch was overshadowed on either side by shopping mall buildings."

"And?" he wondered. "The garden died?" She shook her head with a great smile. "No. She never failed me. Each spring she revived. First the pansies would bloom in the warmer crevices of the rockeries, having self-seeded, I suppose. Then the scillas and squills and finally a whole month of wonderful primulas would make a crazy quilt of color for me to roll around in."

When she was older, in high school and home from college, she'd tend the garden. She did not change a thing since her grandfather, in cahoots with nature, had planned it all so well. She'd prune the hedges, trim the grass from the walkways, pull out the weeds and then she'd just sit there, within its open colonnades of silky green and contemplate its many colors. Others would too, shoppers from the malls, and other passers-by.

"It is still there?" She had nodded. Bored, he asked, "So, what's your point?"

"A tree of heaven," she said. It had sprouted of its own accord, or at the hand of some other gardener, in amongst the arbor vitae, where it grew in secret for many years. Having moved from home to take a teaching job in Ohio, she had not been there to protect the garden from foreign invasions.

Alianthus Altissima, what the Chinese called the smelly tree, was first brought to the New World after the Revolution to grace the Chinese style gardens so popular then among the landed gentry. A fast-growing tree, it was soon discovered to be pestiferous, suckering and scattering seeds, until it came to dominate the gardens it was originally meant to decorate. The tree of heaven!

The tree grew and spread into a magnificent specimen, tall and perfectly crowned, of thick, impenetrable foliage, plunging the garden into deep shade. The iris, the phlox, the peonies still grew in thick clumps, but they no longer bloomed. Even the tall cedars yellowed and grew sparse. A thick mantle of fallen leaves clogs the pathways, fostering molds and funguses and the smell of rotting plants is pungent after it rains.

"The garden is still alive," she mused, her eyes on the patches of sunshine that played across the stands of cypresses that lined the garden pathways, "but it has lost all its color." Caleb had become disinterested in the tale. "Why doesn't somebody just cut the damned tree down?" he asked, flat voiced.

She shook her head. She could have done it. No one else seemed to care. "Maybe it belongs there. Maybe it was I who was the intruder. It is a living thing. It rules a garden. Who am I to say it should not be there?"

"Your grandfather planted the garden and you cared for it," Caleb reminded her. "Otherwise, it would not be there at all. The tree is the intruder, don't you think?"

"Why didn't you cut down your tree?" she asked pointedly.

"Because," he snapped, then softened his tone. "Because; it was my tree." Jo said nothing in response. She merely sipped at her wine and a chilly solitude fell over her, as if she had wandered into the shade of a great tree. Caleb had gotten to his feet and was, once again, wandering off, into his own garden. As before, she saw him only in pieces as he strolled along the tree-lined walkway. The sun was setting, and the afternoon grew colder.

"Goodbye, Caleb," she said.

Leaving the bottle and glasses on the cold stone bench, she pulled her sweater about her and returned to the villa. She ate alone that evening. Caleb had not come down for supper and she was not on close terms with the other less than cordial fellows attending the winter academy. She finished her tea and went up to her room. She did not feel like writing. Instead, she sat in the darkened room for some time, staring first at the door, then at the blank window. Sleep overtook her and she lay back on the bed fully dressed, pulling the blanket over her and curling up within its warm confines.

And, while she slept on one part of the earth, snow fell on another, softly at first, then blanking out the sun. All day it came in a steady, heavy fall of torn curtains, folding over and upon itself in the corners of the garden. Like cold sheets of puckered skin, it enshrouded the terraces, blanketed the spreaders, making small domes over the blasted perennials. A fluorescence of white brought bare branches back to life as crystalline blossoms opened even on the cedars. The sun rose next day as the sky cleared, then set upon a bitter cold night that froze the sap in the early spring branches of even the strongest of trees. But the garden, snuggled and sleeping innocently in its cold beds of insulating snow breathed softly, unaware of the death-grip winds that howled overhead.

As Jo awoke to a warm and sunny morning in Rome, in another garden, a tree of heaven died.

But Jo did not know about the tree of heaven. She awoke with a yawn and a feeling of inexplicable sadness. She lay in bed for some time. The winter was almost over. She was to leave Rome in a few days. Then she would be returning to the States and her teaching job in Ohio. It would be spring there, in the Ohio Valley. She smiled. But would she visit her grandfather's garden? No. It was time, she had decided, to move on with her life and leave the past where it belonged—in memory.

She thought about Caleb. He'd be having his second cup of coffee about now, sitting alone in the dining room downstairs, waiting for her. She decided to join him. Just for old time's sake.

He was not there that morning.

A steady rain chilled the air as Caleb left Trastevere and walked across the Tiber. The grey-green river, swollen from late winter rains in the high Apennines, rolled and tumbled over rocks in the great bend at the Ponte Palatino. The sound of rushing water momentarily overwhelmed the roar of traffic and the stench of diesel fuel. He paused for but an instant and pulled his old leather coat about his lanky body. The rain was not heavy, but steady, just enough to dampen his shoulders and pant legs. His shoes were already sopped from the day before. Caleb had been walking the streets and piazzas of Rome for what seemed to have been days on end.

"Yes," he said to himself. "I'll bet he's at Santa Sabina."

He had not been up the Aventine Hill before. It might prove an interesting adventure. After all, he'd lost interest in his writing. He had to do something with his time, something that, on the surface at least, might have seemed worthwhile.

Having traversed the bridge he crossed the busy thoroughfare to a small, triangular park in which rested a little round temple, supposedly to Vesta. Had Caleb his guidebook handy he would have discovered that the delicate marble temple, the oldest in Rome, though circular and in the Corinthian order, was not in fact dedicated to the goddess of the household but to the patron god of the Greek oil merchants who had built the shrine there in the second century B.C. Even in the ancient world, it seems, oil was a driving force in the market. Where he presently stood, admiring the rotunda, was once upon a time the site of the port of Rome, where merchants from around the known world off-loaded their goods for sale in the city's thriving markets. As a writer, he might have appreciated the irony of the miss-named temple; that things are seldom as they seem.

He rushed across the traffic-clogged *Via del Circo Massimo* to the Aventine Hill, the seventh of Rome's ancient hills. He walked then into a remnant of antiquity as he climbed the *Clivo di Rocca,* a narrow, cobbled lane flanked by high rubble walls overhung with greenery: cedars and cypresses piercing the low-slung clouds at either side. Indeed, as he climbed the mossy way toward a cluster of brick towers, he seemed to transcend realities, from the here-and-now to the once-upon-a-time.

He paused at a bend in the lane and looked back over his shoulders, as if trying to reclaim the past he'd just lost. There, through a break in the clouds, silhouetted darkly against an ice-blue patch of sky was the Victor Emanuel monument, its sculptures of winged charioteers literally flying on banners of mist. Caleb shuddered and continued on his way.

Near the crest of the *rocca*, the lane was cut through a tunnel-like channel with rubble abutments surmounted by high brick and rubble walls on both sides, the boughs of stone pines arching overhead. Even the musty smell here seemed old. The crenelated fortifications had been built in the tenth century when the Aventine was contested land within the Papal territories. Behind the abutments rested the quiet gardens of the fifth century basilica of Santa Sabina, named for a Roman matriarch martyred under the Emperor Hadrian. The carved cedar doors are original and portray the saint as she is lifted into heaven with the help of angels.

The church's vast nave and chapels were empty, but for a couple Dominican monks servicing the altars. Caleb let go with a sigh loud enough to distract the men from their work. He shrugged in their direction and then he left the church, pausing for a moment in the portico. The rain had let up and a brighter light greeted him. He shaded his eyes from errant sunbeams filtering through the bare branches of plane trees. Behind the church was a garden and its pathways led to an overlook. Caleb smiled. Bad weather does not seem to deter lovers, he thought to himself. There was a couple there, pressed together against the wall of the terrace, kissing passionately, a vista of the hills of Trastevere with the glistening dome of Saint Peter's in the distance as their backdrop.

After lingering for but a moment to take in the hazy view, Caleb left the garden of Santa Sabina and descended the hill to the street of the Circus Maximus and its clot of horn-blowing cars and noisy motorbikes.

"I should take Jo up there," he was thinking. "She'd like the view."

He had paused facing the stalled traffic. He didn't feel like crossing the busy thoroughfare, though the cars had come a honking stop, so he turned to his left and returned to the Tiber and the bridge that would conduct him safely back to Trastevere. There, in the lonely confines of his small room he would sit, his pad in his lap, and wait; wait for sleep to overtake him. Next day, after a quick coffee, he would be off again, walking and—Waiting.

It was a warm day in March. Caleb ambled along the Tiber mindless of the noise of traffic and the touch of the sun on the side of his face. He had been walking for some time, following the turns and returns of the river in its meandering way through the old city, as he moved counter to its course, inexorably, away from winter's southerly sun. The cool north beckoned and thoughts of his childhood crowded about him as he walked; his best friend swimming with him off Cole's dock in summer and sledding down cemetery hill in winter.

"I wonder what ever happened to—" He had stopped walking and was leaning on the wall, staring back down the river toward the muscular fortress of Sant' Angelo. The plane trees bent with him to see the river below, channeled and tamed to an orderly flow within its high abutments. The sweeping branches were fuzzy with new life and their tips were pale green and bulging with buds. He realized then that the traffic noises had subsided somewhat, and he turned to look across the thoroughfare toward the Mausoleum of Augustus and nearby, in its own glass house, the *Ara Pacis*—The Altar of Peace. He crossed the street and shaded his eyes to see the pale marble monument where it lay suspended, out of time and out of place, in its crystal reliquary.

Constructed by order of Emperor Augustus and dedicated in nine B.C., it commemorated the Age of Peace that settled for a short and tenuous period upon the Roman people following the Gallic Wars. It was during this same peaceful time that Jesus was born but, ironically, early Christians destroyed the monument for what they interpreted as pagan signs in its decorative carvings. Here, near the entrance portal, we see the allegory of peace as Fortuna, patroness of the prosperity that comes with peaceful times, a beautiful and voluptuous woman resting upon a field altar of rough stones, her twin children and a bountiful gathering of fruits nestled in her lap. How reminiscent the image is of a Renaissance Madonna with Jesus and St. John in her care. The icon of her innocent beauty, the lily flower, blooms nearby, and the reed, a reference to Jesus' sufferings under the Roman Procurator, bends in the gentle breeze. Water flows at her feet. Thus, the three procreative elements—earth, wind and water—are represented while the destructive element of fire is not.

Destroyed and the pieces of exquisitely carved marble carried off to serve as foundation stones for princely palaces, the altar was lost and almost forgotten for fifteen hundred years. It was during the 1930s, when dictator Benito Mussolini was reshaping modern Rome into a fascist fantasy of its ancient grandeur, that a project was instituted to reconstitute the *Ara Pacis*. Researchers, archaeologists and stone workers went to work, looking for, identifying and digging up pieces of the altar as they were discovered throughout the city. Piece-by-piece, the structure was rebuilt, as it was assumed to have originally looked. Two ironies attend this little historical account. The monument to peace was placed not in its original site but on the ancient Roman *Campus Martius*; the military field, and it was dedicated by *il Duce* himself, Mussolini, in 1939, the year of Hitler's invasion of Poland and the start of World War II in which over 60 million people will perish.

Caleb didn't know any of the history of the altar, though maybe, he should have, and, after but a few moments, he walked on. Passing the circular tomb of Augustus, he made his way to the wide *Via Del Corso* and then up the *Via dei Condotti* toward the so-called Spanish Steps. At top of the flight of 137 steps sits the church of *Santa Trinitá dei Monti*. Caleb stood at the bottom of the flight staring up into the bright sky, as if confounded by both the light and the height.

"Maybe he's there."

He had talked of the church as being one of his favorites. But then, he hadn't been in any of the others Caleb had visited over the past several weeks and there had been no answer the several times he had knocked at the door of his flat. Now he pondered: should he expend the energy to climb the steps and visit the church in search of—something? Or should he go back and have supper with Jo?

As he stood there thinking, passers-by nudged him and bumped him as if he was of no importance in their view. So, after a few more moments of thought, he turned his back on the flight of stairs and began in slow motion his walk back down the *Via dei Condotti* toward the river Tiber and beyond: Trastevere. As usual, as over the past few weeks, he returned to the academy too late for supper. Grabbing some bread from one of the empty tables in the dining room, he went up to his room. Piero, watching from the kitchen doorway, merely shook his head and went back to work.

Eighteen

'...It seems the moral of his story, that human beings, of Donatello's character, compounded especially for happiness, have no longer any business on earth, or elsewhere. Life has grown so sadly serious, that such men must change their nature, or else perish, like the antediluvian creatures that required as the condition of their existence, a more summer-like atmosphere than ours.'

'I will not accept your moral!' replied the hopeful and happy-natured Hilda.

'Then, here is another; take your choice...He perpetrated a great crime; and his remorse, gnawing into his soul, has awakened it; developing a thousand high capabilities, moral and intellectual, which we never should have deemed of asking for...'

'Sin has educated Donatello, has elevated him. Is Sin, then—which we deem such a dreadful blackness in the Universe—is it, like Sorrow, merely an element of human education, through which we struggle to a higher and purer state than we could otherwise have attained. Did Adam fall, that we might ultimately rise to a far loftier Paradise than his?'

Hawthorne, *The Marble Faun*

"I've not seen much of you the past few weeks," Jo was saying as the cameriere poured her a cup of tea. She grimaced at the thick, blackness of it, then, sipped at it carefully.

"I've been walking a lot," he said. "Just wandering, mostly. Getting to know this old city a little better, now that the weather is nicer."

"It has been nice," she observed, gazing past him and into the sunny gardens beyond the double doors. Drawing her gaze forward, she noticed his pad, lying lifelessly on the table before him, next to his empty coffee cup. One word was scribbled across the top of it: "Chapter One."

"Starting a new one?" she asked him casually.

"Uh huh." He seemed distant, distracted. They sat quietly for a while, Jo sipping at her strong Italian tea. Caleb asked if her time there at the academy had served its purpose.

"Yes," she responded, even before he had finished talking, but then she added, "whatever purpose that was."

He looked up, a banner of sunshine hanging at the windows behind him. "What?" he asked, befuddled.

She sort of smiled and turned her eyes from his. "I did complete a new book of poems," she said absently.

He seemed to have understood the sadness in her manner as his own expression softened to one of indifference. He turned toward the light from the windows when she asked him the same question.

"Of course," he said, as if to someone else.

"But you haven't finished your story, have you? The one about John and Alison? Isn't that what you came here to do?"

"It has no ending," he said, apparently annoyed with the topic. "There is no story."

"Of course, there is," she insisted. He was moving about uncomfortably in his chair, but she went on, anyway. "What happens to John?" she wondered. "What about Cutler? I liked him the best." Then she frowned and asked plaintively, "and what about Alison? Did she really die like that?"

"You mean, did she take her life because of me?" He laughed. Then he shook his head and added emphatically that he had made that up.

She was stunned, mostly at his tone of voice. "Why?" she wondered. Silence. "It's an awful story," she said. Then, she took his hand. "Nonetheless," she said steadily, "I think you should change the ending, Caleb—"

"I told you," He said, in a cold voice, then relaxing and moderating his tone: "There is no ending."

Silence.

"So," she sighed, "that makes eleven." She was staring past him and into the sunny garden beyond the windows. He asked blankly what she meant. She reminded him that he had told her once, "and you seemed proud of the fact, besides, that you had ten unfinished novels to your credit."

"Well," he said, in a softer tone, uncomfortable with the topic, "I guess that makes eleven, then." They were quiet for a while. They each poised their cups at their mouths but neither of them drank. Jo was looking at the blankness of the tablecloth. "I read a story about Dante Gabriel Rossetti," she mused.

"The English painter?"

"He also published poetry." Caleb admitted he did not know that fact. She was nodding as she went on, in sort of a droning voice, as if reading an epitaph. "He was in love in an almost obsessive way with his wife Elizabeth Siddall. She died young, at only thirty-two. He was inconsolable. He buried his unfinished manuscript in her coffin with her."

"Dead and buried," he said, as if talking about something else. She went on drowsily, keeping her eyes from his. "When he decided to publish his poems a few years later, his publisher simply told him he could not publish a half-finished book. The first half of it was in the ground, you recall, and—" She had paused for effect. He looked up, interested, and asked what Rossetti did about the buried manuscript.

"He had her body exhumed and he retrieved the notebook." Caleb shuddered and hugged himself though the morning was a warm one. Jo went on to say that the published book became a best seller and was still in print after a hundred and fifty years.

"Is that all you care about?" he asked suddenly, raising his voice again, catching the attention of the cameriere across the small room, "being published? Being rich? Being famous, Jo?" Before she could respond, he concluded, getting to his feet and starting away, "Well; some of us don't want to be famous, okay?"

And he left the dining room. Jo watched after him for a while in the silence that followed his noisy departure and then, looking about carefully, she got up and left the table. "Okay," she was saying to herself, as she paused in the doorway to look once more about the room. She nodded in Piero's direction. They exchanged brief smiles and she left. She still had some packing to do.

The sun on the boxwood hedges aroused from deep within their winter stems a heady aroma. Already the pale green flower buds were plumping in amongst their glossy leaves. Beyond them, silvery clumps of lavender and rosemary soaked up the virgin warmth and calendulas reflected the golden glow in their myriad of flowers. Water played in the fountain that rose from the circle of greenery where a maimed Cupid laughed silently. A delicate breeze, gently scented with a mix of musky garden smells and the aromas from nearby Roman kitchens, rustled the palm fronds that arched overhead. The small, formal garden of the Academy lay in sunlight since the plantain trees had not yet awakened from their leafless winter sleep. It was March. The Mediterranean spring was more upon them here than it had been north of the forty-fifth parallel, in Venice. But that was *then*, ancient history as far as he was concerned. Caleb. He sat on a marble bench next to his empty coffee cup, gazing lazily about him. He held his notebook opened on his lap, the first page bare to the sky but for two words: Chapter One.

He breathed in deeply, taking in as much of the fresh air as his lungs could hold. Then he turned his eyes toward the double glass doors that led into the dining room. Piero was standing just inside them, awaiting the crush of Americans intent on enticing an early lunch out of the Italians against their instincts. Caleb motioned for him.

"Piero. Vieni di qua."

The young man came forward, a broad smile gracing his handsome face. He practiced the English Caleb had been teaching him. "What are you wanting, Mister?"

"No. How can I help you, Caleb?" he corrected.

He nodded, dropping the smile as he repeated the phrase to himself, moving his lips. Then he smiled again, as fresh and sincere a smile as he'd begun with, and asked carefully, "How can I he'p you, my fren'?" Caleb returned an encouraging grin. Then he asked in a soft voice if Piero might be able to find him a little wine.

"Bianco o rosso?"

"Red, of course," Caleb said.

"Red," he repeated, trying not to trill the 'r' too much. "O' course."

He took the empty cup and returned to the dining room. Caleb sat back, waiting. Jo stood a few meters away, a valise in each hand. He turned toward her. She was dressed in red, a new suit, and she wore a stylish hat. She set the bags down and smiled beautifully. He nodded his approval as she turned this way and that, like a model in a fashion show. She was almost laughing as she walked over to where he sat.

"Nice."

"You like it?"

He nodded. "Ready to go?"

Her smile faded. "I guess."

He was quiet for a while, looking about as if waiting for someone more interesting to come by. "You sure you don't want me to go to the station with you?"

She shook her head, biting her mouth shut.

"Taxi here?"

"Not yet." He stood and opened his arms and she folded into them. From behind the glass of the doors to the dining room, Piero was watching with a small smile, bottle in hand. Jo said she had a few moments. They sat down together. She looked about her, as he had, as if looking for something she might have misplaced.

"A pity," she said. "It's just getting into spring, and I have to leave. It'll still be winter in Ohio."

"Not for long," he said.

"You're staying until May?"

"My birthday. The twenty-second."

They were quiet for a while. She said she'd been thinking about Botticelli's painting. "The Primavera. Spring: how sad it is in some ways."

"How do you mean?"

"Those lovers; beautiful Giuliano De' Medici and the even more beautiful Simonetta Vespucci, both dead and buried and still longing for each other as Venus ignites the fires of springtime."

"That's one interpretation, I suppose," he said, taking hold of her hands. She turned away from him but kept her hands in his. "I like that one."

"Most beautiful, I think, is the figure of Flora," Caleb said, entwining his fingers in hers. "It is Botticelli's most accomplished portrait of womanhood. Her smile is so—what? Sincere, and yet, tragic." He paused and smiled slightly but genuinely. "Like yours is," he concluded.

"No," she said with a slight shaking of her head. "I am not Flora. But I could be."

He embraced her again, though they were each looking in opposite directions. "Yeah?"

"I am more like Chloris," she said. "I am the goddess of the frozen landscape of winter. Spring seems to be elusive for me, for some reason. All I need is the touch of Summer's warm wind to transform me into sensuous Flora."

"Zephyr's touch?"

She nodded, pushing herself away again and peering up at him. "That's you, you know."

He was slightly amused. "How do you figure?"

"No other man has ever brought out the springtime in me as you have, Caleb. For whatever reason—I mean—" she turned away from him again and stood, her back to him, as if watching for the taxi. "Fuck," she said, mostly to herself. "You know what I'm trying to say, don't you?"

Smiling, he walked up behind her and put his arms about her narrow shoulders. "Wow," he said, at her ear. "Believe it or not, no one has ever said anything like that to me before, Jo." She was embarrassed, lowering her face. "I am a poet, after all." They stood for some time embraced, her back to him. He asked her to recite one of her new poems to him while they waited for the taxi. She lowered her head.

With this face, I pass my hours of minutes away as if it was not there at all. I touch and use it like a friend; one who's beauty I've come by time and practical circumstances to assume is perpetual and self-sufficient:

The voice I hear on the phone that no longer brings to mind the eyes, the hair, the mouth of one so loved once and so ordinary to me now.

Not like then, when every mirror caught me by the hand and greeted me with smiles of gratitude and appreciation.

This face. That friend. Dear God! How much alike they seem to have become!

She stepped out of his embrace and turned to face him again, having sloughed off her emotion in order to return to her more rational self. "Okay?"

"Nice," was all he said.

She wondered what he would be doing the remainder of this sunny day just beginning. He nodded toward his notebook, where it lay on the marble bench. He let out a breath. "It's always hard to write that first word, you know."

"You're not going to finish the other one, are you?"

"Not yet." He returned to the bench and sat down.

She sat next to him and took hold of his hands, both of them. "But I need to know," she began, "Why did Alison die that way?"

"I needed her out of my life," he replied, pulling his hands from hers.

She let out a breath, keeping her eyes away from his. "So, you wrote her out of your story."

He reminded her that Alison was just a character in a piece of fiction.

"Well, I think you should change the ending anyway," she suggested. "It is too sad. Have her just leave town, or something." She paused then and looked him directly in the eyes. "What do you think?"

He merely shrugged, looking away from her.

"Well," she stood up and pressed the wrinkles out of her skirt. "Change the ending, will you?"

He nodded. "Okay."

She asked earnestly, then. "You are going to finish it, aren't you?"

He nodded again, still looking in the other direction.

"But you're starting a new one already?"

"Yes," he said. "I'm working on something a little less—" He didn't finish his thought.

They took a while to stare into their own hands. There was the sound of a car horn and they both looked toward the drive beyond the garden greenery. Jo let out a breath. It hung in the quiet air for some time.

"You have my address in Athens?"

He nodded, his eyes on hers.

Then. "Caleb."

"Yes?"

"How does the story end? You must tell me?" He turned his eyes toward the awaiting taxi. "I told you; there is no ending."

"But. How *might* it have ended, were there one?"

She had asked in a voice both plaintive and caring. Caleb had no choice but to react. He stood up and, taking up a piece of her luggage in each hand, he started toward the sound of the taxi's horn. She pursued him and took him by the arm as they stepped onto the front walkway.

"Did she really die like that?" Jo was asking again. "Did she?"

He stopped walking, keeping his eyes on the taxi and the impatient driver inside. "Yes."

"And you blame yourself for that," Jo mused. He had started walking again but she stopped him with another question. "After all these years?"

"I suppose."

She nodded. "What about Cutler?" Caleb's voice was as dry and flat as a news reporter. "There is no Cutler."

She lowered her eyes. "I kind of liked him." He said simply, as he hefted the bags into the trunk of the taxi, "It was a long time ago, Jo"

He walked her around to the door. The driver was already in his seat, revving the motor. She asked Caleb if he had someplace else to go if he'd do it. He said he might.

"I do like you, you know," he said with a strange smile. "It's something, I suppose."

"Something," she repeated. Then, she raised herself up on tiptoes and kissed him quickly and got into the back seat of the taxi.

"Stazione," Caleb said to the driver.

"Stazione," he repeated.

And off he drove. As the little black sedan rounded the drive, Jo leaned out the window and called with a lilt in her voice, "If you don't call me you can bet your life I'll call on you!"

"Okay," he replied, mostly to himself.

He stood and watched the taxi disappear behind a row of spire-like cypress trees. He stood there a long while, at first listening for sounds of the Fiat as it sped away, then relishing in the silence of a sunny Sunday afternoon in a winter garden.

Postscript

He could even remember, time was, some fifty years ago, he loved a woman. He used to enjoy her company, both in public and in private, both in the barroom and the bedroom. He often talks of it even now, spending long winter hours in his particular kind of semi-sleep, watching memories come and go, emblazoned upon the dark windows of the little bar—like pictures recalled from a book he'd once read—how much he had loved that woman. Then. But he sits alone, now, mostly. Everyone has heard the story. They are strangers to him anyway, now, mostly. The bar even has a different owner and a different name. Now.

He glanced at his notepad, Jo's last letter, yellowed and faded, as a bookmark. He opened the pad. Chapter Nineteen. That was all he had written so far. And even that must have been several years ago, at least. He closed the pad, pushed it aside, and motioned for another drink.

Crockery Township
2022